THE GRAIL
MYSTIQUE

THE GRAIL
MYSTIQUE

BREWSTER MILTON ROBERTSON

For KiTTY...
WiTH GREAT APPRECIATION
AND AFFECTION... I HOPE YOU
ENJOY THE READ.
BEST,
Brewster

Wyrick & Company
Charleston

Published by Wyrick & Company
Post Office Box 89
Charleston, South Carolina 29402

Manufactured in the United States of America

Library of Congress Cataloging-in-Publication Data

First Edition

Dedication

My cousin, Pat Saunders

PROLOGUE

ELEGANT IN HER TAILORED KHAKI SKIRT AND WHITE BLOUSE, Marilee Graham pushed through the ornate copper doors of Colonial Hall Middle School and began walking toward the parking lot. Halfway across the terrace, she paused momentarily to examine the small plaque she carried, nestled in the tissue-lined box:

Marilee Bryant Graham
Mother of the Year 2002
presented
Monday, May 6, 2002
by
Parents-Teachers of the
Colonial Hall School System
Colonial Hall, North Carolina

Frowning thoughtfully, she replaced the plaque in the tissue.

As she resumed her stride across the broad promenade, her attention was drawn to a mockingbird swooping down on a pesky squirrel that had wandered too close to her nest. The mother bird's raucous display of maternal instinct brought Marilee a transitory twinge of guilt.

Maybe I should feel like an impostor, but I don't, she mused defensively. *Regardless of what happens to this rotten marriage, I'm still a darn good mother.* She tossed her head in the useless gesture of clearing her whirling, disordered brain. Lately, her mind had been bombarded by what seemed to be an endless siege of romantic urges and rebellious feelings. Now, she focused on the one thing she had decided with certainty.

To bloody hell with Trip Graham...to bloody hell with Graham

1

International, Ltd....she was sick and tired of playing Mother Goodytwoshoes for old Clayton Graham's tight-assed town. Given another opportunity, she would gladly rush headlong into Norris Wrenn's arms again. This time absolutely nothing would get in her way.

MONDAY MORNING

CHAPTER ONE

ALL MORNING LONG, Norris Wrenn could not shake the feeling he was being followed...but it made no sense at all.

Then, just to add to his discomfort, he had barely settled into his seat on the Delta shuttle at LaGuardia before he knew the Fates were making sport of him again. Right there in the seatback pocket was a picture of Marilee Graham staring at him from the cover of the *Sports Illustrated* swimsuit issue. He opened the magazine to the spread showing the familiar photos of Marilee from her cover debut in 1989 when she was only eighteen. The early poses were contrasted side by side on the page with shots taken for the current issue. If anything, the thirteen years had only served to perfect her beauty.

But Norris certainly needed no reminder of that.

"Thank you for flying the Delta shuttle...we hope you have a pleasant day in the Washington area..." The captain's voice crackled over the intercom as he cut the engines and went through his practiced monologue.

Norris glanced out of the window at the façade of the Ronald Reagan National Airport terminal building. Like many experienced travelers, he had come to think of the place as "DCA," the shorthand used to mark the familiar destination on luggage tags and ticket folders. He wondered how many hundreds of times he'd flown in and out of this place, a staggering number indeed for a man still in his thirties.

Outside, men in coveralls were cleaning the dirty-gray residue from the face of the terminal building. It was a futile exercise. Since he'd first seen it twenty years ago, the building always exuded a resigned air of impending ruin. But, despite dire predictions from anxious naysayers after the terrorist attack on the nearby Pentagon, the FAA had given in to Congress' plea to keep the venerable old terminal open.

Somehow, at this moment, Norris found that oddly comforting.

After the jet engines whined to a halt, Norris stole one final look at Marilee Graham's lush curves in the well-thumbed magazine before he unbuckled his seat belt and stood. Careful not to bang his head on the overhead compartment, he stretched, waiting patiently for the aisle to clear.

A young man in an ill-fitting gray suit stopped in the aisle, offering to let him out. The sleeves of the man's jacket were cut just a trifle too skimpy and his just-too-short trouser cuffs exposed a half-inch of navy wool socks above his heavy dark brown shoes. It was a look Norris had come to associate with newly-released convicts, off-duty career military officers and agents of various covert arms of the United States government.

Norris studiously ignored him.

When the last of the passengers had passed, Norris retrieved his laptop travel case from under the seat and furtively slipped the *Sports Illustrated* into the outside compartment before he ambled up the aisle.

"Always a pleasure to have you with us, Mr. Wrenn," the captain said, standing just inside the cockpit door. "Will you be flying back to New York later today?" The pilot had played basketball at The University of Virginia during the late sixties. He had been a member of Norris' fraternity. Of course, that had been nearly twenty years before Norris' own time in Charlottesville.

"Always good to see you, too, Jim. No...I'm flying on to North Carolina. I've hardly been home in the past six weeks and my wife keeps reminding me this Sunday is Mother's Day. By the way, it's a dirty shame the way our alumni interfere with our athletic program. Meddling caused that prep school super star to go to Carolina. But Wahoo basketball is definitely on the mend."

"Yeah, Pete Gillen is a damn good coach. But Duke and now Maryland and Wake...the whole league just keeps getting tougher. But don't count out football. Coach Groh will kick some serious ass, just wait and see..."

"I hope you're right..." Norris ducked through the door and called over his shoulder, "Take good care, Jim...see you soon."

In the waiting area, Tom Bradley broke into a broad smile when he saw Norris. With his bushy cowboy moustache, Tom always reminded Norris of actors Sam Elliott or Tom Skerritt. Just a few years back, Tom and his father had been the legal darlings at the top of the Washington ladder. But, lately, his former law partner had been down on his luck.

"Well...at last! I was getting worried you'd missed the flight." Bradley stepped awkwardly forward and gave Norris a bear hug. "God...how long? More'n a year?..."

"Longer...much too long," Norris murmured and stepped back, his hand still grasping the slightly taller man by the biceps. Smiling warmly, he was careful not to betray a nagging concern that his old friend looked a little faded at the edges. This man had been closer than any brother—over the years there'd been few secrets between them. Upon careful scrutiny, Norris was relieved that Tom's eyes looked clear. And there was definitely no telltale alcohol odor about him.

"God, let me get a good look at you," Tom blurted happily in his northern Virginia drawl. "Nowadays, I can't pick up a magazine that doesn't have your picture on the cover. This morning's *Wall Street Journal* says Clayton Graham is making you CEO of Graham International, Ltd.—the top spot at Grail is a long way from the good old days at the frat house. Who would've thought you'd still be wiping Trip Graham's no-good ass..."

Looking past Tom's shoulder, Norris caught a glimpse of the man in the ill-fitting suit and brown shoes standing across the terminal, artlessly pretending to examine a schedule folder.

"Well, it's not like that really. I don't see Trip much these days. He rarely comes into the office anymore...I...ah..." Norris hesitated. He had come here to tell Tom he'd cut himself the deal of a lifetime. After tomorrow morning he'd have complete control—virtual autonomy. If Tom had his act back together, he wanted him to be

7

an important part of his future. Still?...he'd heard some horror stories. Cautiously, he stopped short.

Go slow! He admonished himself, deciding to put Tom's involvement aside for the moment.

"I heard about your dad's heart thing...how's the old Chief doing, anyway?"

"Much better. Chomping at the bit again. Can't keep the old warhorse down for long."

"Great. Look, we don't have much time. Like I told you on the phone, Chatham Brookes has been calling me rather frequently of late. Now that the terrorist hysteria is gradually calming down, the White House is showing interest in the Phoenix concept again..." Norris glanced uneasily around. "Is there someplace we can go to talk?"

"Sure...how long before your flight?"

"Almost an hour. Why don't we walk over to United and get me checked in? We can catch each other up on old times on the walk down." Norris had already begun moving through the crowded waiting area.

As Tom fell into step, he saw the *Sports Illustrated* stuffed in Norris' laptop briefcase. "Say?...how about that *Sports Illustrated* spread on Marilee Graham? I've got to hand it to Trip; his wife is some dish. How'n hell did that lucky SOB ever sweet talk a babe like that into marrying him? The crackle of old money is the music of love, I guess..."

Norris ignored his old partner as he felt a blush creep up his neck.

Tom babbled happily on, "Well...are you going to tell me about your taking over as CEO at Grail? Is it official?"

"Tomorrow morning...at ten...if I don't manage to self-destruct. I seem hellbent on doing that lately." The frustration slipped out before Norris could catch himself. He turned slightly and showed a tightlipped grin as he glanced back over his shoulder again. He had to quit all this childish imagining. He was becoming positively paranoid.

Tom caught the tension in Norris' reply and quickened his pace

8

to catch up. "Just what the hell's that supposed to mean?"

Abruptly, Norris stopped short when he saw the waiting line at the United counter.

"Screw this. C'mon. We don't have all day." Impulsively, Norris turned to his left and made a beeline for the exit door in the long concourse. Emerging into the sunlight, he wheeled and hurried back toward the busy main entrance, waving his arms to hail a cab.

An aggressive Red Top driver caught his sign and, ignoring the protesting starter, pulled out of the pattern and stopped at the curb. The Asian driver leaned across, peering up from the window.

"We want to cruise a short way up Glebe Road and back...about thirty minutes in all." Norris opened the door for Tom and pointed in the general direction of Alexandria. "Just drive around...find a quiet neighborhood. But I need to be back here at eleven thirty-five." Norris leaned forward, handed him a twenty and pointed to the face of his watch.

"Hokey-dokey...I catchee." The cabbie brightened, his head bobbing up and down. As the cab moved forward, he switched on a Walkman-like device hanging on the dash and stuck the tiny earplug in his ears.

"Hmm...where were we?" Norris leaned back and swiveled to face Tom across the seat.

"Graham International...so you really are taking over as CEO? Where's Trip in all this—after all, he's next in line? And what about the heat the Court's putting on Grail Tobacco?"

"Forget Trip. He's hopeless. You know when I signed on, Big Clayt hoped I might help Trip take hold and eventually take over, but I think we both knew all along that was never going to happen. And the worst of the cigarette fiasco is history. Except for minor fallout, the major class-action suit is settled. Even before the terrorist attacks brought us billions in military contracts, I'd already moved most of Grail's eggs into other baskets. I'm sure you're well aware that Grail is a prime sub-contractor for both the Pentagon restoration and the World Trade Center project. Anyway, Clayt finally saw the light and offered me the job of running the whole show—as if I wasn't doing it anyway. He about choked when I turned him down. I told him I was damn well tired of...ah...wiping Trip's sorry ass, as you so aptly put it."

"But...I thought you just said you were taking over tomorrow?"

"Oh...I am. With Congress and the White House seeing terrorists behind every tree and the military contracts pouring in, Big Clayt knew I had him over a barrel. I let him sweat a little before I finally negotiated the deal of a lifetime. My up-front cash settlement is a cool seven figures. There are retroactive stock bonuses—not to mention a permanent seat on the board. And that's just for openers..." Norris grinned and paused to let it all sink in.

"No shit? Congratulations...I guess. So? What was all that back there about being hellbent to self-destruct?" Tom was obviously getting more confused by the minute.

"Oh, nothing really. A sordid little personal lapse on my part...ancient history now..." Norris dismissed the subject with an impatient wave. "Anyway, time's short. What I want to talk about is this sudden flurry of calls from Chatham Brookes. That cowboy in the Oval Office can't stand success. The approval ratings from the early days of the terrorist shitstorm went straight to his head. Linking abortion clinic bombings with the other terrorism was a real fuck-up. Congress has been burning midnight oil trying to find a way to overturn this flagrant abuse of emergency powers to shut down abortion. My guess is that his renewed interest in reviving the Phoenix project is just grabbing at straws, trying to divert Congress' attention away from his attempts to stack the Court. Doesn't matter, really...if he's serious, I wouldn't consider it without you." Norris watched for his reaction.

"Well...I'm sure you've heard all about my divorce...the boozing...all that?" Tom averted his gaze and looked out the window.

The driver was turning left onto the Old Richmond Highway. When Tom turned back, Norris was pleased to see him look him straight in the eye...waiting for his reply.

"Well...I've been concerned about you, sure, but, frankly, word is that you've gotten your train back on the track. I know you're working for the Attorney General now. I never gave up, you know?

I've tried to reach you...frequently. You didn't return my calls."

"Yeah...I know. It's been a nightmare...I really lost it...lasted almost a year..." Tom looked down at his hands worrying a button on his jacket. When he looked back into Norris' face, he smiled. "But you're right...I *am* getting my train back on the track. Picked up my six-month chip at A.A. last week. You're right, I am doing a special assignment for the Attorney General, but that's winding down. The answer is '*yes.*' If you want to revive Phoenix, count me in."

"Great. Chatham Brookes called last night...wants to meet sometime later this week. Said he'd call again tonight or tomorrow. The Oval Office is fighting alligators—Afghanistan, the abortion-slanted Court nominations and now Courtland Pike, the holdover from the previous administration, blows his brains out after shredding a dumpster-full of files on the WTC fiasco. And get this, I hear *The Post* is investigating rumors that Pike was boozing, taking the hard-on pill Virecta, playing footsy with some born-again kiddie-porn star from his old district back home. Jeez! With Slick Willy and Gary Condit's stink hardly out of the place. Can you believe it?"

"Yeah...after Slick Willy, I could believe anything. Goddamn politicians are interchangeable—gets worse every time. I've become apolitical really. Whatever happened to the country's statesmen? Can you just imagine Jimmy Carter wigged-out on an overdose of Virecta? We need some real leaders. When are you going to run?"

"Carter on Virecta? That's a picture." Norris grinned. Then he frowned. "Me? Run for President? Hah...be serious!"

"I am serious...this country needs you..."

"Forget it. Freaking job's undoable." Norris rolled his eyes and shrugged. "So...soon as I hear from Brookes, I'll call you. In the meantime, let's get cooking on Phoenix. I'll have Patty overnight you the file. I'll fly back up here and we'll talk again before I meet with Brookes. Maybe Wednesday morning...sound OK?"

"Sure." Tom looked at him again and nervously cleared his throat. "I'm curious what else Chatham Brookes talked to you about. Is Phoenix all he mentioned?"

"What do you mean?" Tom's tone brought a sudden tightening in Norris' belly.

"Well, I don't really know what I mean...well...I mean Dad's old friends drop by to see him now that he's up and around again. Lately, I've heard your name come up once or twice..."

"Oh? In what regard?"

"That's just it, no particular regard. Grail's military contracts...the Pentagon and WTC projects...trade with China...maybe that's what your sudden notoriety is all about—I don't know. All at once your name just seems to be in the air around The District. Something's in the air..."

Norris leaned forward and tapped the driver on the shoulder.

"Better head back to the airport..." Norris pointed to his watch.

"OK...c'mon, let's hear the rest." Norris leaned back and waited. "What's going on?"

"Well...hmmm...weren't you in Wilmington...a little over a month ago?"

"Wilmington? Sure. Agnes and I spent a week at Trip's beach place. The cottage is Marilee's really...she owns it. Always has a big celebrity party during Azalea Festival Week. As a matter of fact, that's where Chatham Brookes tracked me down. He must have called me once a day all that week. How did you hear about that?"

"I overheard Senator Kenan tell the Chief he and his wife saw you there. The guest list at Marilee Graham's party is a big status thing...you know...big spread in *Town and Country*...all that. The Kenans are among the regulars it seems. Old fart was bragging about how he got to crown that ex-porno star Emma Claire as Azalea Queen. Did you know the President flew down to Camp Lejeune for marlin fishing that weekend? One of his rich cronies has a fancy estate somewhere near Wrightsville Beach...Special Prosecutor's office is curious. Seems the First Lady was visiting her parents in Key West. Rumor is that Langley had a whole army of spooks milling around among the Azalea tourists...Bermuda shorts, Hawaiian shirts and all. The way I get it, there were spooks at Marilee's beach party. Your name came up, nothing in particular."

"Wrightsville Beach is right at Wilmington...but our buttoned-down President marlin fishing? Give me a break! And spooks at Marilee's party! I can just see 'em in those godawful brogans and their knee-length blue nylon dress socks sagging around their ankles. They certainly weren't interested in me...I mean why me? Makes no sense—forget it."

"A Company man got off your plane back there." Tom said, not-too-offhandedly.

"Yeah, I spotted him on the plane. Bad haircut...baby-shit brown shoes...tacky gray suit...looked like a motel clerk. Where do they find 'em?" Norris snorted. "You know him?"

"I've seen him around. Tony something. I can't keep up with 'em all nowadays—not like I used to. But you're right; they stand out like a nun at a Shriners' convention. With the money the government spends, you'd think Langley or Quantico or whoever would teach 'em how to dress. They'll never learn..." Tom shook his head. "Do you think he was..."

"Tailing me? No way..." Norris said emphatically, his voice trailing to a half-whisper. He paused and stared out the window. "Then, again...I can't be sure..."

"You think you're being tailed?"

"Uhmm?...I just don't know. Lately, at times, I've imagined things. What you just said about the spooks at Marilee's party really bothers me. Then, maybe I'm just getting paranoid in my old age." Norris tried to smile. Through the windshield, the Washington Monument loomed closer. Norris shuddered involuntarily as—just for an instant—the specter of the 767 crashing into the World Trade Center superimposed itself on the façade of the stately landmark.

"Paranoia? Around this town, it's in the air...like pine pollen...which reminds me, one of the rookie Bob Woodward wannabes at *The Post* called me a few weeks back and asked if I'd ever heard you mention the idea of using Phoenix as a cover for a CIA operation..."

"*The Post*? Are you putting me on? Phoenix a CIA cover? What kind of sick shit is that?"

"Who knows where these things start. Everybody in this fucking town is sick."

"Well, I hope you told him..."

"Oh, I did...still...that might explain the agency clown on the plane." Tom shrugged.

"You've been reading too many Brian McGrory novels."

"Maybe. Well, no sense in letting it bother you. Surveillance is just a way of life around here. Could be anything. Grail has billions in wartime contracts...you're married to the Senator's daughter...besides...with the White House talking about reviving Phoenix, they'd most likely do a routine check on you. You know the drill...carries over from the days of good old J. Edgar. It would fit nicely with there being spooks detailed to attend Marilee's Azalea Festival party."

"*Jeezus*, Tom...I wonder..." Norris suddenly frowned.

"What?..."

"Well...something did happen down there. It really didn't amount to much...still it would be embarrassing. Nah...no way..." Norris shook his head.

"What? What're you talking about?" Tom leaned forward.

Norris gave him a searching look, carefully weighing the moment.

CHAPTER TWO

HUH!…OOOO, SHIT!

Jeezus…that noise! Whazzat fucking noise?…

Wowee! Poor head….oooo…shit…shit…shit! Goddamn! Poor-fucking-head!

Clayton Massie ("Trip") Graham, III tried desperately to claw his way up through the gray gelatin toward the light. It clung to him, trying to pull him back.

Finally, with all the effort he could muster, he opened his eyes to see the fuzzy image of the imitation Thomas Hart Benton "Glory-to-Rural-Americana" wallpaper mural on the wall beside the bed.

Motel?…Where?

In Blowing Rock…yesterday…*Yesterday?*…Sunday?…

In the semi-darkness, his head exploding from the sound, Trip rolled over. Across the far bed, through the narrow crack between the heavy drapes, he could see daylight.

Sweetjeezus, please let today be Monday!

The sheet stuck to him. Lying in a pool of sweat. Sweat?…heh, heh?…

He wiped his fingertips cautiously across the damp sheet and put them to his nose.

OH, NO!…Not again…

Fuckin' bummer. Heh, heh!…hadn't done that little number in a while…not since Boca, anyway…

Time? What time?

The digital clock on the lamp table between the beds displayed 11:11.

Monday…Please, God…just let it be Monday…Monday morning!

Slowly, he focused on the desk built onto the wall across the room.

15

Ice bucket. Grail logo! A bottle? He squinted hard...Stoli? *STOLI*! Good old Stoli...God bless you vodka-loving, commie bastards.

Any left? Please...God...just one good stiff one would help.

Finally, he struggled erect and lurched over and hit the OFF button on the TV.

He picked up the bottle. Half-full. Yes, praise Jesus...*YES*...and yes again.

And what have we here, m'lord?...dainty little cans of grapefruit juice...good old Bluebird!

Ice, m'lord?

Ah, one...two-o-o...ah...come here, you slippery little mutherfucker...Hah! Gotcha! Ah...three...four...ah...gotcha!...five little pieces...

Good old Stoli and Bluebird. Hair of that wonderful dog...man's best friend. Ever get me another dog, name him Blue!

He lit a Colonial Hall filter and idly examined the motel matchbook cover.

Grail MASSIE HOUSE. Greensboro. I-40 at High Point Road. Greensboro's finest...named for his sweet old granddaddy...rest his long-gone ass.

Well, now, Granddaddy Massie, your grandson Trip had the sense to get his drunk ass off the road. Ain't you proud, Granddaddy? Gonna have another one jus' fo' you, Granddaddy Massie, you moldy old fart.

He pulled on his jeans and headed for the door. Get outside...find a paper quick.

There! By the drink machines...*Charlotte Observer*... *Greensboro Record*...*Raleigh News and Observer*...*The Roanoke Times*. All of 'em...*Wall Street Journal* and, God bless 'em, *The New York Times*...all the fucking news that's fit to print...All of 'em...M...O...N...D...A-fucking-Y. MAY 6th...

"Stelle, this is Trip...is God there?"

"No sir, Mr. Graham, he just called...had to speak at the Rotary breakfast in New Bern... he's on his way. Where are you?

You know he's expecting you..."

"Yeah, yeah...I know. Tell him not to worry. I'm in Greensboro. I'll be on time."

"All right...but he said if you called to remind you about dinner at the club for Mrs. Graham tonight..."

"My mother or my wife?..."

"Your wife. The Governor is naming her Mother-of-the-Year tomorrow, remember? We're all so proud..."

"Huh? Oh, sure. Well, thanks...tell my father I'm on my way." He hung up before she could reply.

Idly, he examined a lipstick-stained cigarette in the ashtray by the phone. Jeezus! Got to start remembering better. Shaking his head, he headed for the shower.

As he toweled dry, he winced at a freshly-bruised area high on his back, just below his right shoulder.

Heh, heh!...what the fuck had he done to get that? The goddamn party at Blowing Rock had gotten a bit out of hand Friday when it started raining and the prospect of golf had gone sour.

Oh well, plenty of time to get spiffy and be in his daddy's office at three.

Now, was that good news or what?

CHAPTER THREE

"MARILEE...WAIT UP!"

Marilee Graham stopped in mid-stride, turned and watched as Superintendent Byron Jones emerged from the ornate copper school doors and walked briskly across the wide brick promenade.

"Byron...what a nice surprise..." she said as he caught up with her at the top of the steps leading down to the parking lot.

"I tried to say hello back there in the auditorium, but Henry Stewart grabbed me about a problem he's having with the new PA system. Anyway, I just wanted to say congratulations. We're all proud of you. It's not everyday the Governor honors one of Colonial Hall's own as North Carolina's Mother of the Year. Let me walk you to your car." He took her lightly by the elbow as they started down the steps.

"Thank you, Byron, but you don't suppose this award has anything to do with the fact that *Graham International, Ltd.* provides about seventy thousand jobs across the state, do you?" She laughed. "In North Carolina, governors can run for reelection. I'm not implying Lonnie Reynolds could be influenced, but in the twelve years I've been here, I've noticed no one becomes governor without Clayton Graham's support."

"Don't be such a cynic. And don't sell yourself short. You're our claim to fame. Everybody here is a fan. I saw your spread of bikini poses in the recent *Sports Illustrated*. It was...ah...in the very best of taste. It's hard to imagine you'll have a son starting middle school...I...ah...I hope I said that right."

"You said it perfectly, Byron...and thank you. You made my day. Will I see you tonight at Mabel's dinner party?" She squeezed his hand and slid beneath the steering wheel. Marilee liked Byron. He was a real Boston gentleman.

18

"I wouldn't miss it. You know, a school superintendent has to play a little politics, too."

"Don't kid me, Byron. Clayton handpicked you himself. I happen to know he's always bragging about how he stole you right out of Harvard. Clayt's a staunch believer in the public school system. Wouldn't hear of it when Trip wanted me to send Ivee to Country Day in New Bern. Come early tonight. I'll need your moral support." She smiled and started the engine.

Reaching up, she pushed the button to open the sunroof. The warm spring air was heady with a scent of honeysuckle. It was a lovely day, but she had disturbing consequences to ponder.

Driving along, Marilee's head was besieged with erotic thoughts of Norris Wrenn. She had read just last evening, in the current issue of *Cosmopolitan*, that Dr. Kinsey's original 1953 study on Sexual Behavior in the Human Female had estimated 26% of American housewives have an extramarital affair.

Twenty-six percent. One of every four. One at every table at her bridge club!

Who else? she wondered, half aloud.

Her thoughts drifted back to the previous evening. She recalled placing the article on infidelity on the footstool while she had sorted through the heavy stack of unopened mail. Putting aside the rest, she had opened the bulky manila envelope containing magazine and newspaper articles she had ordered from a New York clipping service. Spanning a dozen years, the articles were a testament to Norris Wrenn's career.

Leafing through the clips, a cover feature from *The New York Times Book Review* had caught her eye. Entitled PHOENIX RISING, the date "April 4, 1995" was noted in pencil. She had replaced the other clips in the envelope and had rapidly scanned the article. Then she started over, reading slowly from the beginning.

"Hi, Mom." Ivee had walked unnoticed into the room. "All the kids are giving me a hard time since they heard you were voted Mom of the Year. They announced on the intercom that you're coming to the assembly tomorrow."

She had lowered the clipping and smiled. "I wasn't exactly

elected. I guess the PTA was kind of forced into it. You know...because Governor Reynolds is honoring me day after tomorrow in Raleigh. Don't sweat it...it's just a lot of fuss over nothing. It will all blow over by next week."

"Oh, I don't mind. First *Sports Illustrated*, now this. I think it's great. Jody Harris told a bunch of snooty girls on the way up Red Barn Road from the bus stop they were just jealous. Jody's neat. By the way, thanks for talking to his mom. She finally gave in and said he could go to golf camp with me. How about that? Give me a high five."

"High five, Tiger!" She slapped his palm. "Don't mention it. I think Jody's mother's pretty nice, too."

"I'm going over to the putting green awhile before it gets dark." He had turned to leave.

"Do you have homework?" The question was rhetorical, really. Marilee didn't know why she always asked. You never had to worry about things like that with Ivee.

"You sound just like the Mom of the Year." Ivee had grinned and skipped out of the room.

She had watched him go, then picked up the magazine again and absently flipped through its pages until a feature about model-turned-film-actress Sadie Bailey caught her eye. Marilee could count on the fingers of one hand the women she truly regarded as friends. Of those few, Sadie Bailey was the best friend she had in the world. Sadie was closer than a sister—there were no secrets between them.

Ironically, it had been Sadie who had introduced her to Trip. But, later, it had been Sadie who had pleaded with her not to marry him, so the score was even.

Anyway, marrying Trip wasn't Sadie's fault. Nobody could have talked her out of it then.

Marilee examined the fancy *Cosmo* spread. Good old Sadie; her career was soaring—higher now than ever. Her success gave Marilee a deep sense of satisfaction. Sadie was a class act. She deserved the very best of everything.

She had known Sadie since 1987, the summer just before she

started her second year at the University of Miami. They had met on the same modeling assignment in Nassau. It was at a time when Marilee's own career was just beginning to blossom, and Sadie, even though she had not yet reached her twentieth birthday, was already at the top.

Right from the very start, they had hit it off. The friendship began with a remark Sadie had made during a break in the shooting on the first day. They were sitting under an umbrella by the pool. Marilee sat watching as the frustrated camera crew struggled to anchor a large reflector against the whims of a gusty Caribbean breeze. Sadie had been very quiet—pensive. Finally, she turned to Marilee and waved her hand across the expanse of the lush island landscape.

"You know, five years ago I wouldn't have believed there were places like this. I know that's hard for a college girl like you to understand. You have to be raised in the Bronx in a single room with eight other people to know what I mean." There was no edge of bitterness in her voice—not even a plea for sympathy. It had been the simple statement of a wide-eyed Cinderella who had just arrived at the ball.

"All college girls don't come from the right side of the tracks, Sadie. There are some of us who know exactly what you mean. And Sadie," she had added, "there are things just as ugly as sharing a room with eight people."

Sadie looked at her a moment. Then she broke into an easy smile. She raised her glass and murmured, "To a very dead past."

She met Sadie's serious eyes over the rim of her glass and drank her toast.

In those days, Sadie had been highly sought after for swimsuit work and could take her pick of the Florida and Caribbean assignments. Marilee ran into her fairly often that first year of modeling, her final year at college. Their friendship had quickly grown. Sadie had helped set up Marilee's famous first *Sports Illustrated* shoot and Marilee's career had skyrocketed. It was at Sadie's urging she moved to New York after graduation. There had been plenty of work. She could thank Sadie and her agent, Athena, for that. The moment Marilee graduated, she jumped at Sadie's invitation to move in with her. For Sadie, not having enough room was a thing of her past.

"My God, I'll need a floor plan to find my way around," Marilee remembered saying in amazement, the first time she set foot in Sadie's place.

"Just look here, Marilee. My bathroom is larger than the room I shared with seven—sometimes eight—other people for sixteen years." Sadie smiled quietly. There was a husky undercurrent of emotion in her voice. "In those days, the crapper was down a dark hall with rats brushing against my ankles and nasty old condoms sticking to my bare feet. I remember I bought a pair of cheap felt house slippers with the money I made from the first trick I turned. I was fifteen...almost sixteen. I walked out of there on my sixteenth birthday. I bought my family a big house out on Long Island two years ago."

Sadie stopped and smiled again. Then she shrugged. "Ancient history...you really like it?"

"Yes." Marilee hugged her. "I love it...and Sadie, I know about rats and roaches, and I've stepped around a used condom or two in my day."

Marilee missed talking to Sadie. For the past month, Sadie had been in California wrapping up a film. Sadie never called when she was on the coast. They hadn't talked in weeks. Shooting schedules were made in hell. Marilee had long since given up trying to reach her out there.

On impulse, Marilee had put the magazine down, picked up the phone and dialed Sadie's New York number. It rang twice before the recording came on...

"Hello, this is me. Sorry I'm not here to...." There had been the sound of a sharp click and then a loud noise as if the phone had been dropped.

"Sadie?...Sadie...is that you? Are you there?" she had asked, puzzled by the noise.

"Goddamnit...I hate these frigging things...hello...hello. Marilee? Is that you? Hold on 'til the message stops..." Sadie's voice had come over the recording.

"Yes...I'm waiting," Marilee had assured her.

"There!...Finally! You still there?" Sadie had asked, when the recording ended.

"Yes, Sadie, just take it easy...I'm here."

"Marilee, oh baby, am I ever glad you called! Do I ever need someone to tell me I'm OK. I just got back from that frigging cracker factory last night, and I've slept the clock around. When are you coming up here? Have I got a story to tell you. Forget all those rumors about real live men roaming the face of the planet. Marilee, it ain't so. The male animal is extinct..." Sadie's words had rushed out nonstop.

"Oh, Sadie, I've missed you. Don't worry, you've just been around those Hollywood people too long. Don't let them sour you on men. Six weeks ago, I might have agreed. But take heart," she had said and laughed. "I'm here to tell you you are definitely wrong. There are still a few good men out there."

"No...you're wrong. Trust me on this, Marilee...and, anyway, you're the last one on earth I'd expect to argue that point. I know you could write the book on rotten men. First your father and then Trip...you've had two of the worst," Sadie said emphatically. "I'm sorry to be so blunt...but Trip is...well...Trip is a rectal orifice."

"I can't argue that...but there are still some fantastic men lurking about, Sadie. You just haven't found them yet," Marilee persisted happily.

"What? Fantastic men? Who is this? I thought I was talking to Marilee Bryant Graham, my oldest and bestest friend. Marilee, what are you saying? Don't tell me...Trip's finally in AA. I don't believe it."

"No. No...Trip hasn't changed. Not for the better anyway. I practically never see him now. He was in Palm Beach for two weeks and hardly got home last week before he headed up to the mountains to play golf," Marilee had admitted. "Poor Ivee...he doesn't understand why his father never spends any time with him. He notices the drinking. He doesn't say much, but it hurts him. I look at Trip and I remember my father...oh well, no sense going into all that."

"Oh God, Marilee. Why doesn't Clayt do something about it? Surely he can see. Trip is his only son. It's been going on forever. I thought Clayton Graham was such a no-nonsense guy. Why does he?...why do either of you?...put up with that asshole?"

"I guess I just kept on hoping...still...I wouldn't have put up with it at all if it hadn't been for Ivee. But now I can see how it's affecting him. I'm sick of it," Marilee had said. "And Clayt?... Clayt's simply given up. He's just waiting now until Ivee is old enough to take his place at Grail. Clayton's not going to let Ivee out of his sight. I don't know what he'd do if Ivee suddenly decided he wanted to be a brain surgeon or an astronaut. Clayt would simply pitch a fit."

"And you're telling me there are still some good men out there? Bullpucky! They're all alike. How can you of all people defend the bastards?"

"Listen to me. I'm telling you, they're not all like Trip...there are some...ah..." Marilee hesitated, took a deep breath and put her toe in the water. "Remember Norris Wrenn, Trip's best man...do you remember him from the wedding? Did you know he's here with Grail now?...lives next door...plays golf with Ivee. He's a wonderful man."

"Sure. Of course I remember. He wrote that book...*Phoenix* something or other. I saw his picture on a magazine cover yesterday on the airplane. Marilee, everybody knows who Norris Wrenn is. What about him?..."

Silence.

Suddenly, Sadie had gasped.

"MAR-I-LE-E-E!...oh my God...what are you telling me? Not you and Norris Wrenn?"

"Wait now, Sadie...don't jump to any conclusions. I didn't mean anything, I, uh..." Marilee had stammered weakly.

"C'mon, now. Who do think you're kidding? What's going on?"

"Nothing. Really. You know...nothing like that." Suddenly, she had felt more than a little foolish. She was sorry she'd said anything.

"Don't give me that 'nothing' crap. You sound different. This is your old Sadie gal you're talking to." Her voice had dropped to the special tone Marilee recognized from the many late nights they had spent together over the years, usually on Marilee's rather frequent visits to New York. "OK, come on now, what's happening between you and Norris Wrenn?"

"Oh Sadie, I'm serious. Forget it. It's really nothing. I feel silly for saying it that way."

"Marilee, why are you doing me this way? Quit teasing. I could have called my agent and been treated better. Come on now, tell me all," Sadie had persisted. Marilee had never had any luck trying to fool Sadie.

"Well, OK, something did happen...sort of...when I had my annual hail-hail-the-gang's-all-here down at the Caswell Beach house during Azalea Festival week. But honest, it didn't amount to much." She'd felt rather defensive once she heard herself talking about it.

At that point, she had decided to change the subject.

"Oh Sadie, I missed having you there with me this year. Talk about men, that reminds me. I met this writer who just moved down there. He's living in Southport. He's perfect for you...you've got to meet this one! He's so funny, you'll adore him. You have to get down here right away. Ivee's going to camp as soon as school is out. Come down and we'll go to the beach. We'll have the whole place to ourselves. I'll introduce you to this guy. I think you'll change your mind about there not being any real men left."

"Uhmm...sounds yummy. Tomorrow I have to fly back to California to wrap up some studio shots. I'll be gone about another ten days. After that, say around the first of June, I have nothing but time on my hands for the rest of the summer."

"Oh, the timing would be perfect. Ivee will be gone for a month to all these camps...and Sadie...I kid you not...you have got to meet this man. He's not just smart. He's a hunk."

"OK, that's settled. I'll come down the first part of June. Now, let's get back to the subject. Quit stalling. Tell me what happened between you and Norris Wrenn at the Azalea Festival. Cut the bull. Just tell me, damnit!"

"Well...all right, but you're never going to believe it. I almost...I almost fell into bed with him." Marilee had held her breath while she waited.

"Bed? No shit? You're talking self-destruct. You're frigging right, I'm not believing this."

There had been another brief silence.

"What do you mean, almost?"

CHAPTER FOUR

ALL THE WAY DOWN THE HIGHWAY FROM GREENSBORO, Trip Graham tried to piece together the events of the weekend that had started in Blowing Rock.

One thing he remembered for sure: he had played no golf.

The weather had been promising when he left Colonial Hall, but, as was often the way in the mountains, it had turned bad by the time he had arrived at the condominium. He had met the others at the clubhouse and they had hung out in the grill, drinking, playing cards and watching golf on cable in the afternoon. Later, there had been a party at someone's house...

There was at least one other party. Almost certain. And...oh yeah...he had run into some New York people late Friday...or maybe that had been Saturday afternoon...the club bar?...

Shit! All a blur...

Trying to remember made his head hurt. And...Jeezus...he knew every-fucking-body.

Goddamn nose was sore. Probably snorted some blow. A lot of fucking nose candy around these days. Got to stop all that shit. Feeling bad. Bad, bad...bad...that bad.

He pulled a can of Coors from the little cooler he'd bought at the Quick-Stop and popped the top. Better...uhmmm...Wish he could skip this dumb thing with Clayt. Who cared if Norris was taking over?

Radio? Frigging farm reports...Paul Harvey...goddamn hillbilly music...news?...hmmm?...

"...DESPITE LATEST RUMORS OF PROBLEMS WITH CHINA TRADE, THE PRESIDENT REFUSED TO DISCUSS LEGALITY OF THE ABORTION SHUTDOWN..."

Freaking bluenose clown shut down legal abortion.

"...AND THIS JUST IN FROM GREENSBORO...THE BODY OF MOVIE ACTRESS EMMA CLAIRE WAS FOUND DEAD EARLY THIS MORNING IN A GREENSBORO MOTEL... RUMORED TO HAVE ACTED IN KIDDIE-PORN, MISS CLAIRE WAS CROWNED AZALEA QUEEN IN WILMINGTON AT THE ANNUAL FESTIVAL EARLIER THIS SPRING... DETAILS ARE SKETCHY, BUT AUTHORITIES SAY MISS CLAIRE HAD BEEN VACATIONING WITH FRIENDS IN BLOWING ROCK OVER THE WEEKEND..."

Emma Claire? The Azalea Ball?...Blowing Rock? Greensboro motel?

Blowing Rock? Had he seen her?...sexy little bitch.

Emma Claire? Dead?

The entire goddamn weekend...all just one big fucking blank...

CHAPTER FIVE

As they turned back into the airport traffic, Tom looked across at Norris expectantly. "C'mon, man, we've got enough shit on each other to wind up behind bars for life. Since when have we had secrets? What's bothering you? Spit it out."

"I'm sorry. You're right. I need to tell someone. It's been driving me crazy. One minute it's a trifle and I want to laugh...the next, I see my whole life coming apart. That's what I meant when I made the remark about screwing things up..."

Norris watched an anxious look pass across Tom's face. Now, he had to laugh.

Reaching over, he touched Tom's arm.

"Relax. Don't look so goddamned serious. It was just a silly episode...more adolescent flirtation than an indiscretion, really. Still it bothers me. You know me. Always in tight control..."

"What the hell are you talking about anyway...wha'ja do?...have one too many and grope some babe's ass?"

"Well...sort of, but it could've been a lot more, I'm afraid. I nearly made a mess of things."

"All right, start over. Let's hear it. Probably not as bad as all that." Tom shrugged.

"Well...I got no one to blame but myself. I didn't want to go down there and spend a week at that damn beach with that stuffy crowd in the first place. I should never have let Agnes badger me into it. And then, when Marilee walked out there on the beach before dawn that first morning...what can I say?..."

"Marilee? Jeezus, Norris...not Marilee Graham?"

"Sure. Who else? Why else would I worry about it? Have you ever seen her?"

"Not in person...but I saw that spread in *Sports Illustrated*."

He nodded at the magazine sticking out of the briefcase. "That is one super-gorgeous female. Still, man?...it's just not like you to fuck around...and the boss' daughter-in-law. You're fucking with mega-billions, man."

"I know...I can't believe it either. Worse...I can't really explain it. I confess, I always envied Trip...how could that stupid asshole have been so lucky? And, more—how could a woman that beautiful have made such a choice? And, I was pouting too...resentful that I'd let Agnes talk me into going down there. Agnes is such a total goddamn airhead. Still...I don't know what came over me. I was bored. With Trip routinely getting half in a bag every night and making an all-around fool of himself, it was like shooting fish in a barrel. I thought, why not show her—play 'King of the Hill.' I couldn't help it. I had to strut my ego...make her see. Jeezus, I quoted poetry...showed her the local color...taught her the finer arts of kite flying, played my guitar and sang to her. You wouldn't believe it. But I swear it started out as just an innocent pastime—it was all so easy. She was so eager, so childlike...hungry for attention...and so goddamn beautiful."

"Is that all?...doesn't sound like much to me." Tom chuckled. "Did you promise to run off into the sunset? Hell, you didn't even pull her panties down..."

Tom stopped short as a guilty look crossed Norris' face.

"Oh?..."

"Yeah! Oh. Oh-ho-ho!..."

"Hmmm...ah...well...lucky you...I guess."

"Before I knew it, it just got out of hand."

"Sounds to me like it's still out of hand. Are you still?..."

"No way. It's done. Over with. She understands...I made that crystal clear that same night...afterwards. Trouble is...I've been hiding from her for six weeks. I can't stand the thought of facing her. Can you imagine? She lives next door. I feel like a goddamn idiot."

"Why are you so afraid of the lady?" Tom's laugh was hollow. "Not in L-O-V-E...are you?"

"Love? Give me a break, Tom! I admit this one is prettier than most...and she's scary bright, definitely the exception. But, listen, old buddy...this is Norris Wrenn remember? We go back a long way. Love is just another four-letter word...and I'm not looking to chase strange pussy either. Besides, if I was, I wouldn't pick the boss' daughter-in-law—and my next door neighbor in the bargain. In over thirty-seven years, I've never been a life support system for a runaway penis. I'm not about to start now."

"C'mon, now, Norris. Who are you trying to convince? For a guy who's been hiding out for six weeks, that's pretty unconvincing talk. So why have you been afraid to even say hello to her? If you're so cynical and altogether intact, my macho friend, why haven't you told her all about love and four-letter words and men with all their brains in the heads of their dicks? Don't be telling me. Put her in her place, for chrissake. I thought you made it crystal clear to her...that very same night? Didn't you just tell me? Is this the same Norris Wrenn they write about? The man who says 'No' to presidents and kings?"

"OK, OK...so, just maybe she got to me. Goddamn, Tom, did you ever see her? Jeez, I don't remember the last time I wanted to read poetry to a woman. I don't like feeling like this. I feel so goddamn vulnerable. Listen...I may not know much about fucking around, but I don't need you or anybody else to tell me not to fuck around with about twenty million bucks. That's what I'll make at Grail in the next few years with just ordinary luck...and I believe the less I depend on other people, the luckier I get."

"Sounds like good advice...like the old Norris Wrenn of song and legend."

"Anyway, Mabel Graham is having this big dinner party tonight. The Governor's proclaiming Marilee Mother of the Year or something. I've made up my mind, I'll talk to her...straighten it all out."

"Well, I certainly hope so. If you don't, we're going to have you taken off the streets for your own protection. And what the hell, she's probably sorrier than you are. After all, she has just as much to lose as you do. Talk about making a mountain out of a mole-hill."

"Same old Tom. You've always had a knack for keeping me in

perspective..." Norris smiled and relaxed a little.

"United," the driver announced. He took the earphones out of his ears as he pulled the cab to a stop at the terminal.

"I guess you're tired of hearing my shit, huh?" Norris laughed and reached for the door handle.

"Not at all...like old times. But, cheer up. You're depressing. Think about us poor ordinary earthlings. You breeze through life leaping tall buildings in a single bound without even pausing to change in a phone booth. Be grateful, for chrissake. This time tomorrow you'll have the power to make all those idealistic schemes you used to talk about—the dreams you wrote a book about—come true. Forget all the garbage about power corrupting. True power is freedom. There won't be many men in the world with more power than you. Not even the President—now you want to talk about a real fuck-up..."

"OK, OK...you've made your point. I feel better already. I always do when I talk to you." All at once Norris made a decision. "Listen I want...no...I *need* you here in DC to help me with this new job at Grail—you know that. We'll be a team again...like old times. Sound like fun?"

"Sure. Like I said, just give me a call as soon as you know your schedule."

"We're signing the Grail contract tomorrow morning around ten. Chatham is going to call tonight. If he says the President wants to revive Phoenix, then you and I have to talk first."

"OK. And, for godsake, relax. Marilee Graham ain't gonna do anything you don't want her to."

"Yeah?...maybe that's the problem."

"Norris..."

"Yeah?"

"You're probably just plain garden variety horny. When was the last time you patted Agnes on the bottom? Never underestimate the therapeutic value of a good piece of ass."

"Sure." Norris laughed and opened the door. He leaned across the seat and handed the driver another twenty. "Driver, take this gentleman wherever he wants to go."

As he turned to leave, Norris watched the driver remove the headset connected to the device hanging on the dash. Briefcase in hand, he strode into the terminal and headed at a trot toward the boarding gate.

CHAPTER SIX

ABOUT TEN MILES PAST GOLDSBORO, Trip could see the Grail Tower shimmering through the summer heat haze off in the distance. To be suddenly confronted by the sight of a monolithic spire looming like the turret of some ancient castle above the gently undulating farmland was an experience not soon forgotten by many an unwary pilgrim passing through the area. The involuntary blink of eye and sharp intake of breath at first glimpse, and—as the beholder drew closer—the increasing hypnotic fascination as the emerging skyscraper on the horizon slowly came into sharper focus, was a reaction which remained much the same today as it had in 1928 when the legendary tower had been completed.

That year a famous writer who had been invited to cover the weeklong dedication ceremonies for *The London Times* wrote of the experience: *The moment was indescribably magical. I was immediately moved to recall the lines from the Rubiyat: 'And the hunter of the east has caught the sultan's turret in his noose of light.'*

For years, the Grail Tower stood as the tallest commercial structure east of New Orleans and south of Richmond. Now, even though it had long since lost that distinction, the Tower still emanated a majesty unequaled by taller structures lost among the steel and concrete spires of cities like Charlotte and Atlanta.

But to those more erudite, it represented far more than mere architecture. *Time* magazine had once written in a cover story about the Grail dynasty's rise to power: *Originally, the Graham empire was formed as Graham Tobacco and Cotton Company, a name it held until 1900 when it was changed to Graham Enterprises. By the late 1930s, expansion into a holding company that included the diverse manufacturing and worldwide distribution of plastics, aviation products, textiles, electronic communica-*

34

tions and other industries vital to the approaching WWII, the name was finally changed to Graham International, Ltd. and was listed on Wall Street with the stock symbol GRAIL. Apocryphally, sometime shortly after Pearl Harbor, the acclaimed columnist H.L. Mencken...or Walter Lippman (or both)...began waggishly referring to the powerful conglomerate as 'The Holy Grail.' Typically, the nickname caught on among journalists and was quickly shortened to become simply: Grail. Corporate meetings held in the austere boardroom at the top of the Grail Tower are reminiscent of the imposing scene from "The Wizard of Oz" where Dorothy is ushered into the electronic presence of the mighty Oz. When it comes to spectacular productions, Clayton Massie Graham could have taught even the great filmmaker, Cecil B. DeMille, a thing or two.

If any of the executives of Graham International, Ltd.'s subsidiary companies tended to have a short memory about who pulled the strings that made them dance, they were quickly restored to a proper condition of humility in that impressive chamber. Each year, after their annual refresher pilgrimage, these junior officers were returned to their own corporate settings with that same renewed but uneasy feeling of gratitude well understood by serfs in medieval times after having survived another tense, but successful, harvest. It was a profoundly affecting trauma.

As a boy, Trip had sailed paper airplanes from the top of that tower. Now, at the age of thirty-eight, this first view always made him feel as if he'd gotten away with some monstrous sacrilege; in his bones, he knew that sooner or later he'd have to suffer divine retribution.

The Corvette's digital clock indicated 2:06.

Plenty of time to stop for a cold Corona before he saw Clayt.

The outer walls of the entire top two floors of the twenty-five story Grail Tower were glass. Underneath this double-decked tier of luxurious penthouse suites housing the top brass, in descending pecking order, were the offices of the unsung heroes of the corporate hierarchy. Ducking into his own office, Trip sneaked in a hasty fortifying drink before he walked into his father's adjoining suite.

Trip could see his father standing by the window in the spa-cious sitting area removed from the working area around his desk. Boasting a wet bar, the sitting area also doubled as a small conference room.

Clayton Graham turned from the window as Trip came into the room. With his left hand, which was already holding a glass, he gestured toward the bar.

"Help yourself."

"Uhmm, thanks." Trip poured himself a healthy slug of Jack Daniels and filled the remaining third of the glass with 7-Up.

Clayton Massie Graham winced at the sight of his only offspring desecrating such fine whiskey. But he had long since given up any hope of Trip developing a real appreciation for the quality of liquor. To Trip, booze was just booze and that was simply that.

Clayt moved across the room to a small table and picked up a yellow legal pad and a couple of file folders. Moving back to the sitting area in the windowed corner of the room, he settled himself in one of the chairs and quickly glanced through the folders.

Trip waited until his father had seated himself with his back turned and took a big swallow of the drink. He quickly replaced the depleted quantity with more of the whiskey before he moved to the chair opposite his father.

"How was Blowing Rock? The Weather Channel said weather was rotten in the mountains. Were you able to play any golf at all?" Clayt asked without looking up.

"Nah. Didn't even try. Kept hanging around hoping...it just got worse," Trip said. "It's pretty up there, but the weather's the pits...never can depend on sunshine in the mountains."

"Oh, I think you're exaggerating. You just got back from Palm Beach and you're spoiled," Big Clayt chuckled, as he shuffled the file folders and placed them underneath the legal pad.

"Hmmph..." Trip snorted, the objection barely audible.

"Sit down. I want to go over this thing about Norris' new contract as CEO." His daddy handed him the legal pad. "The left-hand column breaks down his compensation for the four years beginning January. The right-hand figures outline the new terms he asked us for."

Trip leaned forward and took the pad. Taking a deep drink from the glass, he set it on the low table between them and leaned back in the chair to study the number-filled pages.

He had scarcely gotten comfortable when he sat bolt upright again.

"Who the fuck does he think he is? He's asking us to pick up his unexercised stock options just as a bonus for staying on...and be put in control in the bargain. Goddamn! We'll be paying three-quarters of a million just to have the privilege of promoting him. That's bullshit!" Trip picked up his drink and angrily thrust the pad back at Clayt. "Daddy, you must be out of your mind. This is the same guy I fired as a caddy at Pinehurst when I was thirteen or fourteen. Look, I know Norris is a prima donna, but he's really just the hired help...a goddamn flunky."

"Whoa! Calm down." Clayt clucked his tongue. "Kinda tightens your pucker, doesn't it? But you seem to forget that caddy was a year younger than you. It was that very same kid who whacked your donkey for the state junior championship. Your ex-caddy has come a long way from the caddy shack."

"Big deal..." Trip waved his hand in dismissal. "According to these figures, that bonus is nearly four times his current salary. That's one hundred grand more than he made in salary in the entire four years since he came on board. And he's already received a cool million in stock bonuses over that period. Goddamn! I didn't realize we were paying him that much. That's frigging ridiculous for a hired hand. Jeezus, I don't get paid that much...how come?"

Trip stopped to light a cigarette. "In the first place, he's getting the title and authority of Chief Executive Officer. That's enough. It's nothing new in the way of responsibility...he's already doing most of the work, anyway. He ain't worth it to us. What does he think he'll do if we don't make this deal? Quit? Where the hell is he going to find another deal like he has here? Shit. He's got it made. Sounds to me like he wants us to hand him the company on a gold platter. Screw the ungrateful S.O.B. He's still a glorified flunky as far as I'm concerned..."

Clayt remained silent.

"Now he's asking for three-quarters of a million just to hang around and do what we're already paying him to do in the first place. He sure has a fucked-up idea of how far he can push friendship. We need to straighten him out quick. Before this thing goes any farther..." Trip paused again.

Clayt made no response.

"...and while we're at it, how come he's taking more out of the company than I do?"

Clayt's eyes went icy.

"Because he works for it..." Clayt's tone was flat.

"Works for it? I'm your son, for chrissake! I'm a fucking Graham...what does that count for? This guy's just a goddamn flunky..."

Clayt raised his hand.

"Back off, Trip." Clayt's tone was dead serious. "We're going to give it to him. He's worth every cent and he knows it. He was already a hot item when he came here. Now he can go anywhere he wants to. Phillip Morris—or any of the other vultures that are dying to eat our lunch—would grab him in a heartbeat. Since he came here, our corporate worth has doubled. Despite the recession since the terrorist attacks, Grail stock has increased in value. That's not luck. Norris Wrenn did that. And half the time he had to fight me to get it done. He's worth every penny."

"Well, shit. Come on, Daddy, I know he's made some lucky guesses and pushed a few of the right buttons with the Senator and the White House, but he just wants to bargain...to sweeten his deal. He doesn't really expect we'll sit still for this. He'll settle for a quarter-million in stock. Bet on it..." Trip stubbed out the cigarette and leaned back confidently.

"Wrong," Clayt said emphatically. "Norris has given this careful thought. He won't play games. We're going to give him what he wants. Norris Wrenn's one of a kind. There's only one other name that comes to my mind...and that's Ted Turner and Norris is thirty years younger. Face it, son, your old college roomie—that lad you fired as a caddy—is an eight-hundred-pound gorilla...and you know where they sleep?" Clayt glared at him.

"Huh?...Oh!...'anywhere they want to'...right? That's really corny." Trip was not amused.

"Corny or not, we're meeting here at ten tomorrow morning to sign the papers. It's all set up. We can lunch at the club to celebrate, and I thought we could all play golf afterwards. You can have the pro. I'll take Norris. Look at it this way: Norris does the work, we make the real money. This way we don't lose sleep over him taking a better deal at Phillip Morris tomorrow."

"Goddamn it, if you put in the perks, he'll be making triple what I am. How can you justify that?" Trip lit another cigarette and picked up his glass.

"Well, do you want to handle this call from the Pentagon about Grail's Janus missile shield contracts...go to Houston next week and negotiate the Alaskan leases? The snarls in the Japanese electronic conglomerate merger...want to iron them out? Or, this snag in the class action still pending against Grail Tobacco?..." Clayton wasn't smiling. "Do you even think you could?"

"Well..." Trip drank the remaining swallow of bourbon. He stared into the glass and swirled the ice cubes. "OK...OK. I know I haven't exactly been keeping up with the day-to-day operations lately. But I could if I had to."

"Oh sure. If the Queen had balls, she'd be King." Clayton sniffed. "Are you telling me all of a sudden you want to take over day-to-day operations? Come to the office for a change?"

"Don't be so dramatic. No, I don't want to do that. That's a job for...for people like Norris. The woods are full of bright young corporate types with MBAs from Harvard or Babcock...and for a tenth of that." Trip pointed at the legal pad, obviously sulking now. "I'm trying to build a house in Palm Beach...I love overseeing the management of the Grail Hotel division at our flagship facility. The new Grail Beach and Golf Villas are a dream. God, I love it down there...they're our kind of people. Grail stockholders. It won't look good in the annual report that Norris will be taking more out of the company, than I am. I'm your son. I'm on the board. This is my company too. Old Massie meant for it to stay in the family."

"I mean for it to stay that way too. God knows my dream has

39

always been that you'd take my place...but that just hasn't happened, for whatever the reason. Now...for Ivee's sake, I...we...we all...need Norris. Just think of it as making it easier for you. And now that you mention it, I notice Norris has been playing golf with Ivee and his little buddy late afternoons. I'm sure Ivee would appreciate it a lot if his own daddy would play with him sometimes.

"By the way, your mother told me to remind you we are all eating at the club tonight. Agnes and Norris are coming. The Governor...Griff...both Senators...you name it—you know your mother. It's a private celebration for both Marilee and Norris. Marilee was honored with some Mother's Day thing today by the school PTA. Did you know the Governor is proclaiming her North Carolina's Mother of the Year 2002 tomorrow? That wife of yours is quite a girl."

"Oh, yeah, tell me about it. This spread about her old covers in *Sports Illustrated*...I've taken quite a kidding everywhere I go." Trip picked up the magazine from the cocktail table and opened it to the page with the photos of Marilee. There was a small photo of the two of them with Ivee at the Masters tournament in Augusta.

"I hope you appreciate what you have at home," Clayt said, absently, as he glanced over at the magazine cover. Gathering up the legal pad and folders, he started back to his office. "Griff and Nan are coming. I'm about ready to leave. See you at the club around seven."

"OK, I'll be there. Listen, I don't want you to think I don't value what Norris has done for this business. It just seems to me he's being a little pushy. A bit ungrateful. And you're right...I should take a more active role. I'll see you later." Trip tried to affect a tone of deep respect, but it was something he did not feel. Still, his father's reminder about how well the corporation was doing under Norris' leadership had started him thinking again about building the new house at Palm Beach...all the beautiful people at the Everglades Club...Sunday brunch at Palm Beach Polo and Country Club. The images brought about a sudden change in his appreciation for his old college roommate. The implication was clear. As Grail's CEO, Norris would take the pressure off.

He was looking forward to the evening at the club. He felt particularly satisfied that Marilee had been honored by the school today. And, tomorrow, the Governor was going to make her a celebrity...well, she was already a celebrity. This made her what? Motherhood was the next thing to sainthood. Hah! Sainthood...that was a good one!

From the first moment he'd met her, Trip had decided Marilee was the perfect trophy. When she steadfastly refused to go to bed with him, that had clinched it. He had put on a gaudy campaign to win her hand and, five months later, he'd brought home his famous cover-girl bride. Near the end of the first year, Marilee had borne him a son, right on cue. To Trip, that was only to be expected. He was happy with the way she saw to Ivee's upbringing. All in all, when he thought about it, he was quite pleased with his marriage.

Even her disappointing frigidity became OK with him. Besides...she really had been a lousy fuck. But, what difference did that make? Being Trip Graham's wife was just window dressing. The most overrated thing in the world was homefucking. Homecooking and the goddamn United States Marines ran a close race for second.

Glancing at the cover photo of the woman in the swimsuit, a wistful pang betrayed him.

Saint Marilee? Maybe. But who was he trying to kid? She certainly wasn't frigid.

Truth was—Marilee despised him. He flushed with shame, remembering his embarrassing performance in their honeymoon suite at The Greenbrier. Maybe, if he cleaned up his act, the Ice Maiden would give him a second chance...

All at once, Trip felt better about the thing with Norris.

Good old Norris, he mused. Keep my daddy off my back, keep Saint Marilee and my kid off my back, and you're worth your weight in gold. Maybe I'll just show Marilee...my kid...my daddy...Norris Wrenn...everyfuckingbody...that I'm as good a Graham as any of 'em.

"Wait up, Daddy," he called. "I'll sign those papers now. It'll save a lot of time."

CHAPTER SEVEN

THINKING BACK ON LAST NIGHT'S CONVERSATION with Sadie, Marilee smiled, remembering that Sadie had been shocked speechless when she'd told her she'd almost fallen in bed with Norris Wrenn at the beach.

"What do you mean, almost?" Sadie had asked, when she'd finally regained her composure.

"Well...we didn't. I mean we would have—we almost got caught stark naked. Anyway, it doesn't matter...we didn't actually do anything." Marilee had held it in so long, she suddenly felt relieved to have told someone. She had held her breath, waiting for Sadie to say something.

"Uhmm, I don't know why I'm all that surprised. Trip's such an asshole...serves him right. I sort of wondered when the lid would blow off," Sadie said, thoughtfully. "Don't stop talking now. For god's sake, what happened?"

"I...I'm not even sure what happened. Norris and Agnes were with us at the cottage during the entire festival week. Clayt and Mabel, too. I'll give Mabel credit for one thing: she tries. She fights with Trip constantly about the drinking. But it's useless. After a day or so, it just gets on my nerves. But that's beside the point. You remember how it goes. The women play bridge and lie around in the sun...or go into Wilmington and tour the gardens...and shop. The men play golf...or fish. And drink. Anyway, it's still my favorite thing of the year. Everybody we know comes down there."

Marilee paused, trying to find the words.

"I know this sounds...well...kind of corny. I just sort of looked up the first morning and there was Norris Wrenn. Before I knew what was going on...oh Sadie, I don't know how to tell you...it sounds like some breathy novel by Nora Whatsherface. It was unreal. He's been our next door neighbor for four years, and I'd never noticed him. Isn't that wild? He's famous—of course you know all that..." Marilee paused for breath. "You're right about his book. The title is *Phoenix Rising*. I have some clippings...just listen to this."

She had picked up a clipping and read, " '...*in Phoenix Rising, Wrenn has revived hope of rescuing the vast untapped wealth of the truly gifted young minds from the free world's wasteland of the disadvantaged. Wrenn's brilliant concept not only promises that mankind can save itself from the inexorable crawl back into the slime of the sea, but he openly dares us to turn away from the responsibility.*' That quote was from *The New York Times* and it was on the dust jacket of the book he signed for me at the beach. You know what he said? He laughed and said, 'Save the world? I'm not sure if I can even save my own ass anymore! Some days I look around and wonder if I'm not starring in the wrong movie.' He's so serious and...so clever. Can you imagine? In that one week down at the beach, he got a jillion calls from the White House. He told me they were bugging him to come back to Washington...but...God, Sadie, if he left now, just when I found him, I'd die!..." Marilee hesitated, lost momentarily in the thought. "Anyway, did you read his book?"

"Read his book? What goddamn difference does that make? And famous? What's with famous? Marilee...*Sports Illustrated* just published a cover and four pages of you in their special anniversary issue. Your husband is heir to one of the largest corporations in the world. Think about it. When was the last time you had lunch or dinner with a senator or a former astronaut? If not yesterday, then tomorrow, most likely? You've come a long way from Hicksville, babe. What's the big deal about the rich and famous all of a sudden? It's your way of life. Will you get real?"

"I know...I'm sorry. I guess I'm not making much sense," she'd replied, sheepishly. What Sadie said sank in. For six weeks she had been carrying it around, all locked inside her. It had all been so secret, so wonderful, she hadn't really thought about how it would sound to someone else. She was babbling like a teenager. But she felt like a teenager...what was so awful about that?

"And what about his wife, good old Angie...or whatever her name is...I guess it doesn't matter that Norris Wrenn is married, too? I don't quite know whether to laugh or dial nine-one-one," Sadie said flatly.

"Her name is Agnes...but he doesn't love her, Sadie...believe me, I know..." she had begun, but Sadie interrupted impatiently.

"OK, OK, we can skip all that for now...let's get back to the subject. I still can't believe it. Right in the middle of all those damn people, did you just walk right up to each other and do...ah...whatever? And by the way, what did you do?"

"Well, it was kind of...you know...an accident. After the first morning, I guess we both were sort of making it happen. That first morning was incredible. I got up just before sunrise and slipped out to walk on the beach. Norris was already out there. It was all so natural. We just started walking and we talked. It was wonderful."

"Oh, my God. He talked to you," Sadie said sarcastically. "Did he quote you poetry?"

"Well...yes he did. And, Sadie, did you ever fly a kite?"

"Oh, shit!" Sadie muttered.

Marilee ignored her. "Before we left, he gave me a book of poetry...and he read to me. He can quote passages from Steinbeck and Hemingway...and he told me about H. L. Mencken...I got a copy of Mencken's *A Treatise on the Gods* from the library when I got back. You should read him...you'd love Mencken. He was such a cynic."

"Mencken? How about Sartre...or Kierkegaard? He didn't leave out Kierkegaard, did he? Jeezus!"

"Oh yes, Kierkegaard...him too! You know about him?" Marilee hardly paused for breath. "And, would you believe it, he plays guitar...he's crazy about country music."

"Oh shit! Mencken...Kierkegaard...kites...guitars...and country music. What's a poor girl to do? Christ, Marilee, I could take him to Monterey and start a frigging cult."

"Oh Sadie, don't make fun. It was the most wonderful week of my life. We walked and talked every morning. Well, until the morning after the Azalea Ball...after the night we...after it almost happened." Her excitement had slowly faded. "That last morning, he and Clayton walked on the beach for awhile and were talking...about business I'm sure. I tried to find an opportunity to talk to him but in the confusion of the packing Agnes kept...."

"Oh Christ! This is worse than I thought!" Sadie interrupted. "I can understand the little tête-à-têtes on the beach, but you keep avoiding the punch line? Tell me about the fireworks."

"Well, Friday night after my cocktail party, the Governor and all the big shot players...anyway, afterwards, Norris got a call from Washington, and I had to stay behind and pay Marcellus and the extra help. We suddenly found ourselves alone at the cottage. All the others had run off to Wilmington to the Azalea Ball. And it just happened. We were in each other's arms and we couldn't keep our hands off each other. The whole thing was out of control. We hardly said a word. In less than five minutes we were upstairs...headed for bed..."

"Holy Mother! Poetry is one thing, but headed for bed! What stopped you?"

"Nothing would have stopped us, I promise you that. But Marcellus came back and damn near caught us." Marilee caught her breath, remembering. "As a matter of fact, if Marcellus hadn't run over a conch shell in the driveway that exploded like a cannon, it would have been more than just embarrassing. I'm not so sure he didn't suspect something anyway. But, you know Marcellus, he would never be disloyal to me."

"Oh, I'm not worried about that, but don't just leave me panting, dammit. Gimme the juicy details."

"God, Sadie, we...were undressed...buck naked. He is so...so beautiful. You'll never believe this, but he just barely touched me and little red lights exploded inside my brain. God, I've never felt so out of control."

"My God! Marilee, you must have been crazy. Were you drunk? You weren't smoking anything, were you? You just can't dive into bed with your husband's best friend...and your next door neighbor at that."

45

"I know! It's crazy. But we weren't drunk, and I've never smoked pot in my life." Marilee was indignant. "You're not even trying to understand."

"OK...OK. This just isn't like you. Marilee, you aren't plain Jane Doe. We ain't talking about some two-bit company. *Graham International, Ltd.* is *Fortune* top ten! Have you thought about that? This is scary!"

"Scary? You're telling me about scary? I was scared to face Agnes at church or the club for about two weeks. I was paranoid. I was sure that somehow everyone knew. I imagined all sorts of things. But I keep thinking about it. I keep on remembering."

Marilee caught her breath. "God, Sadie I want him so bad. I haven't felt anything at all in years. I had forgotten how it was to feel. And besides, Sadie, I've never felt anything like this in my life. I want him, Sadie. I keep scheming, building little scenarios about how I can have him."

"Forget it, Marilee, you're married, remember? All that was just a...a flirtation...whatever. The beach. The moonlight. Shit happens! C'est la vie! It was 'just one of those things,' like the song goes. It's been a long rotten marriage. You've just been building up like a...a volcano. Believe me, I understand. It had to happen, I guess, but it isn't real. Trust me, Marilee, I know men like Norris Wrenn. He might wind up as President, but he won't fall in love. Norris is too smart to get his fingers caught in the boss' honey pot. He's not about to get involved. Take a deep breath and be glad you escaped."

"Oh, but you're wrong—you don't know him. That week at the beach, for the first time in my life I found myself talking to a man who gave me permission to just be me. I was a person again. Don't you see? I'll never be the same. And that night...I've never...never ever...felt like that. He's not at all like you say. He's wonderful."

"My God...do you know how you sound? You've said every frigging new age cliché except 'he's the only man who has ever understood me.' Just listen to yourself. You're bored, you're frustrated...and you're just horny. Nobody dies of horniness...praise the great goddess Aphrodite."

"Yeah, maybe...maybe I'm that too." For a moment Marilee sounded contrite. Then she fired right back. "Well, what of it? I don't care anymore."

"Marilee. Go take a cold shower. Go to Raleigh, catch a plane to Alaska...then take the shower."

The line had fallen momentarily silent.

"I don't blame you for making fun of me, but you're wrong. It's not just an attack of hormones. I'm up at five-thirty peeking out my window hoping to catch a glimpse when he starts his morning jog. I've been mooning around here for six weeks in my back yard just hoping he'd come out and prospect for uranium or send up a weather balloon...or something...anything. I can't help it. I'm miserable. Oh, Sadie, I wish you could come down here," she wailed.

"OK...OK. Just hold on for a few days. Why don't you get away...go to the Greenbrier and check into the spa...or come up here for a few days and shop. Honestly, I'll be there before you know it," Sadie had pleaded earnestly. "For godsake, don't do anything crazy. I know I sound like a parrot, but you've got Ivee...and what about Agnes, remember her?"

"He's not in love with her. But, don't worry Sadie; I'm not going to march next door and tell Agnes I'm taking her husband. I may be crazy, but not that crazy. Besides, if I'm crazy, it's his fault. He makes me sick, being so damn noble. He told me that night he was going to stay away from me. He hasn't been within a hundred yards of me for six weeks."

"Well, good for him. At least it sounds like he's got his head screwed on straight." Sadie was silent for what seemed like a long time. "Oh, well...either way, Marilee, the man upstairs is looking out for you. God knows, in your present condition you can't look out for yourself. You need all the help you can get."

CHAPTER EIGHT

As FAR AS NORRIS COULD TELL, no one followed him off the plane in Raleigh. All that cloak-and-dagger talk with Tom Bradley about spooks poking around Marilee's Azalea Week beach party had left him feeling unsettled.

Heading east on I-40 toward Colonial Hall, he passed a National Guard parking lot full of military vehicles and he was struck by an unexpected wave of nostalgia.

Hopkins? Tom had said. There'd been a Toby Hoskins... Colombia...'87?...Panama maybe? A very busy time. Except for poor old Ollie North, he couldn't put names to all the faces. Most of the names probably weren't real anyway.

Almost fifteen years had passed since he'd limped off that plane at this same airport on his return from Colombia. Back then, he believed he was through babysitting Trip Graham's sorry ass. When he had graduated from Virginia, he had made a solemn vow that he was through dragging Trip around.

So what was he doing back here when the whole goddamn world was suing Grail Tobacco? Was he really doomed to a lifetime of rescuing Trip Graham? Maybe he was like a moth and all that lovely Graham money was the flame?

So, what about himself? A good moth just keeps coming back for more until he finally gets burned.

A few months before graduation in May of 1985, Clayton had offered to get him a scholarship to Harvard Law. He had told him, "Thanks, but no thanks," and headed off to law school at Washington and Lee that fall.

At W&L things went well as usual. He'd had everybody impressed...and he'd really liked studying law. But, spiritually, that

48

fall had been a difficult time for him. His father had gone to Washington and Lee, and Norris found himself on a campus inhabited by the ghost of a father he'd barely known.

He had rarely seen his father, career Army officer, over the several years before he was killed in late April 1980 on an infamous covert mission to rescue the American hostages in Iran. All at once, the world's turmoil seemed very personal. For perhaps the first time in his life he was asking himself heavy questions about who he was.

That fall of 1985, thinking about his father, the craziness in the Middle East, and the Communist sellout by the Sandinistas in Nicaragua...it was all heavy on his mind.

It was inevitable. In January of 1986, Norris left his newly begun law studies and enlisted in the Army as an officer candidate. He suddenly found himself in an unfamiliar world where the personal pronouns were impersonal and identity was a long number which distinguished him only as being one digit different from the guy ahead of him in line.

For the next four months in basic training at Fort Sill and the following six months in OCS, he dedicated the time usually spent for prayers to cursing himself for not taking Clayton Graham up on the offer to get him a direct commission.

For those ten surreal months it took to bring him to the moment when he walked across the stage of Post Theater No. 1 and received his commission, he remained devoid of pride. But in that instant, pride returned to him, a much better and finer thing than Norris had ever felt before. It became something he could feel on the occasion of unusual achievement. Something a young officer newly graduated from a crash course on hush-hush military operations could still feel after his patrol in Colombia had been ambushed by Medellin drug enforcers and he had stood, insane with fear, slashing out again and again, ripping human flesh that had no humanity.

It was all the same to the men who were there. In their simple way of looking at things, the shooting and killing seemed a lot like their idea of war.

When he'd limped off the plane back in Raleigh and suddenly

realized he was still alive and everything still worked, only then could he allow himself to be proud that he had not accepted Trip's father's offer. Nicaragua...San Salvador...Honduras...Panama... he'd been a non-presence in forbidden lands. In a war that was non-existent, he'd walked away his own hero at least.

Norris Wrenn—the All-American Dream.

CHAPTER NINE

MARILEE SLOWED AS THE LITTLE CAR she had followed from the school turned into a drive up ahead. The driver got out and ran down to the street waving for her to stop.

There was no traffic coming from either direction, so Marilee pulled to the side and lowered the window.

"I wanted to catch you at the school, Marilee, but there was such a mob...and I had to hurry back to relieve my sitter. You were wonderful, simply wonderful! We're all so proud of you. Mothers don't get enough credit," the young woman gushed.

"Thank you, Penny. I'm not much of a speaker, I'm afraid," she said, embarrassed by the woman's adulation.

"Anyway, I just wanted to ask you when we could get together to make plans for the Cub Scout picnic. Saturday after next doesn't give us much time. I talked to Jaynie and Marie and Anne and Sue. They say they can come over tomorrow or Wednesday night, whichever. We can't meet without you. What suits you best?" Penny looked to her anxiously.

"I have to go to Raleigh tomorrow morning, but I plan to be back by late afternoon. I have a tennis lesson at five-thirty. Would eight tomorrow evening be OK?"

"Oh, Marilee, that would be wonderful. I'll call the others. We'll meet here if that's all right. I'm having trouble getting a sitter for the new baby."

"That's fine, Penny. I'll see you then." Marilee knew better than to ask about new babies; you always got more of an answer than you bargained for.

"Oh, Marilee, thank you. That would be really super. See you tomorrow night then." Penny reluctantly stepped away to let her move on.

A few blocks further along, Marilee turned into the entrance of a lane which was eloquently imposing. Lush, meticulously manicured hedges ten feet high ended at two antique-brick columns which served as solid, austere gateposts. There, the lane was divided by an island planted with a riot of colorful flowers. In the center was a colonial-style sign hanging from a white cross-arm, lettered in Times Roman:

THE COUNTRY CLUB
Private

It was a statement of unrelenting exclusivity seen only here and—she'd heard Clayt brag many times—in Brookline, Massachusetts.

Once inside the gateposts, the surroundings changed. The security guards wore sharply creased grey slacks, pale-blue button-down oxford shirts with a distinctive ancient madder medallion tie of loden green and blue. Their blazer jackets were deep hunter green with The Country Club crest on the breast pocket. Their shoes were meticulously polished tassel loafers.

As she passed the gatehouse, Marilee nodded an acknowledgment at the guard's salute.

Club Drive was the only way in or out. Like an enormous, brick-scaled snake biting its own tail, it began where Red Barn Road bordered the twelfth fairway. From there, it wound ingeniously in and out between fairways cut through dogwood and pine woods. The Drive was a marvelous maze of little cul-de-sacs darting off here and there into the trees. It eventually ended back at the little Williamsburg-styled brick guardhouse just inside the gateposts.

Only the residents and non-resident club members had free access through the gate. Every vehicle not identified by the distinctive sticker on the windshield had to stop and be cleared by the security police. If an outsider had not previously been cleared and was not entered on the expected list, then a resident or The Club had to be called and the visitor given clearance.

There were only sixty-one homes on Club Drive, which left most of the property yet to be built upon. There was no danger of crowding. The Grahams quietly and implicitly controlled it all. It was their domain.

Since she had come here, Marilee could recall only a dozen or so outsiders who had been permitted to acquire property on Club Drive. It was a complicated process of being proposed for approval by at least two property owners and the proposal being placed before The Committee with the required endorsement of three other residents. And there were details to be taken care of, like the prior approval of both the architectural drawings and landscaping plans by the Architectural Review Board.

To the locals, the austere street was simply "The Drive."

Most of the women she saw at the Club lived outside Club Drive, of course. Not many, if any, would ever make it inside the gates. Many of their husbands were bright young men working for Grail.

By definition, an outsider in Colonial Hall was anyone whose family did not already live there. But to the residents on The Drive, the philosophy was a far more critical one. By no means did you have to be from outside Colonial Hall to be an outsider to the residents on The Drive. Rarely did a "homeboy" or "girl" move that far up in social standing. In reality, it was far more likely that additions to the list of families living on The Drive would come from the ranks of socially prominent families migrating from elsewhere in the South. There was no rule. Marilee had never heard it discussed. But, except for the highest ranking officers in Grail, there were few real Yankees on Club Drive. And Marilee knew that even those had undergone a period of watchful scrutiny by Clayton and Mabel before the barriers were relaxed and the exceptions were made.

Driving along, here and there Marilee waved at the women inspecting their gardens and lawns. Immaculately dressed for golf, or tennis, or luncheon at the club, these women all looked as if they'd just stepped off the pages of *Town & Country*. It amused her to contrast the young women she had passed in Penny's neighborhood, a mile or so back on Red Barn Road. They too were moving about their lawns, but they were dressed in boutique-cute denim things with gingham appliqués of flowers and sprinkling cans...or white tennis shorts. She knew them all and waved at them, too. The lawns back there had been somewhat narrower, more evenly spaced plots fronting the less pretentious but affluent homes in Country Club Downs along Red Barn Road. She would also see most of these women and their husbands at The Club. But the identifying stickers on the windshields of their cars were red, not green. Only a few would ever make any real progress toward closer relationships with their contemporaries along The Drive.

It was difficult to decide which group deserved the most disdain. Marilee felt no kinship with either. Deeply imbedded in her subliminal self, both groups represented the same snobby women who had made her life a hell growing up back in Virginia. Yet over her years here, she had become their symbol of attainment—both insiders and outsiders alike looked to her example.

"It's a miracle they ever let you in the gate," Sadie had reminded her. "Remember how that Richards woman rescued you from Mabel's clutches? Now that is an incredible story."

Thinking about it now, Marilee laughed out loud. It was an incredible story all right.

CHAPTER TEN

DRIVING ALONG U.S. 70, thinking about Mabel Graham's dinner party, the thought of having to face Marilee tonight at the club gave Norris butterflies the size of 767s. Tonight he'd say his little speech to Marilee and tomorrow, after the contract signing, he'd get on with his life.

As he approached the town limit of Colonial Hall, Norris looked out the window at the looming presence of the Grail Tower.

He was suddenly overwhelmed by the enormity of it. Tomorrow he would have it all.

Incredible.

He knew that life was a process. Inspirations that lead to landmark achievement begin with one usually ill-defined moment and then, like seeds germinating just below the level of awareness, they grow until they finally emerge at some point into the realm of consciousness.

Norris would never forget the day he had first recognized the opportunity that had brought him here to Grail. He could still pinpoint, with the greatest clarity, the precise moment he first realized the enormous power that he held over Clayton Graham.

At Virginia, Norris had quickly learned that Trip Graham's academic problems usually precipitated a fatherly visit by the senior Graham. Although he had met Clayton Graham briefly at golfing events where Trip had been his teammate, Norris had hardly more than a nodding acquaintance with Trip's father. And that had suited him just fine. One year as Trip's roommate taught him: one Graham was enough.

The momentous day of Norris' epiphany occurred the first time the elder Graham had joined the two of them on the golf course.

Trip had taken the golf coach, a former touring pro, as partner. There had been an undercurrent of hostility seething between father and son, and Norris, wanting to stay out of it, had resisted joining the group at first. But Clayton, fresh from watching Norris' performance as low amateur in his first Masters appearance, had doggedly overridden his excuses to defer.

Sly old Clayton had chosen his partner well. He was exuberant by the time they had made the turn. His unworthy son and the hapless coach were getting their donkey soundly whacked.

For Trip, it was a major setback in the larger war between father and son. To be losing to his father at a time when he was already in the elder man's bad graces was intolerable.

"You guys have us dormie. Give us a chance...let us double everything on the last three holes," Trip whined in frustration.

It was really a meaningless bet for Norris and Trip. But money was not the real issue here. This represented a mortal combat...the infinite struggle.

"Why not? It's your funeral. Right, partner?" Clayton hadn't even looked to Norris for approval.

The bet renewed, Trip stepped up to the tee and smacked a screamer down the left center of the narrow fairway. Smirking arrogantly, he turned and said, "Eat your fucking hearts out, gentlemen."

It was a statement of the war between father and son and made Norris uncomfortable. He didn't really understand father-son relationships anyway.

The elder Graham had come storming angrily into Charlottesville the day before, after being hastily summoned by a member of the University hierarchy well aware of the benevolent, and virtually bottomless, wellspring of resources for the grand new Science Hall—and the even grander Classics Building last year—an administrator who kept Clayton informed with disconcerting accuracy of the current status of Trip's progress or, most often, the latest of what seemed to be a never-ending sequence of Trip's minor disharmonies with life, both on and off campus.

Norris knew the current situation was grave. Trip's usually precarious academic standing loomed almost beyond repair. Unless heroic intervention was immediately forthcoming, he was going to be kicked out at the end of the spring semester.

"Coach tells me you are at the head of your class. And the top golfer in the conference, too. I wish some of that would rub off on Trip," Clayton Graham had remarked. The senior Graham seemed tired, older than his forty-odd years. "What'n hell's wrong with him, anyway?"

"He's just having a bad putting streak, sir. Trip's game is coming around. He'll be in top shape by the time the conference tournament comes up." Norris understood full well that Clayton's question had nothing to do with Trip's golf game, but he wanted nothing to do with the problem between father and son. He certainly had no ambition to be part of the solution either. Norris was sick of trying to reason with Trip about his grades and the constant partying. Trip had already told him—one time too many—to mind his own business. It was advice Norris had been happy to take.

"I don't give a good goddamn about his golf game," Clayton had snapped in frustration. Then, suddenly aware he was unfairly venting his anger on Norris, he added apologetically, "I just wish I had a clue. Why can't he get serious about school?"

Norris pulled the cart up to where Clayton's ball rested near the center of the fairway. The elder Graham didn't hit it as far as the rest of them, but he carried a five handicap and played a first class game. "Hit it close, sir. We don't want these turkeys to win the press; that would be embarrassing."

It was a tricky shot of about 150 yards over a yawning bunker guarding the pin closely tucked in about ten yards behind it. Clayton looked to Norris. "Hard eight or easy seven?"

"It's a six, sir. There's a little wind up there you can't feel down here. Hit the six as good as you can."

Clayton had taken his advice and jumped all over the shot. The ball hit just over the trap and skipped nicely up, fifteen feet past the hole.

"Great shot, sir. That'll hold 'em."

After they all had hit their second and they were riding to the green, Clayton spoke again. "What can we do? Is Trip a lost cause? Can he get his grades up?"

"A lost cause? I don't believe in lost causes, sir. I guess he just needs to learn how to study and how to discipline himself. I think a good tutor might help. But..." Norris let the thought trail off, into the spring afternoon. They had reached the green and he jumped quickly from the cart trying to avoid further conversation about the matter.

"But what?..." Clayton tried to call him back, but Norris had already grabbed his putter and was walking onto the putting surface.

Riding up the next fairway, Clayton persisted, "Do you really think a tutor would help?"

"Sir, I doubt anything is going to help as long as Trip has unlimited money and a car to drive. Why should he give a rat's ass about staying in school anyway? After all, he doesn't have to worry about making a living. School's just a party for him."

"But he's going to be head of a major corporation someday. He sure-as-shit needs to prepare for that...Grail isn't some goddamn family hardware store," the senior Graham protested.

"Does he know what that means? I don't think he has the foggiest notion, sir."

"Why, it means running a multi-billion-dollar international conglomerate. Do you know how much a billion is, young man?"

For the moment Norris seemed to ignore the question. He looked over the shot facing the elder Graham and said with a tight smile. "Hit the sand wedge as good as you know how, sir. We've got 'em on the ropes. Go for the kill."

Clayton was getting more irritable by the minute. "Fuck the golf...goddamn it, this is serious. Don't you care whether Trip stays in school? Do you have any idea how much a billion dollars is?"

"In American numbers it is one thousand millions. That's a cardinal number followed by nine zeros in New York...in London it's twelve goose eggs after the number. Over there, it's a million millions...I guess? Anyway, who cares? We're talking American. At Graham International, Ltd., it was twelve billion American, and some change, last year. I know what it means, sir. But it's not me who needs to know." Norris moved to a position just behind him and pointed with his right arm over Clayton's shoulder so he could see the line. "Hit it just over to the right edge of the bunker, sir. It'll kick left down toward the pin."

The elder Graham executed the shot nicely and the ball kicked just the way Norris predicted.

"Certainly I care whether Trip stays in school. He's my roommate, my teammate...why, he's almost like a brother...he's my best friend." Norris stopped short. Suddenly, it occurred to him twelve billion was quite a lot to think about. Suddenly, he was overcome with a rush of warmth for Clayton Massie Graham the Third—and genuine sympathy for a perplexed father who was trying to make a man out of his recalcitrant son. At that moment, he made a decision to take an abiding interest in Trip.

"Great shot, sir."

"They told me you were bright...how come you know that much about Grail...I'll bet Trip doesn't know that."

"Oh yes he does, sir. He told me, himself," Norris lied. "Don't sell him short, sir. Don't count him out. He needs a firm hand, sir. Do you know how to train a mule?"

"If you mean hit him in the head with a two-by-four? Yes, everybody's heard that one. If I thought it would help him I'd go hit him in the head with this putter right now...as a matter of fact it would at least make me feel better." The elder Graham suddenly laughed and shook his head. "What can we do to help him? You're his roommate."

"Here's what I'd do, Mr. Graham. Spring break begins next week. Trip's planning to go to Bermuda. I'd insist he come home and spend that time with you at the offices of Graham International Ltd. All day...every day. And, I would go to his faculty advisor this very afternoon and identify the best tutor money can buy and I'd have that tutor start tonight...and continue night and day, including the spring break trip to Colonial Hall. And I'd ground him...take his wheels, right now. And cut off his money. All of it. If you're serious, sir, don't tell me. Tell him."

Norris walked over to his ball and hit a knocked-down sand wedge that bored through the wind and almost tore the flag off of the pin. It fell within a foot of the cup.

"That should put us one up, sir." He smiled quietly and walked over to the cart. "And, sir, I'll deny I ever had this conversation or that the subject ever came up. I have to live with him. He's my best friend...I don't want him to think I'm a traitor."

"I think you've given me good advice. I just hope it's not too late." The elder Graham gave Norris a fatherly pat on the shoulder. "Why don't you come down next week with him and I'll show you how twelve billion looks from the top."

Norris never forgot that fateful day eighteen years ago when he had decided he would take a serious interest in Trip's future.

Twelve thousand million—the number kept echoing inside Norris' head.

As the Tower loomed larger, his thoughts turned to the present. The bottom line for Grail was over eighty billion now. He had increased it over sixty billion himself.

Not bad for a rookie!

He had to shake all this current uncertainty about his job, and his wife, and his life in general. There was too much going on. This crazy preoccupation with Marilee was affecting his objectivity—threatening to destroy everything. After all, he knew what he wanted.

All of a sudden, he noticed the sun had come back out again. Trying to escape his mood, he opened the sunroof and was greeted with the aroma of tobacco warehouses and plowed earth and the unmistakable stink of hog excrement clashing with the sweet bouquet of honeysuckle and pine rosin—all commingling with a faint smell of factory smoke.

The wonderful smell of old money...the most seductive of perfumes.

CHAPTER ELEVEN

CONTINUING SLOWLY ALONG THE DRIVE, Marilee marveled that she had ever been naïve enough to believe that Mabel Graham would be happy to have Trip marry her.

Back then, her overnight international celebrity notwithstanding, she had been totally wide-eyed—a strange mixture of New York chic and small town innocence.

When she first met Trip in 1988, she had only been out of college for seven months. Her head was still a whirl from seeing herself on the cover of every fashion magazine and on billboards in Paris and Rome.

Trip had been making the rounds in New York, celebrating his return from a post-college trip abroad—a graduation present from Mabel which had stretched out to over three years on his pretense of touring overseas offices of Grail.

A friend of Sadie's had introduced them at a cocktail party and Marilee had found him to be pleasant and unbelievably generous. It had been easy to allow herself to be swept into the kaleidoscopic pattern of his extravagant courtship. Trip was handsome, well-mannered, and, of course, he had money. But, in her naïveté, she'd had no idea just how rich he really was.

It all had been like a fairy tale. She had hardly known him two weeks when he had herded her, along with Sadie and Sadie's "boy-toy" of the moment, a famous cover boy for romance novels, as chaperones, onto a corporate jet and flown the lot of them down for a whirlwind tour of "the old home place."

On that impromptu weekend visit, Marilee had seen enough of Colonial Hall to fill her with longing. The brief glimpse of the life she might have on Club Drive revived much too sharply the hunger of her childhood growing up in shabby rooms over the pool hall.

She had been too starry-eyed to let Mabel Graham's not-so-subtle questions about her family background put her on notice—not that it hadn't made her more than a little resentful at the impertinence of it all. Besides, she really hadn't dared dream it would ever amount to anything serious.

The ensuing courtship had proceeded at such an incredible pace, it was over before she realized what had happened. In less than a month, Trip had proposed. And, of course, she'd been powerless to say no.

Mabel Hodges Graham had struck like a cobra as soon as she heard of the engagement. Her scheme to nip the wedding plans in the bud had been diabolically calculated to completely dehumanize Marilee and send her running for cover.

Not yet twenty and a total stranger, Marilee had not yet gotten used to the feel of Trip's gaudy Cartier diamond solitaire when Mabel's summons had come like a thunderbolt on a Monday morning. Trip had gone to San Francisco with his father, leaving Marilee no warning.

"Marilee, this is Mabel Graham. I've hardly had a chance to get to know you. I want you to come down Friday for the weekend to meet some of my friends."

"*Friday?*...not *this* Friday?"

"Yes...I've already arranged for the company plane to come pick you up."

"Oh...my! I...ah...well...I thank you, of course. Certainly I'm anxious to get to know you better and I'd love to come...but..." The thought of having to face Mabel alone had scared her half to death. And with no preparation! She sat down and frantically busied herself, looking at her calendar. When she saw the conflicting date, she suppressed a sigh of relief. "...but...I can't. I'm scheduled to do a *Vogue* cover shoot that day."

Of course, sooner or later she knew she would have to face Mabel alone, but for the moment at least, she was overjoyed that she had a legitimate excuse.

"But, I don't understand..." Mabel replied.

"I'm sorry, Mrs. Graham. I have a crushing schedule for the next few days. Anyway, Trip and I plan to come down on the way to the Masters Tournament. That's only a few weeks off."

"Oh, my dear, that wouldn't do at all. I've planned a little tea for you Saturday. I couldn't disappoint my friends. The Governor's wife is coming from Raleigh and the wives of both of our Senators. I couldn't possibly cancel on such short notice," Mabel interrupted, imperiously.

"But, Mrs. Graham...I...I don't know what to say. This puts me in an impossible situation. Why didn't you let me know sooner? I have commitments." Angry and resentful, momentarily she forgot her intimidation.

"Oh, bother! Trip said you were quitting that silly modeling thing. I *know* it's short notice and I'm sorry, but, after all, you and Trip didn't give us very much warning about all this—not that it isn't all so exciting...and...well, three months isn't much time for us to plan a wedding, now is it?"

In the end, the *Vogue* shoot had been rescheduled.

Trip had been pleased when Marilee finally reached him in San Francisco. "Cheer up...the old girl just wants to make you feel at home."

From start to finish, Mabel's entire charade had been a diabolically plotted assassination, artfully orchestrated to put her in her proper place. Determined to humiliate her, Mabel was intent on sending her back to New York tearfully despairing that she could ever be able to assume the role of Trip's wife.

Impeccably dressed in a dark green blazer with the Grail crest on the pocket, the limousine driver had taken her directly from Sadie's town house to the corporate hanger at La Guardia. With the handsome pilot and pretty attendant smiling in the open passenger door, the sleek jet with the Grail emblem high atop its vertical tail section stood waiting.

She was the only passenger.

Being left alone in the richly outfitted airplane had been malevolently disconcerting. Suddenly weak-kneed at the prospect of her family background coming under Mabel's inquisition, Marilee had tried desperately to collect her wits. Since she had left Melas, Virginia, she had not found it necessary to make any detailed disclosures about her past—not in any personal way, beyond the vital statistics required on official forms.

It would be an empty exercise to try to explain that her father, a national hero—but medically addicted to morphine—had been retired from the service with full honor; he was a military embarrassment, a flagrant advertisement that the system had failed. The Pentagon didn't like to be reminded of their failures. How do you explain that your mother is dead and that your father is doomed to rot on the back ward of a VA Hospital due to a drunken stumble down a flight of stairs?

A hopeless, brain-dead alcoholic father...a sordid existence over a rundown pool hall...a girlhood of poverty and shame...her father's accident...the tragedy of her mother?

On the plane, Marilee had rehearsed what she would say, if she were questioned by Mabel.

"My father Bedford Forrest Bryant was a career officer and a hero. He was wounded severely in combat and decorated for bravery. Poor man never recovered. His brilliant military career was tragically cut short by a medical discharge. My mother died of a broken heart."

That was enough. Besides, who cared about things like that anymore? She had consoled herself as she watched the countryside passing far below. But, she knew she was fooling herself. In the end, she knew that her family background was a thing that sooner or later she would have to reckon with in a place where private jets and chauffeured cars were commonplace.

By the time the plane landed, she had been a nervous wreck. Momentarily, she had considered taking a bus to Raleigh and grabbing a commercial flight back to New York.

It was hardly a surprise that Mabel had not been waiting to meet her at the Grail Air Centre. At the small administration building, there had been another corporate limo waiting—the same green Cadillac driven by a young man wearing the same green blazer with the Grail emblem.

64

When the limo arrived at the front of the Graham manor house, she had been relieved to find that she had been spared the ultimate indignity of being deposited, luggage and all, on the front steps of the downtown Holiday Inn.

Of course, word of her arrival had been phoned ahead. Right on cue, Mabel had stepped through the massive front doors, all smiles.

Even up close, the regal woman had seemed ageless. Her skin was flawless, a healthy golden tan. Only when she smiled did the tiniest suggestion of crinkles show at the corners of her mouth and eyes to give a hint of her years. She wore a light cotton shirtwaist dress in a pewter shade with a simple ecru cardigan of knit silk casually draped over her shoulders.

"Marilee, my dear, let me look at you. You are so much lovelier than your photographs. But, I'm sure you'd rather I didn't mention those swimsuit things..."

Tongue-tied, Marilee had wished desperately for a place to hide.

Later, when they were seated in the dining room at The Country Club, she had regained her tongue. "This is so...so...so majestic. The gatehouse...and the architecture of the homes, it's all so reminiscent of Williamsburg. The College of William and Mary...the Christopher Wren influence?" she gushed, wanting so desperately for this woman to like her.

"You recognize the influence? Trip must have told you. Old Massie, Trip's grandfather, had this building modeled after the Governor's Palace in New Bern," Mabel replied.

After lunch they had walked back across the terraces to the house and were seated facing each other in the large sitting room at the rear of the house. Mabel lost no time in getting down to the heart of the matter. "We are all so pleased Trip has given you that Cartier diamond. But I don't mind telling you—as I have already told him—I think he may be going a little too fast in this relationship. I was totally unprepared when he told me you two were engaged...and then...when he said something about a June wedding? Frankly, I had hoped if you and I could talk...ah...when you see what a responsibility being married to a Graham can be, then...well...ah... then you would not be in such a rush. I just don't think you realize the responsibility...but, then, of course you couldn't."

"Oh? And just why is that?" Marilee had bristled. She resented being talked down to.

Momentarily, Mabel was taken aback. "Well...you're so young—it's a heavy load to be the wife of a Graham. Graham men have always married women who were raised in an atmosphere of the highest social responsibility...you can't possibly imagine what a burden it can be," Mabel said, bluntly.

"What makes you think I couldn't manage, Mrs. Graham?" Marilee stared defiantly into the older woman's cold unwavering eyes, somewhat amazed at her own audacity. It was suddenly as if someone else was talking for her.

"Well, naturally, I want to get to know you better, to find out a little more about you. I think Trip said you're from Virginia... Melas? A little town near Roanoke, I believe. Tell me about your poor mother. She's no longer...ah...oh..." Abruptly, Mabel broke off in mid-inquisition and stood as another woman walked into the room.

"Why...Nan, hello..."

From her tone, Marilee could tell that Mabel wasn't at all pleased at the interruption.

"How are you, Mabel?..." The woman acknowledged Marilee with a smile.

"Nan, dear...at last. I was disappointed you couldn't make lunch. Is that for me?" Mabel reached for a thick manila envelope the woman was carrying. "Nan Moss, I'd like to present Trip's friend from New York, Marilee Bryant."

The way Mabel said it, "friend" sounded like a euphemism for "whore."

"I'm delighted. We've all been dying to meet you. I feel as if I know you already. Your picture was on the covers of at least two magazines that came in my mail this week. You're even lovelier than you photograph," Nan Moss said sincerely.

"Nan is my dearest friend...family, really. She's come to give us moral support for our big tea tomorrow," Mabel explained. "Nan is the real genius behind Griff Richards, Clayton's personal attorney and...best friend. They are...ah...devoted...been together for...ah...forever."

"What she's trying very hard not to say is that Griffin and I are living in sin." Nan smiled. "Well, now, I can't believe our own little Trip is lucky enough to have captured you. You're the talk of the town. Everyone's dying to meet you."

Marilee had liked the woman instantly. Now, driving along, she still recalled how much she had felt the need to see a friendly face that dreadful day. But, her hope that Nan's arrival had brought a welcome postponement of Mabel's inquisition into her past had quickly gone a-glimmering.

"I believe Mabel said you were from Virginia. Where in Virginia?" Now, suddenly, it was Nan asking. Was she just another interrogator, Marilee wondered, crestfallen.

"A little college town named Melas." Marilee nodded, warily, and took a sip of coffee.

"Oh, really. I know Melas. I grew up in Roanoke," Nan had exclaimed.

This unexpected revelation had pushed Marilee to the edge of panic.

What was going on here? Were they ganging up on her?

Suddenly frozen with terror, she was taken with a minor choking spell on the coffee.

Nan leaned forward anxiously. "Are you all right, my dear?"

"Uhmm..." Marilee nodded and waved her away. She composed herself as best she could and sat the cup on the table in front of her. "Too hot...I'm sorry...went down the wrong way..."

"I was wondering...is your family still in Melas?" Nan pressed ahead.

"No, my family's all gone." Marilee wished desperately she could run and hide.

"Gone? You mean dead?" Mabel gasped.

"Well?...except my father...but he's no longer there." She knew better than to lie.

"You were a Bryant? B-R-Y-A..." Nan Moss spelled it out slowly and correctly.

"Yes," she almost whispered and nodded numbly.

"Were you by any chance related to Bedford Forrest Bryant?" Nan asked.

It was the first time Marilee had heard her father's name spoken aloud in four years.

"Why...ah...yes..." She was certain they both were playing a cruel game now. It was no accident this woman was asking her about her father. These women were trying to humiliate her. Her first impulse had been to flee the room in tears—but it was too late to run. Might as well get it over with. Sooner or later, it was bound to happen.

Then, her impulse to flee had been quickly replaced by anger.

What right did they have? Who were they to judge her, anyway? She couldn't help who her father was, no more than she could help having red hair. She was tired of this. These people were no better than anybody else. She lifted her chin and said without batting an eye, "Yes, my father's given name was Bedford Forrest. Did you know him?"

"My word...you're Bedford Forrest Bryant's daughter! Then, your dear mother, the lovely Nancy Botetourt, is dead? Oh, my, what a shock! I didn't know...when? My God, she couldn't have been much past forty." Nan had leaned forward and touched her hand.

"When she died three years ago, Mother was barely thirty-nine..."

"You...you actually knew her parents?" Mabel interjected, unbelieving.

"Oh, yes, I knew her mother from girlhood. She grew up near my aunt in a pretty little town named Fincastle. It was founded by Lord Botetourt, an English aristocrat, sent by the King to be the first Governor of colonial Williamsburg. Nancy's family was descended from Lord Botetourt himself. And your father, Marilee? Is he well? You must be very proud of him," Nan said.

What was happening here? What was this woman saying?

Marilee had been confused. This Moss woman had the names right—but proud of her father? Surely Nan was mistaking him for someone else.

"No...not well at all. He's in the Veterans Hospital...from the war, has been for years." She wished the woman would change the subject. Still, she couldn't help but be curious now.

"How sad. There aren't many heroes like Bedford Bryant. We were all so proud when we heard it. Bedford was so dashing. His pictures were in all the papers. Not many men live to receive the Congressional Medal of Honor. Former President Nixon presented your father his medal. I believe your grandfather may have been Dwight Eisenhower's classmate at the Point. The Bryants are an illustrious family. You come from a fine heritage, my dear." Then Nan seemed to have sensed her discomfort. She hadn't questioned her about her father any further. "It's a small world, isn't it, Mabel? That will make interesting conversation at the DAR. Trip's fiancée is the daughter of an honest-to-God national hero."

"Remarkable." Mabel obviously didn't know what else to say. Then she said, "Your mother must have belonged?..."

"Belonged?..." *What in the world was Mabel talking about now,* she'd wondered.

"The Daughters of the American Revolution," Nan explained.

"Oh? I really couldn't say..." she'd said lamely.

"My word, child, certainly anyone would know a thing like that," Mabel said archly.

Afterwards, Mabel had excused herself to take a nap, and Nan found Marilee alone on the terrace.

"Would you care to walk? It's lovely walking down the cart paths. The view looking back here from the eighteenth tee is spectacular. It's going to be home for you soon," Nan offered.

She hadn't really wanted company, but she didn't know how to refuse, so she nodded and quietly followed along.

"Here...I think you should take care of these..." Nan opened her purse and took out two photocopied pages. The first was a bill for $250 from the Coral Gables Women's Clinic for an abortion;

the second was a clipping from *The Roanoke Times*, dated March 7, 1986. The headline read: WIFE OF WAR HERO DEAD FROM TRAGIC FALL AFTER FAMILY FRACAS. The article described her mother's death and her father's injuries from his drunken fall.

CHAPTER TWELVE

CLAYTON MASSIE GRAHAM, SR. SMILED AND WAVED at the young security guard as he drove by the gatehouse. When he had passed safely out of view, he pushed the memory call button on his console-mounted cell phone. On the other end, his party picked up on the second ring.

"Hi, baby."

"Oh, Clayt honey, I was hoping it was you. I miss you....two weeks seems like forever. Are you still coming tomorrow? No pun intended, but it's a delicious thought. You coming...so I can come, and come and come...don't tell me something's happened...you are coming, aren't you?"

"No. Uh, I mean no, nothing's happened and, yes, I'm coming and you can come and come..."

"Stop, you're making me horny. By the way, I got a new little love-toy from that place in California. It will drive you crazy. We will be vibrating on the same wavelength, as the saying goes. I can hardly bear to wait." Glee Craige's voice came in breathless Marilyn-like sounds.

He wriggled at the sudden tingle in his crotch. Glee could get pretty wild sometimes.

"Me either. How about the movers? Are you packed? Griff is coming down to handle the closing Wednesday. If the carpenters are finished, we should be able to get you moved to Starfish Wednesday afternoon...how's that sound?"

"Uhmm...delicious. I can hardly wait...we're going to love it...it's so private. I don't think I can stand it if something happens to postpone your trip. I love you so much. Do you love me?"

"You know I do. Don't worry, everything's all set, it'll be OK. I'll get the business here over early. I'm flying the Lear, be leaving no later than six. I'll be there by nine. Be ready, baby. It's OK to start without me, but don't waste it all on that toy; save the best for Daddy. I've got to run now, see you tomorrow night."

"Hurry, darling. Try to cut your silly business short. You can't be here soon enough for me. Bye, bye, sweetheart." The phone clicked in his ear before he could say goodbye.

CHAPTER THIRTEEN

EVEN NOW, AFTER ALL THE INTERVENING YEARS, Marilee's hands tightened involuntarily on the steering wheel as she remembered that long ago afternoon when she'd had the fateful confrontation with Mabel and Nan Moss. She'd gone weak with shock when Nan had handed her the receipt from the abortion clinic and the clipping about her mother's death.

Nan had reached out and taken her elbow to steady her.

"The manila envelope I gave Mabel. You know that Mabel Graham had Griffin Richards check you out. I read the entire report last night. I've seen her in action before and I wasn't about to let her send you away without a fair fight," Nan had explained. "Before last night, I really never knew your mother...or ever heard of your father. I got all that from the investigator's report. But it's OK now. You have to understand Mabel—and you have to understand the rules. Things like the DAR, they're important here."

"I don't understand." Marilee had stopped and turned, suddenly angry and humiliated. "All this superiority...the bloody DAR? What does that make her, God?"

"No, unfortunately, she is well content she is Mabel Hodges Graham. Even if there was conclusive proof God was female, Mabel would never stand for God being in the DAR..." Nan smiled, mischievously.

"Oh, bother! The DAR doesn't mean anything to me." She had drawn herself up proudly. "I don't have anything to be ashamed of."

"Well, here it means more to you than you think. The report said both of your grandmothers were DAR. I'm surprised you didn't know that," Nan told her kindly.

"No. I never knew either of my grandmothers..." she'd confessed.

"How sad. Anyway, Mabel may not ever be your best friend,

but if you're smart, you'll lean on her. She'll make a powerful ally. You can depend on that. Without her, you don't have much of a chance. It's a different world here on The Drive," Nan said.

"I'm smart enough to see that," she'd replied. "But I still don't think she's God."

"Don't be too judging. Mabel's quite a force, believe me. I've known her from way back—way, way back. The old girl has a history of her own. Underneath that southern belle/china doll exterior, she's tough...a survivor. I don't suppose you've ever heard of Madie K's?"

"May-dee-kays?" She had pronounced it slowly and phonetically. "No, should I have?"

"No, oh no. It's really sort of local lore, ancient history, really. It's not at all likely you would. I was just curious."

Marilee was confused again. "Was this May-dee-kays a private school?"

"Well...no...not a school. Let's say Madie K's was just one of life's little classrooms..." Nan smiled vacantly and had a faraway look. "No matter...that was a long time ago. It was more a practicum than anything else."

"It's no longer around, then?" she'd asked politely, her head spinning. All this was too deep for her. She still couldn't get over the fact Nan had conspired to save her from Mabel.

"Oh no, Madie K's has been closed for years." Nan looked away before she spoke again. "It takes time to understand the way things are...the way people are...and how they got that way."

"Why did you help me? You don't even know me," Marilee couldn't help but ask.

"I read your file. You're a survivor...strong. I like that...I'm a tough old broad myself. Besides, Mabel can be such a goddamn pompous bitch. And Trip Graham will need someone like you." Then Nan touched her arm and exclaimed, "Oh, my dear, look! There's a bluebird. It's early in the season for bluebirds...that's a lovely omen."

The weak sun of early spring was setting now. The shadow of the huge clubhouse had fallen across the area where they stood on the cart path below the ninth green.

74

"It's getting a little chilly. Let's walk up to The Club. A cup of coffee would be nice. It's after five...Irish Coffee, perhaps? I think we should celebrate." Nan turned to retrace their steps.

"Uhmm..." Her head was reeling. Things had happened too fast. If this newfound friend said it was time to celebrate, then Marilee had wanted desperately to believe her.

They moved slowly back across the wide terraces. The white wrought-iron tables and matching chairs with green and white umbrellas were deserted in the chill of the late afternoon shadows. The climb was steeper than Marilee had imagined. She was puffing slightly with exertion when they reached The Club. They sat inside the lounge overlooking the golf course. Through the bare-limbed, newly-greening trees, the stately, widely-spaced homes lining the fairways stretched before her.

When their drinks were served, Nan lifted her cup. "We should make a toast." She looked to Marilee and her eyebrows lifted quizzically, silently questioning.

"How about to the DAR?" Marilee giggled.

"Uhmm...the Irish have a wonderful way with words. Have you ever been to Ireland?" Nan asked.

"Yes, twice on modeling assignments. I love the people...they are...ah...expressive." She couldn't keep up with the older woman's train of thought. What did the Irish have to do with the DAR? In this place she never knew what was coming next.

"Good, then you'll understand this toast: 'Up the bloody DAR!'" Nan lifted her cup and gave Marilee's a resounding clink.

"*Up?* You mean?..." She was totally lost.

"Yes, yes...you know. Up them and the bloody 'orse they rode in on." Nan clinked their cups together again and her eyes twinkled as she looked over the edge of her cup to see Marilee's reaction.

"I'll drink to that." Marilee drank the toast. Then she clinked her cup against Nan's a second time and added, "But, God bless 'em, too,"

Nan laughed. "By George, I think you've finally got it!"

It was a long time before Marilee came to understand exactly what it all meant, but at that moment she knew that she had won.

Wherever and whatever it had been, she mused, that Madie K's sure had handed out one hell of an education.

It had been to Marilee's amazement and relief that Mabel surrendered later that afternoon. Gracefully, without further questions about her past, Mabel lost no time in getting her alone to say her piece. "I'm sure it comes as no news to you that I did not want this marriage for my son. But that is all settled now. You are going to be Trip's wife and that's that...but you're barely a woman. It's going to be a great deal of responsibility you didn't bargain for. Being married to Trip is, in a real sense, being married to the whole town—to the corporation, *Graham International, Ltd*. And that is quite a lot. This town has looked to the Grahams for leadership for over a hundred and fifty years. It may seem overwhelming at first, but I will always help you as long as you need me."

On Saturday at the reception at The Club to introduce her to the elite universe of Mabel Graham's friends, she had been given the final stamp of approval.

Mabel knew everything now—all the sordid details. But her subtly creative presentation of the dreary tale had become an official document of a glorious genealogy.

After the guests were gone, a very happy Marilee had given Mabel a big hug. "Oh, Mrs. Graham...Mabel...thank you. You won't be sorry. I'll make you all proud I'm a Graham."

"Well, I'm sure you will do just fine," Mabel had replied coolly, turning to go upstairs.

"Oh, by the way, Mrs. Graham...ah...I mean, Mabel...I wish sometime you'd tell me all about Madie K's," Marilee had called up to her as she neared the top of the spiral stairs.

"W-what?...w-what did you say?..." Mabel had turned and grabbed the rail, blood draining from beneath her glowing tan. For an instant, she looked as if she was going to faint.

"Mrs. Graham!...Mrs. Graham, are you all right?" Marilee had started toward the stairs.

Mabel had straightened and, without a word, turned and disappeared into the upstairs hall.

CHAPTER FOURTEEN

IT WAS BARELY PAST 4:00 when Trip stepped into the warm afternoon sunlight and walked across the parking lot to his car. There had been a fleeting, late spring shower and the steam rising off the pavement was fresh with the scent of hot tar and new-mown grass.

Now, guiding his car into the trickle of light traffic, he caught a glimpse of Norris in the dark-gray Riviera at the top of the long gentle slope ahead. Trip watched as he turned off Main Street headed in the direction of Club Drive.

Since it was still early, Norris would very likely stop at The Club. Trip didn't particularly fancy running into him at the moment. He'd have to see him tonight anyway.

When he reached the intersection, he did not turn. Instead, he continued out Main as the thinning concentration of houses quickly gave way to the openness of the countryside. Absently, Trip pushed the button on the radio, "...AUTHORITIES ARE REMAINING QUIET ABOUT THE MYSTERIOUS DEATH OF EMMA CLAIRE, SENSATIONAL NEW STAR OF TV AND MOTION PICTURES, WHOSE BODY WAS FOUND IN A GREENSBORO MOTEL. MISS CLAIRE WAS HONORED AS QUEEN OF THE AZALEA FESTIVAL IN WILMINGTON SIX WEEKS AGO. THE TWENTY-YEAR-OLD ACTRESS WAS SAID TO HAVE BEEN VACATIONING IN BLOWING ROCK UNTIL YESTERDAY MORNING...THERE ARE RUMORS MISS CLAIRE'S DEATH WAS INVOLVED WITH DRUGS, BUT CHIEF OF POLICE D.C. MILLS..."

Troubled, Trip quickly turned the radio off.

Emma Claire?...Blowing Rock?...Drugs?...

A total blank...the news made him uncomfortable.

Emma Claire! He'd made a drunken spectacle of himself over

the little fox last month in Wilmington. Hard to imagine her dead in a Greensboro motel this morning.

Damn all the memory blanks lately. Spooky! Fucking crowd he ran around with drank too much. And pot...pills...and coke, of course...lately heroin was showing up with regularity. Absently, he rubbed the inside of his left elbow. He'd found a suspicious mark there this morning.

A few miles out, just before he reached the bridge where the stretch of highway crossed the river, Trip pulled into a steep driveway leading down through the lacy overhang of trees, dead-ending at a ramshackle roadhouse perched on the high wooded bank of the river.

The sparsely-graveled red clay parking area held an assortment of cars, farm trucks, and one lone John Deere tractor, fresh from the fields, cultivator still attached.

Trip drove to the far end of the building, nearest the riverbank, out of sight from the highway. He backed in, got out and noticed a small square of waxy paper on the floor almost under the driver's seat. His heart skipped a beat. Nervously, he reached in and picked it up and checked thoroughly under the seats and in the back.

Nothing else—not that he could see at least.

He examined the paper carefully—a trace of white powder. Rolling it into a tiny ball, he threw it into the underbrush that grew up from the steep riverbank to the edge of the parking lot. How did it get there? The implication made him uneasy. He didn't really want to think about it. Abruptly, he wheeled and walked back around the car toward the old building.

In weather-faded green letters on the roof of the sagging porch, a rusted metal Coke sign displayed the legend GINGER'S PLACE. Over the battered door, a neon-orange electric BEER sign sputtered unsteadily.

Inside, Trip blinked to adjust his eyes to the murky room. Bright tendrils of blue smoke swirled in lazy, ever-changing patterns as slanting rays of the late afternoon sun probed the heavy cigarette haze. A small counter without stools ran part of the way along the left wall toward the rear of the room.

There were perhaps two dozen men drinking beer at the tables crowding the room. About a half-dozen overly-made-up young women were scattered about. Two wearing shorts and skimpy halter tops were seated at the big table nearest the door. The other women—there were five more, now that his eyes had become accustomed enough to count them—wore jeans and were seated with other groups. The males were mostly wearing denim work clothes, except for a few salesmen-types that could always be found here on weeknights.

Trip had been coming here since high school. He had been sixteen the first time he walked through the door, almost twenty-two years ago. At the time, although she was barely thirty herself, Ginger had a daughter, Amy Lou, who had been in Trip's third grade room at the public school before her mother had placed her in the new private all-girls' school.

"Howdy Trip, long time no see." Ginger herself, tastefully dressed in a tapestry silk suit, was back of the bar. A very rare occasion indeed. In recent years, Ginger almost never showed her face out here.

"Hey, Ginger...been out of town some lately. Gimme the usual."

"Bud in a long neck?"

"Yeah." He took the beer, put a bill on the bar and waited for his change. "Good to be back home. Where the hell you been, all dolled up like that?"

"Junior League. I looked for Marilee...she had that thing at the school, I guess."

"Jeezus, Ginger...Junior League! Not you..." Trip shook his head. "I thought you had too much class."

Ginger ignored him. "Marilee was named Mother of the Year today at school. She's a credit to our community. We're proud of her...and that boy of yours is quite a fine young man."

"Yeah, the kid's a chip off the old block, huh?" He picked up the beer and headed for an empty table, nodding as he went, playing the good old boy as he made his way across the room. He seated himself at an empty table. Slouching low in the chair, he idly held the beer bottle up to the dull shaft of light that filtered into the far corner of the room through the layers of red dust on the window.

When he looked away from the bottle, he saw the assistant golf pro, Zeb Long, waving a salute from across the room.

Trip saluted back and motioned him to join him. Zeb gathered up his cigarettes and loose change from the table and snaked his way across the room.

"How ya hittin' 'em, Bubba? Have a seat."

"Straight as a mule's dick. How 'bout yourself? Didn't see you today. As a matter of fact, it's been awhile..."

"Three weeks. Been in Palm Beach. Ever been there? The new PGA headquarters is close by," Trip said.

"Yeah, I was pro at Mariner Dunes just up I-95 in Stuart for a couple years. Man, you've never seen so many good-looking women..."

"Yeah...I know all about that stuck-up pussy. Mostly trouble. Sometimes a man better ask himself, 'Is the fucking I'm gonna be getting worth the fucking I may be taking.'"

"You're right about that," Zeb laughed. "How come you didn't play today?"

"Well...I got tied up in a meeting with Clayt. Every once in awhile I fuck up and have to do a little work." Trip snorted and shrugged. "Makes me feel sort of good though...to give you pigeons a break. I get to feeling real guilty sometimes about taking your money."

"I hear you talkin' that shit...I been playing good lately. Just waiting 'til you got back." Zeb smiled. Outside the club and on the golf course, the young assistant was on familiar terms with the younger, low-handicap golfing members. He and the head pro, Clem Johnson, were regulars during the members' friendly money games.

"Sounds just like a turkey waiting to be plucked," Trip kidded. Lately, he was hitting it pretty good himself.

"Speaking of getting plucked, where's Norris been hiding the last few weeks?"

"Do I look like that goodytwoshoes' keeper? Who the fuck

cares, anyway?"

"Me, for one. He's got a pocketful of my money...I been playing real good since Easter. I'm ready for that dude. I want a chance to get my money back. How does that guy play once or twice a month and still play under par? Hell, unless you count the late afternoons when he plays with your boy and his little buddy, that Harris kid, I doubt he plays that often if you average it out over the year. It's damned unreal."

"You're the second person today who told me Norris has taken up playing with the kindergarten crowd. How long has that been going on, anyway?" Trip scowled.

"I don't know...awhile. He seems to get a big kick out of it. He really has that boy of yours playing like a pro. Ivee's a shoo-in for club juniors champ. There aren't any of the other kids who can touch him. Norris said he was going to the membership and see if they won't waive the age restriction on weekday play to accommodate him and that Harris kid he plays with. It's really not fair to make him play early and late like that. Your kid's too good...I give Norris credit...he's a real gentleman." Zeb shook his head in wonderment. "But, I still don't see how he can score as well as he does and not play."

"He was like that in college. Makes me sick. But just who the hell does he think he is, trying to let kids on the golf course during daylight hours. It's bad enough they let the women play on Saturdays and Sundays," Trip said disgustedly. "Wait 'til my daddy gets wind of that."

"He already has. Big Clayt said he thought it was probably fair and maybe worth a try, just to see if the boys could handle the responsibility."

"Well, goddamn! Clayt never even played with me until I was sixteen." Trip couldn't believe his ears. "As a matter of fact, he took my clubs away once for not letting a group of old farts through when I was about my kid's age. I guess the old boy is going soft in the head."

"Well, you know granddaddies." Zeb winked. "So when are you going to play again? Why don't you round up Norris tomorrow? His money's good too."

"As a matter of fact, he's gonna play with my dad and me tomorrow. How'd you like to partner me? You say you're playing good lately? Clayt wants Norris. Clayt set it up for me to play with Clem. I'd a lot rather have you. At least Clayt should let me pick my own partner."

"Suits shit outa me...but you'd have to speak to your dad. I know Clem won't mind."

"OK." Trip lit a cigarette. "Just don't let my daddy con us out of too many shots. If Norris is on, he can beat us both."

"One a side. Trust me. We're safe..." Zeb spread his hands in a baseball umpire's sign.

Trip threw back his head, blew smoke at the ceiling and snorted. "Don't bet on it. The-son-of-a-bitch has been beating me like a clock ever since I first set eyes on him."

"How long you known him anyway? Did he grow up around here?"

"Naw, he's from Raleigh. My dad sent me to Pinehurst to take lessons from Bob Toski the summer I was fifteen. I had gone to high school here that year as a freshman and had won all the major junior titles in the East, except I hadn't played in the North Carolina Junior because it conflicted with a bigger event somewhere. Anyway, there was this kid at Pinehurst who caddied for me the first day at Toski's school, and I fired him on the first hole because he told me I needed two clubs more than I thought I did on the second shot. He was right, of course. The sumbitch is nearly always right. Never forget it!" Trip took a drink of beer and looked at Zeb. "Well, I just about shit when I met him the next spring at the state high school championship. I had heard a lot about this kid who was such a hotshot player from Broughton High School in Raleigh. We met in the finals and he cleaned my clock. The next year my dad shipped me off to prep school at Fork Union. Norris had to work in the summers and didn't play in the big junior events and, of course, I was going to school out of state and wasn't eligible for the high school championship. Fortunately, I didn't have to see him or play him again for two years. I've won a lot of big titles, but I've never beaten the bastard in a major championship."

"Well, if he kept whackin' your donkey, how come you got to be such good friends?"

"He wound up at the University of Virginia on a scholarship and beat me out for captain of the golf team. Anyway, we became roommates when we pledged the same fraternity. School was never my thing. I never did figure out why I was there if it wasn't to chase pussy and drink likker. I would have never made it through school if it hadn't been for him dragging me, kicking and screaming, all the way. Of course, it helps a lot to have the head of your class for a roomie. I'm pretty sure my dad kinda put him up to being my guardian angel. It doesn't matter. I'm sick and tired of the sumbitch beating my ass. If you think we can take 'em, call Clem and talk to him if you want to play with us tomorrow. It's up to you."

"Does a bear shit in the woods? I'd love to get some of Norris' money. You ought to see the way I'm playing. Nothin' but frozen ropes out there. Looks like I got a bag full of stepped-down three irons." The young pro made a low sailing motion.

"We'll take the muthafuckers apart," Trip gloated. "I'd purely love to get in my daddy's pocket."

Trip finished his beer. He looked at his watch and pushed back his chair.

"Gotta head for the barn...Mabel's throwing some kind of dinner party for Marilee. See ya tomorrow." He headed for the door.

"Well, shit!" Trip muttered aloud and stopped short as he approached his car. He stooped over and examined a tiny, almost invisible, scraped area and a smudge of red paint on the front of the Corvette by the cornering lights on the driver's side. The blemish was minor and would come off with some rubbing compound. But, still, it bothered him. For the life of him, he had no memory of how it happened—some careless asshole in a parking lot most likely.

CHAPTER FIFTEEN

As she neared the club, Marilee absently reached down and turned up the radio:

"...AUTHORITIES ARE REMAINING QUIET ABOUT CIR-CUMSTANCES SURROUNDING THE MYSTERIOUS DEATH OF EMMA CLAIRE, THE SEXY NEW STAR OF TV AND MOTION PICTURES. MISS CLAIRE, WHOSE BODY WAS FOUND EARLIER TODAY IN A GREENSBORO MOTEL, WAS HONORED AS QUEEN OF THE AZALEA FESTIVAL IN WILM-INGTON SIX WEEKS AGO. THE TWENTY-YEAR-OLD ACTRESS IS SAID TO HAVE BEEN VACATIONING IN BLOW-ING ROCK UNTIL YESTERDAY MORNING...THERE ARE RUMORS DRUGS ARE INVOLVED, BUT D.C. MILLS, CHIEF OF POLICE IN GREENSBORO REFUSED COMMENT...MISS CLAIRE'S FIRST MAJOR MOVIE IS TO BE RELEASED NEXT WEEK. RECENTLY MISS CLAIRE MADE INTERNATIONAL HEADLINES WHEN HER ATTORNEYS FILED FOR A COURT ORDER TO STOP THE DISTRIBUTION OF THE UPCOMING ISSUE OF PLAYBOY MAGAZINE WHICH WILL CONTAIN A CENTERFOLD SPREAD OF NUDE PICTURES OF THE YOUNG ACTRESS...NOW LET'S LOOK AT SPORTS..."

Quickly, she turned the radio off. Vaguely, the news was trou-bling.

She recalled meeting Emma Claire at her Caswell Beach house during the Azalea Festival. It was hard to imagine the young woman dead.

The report said the actress had been in Blowing Rock...

Trip had been at the corporate condos near Blowing Rock since Friday.

As difficult as it was to believe, in less than a month, it would be twelve years since she had cruised down this same street with tin cans jangling from the rear of Trip's Corvette, like a scene from an old-time movie.

Before the wedding, Sadie had remarked, "I just hope you know what you're letting yourself in for. Don't let all that phony glitter blind you."

"Oh Sadie, don't worry." She had been too excited to think anything gloomy.

Sadly, the wedding was hardly over when Sadie's words had come back to haunt her.

Being swept from the happy confusion of the wedding reception at The Club to the Grail jet and whisked away over the cloud-topped Virginia mountains had filled her with fairy-tale wonder. Speeding from The Greenbrier's private mountaintop airstrip, the limousine glided through the tree-lined avenues along the wide, perfectly manicured lawns fronting a white-porticoed Grecian temple with magnificent columns ascending into the clouds.

Efficiently escorted across the expansive checkerboard of black and white marble through the lobby, they had entered an elevator. Then, gliding down a wide, green-carpeted corridor, Marilee had watched transfixed as the door to their honeymoon suite stood open. The room was a Dorothy Draper fantasy of magnolia blossoms.

Body and soul bursting with anticipation, she had fairly danced into their enchanted castle. For weeks, Marilee's imagination had been afire with fantasies of erotic delights. A handsome prince...a manor house on the hill...at last, she had it all. The weeks before the wedding she had imagined enough pink-tinted versions of her honeymoon night to fill a hundred romance novels.

Freshly showered, glowing and blushing, pristine in an ivory silk negligee, she approached him shyly—expectant, tingly...aroused! Stepping forward into the reach of his arms, she turned her face up to be kissed.

"Here, drink this. It'll help you relax." With the first pop of the cork, her handsome prince turned into a toad. Trip handed her a glass of champagne.

"All I need is you." She took the glass and set it carefully aside after taking only a token sip.

"Don't you want your champagne? Go ahead. Look. Dom Perignon." His speech was a trifle slurred and he had a vacant leer on his face. There had been a lot of toasting at the reception.

"Really, Darling, I don't need a thing..."

"Aw, come on now. Let's don't rush. We have plenty of time. I know you're nervous. It's OK...happens to everybody," Trip protested, snatching his glass away from her reach.

"Umm-m. I am relaxed...very..." she crooned, undoing the top buttons on his shirt and running her hand over his nipples.

He jerked back, unexpectedly.

"Ah...ah hah...ha! Come on now. I can undress myself. Relax, honey." He turned and refilled his glass. "C'mon now, let's ah...unwind. We're hitched...no need to be in a hurry."

"But I am in a hurry. Aren't you? You were in an awful hurry on our first date. Remember?" She teased, prettily.

"Well, ah....I shouldn't have tried to get fresh then. I had too much to drink. I had just gotten back from Germany. I thought you were fast. You know, being a famous model and all that. I didn't know you—didn't know you wouldn't..." He nervously sipped his wine.

"Well...I will now...." Her hands were busy.

"Judas, Marilee. Wait. I can take off my own pants...let me...at least let me finish my drink...and...grab a quick shower. Jeezus. Marilee..." He watched as she stepped back a half-step.

Loosing her robe, she was naked underneath and she put his hands on her breasts.

"Oh, my god, so big. I can't get over how they're so big when you're so slender everywhere else? Before we dated, I thought it was just a cheap camera trick."

"I'm glad you like me...hmm...you have such a wonderful, strong body." She undid his belt.

Lowering herself to her knees in front of him, she pulled down his khakis and coaxed him to step free. His undershorts were the next to go.

Standing above her naked now, he had not yet begun to respond.

"Uhmm...let me..." She had cupped his scrotum in her palm and flicked the head of his penis with her tongue.

"Oh, no, NO! Don't do that." He pulled back and moved away. Abruptly he lifted her to a standing position facing him. "What made you think?...ah...where did you learn that?" He took another swallow of champagne. "We're married. C'mon, have a drink now and let's relax. I'll get in the shower in a minute."

Crushed by his abrupt rejection, she rose and closed her robe.

He turned away, oblivious to her hurt. "It's early yet...what's the rush? Let's go take a walk around? We have enough time before dinner? You can see the spa...you'll love the shops...you won't believe it...c'mon. There's no other place like this in the world."

Woodenly, she'd sat there watching as he refilled his glass and moved a little unsteadily toward the bathroom.

Incredibly, she dressed for dinner and watched numbly as he drank away the evening. Finally, he passed out on the chaise.

She had cried herself to sleep. Sometime in the night, she roused to hear retching in the bathroom. In the morning she feigned sleep, watching as he drank some vodka before he showered and shyly came back to bed drunkenly seeking her favor.

Dutifully, she had submitted.

Dutifully, he had performed.

Afterward, he had been sheepishly contrite.

"What do you suppose I ate that made me ill? I should complain to the concierge."

Marilee couldn't believe her ears.

She hadn't had the heart to tell him he hadn't eaten anything...or done anything either.

She had been too devastated to be angry. Had she offended him in her rush? After that, she had tried to be less aggressive...always letting him take the lead. But nothing changed. Trip withdrew even further into his drinking. From the first day of her honeymoon, slowly she had begun to die. The premature celebration of her womanhood began to shrivel up and languish deep inside her.

After their honeymoon, Trip continued to be reasonably pleasant and he saw to it she had everything she wanted. Except in bed.

There she found him self-conscious and inhibited...and most often reeking of alcohol. She had been passive...submissive...dutiful.

Near the end of the first year of their marriage, she had borne him a son. Of course, there had been much celebration among the Grahams—Big Clayt and Mabel had been ecstatic. Trip never suspected she did not love him. Secretly, Marilee always felt she had cheated her son in the choice of a father. But, now that Ivee had just turned eleven, she no longer worried about him being too much his father's son. He possessed all of the strength and intelligence his father lacked. Like Big Clayt, his grandfather, Ivee was going to be a fine man.

As time went by, Trip's drinking had worsened, and there was the increasing travel. In the last few years he was home very little. In their circles, it was no secret that Trip had other women.

Gratefully, Marilee found herself finally freed from obligations of the marriage bed.

But now, after the time with Norris at the beach house, what was she to do? After all the years of denial, Norris had left her aching to be a woman again. Suddenly, she wanted to run across sunlit fields of wildflowers, arms spread wide, grabbing happiness in double handfuls.

At its highest point, The Drive ended abruptly at two brick pillars which marked the entrance to The Club parking lot. Marilee threaded the car through the network of landscaped islands and parked near the entrance to the tennis shop. Inside, she found the assistant pro, Jimmy Lane.

"Good news. The outfits came this morning. Monograms look great." He turned to get them.

When he returned, she examined the monograms. "Uhmm...they do look great. It was worth the wait. Thanks, Jimmy. I've got to run."

She whirled and almost crashed into Agnes coming in the door.

"Ooops! Glad I saw you come in." Agnes laughed, a little out of breath.

"Hi. I'm glad too. Are you coming tonight? I mean you and

Norris will be there, won't you?" Marilee was suddenly afraid that the elusive Norris would manage to escape again.

"Uh?...Mabel's party? Yes...of course. I'm looking forward to it. We really haven't gotten together since your party at the beach. And, by the way, congratulations. I heard your speech was wonderful. But then I'm not surprised. Now!...Marilee, please don't hate me but what I really needed to see you about is to ask if you'll help me with the flowers at the church on Sundays during July. In a moment of weakness, I volunteered," Agnes confessed sheepishly.

"Of course. We'll just have the florist do them and we'll supervise like we did last time. Everyone seemed pleased," Marilee agreed.

"I knew I could count on you. Sorry, I've got to run...can't leave the girls at the pool by themselves. See ya tonight. *Ciao!*"

Agnes turned to leave, then stopped and turned back to Marilee. Her voice dropped to a more confidential tone. "Did you hear anything at the school about Dr. Jones?"

"Like what?" Marilee was puzzled.

"Well, there's talk he and Nora Clarke were seen having lunch in Winston-Salem at the PTA conference. I just wondered if anyone said anything?" Agnes seemed pleased Marilee hadn't already heard.

"I don't understand. Nora is president of the PTA." Marilee was irritated at Agnes' irresponsible gossip. "What's so unusual about them having lunch in a public place?"

"Well, Nora seems to be spending a lot of time at his office lately. People notice things in Colonial Hall." Agnes raised her brows in a knowing way.

"Agnes, who did you have lunch with yesterday?" Marilee knew Agnes had brought the new young assistant rector to have lunch at The Club buffet after services.

"Be serious, Marilee, you know that's different." Agnes headed back to the pool, clearly exasperated at Marilee's inability to see the difference.

Watching her go, Marilee found it hard to dislike her.

She suddenly felt the strangest sense of detachment. It was as if the person she was watching, the person she was going to have dinner with, the woman she would supervise the decoration of the church with—and the wife of the man she wanted to jump into bed with—were two separate people.

Marilee walked to her car and headed home.

CHAPTER SIXTEEN

CHATHAM BROOKES WALKED TO THE WINDOW overlooking 1600 Pennsylvania Avenue. The voices coming from the recorder on his desk had a slightly tinny sound.

"*Why are you so afraid of the lady? Not hung up or in ell-oh-vee-ee or anything, are you?*"

"*Love? Give me a break! No...no. Hell no. I don't even believe in it...*"

He picked up a thick folder from his desk and turned off the recorder. From his third-floor office in the anonymous brownstone close by Blair House, the elder statesman could see a straggle of war protesters marching along Pennsylvania Avenue in front of the White House denouncing the latest missile strikes on Afghanistan. Alongside the usual dispirited panhandlers, others carried placards condemning the Attorney General's sudden shutdown of the abortion clinics under the aegis of the current military alert. Across the White House fence, he watched a nondescript beige government motor pool vehicle entering the gate to the West Wing.

Brookes' eyes misted slightly as he was struck by an unexpected wave of nostalgia.

Thinking back over nearly fifty-one years, he'd been only twenty-five the day he'd first walked under the portico of the West Wing. A Purple Heart combat vet, newly-graduated *summa cum laude* from Missouri Law, he'd been chosen to serve an apprenticeship in the Oval Office of Harry S. Truman.

Barely a year later, Truman had invited him in and introduced him to Eisenhower.

Ike had shaken his hand and put his arm around him in a fatherly way. "Brookes, your country's counting on you to stay on, at least for a few months. I need you to help me learn the ropes and make a smooth transition to command."

What could he say?

For political appearances' sake, Ike had moved him across the street to this very office. Of course, those "few months" Ike mentioned so offhandedly had stretched into eight years.

Then, almost before he knew it, young Jack Kennedy summoned him to the Hyannisport family compound and told him, "Chatham, old sock...by virtue of experience, you've become irreplaceable...it's unprecedented...you're a personal advisor without political portfolio. You, old sport, are the real power behind the Oval Office."

He'd just turned thirty-five.

LBJ, Tricky Dick, Ford, Carter, Reagan, Bush, Clinton... and...now this...this...ahhh...whatever... He stopped and considered the protesters. *Only history should really judge the worth of a man.*

The jangle of the direct line jarred him out of his reverie.

"Yes sir...I heard the news. I was just going to call. Given the circumstances, I think we should move without further delay..." He listened to the raspy voice on the other end.

Absently, he glanced down at the official file folder he held.

TOP SECRET

Norris Garrett Wrenn

CHAPTER SEVENTEEN

"A FLAMING REDHEAD IN A MARILYN MONROE BEDROOM." The first time Sadie had seen Marilee's bedroom, she had teased her about it. Except for the colors in the framed art on the walls, the suite was done in a soft ivory-white. The layout was as large as a small apartment. There was a windowed alcove containing a small desk, a wide chaise, a table and a chair. On the side opposite the foot of her bed, a door opened onto a large dressing room and bath.

Deep in thought, Marilee moved into the sunny, skylighted bathroom and started the shower before she began to undress. There were mirrors on every panel of folding doors at the foot of her bed, which concealed large closets with built-in shelves and drawers. At the far end—if the doors were closed entirely—they separated the bedroom from the large dressing room and adjoining bath and made an unbroken mirrored surface across the room.

Moving about the room she could see her reflection in the sharp, angular mirrored panes of the partially opened doors as she took off her clothes. The broken reflections taunted her. Unconsciously at first, then with a fierce defiance, the undressing became a striptease...a pantomime, a burlesque. Restless, she prowled the large room, putting each article of her clothing and jewelry back into its proper place. She was so sensually charged that even the sensation of the delicate fabrics teasing across her skin heightened the tension. In her frustration, she felt as if she wanted to kick something.

All the way home from the school she had felt warm. Flushed. Unfulfilled. Angry.

She kicked a shoe and sent it flying. *Go ahead, scream! NO!* She resisted.

In the shower, she adjusted the control until the spray was barely above room temperature. Closing her eyes in an effort to shut out the world, she tried to imagine that the hands gliding over her body belonged to Norris. With tiny teeth, desire nibbled her. The illusion floated up and back, teasing each time it slipped away. Angrily, Marilee opened her eyes. Out of the shower, she toweled herself roughly, trying to rub away all sensation.

She moved to the dressing table and dusted herself with the huge puff. *Pollen*, she thought. *All this damned pollen and no honeybee—no hummingbird to taste the sweetness.*

Let me have Norris...please, God?

She turned this way and that, posing. Her stomach? Flat. Hips? Not a trace of cellulite. Her breasts? Hmm...no real sagging yet—a miracle really.

Slinging the puff carelessly aside, she leaned forward, both hands flat on the surface of the table and arched her neck back, trying to relieve the tension. In an exaggerated gesture of contempt, she stuck out her tongue at the reflected likeness in the mirror.

With a sigh, she moved naked across the room back into the dressing room. Still watching her reflection, she stepped into a pair of delicately monogrammed, lace-edged, ivory satin panties. Sadie had introduced her to the tiny Frenchwoman who made them. To Marilee, they had become a statement of personality. In her loneliness and isolation, she had taken refuge in such things. They had become her identity.

On the floor beside the chaise, a giant album of wedding photographs lay open to the page displaying the picture of Trip and Norris, arm in arm, grinning happily into the camera. The envelope from the New York clipping service was beside the album where she had left it last night.

She moved to the small rolltop desk near the chaise in the windowed alcove. Opening the drawer, she removed two thick envelopes of color prints that had been taken during Azalea Week at the beach. Originally, there had been several hundred snapshots, but she had carefully screened out the ones in which Norris appeared and put them into a separate envelope. Some of them she had taken during the mornings they had shared at the base of the lighthouse and around the ruins of the old fort.

These had become her secret treasure.

She stooped and gathered up the album, the thick package of clippings and the envelopes of snapshots and dropped them on the floor beside her bed. A few of the snaps spilled out near the envelope. She left them where they were.

All at once she felt exhausted. Drained.

Without bothering to put on a brassiere, she moved across the luxurious expanse of pale carpet to the far side of the bed and toppled, face first, onto the cool cloud of the satin comforter. She lay there, unable to sleep, her mind aimlessly drifting in that semi-suspended state which is not quite consciousness. With her elbows tucked in tight to her sides, her hands cupping the fullness of her breasts, she closed her eyes in anguish and tried to shut away the images of Norris. She couldn't order her thoughts, and she lay there helplessly as she watched the fragmented montage of recollections flickering across the screen in the darkened theater of her mind.

She'd first met Norris when he had been Trip's best man at their wedding. After that, they hadn't seen much of him until he'd become a part of the corporate hierarchy of Graham International, Ltd.

Counting back, they had been together three successive years at Pebble Beach where both Norris and Trip had been invited to play in the big Celebrity Pro-Am. The first year, they had met there quite by coincidence. The following two years they had arranged it, and it was enjoyed and looked forward to by everyone. Then, after having to cancel the Pebble Beach outing for the second year in a row, they managed to get together again at the Masters in Augusta. It had been there when Big Clayt offered Norris the position of Vice President and Chief Counsel for Grail.

So, it was four years now since Norris, Agnes and their two baby girls had taken up residence on Club Drive. Up until then, Marilee really hadn't had to consider either Agnes or Norris, not critically in the way you must when you know you are stuck with someone—like it or not. She had considered them only in the casual way that is the luxury of knowing the association is to be short-lived and not often repeated. Then, the little clashes of personality are so trivial they tend to build the enjoyment of the relationship because they give a sense of being able to overlook, or forgive, whichever may be the case. But when they moved next door, Marilee immediately found herself being overly critical of them both, and, at the same time, becoming annoyed with herself because she was.

The real paradox was that Agnes had become the first woman in Colonial Hall with whom Marilee had established a regular companionship. She'd drifted into it as a practical matter.

She found Agnes to be dependable and a natural participant. The local women found Agnes charming in an unobtrusive way. She fit in nicely and entered into local activities with enthusiasm. In Marilee's book, Agnes was, in some ways, a world-class airhead, but having her around was quite useful. Marilee was the first to admit that, with Agnes around, life was more enjoyable not having to be so occupied with the nitty-gritty.

Marilee wriggled forward to the edge of the bed and reached down and dumped the pictures out of the envelopes. Careful not to let the ones of Norris get mixed in with the others, she idly started shuffling them around.

It had become almost a crusade with her to get Agnes and Norris to join Trip and her for Azalea Week at the Caswell Beach cottage. She had first begun inviting them while they were still in Washington, long before they had moved to The Drive. If she had felt such antipathy toward them, why had it become such an obsession? This year, when Agnes finally told her they would come, the event had taken on a special meaning for her.

The Azalea Week party was her signature event. A production...a happening. To Marilee and the selected few, it was all that...and more. It had become a tradition. *No, by God!...it was an institution.*

Southern Living had done a little spread several years back. *Town and Country*, too. But because the Wrenns had finally agreed to come, this year the week had become even more special.

She shuffled photos. *Dear Marcellus...grinning like he'd just found a pot of gold.*

Marcellus was magic—he made it all happen. Marilee sometimes believed he was a sorcerer. In his management of the beach household, he performed miracles.

For several years, Marilee tried in vain to induce and cajole the old man to return to Colonial Hall with her to manage the household here. Marcellus wouldn't budge. The extra money didn't matter to him. Life for a black man in the Carolina lowcountry was a far different thing compared to living in the black quarter in Colonial Hall. Besides, Marcellus knew that she would not risk losing him and would pay him on an annual basis anyway. The leisurely off-season at the beach was what made the job attractive.

In the final analysis, the magic was in the devotion and respect that had grown between them. Deep inside, she nurtured the fantasy that someday, after Ivee was a man, she would make the beach place her permanent home.

Marilee poked her finger through the pile of photos until she found some exteriors of the cottage. She loved the place. Just thinking about it gave her a warm feeling. Except for her bedroom here at home, her beach house was the only place she had ever been really able to think of as her own.

When she had bought the old survivor of countless storms, it had long been neglected and was considered a local eyesore. Towering iconoclastically above the newer, uninspired cottages that had been built on the dunes where Hurricane Hazel had cleanly blown—or washed—away most of the existing structures north of Myrtle Beach, the house was of a weathered, cypress-shingled, vaguely Victorian Gothic, but rather aimless, style of architecture she'd come to think of as "Seaside Charles Addams."

Most importantly, the house was hers—hers alone. And it was totally removed from Colonial Hall. Here, she had only this bedroom suite. At Caswell she could be herself. The beach house brought her the happiest moments of her life. She fairly bubbled for days at the prospect of going there for any reason. But to her, the Azalea Festival Party was the best reason of all.

Usually the moods of early springtime are unpredictable at the Carolina beaches, but the weather had been perfect this year. Looking now at a photograph of Norris with the lighthouse in the background, she remembered that first Saturday morning had been the kind of lovely early April day that comes often to the Carolina coast.

She had awakened just before sunrise and quietly slipped into light cotton warm-up pants and jacket for protection against the chill of the pre-dawn wind and started to walk on the deserted beach. With her head down to avert the full effect of a fresh breeze blowing lightly across the mirror-calm sea, she had walked perhaps a mile. As the sky began to lighten slightly, she looked up, expecting to see the lighthouse towering above her. The lighthouse was there just as she knew it would be, but almost directly in front of her, outlined against the clear, still star-filled sky, was the shadowy figure of a man. Thinking herself alone, momentarily she stiffened in fear and surprise.

She had almost collapsed with relief when she realized it was Norris.

"Norris Wrenn, my God! Where did you come from? You almost gave me a heart attack," she had breathed. Impulsively, she had leaned forward and held on to him with both hands.

"Sorry. I thought you saw me. I've been watching you...all the way...since you left the cottage." Companionably, he hugged her and laughed. "I didn't mean to scare you."

Leaning against the full length of him, she had been jolted unexpectedly by her strong physical reaction. Suddenly, her senses went skittering around in her head and tingling on her skin. There had been the smell of him, the clean, unmistakable male essence. But Marilee remembered most vividly the feel of his maleness pressing against her.

She had been totally undone by the sensation.

Momentarily confused, she had pulled back slightly but Norris had held on firmly. It seemed so natural...he held her lightly. All a-tingle, suddenly, she never wanted to move away. In that one moment, her awareness of him...and of herself...had been forever altered. All week long, the feeling had kept her on edge...expectant. On their daily morning walks that followed, when they had occasionally bumped together in the unsteady tramping across the uneven surface of the sand, she reacted as if she had touched an electric wire.

"Do you like the ocean?...there's something about the water that fills me with the strangest sense of...harmony...peace. I don't know how to say it."

"I know what you mean...there is something special about the water all right. I have an island place off Maine, almost to Canada...not much of a beach, it's rocky there...but it has a lighthouse...and it's very peaceful. I go there sometimes when I feel lost...it's my secret."

"Oh...it sounds wonderful...do you go by yourself? I mean... doesn't Agnes go, too?" The question slipped out before she thought how it might sound.

"No. Agnes doesn't even know about it...I go alone. Not often enough, I'm afraid. It really is my secret. When I bought my hideaway, I still had dreams that I might write again. But now I don't know what I have to say anymore." He shrugged.

"Oh, I'm sure you have a lot to say. I have a copy of your book back there at the cottage. *Phoenix*...ah..." Flustered at her lapse, she'd felt like a fool. She hadn't read the book.

"*Phoenix Rising*...you have a copy here? Lately Washington has been calling me...might be a good time to do some homework. It's been a long time since I wrote it—wonder what I had to say?" He laughed a deep chuckling sound. Whatever the joke, it was clearly on him.

"Maybe you wouldn't mind signing it for me..." She resolved to start reading the book the minute she got back—before she handed it over to him.

"Sure. Has this place been in the Graham family long? It looks like it has a history."

"This was *never* in the Graham family...this place is mine..." she had snapped with an air of possessiveness. "I bought it back in the early nineties...but I spent one entire season having it restored.

99

This is the eighth Azalea Week I've entertained here."

"Was that the idea...to have a place to entertain? It seems perfectly suited..."

"Well...no...the first party just happened. I don't know...when I came down here from New York, I had a hard time feeling at home back there on The Drive...you know how exclusive it is...a real closed society. I really didn't feel like I had any privacy. Did you ever see a dog roam about a new place until he finds just the right spot to call his own? Well, the first thing I did was have my bedroom in our house in the Graham compound on The Drive completely remodeled...I thought Mabel was going to have me arrested for desecrating a national shrine...I mean, that lady pitched a fit. Trip didn't care, but he isn't very assertive when it comes to Mabel...or Clayt either." Marilee laughed at the memory. "No matter, I got my way. I was pregnant with Ivee and I think Clayt took my side. He didn't want to upset the 'little mother,' I guess. Anyway, personalizing my bedroom helped, but I still felt the need to have some place where I could go...a retreat when I felt like you said: 'lost.' And believe me, I still feel 'lost' a lot."

"I know that feeling well..." He nodded.

She'd found herself talking easily as they walked slowly along with little sandpipers dancing just ahead of them at the edge of the surf. "My first year out of New York, I missed being the sensational cover girl...and...being pregnant in the bargain...I was feeling not very pretty, but *pretty* damned sorry for myself. Trip was gone all the time. I started coming down here and spending time at the Grail family condos, and I began to think a lot about how I always looked to someone else to define who I was. I didn't really have a sense of *me*. I wanted to feel like my own person. So I decided a good way to start would be to get a place of my own...I was raised in the mountains. I always wanted a place at the beach. Except for Sadie Bailey I didn't tell a soul. But I started to look...I took my time. I wanted it to be exactly right. Funny, I'd seen this old eyesore before. From a distance, driving across the bridge, it sticks up against the horizon. One day it just clicked and I drove up here. *Voila!*" She shrugged and smiled.

"It really is a marvelous place."

"Well, thanks. The design, all of it, is mine...of course I hired a contractor, and he had an architect translate my sketches into plans and specs, but...you should have seen it. It was a mess...a magnificent ruin...probably would have been condemned in a year or so."

"Well I have to admit, first time I saw it, I thought of the house on the hill above the Bates Motel."

"Huh? Oh?...you mean from *Psycho*?"

"Yeah...think about it."

"Uhmm? I do see what you mean."

They'd laughed.

"Even after I had it restored, the locals still thought it was an eyesore...then *Architectural Digest* and several of the hoity-toity women's magazines ran cover features and big photo spreads, and, all of a sudden, the old relic took on an air of newfound respectability...anyway, *I* love it..."

Now, Marilee looked up sharply from the spill of photos as the sound of a car broke her reverie.

Next door?...*Norris?*...

Sliding off the bed, she hurried to the window. Across the lawn, Norris' Riviera was in the drive. She caught a glimpse of him just disappearing through the front door. Out back, across the terraces, Marilee's eye caught a flash of orange through the trees.

Agnes...coming across the lawn...obviously, she must have seen Norris drive up.

Well, well, Norris Wrenn home at last. Marilee shuddered a little sigh of relief.

Agnes had seemed quite positive they were coming to the dinner party tonight...

Well, now!...best you just look out, Mr. Norris Wrenn!

MONDAY EVENING

CHAPTER EIGHTEEN

For perhaps the first time since the Azalea Festival weekend, Norris arrived home in a civilized mood.

Tom Bradley had given him sensible advice. Tonight at Mabel's party he'd set the record straight with Marilee. Then, he'd come home and take Agnes to bed. Tomorrow was his big day. He needed to get his life back on track.

Finding the center hall deserted, he sorted through the stack of mail, dismissed it as unimportant and proceeded through the double doors into the drawing room. As he crossed the drawing room and approached the dining room, the scene evoked a sudden tug of sentimentality. There at the huge dining table sat his two daughters, alone and forlorn in their white antebellum dresses with eyelet-threaded ribbons of pink. It was a setting right out of *Gone With The Wind*. At any moment, he expected Hattie McDaniel or Butterfly McQueen to appear through the door from the kitchen.

However, in less than the time occupied by one step of his long strides, his daughters destroyed the poignancy of the illusion with an outburst of giggles.

Then, in rapid-fire order, Linda Susan, at five the youngest, flipped a pea at her older sister, Sarah Lucy. With all the disdain she could muster for the utter childishness of the act, Sarah Lucy demonstrated she was above such conduct by calmly putting an ice cube down the front of her younger sister's dress.

Norris coughed politely. Magically, the scene returned to a picture of ladylike decorum.

"Please excuse the untimely intrusion upon the privacy of your dinner, ladies. If you will permit me, I will retire to the terrace and allow you to finish your dinner undisturbed."

"Oh, Daddy, you talk so silly," Linda Susan said with a little giggle.

"Enjoy your dinner, ladies." He kissed them each on the forehead and exited through the serving pantry.

Smiling inwardly, Norris made his way back through the house into his study to where the French doors opened onto the brick-paved terrace. Through the doors he could see Agnes down below the rose garden in the trees which separated their lawn from the eighteenth fairway.

Norris watched her walk back across the meticulously manicured lawn. She was wearing tight-fitting silk shorts in a bright orange paisley pattern and a white bolero top that dropped down from the points of her breasts to stop abruptly a couple of inches above the waistband of the shorts. The contrast of the bright orange and the narrow circle of tanned flesh made the blouse seem even whiter and her breasts even fuller.

Agnes was tall, as tall as Marilee. But the extra heaviness, distributed over the larger bones of Agnes' frame, gave her a quality of earthy womanhood Norris vaguely associated with Italian movie queens. Agnes was forever talking about losing fifteen pounds. Norris didn't mind that she never had. He understood that the loss of fifteen pounds would undoubtedly produce a remarkable streamlining effect on her figure, but he couldn't imagine her as being any sexier than she already was. It bothered him that, despite the overpowering emotional and physical attraction he felt for Marilee, he was still aroused by the sight of Agnes walking up the lawn.

The morning following the explosive episode at the beach with Marilee, he had taken Agnes in a powerful surge of desire that he realized was fraught with overtones of hostility. Since then, the same powerful experience had been repeated, and always there was the ever-increasing element of hostility giving raw force to the act.

Norris sensed that Agnes also drove herself against him in bed with some of the same grinding sense of hostility. She had fought bitterly against having to move here, and she resented him for it. The consummate career politician's daughter, she missed the social swirl in Washington. He had snatched her away just when they were atop every guest list in town, especially the White House.

Norris remained a favorite there, despite the change of administrations.

Their relationship had been born the child of conflict and nursed at the breast of frustration. From the moment it began, he had hated himself for not being able to break away from it. That they were worlds apart, intellectually and philosophically, he had always recognized. But despite the maddening prospect of being married to a woman who would never have even the barest understanding of his perception of things, at the time he had been helpless to stop it.

Had he ever really loved Agnes?

At the time he'd thought he had—as much as he could love anyone, he'd guessed. Although he had locked it away somewhere just beyond his awareness, Norris understood vaguely that his love for Agnes and a nagging hatred of himself had begun the same night. As Norris saw it, the alchemy of love was a strange collaboration of devils and angels. Side by side, they brewed their capricious spell, mixing a seemingly careless potion of vanities and desires in the same pot. They clung to each other, orbiting somewhere in limbo between twin planets: Ego and Sex.

Their courtship had been a blur of Virginia landscape stretching from the Washington and Lee law school campus in Lexington to Lynchburg, over fifty miles of narrow mountainous road. Even now, after all these years, Norris felt he could drive that hazardous road in his sleep. That it was an aesthetic experience of hazy, blue-green-violet mountains and deep, moonlit river valleys, he never quite had time to discover.

The summer of 1988, Norris had taken a student job in the library of a Lynchburg law firm. That June, after her graduation from Randolph-Macon Woman's College, Agnes Farnsworth, daughter of the legendary Senator Dabney Thoroughgood Farnsworth, had stayed in town to work with the retarded children at the State Colony. Looking for a husband, she had planned to integrate her search with the graduate work she was to begin at Columbia in the fall. But then she had met Norris and there had been no need to go husband hunting in New York.

Norris had taken the summer job in Lynchburg not so much because of the practical law experience it offered, but because the senior student who had the job the previous summer had assured him it was more like a vacation than work. Norris had reentered law school at W&L almost as soon as the airplane had landed from Nicaragua. It had been well over three years since he graduated from Virginia and almost as long since he had left his law studies at W&L to go into the Army. Although his professors and classmates marveled at the way he seemingly breezed through the first year at the head of the class, it was far from relaxing for Norris.

Norris had no intention of losing his standing at the head of the class, so he had hardly eased the pace. Not that he had been a complete fanatic about it. There had been occasional trips to Roanoke to visit an attractive and rather uninhibited schoolteacher. All the same, he had kept himself under tight discipline too long. So he indulged himself by taking the Lynchburg job.

As part of the deal, he was furnished quarters with two young bachelor members of the firm who lived in a sprawling house several miles out of town on a wooded lake. Every night was a minor social event. Weekends were even better. Weekends, there were more women around.

Agnes Farnsworth had been merely one of a number of attractive young women he'd met there. He'd quickly perceived that she had attained some sort of senior status in the group because of her four years at Randolph-Macon. From the beginning, she had been just someone else's date. But as the summer progressed, Norris noticed that she came often, and somehow, even though she was with someone else, they wound up spending an unusual amount of time together.

Mostly, she liked to talk. She seemed fascinated by his ideas and was forever baiting him about religion or politics, or something equally philosophical, in an effort to get him going. He was both flattered and annoyed. He toyed with the idea of dating her, but before he had gotten around to it, Agnes rather abruptly took the matter out of his hands.

He recalled the occasion in the greatest detail.

Both his housemates had been at the beach that weekend, and he had been looking forward to indulging himself some time alone. The thought of complete isolation for an entire weekend was seductive. Friday following work, he stopped at the pharmacy on Rivermont and purchased three paperback novels, carefully choosing works by writers who were unfamiliar to him.

He really should have known better than to stop by The Keg for an icy mug of German draught beer before he started home. That was as far as he got with his plan for a private weekend. Before he knew quite what was happening, the gang at the Keg was organizing a party—at his place! He quickly shrugged and good-naturedly gave in.

The only thing he could remember about the paperback novels now was that he had carted them back to school that September—unread!

As is often the way with parties which generate on the spur of the moment, this one turned out to be fun. Even so, Norris couldn't help but breathe a sigh of relief when, shortly after midnight, he found himself alone at the front door watching the last taillight disappear through the trees. Closing the door, he considered briefly the idea of dousing all the lights and heading off to bed. But, he really hadn't been sleepy.

Norris turned out most of the lights and headed for the kitchen to fix a nightcap. Dumping the watery remains of his drink into the sink, he located three fresh ice cubes and slopped in a macho slug of bourbon. Swishing the ice cubes around in the glass, he made his way out into the darkness of the wide porch overlooking the lake. Standing at the rail in the warm, parchment-hued shaft of light from the open door of the living room, he watched the lights from the houses across the lake as their striated reflections danced on the midnight blackness of the water.

"Isn't it just too beautiful?" The sound of her voice, breaking the utter silence of his preoccupation, startled him into momentary paralysis. At first he couldn't locate her in the darkness of the moonless night. Gradually, he made out the anonymous lightness of her dress.

"Agnes?..." He stood peering into the shadows, still uncertain who she was.

"Just little old me...I thought you were trying to ignore me. But I can see now you didn't realize I was still here." She laughed at his startled reaction. "I wasn't sleepy...so I thought you wouldn't mind if I helped you straighten up the mess. You don't mind, do you?"

Still speechless, Norris walked slowly back to where she sat on the cushions of the metal porch glider. He stood looking down at the indistinct softness of her in the darkness. Feeling a bit shaky in the knees, he plopped down beside her before he finally collected himself enough to speak.

"Whew! Goddamnit, Agnes, why didn't you cough or something? You scared me out of ten years!" He clutched his hand to his heart. Instinctively, she leaned closer and put her hand there, too.

"Well. He has a heart after all," she laughed.

Norris leaned back, put his feet up on the rail and sipped his bourbon.

Almost at once, Agnes relaxed. "How smart are you, Norris Wrenn? I mean, seriously? Everyone says you're a genius."

"Hardly," he muttered, not considering the question.

"Are you really brilliant?" An edge of impatience crept into her tone. "I mean, really."

"Well...certainly. Can't you tell? What do you think about Kierkegaard?"

"Oh, poo! I can't read enough of that garbage to understand. Or at least I can't understand what I read. I keep reading the same paragraph over and over and still not getting any sense out of it. Do you understand all that stuff? You must be brilliant. I mean, really."

He could feel her beside him, just barely touching at the shoulders and at the hips.

"Norris Wrenn, you're not paying the slightest attention to me."

When he turned, her face was so close. She turned toward him.

With swift, miraculous maneuvers of unloosening and unfastening, she welcomed his explorations.

After that he could only remember a blurring of days, months, a year of touching, talking and the frequent trips over the mountains from Lexington to Lynchburg.

Thanksgiving weekend she had taken him to meet her parents. The Senator's estate was in the Virginia horse country near Upperville. Enclosed within miles of white fences, it seemed to Norris a walled feudal fiefdom, remote and out of touch with the world. As they were leaving, Agnes had suddenly asked him to stop as they made their way down the long tree-lined drive.

"Look, Darling! The house, the orchards, the stables, and all the land you can see in every direction. I love to stop here once in awhile and just let the whole thing sort of sink in. Just looking at it reminds me of all the important things...the deeper meaning of life. It all comes clear. The way of life it represents. That's worth fighting for...worth dying for. That's what you fought for in Nicaragua. Doesn't it make you proud? I mean, really?"

"I think I know what you mean." Norris let his voice drop in a burlesque of reverence which went completely undetected by her. "It's like that good feeling you get just in the knowing your children can belong to the right country club and sit at their very own pew in the very best church. It's knowing your children can go to the right college, where only the children of the right families can get in, no matter how smart they are. Sometimes being smart can be a bad thing if you haven't had the advantages of upbringing."

"That's it exactly! Oh Darling, you can say things so much better than I. I understand it but I could never put it into words the way you can. I never stopped to think about how important it is not to be a snob. But you are absolutely right. I mean, really. That's the most important thing of all."

Agnes snuggled up to him with a sigh of contentment—at peace with her world. She kept babbling away, the unwitting foil for his wasted dissection of her shallow values. "I'm glad our parents got over our grandparents' prejudices, aren't you? After all, the black people have a right to go to our schools. My brother had a colored man living in the same barracks with him at VMI. He never complained a bit—just went on like it was OK. Of course, the colored

111

Keydet was an exceptional student. He led the class."

"Yeah, we didn't have any prejudice in Nicaragua. We buried the blacks right beside the whites…" Norris stopped, sick to death of the empty exercise. It was beyond her to understand.

What was it that made him parody his own ideals? What kind of sickness made him cling to her when he held her in such low esteem? The Senator's money was the cancer, of course.

The following June he graduated. They were married and he had taken a position with the Senator's law firm in Washington. Their wedding gift was a deed to a house in Georgetown. He convinced himself Agnes had been right. There was no reason why he couldn't pursue his own idealistic dreams and live in comfort too…after all, he deserved it. No, no reason at all…

Except the flaw in his character.

Just when and where he had gotten lost was impossible to say. He knew there is seldom, if ever, a precise, clearly defined moment, which changes the course of life and personality. If it were that simple, then getting back on the right track would be easy. And life is never a single silken thread that runs without intersection, straight from the womb to the tomb. It is truly like a spider web, spiraling upward and outward, laid upon the countless other life strands it must intersect, even depend upon, for its existence. The trouble was people, unlike spiders, were seldom able to make a neat job of it. Even the best examples of the human web were patchwork creations, characterized by many backtrackings to pick up the imperfect and broken strands.

Now, standing there by the French doors watching Agnes walking across the terrace toward him, Norris knew that he had no one to blame but himself. He alone had understood the vastness of the gulf that separated them. That he had tried to explain it to her before the marriage made no difference, for he had known all along she could never understand. The explaining, though he hadn't understood it then, had been his cowardly mechanism to transfer the responsibility to her.

It occurred to him now that he had been trying to deposit to his "moral" account an excuse to get out of the marriage by banking

112

all the "I-told-you-sos" for future withdrawal, if and when the need should ever arise. Oh, yes, the wry thought passed through his head. I guess none of us is exempt from constructing a few convenient loopholes when we are laying the groundwork for a marriage contract. Funny, though, how you forgot all about them when you were busy playing "wonder boy" in the executive suite. Getting rich and famous can be a fascinating pastime. You can overlook a lot of things.

Tomorrow he was going to become one of the most powerful men in the world...and rich.

Why didn't he feel good about any of it?

CHAPTER NINETEEN

FROM HER BEDROOM WINDOW, Marilee watched Agnes walk up through the trees from the golf course. Agnes crossed the terrace and waited for a moment before she disappeared into the house. Feeling relieved that Norris was home, Marilee went back and sprawled across the bed and resumed looking at the jumble of beach party photographs on the floor.

An all-around night to remember...for a lot of reasons....

Saturday afternoon, the big show had gotten off to a doubtful start. About 3:00, Mabel had returned from the hairdresser announcing that she had run into a number of Colonial Hall people checking into the hotel in Wilmington which served as headquarters for the festival and its visiting dignitaries. They were all looking forward to Marilee's party and the first of them could be expected to begin arriving early, around six.

Around 4:00, Big Clayt had called to say, "Never mind sending Dupree with the car. Martin Stowe is going to bring us over."

Martin Stowe was a politician's politician. He was Colonial Hall's mayor and had been since long before Marilee had come there. Although he had never actually run for any other office, he had been state party chairman one year and had served on the staff of every governor for more years than even Martin himself could accurately remember. He was the party's strong right arm, every man's friend and a joiner *extraordinaire*. There were virtually no organizations, except perhaps the Girl Scouts, to which Martin did not belong.

Marilee could not remember being in the presence of Martin Stowe when he was not sparking some membership drive or another. To speak one word against Martin in the presence of the good people who comprised any of the virtually innumerable civic organizations and social clubs of Colonial Hall was second only to denouncing God. Marilee disliked Martin Stowe intensely, simply because he would not allow himself to risk being disliked by anyone.

When she saw him coming up the steps, Marilee tried to shake off the feeling of dread she had for having to suffer the boorishness of the Martin Stowes of the world. Fighting back the intense dislike welling up inside her, she'd shrugged, pasted a smile on her face and moved across the room to greet the men back from the afternoon's fishing expedition.

"Marilee, derned if you don't get prettier every time I see you." Martin Stowe turned to the two men with him for agreement.

"Where are the girls, Martin...isn't Ora Mae with you?" she'd asked.

"Well, sure she is, Marilee. You don't think she'd trust me to come by myself, knowing that you were here? We boys just came over early for a little fishing with Big Clayt and the rest of the menfolk. Going straight back to the motel and clean up and bring the womenfolk back...right now, in just a minute." The last was said with a meaningful look in the direction of the Victorian bar where Marcellus stood in readiness.

"Surely you can stay and have just one drink before you rush off." Marilee resisted her impulse to ignore his shameless hint and played along with the man's dishonesty. She knew the tiresome game by heart.

"Well now, you know I don't usually touch the stuff...I'm a deacon, you know. But old Doc Hardy said a toddy or two...in moderation, of course...might be good for my blood pressure. I've been under a lot of stress lately. Wouldn't do to have a stroke, you know."

It was all Marilee could do to hide her irritation. Before the evening was over, she would hear it from at least half of the people who came. It wasn't hypocrisy to them. They believed it. They didn't drink. No good, God-fearing, church-going, Bible-quoting Christian did. Of course, their livers got pickled just the same and their speech invariably got just as slurred. But, even when they staggered back for the one that turned the lights out or the stomach inside out, they still didn't consider themselves drinkers. It was the same old rule she had learned from Mabel: *It's all in the way you look at it!* The contradiction was a masterstroke of denial.

"God knows I never could be much of a drinking man, but I enjoy an occasional drink with old friends," Big Clayt said. Then he added, "On the rocks, Marcellus." From Colonial Hall to Cairo, everyone who knew him knew that meant Jack Daniels Black Label.

"It's a little early, but I'll have the same…with Seven-Up, Marcellus," Trip chimed in.

Early? Marilee almost choked. Trip had started the day with a Bloody Mary that morning before 9:00.

Like his father and Martin Stowe, Trip practiced the same deceit. Marilee had long since given up trying to bring the subject up. Lately, it was getting worse.

One of the increasing number of things Marilee had discovered she admired about Norris was that he didn't play these games. While Norris was a very conservative drinker, he didn't have any hang-ups about it. As if he had read her mind, Norris had caught her eye and winked when both Big Clayt and Trip echoed Martin's example.

"I guess I'm the only honest-to-God drinking man here, Marcellus. Save some for me," Norris spoke up in a loud clear voice.

"Me, too. Save some booze for a doomed-to-hell drinking woman, Marcellus," Marilee said with a straight face and watched as a disapproving frown crossed Clayton's face.

Norris walked straight over to her and gave her a proprietary hug. "Well, it's good to know there are two real drinkers left in this Baptist world."

Thinking back, Marilee realized now, it was in that early part of the evening she had begun to admit the powerful sexual attraction she'd felt for Norris. All those mornings on the beach, the wanderings in Southport, something had been happening between them. Those shared moments, in a special way, had evolved into a contract of intimacy.

"Say, that reminds me, we're having a big membership push at the Veterans Legion. If we get a hundred new members, we get to add a delegate to the national convention. It's in San Francisco next year. Already have a promise of a starting time at Spyglass. Hot damn! Excuse the French, Miz Marilee. I get carried away, sometimes. My mama would wash my mouth out with soap if she knew."

Martin turned to Norris and produced a thick stack of membership cards from his pocket. "How about it, Norris? It's only five bucks. Big Clayt and Trip renewed their membership after they took all my money at the poker game Monday night. Both of 'em have been members for as long as I can remember."

"Yeah, Norris, you should start to support our local organizations. You've been here long enough, it's time you became one of us. It's your civic duty," Clayt spoke up.

"Yeah, Norris. Daddy's right," Trip parroted his father.

Marilee felt a rush of shame. Trip's being such a daddy's boy was a joke around town.

"Really? My schedule is pretty full. How often do they meet?" Norris spoke directly to Trip. There was an edge in Norris' tone that suddenly alerted Marilee. She was sure the others hadn't caught it.

"Oh hell, Norris! You don't have to worry about the meetings. When *do* you meet, Martin?" Clayt intervened.

"Once a month...on the second Tuesday, I think...or...first Wednesday, maybe. What durn difference does it make? Veterans Legion's got a strong lobby in Congress. Our boys are fighting them terrorists, man." Martin was getting red-faced and flustered. "We're talking about your patriotism here."

"Hmm?...a strong Congressional lobby? What's this organization stand for, anyway?" Norris persisted, nudging Marilee imperceptibly with his shoulder.

"Stand for? Why, hell's fire, man, they're just a bunch of good old boys who love their country."

"Come on now, Martin, you're standing there telling me in one breath how serious this organization is and they have a strong Congressional lobby and you won't tell me what it stands for. I don't feel I can afford to belong to groups unless I'm sure they represent the things I stand for." Norris gave Marilee another nudge with his hip.

"What's this hang-up about Washington lobbies? Goddam...ah...goshdurnit...I just told you. They represent responsibility in government. I take that seriously, don't you?" Martin was trying hard to control his frustration and anger. "What are you, some kind of a communist cheapskate? It's just five lousy bucks. These are your neighbors in Colonial Hall. I go to their annual Fourth of July picnic, take the family, eat hot dogs, have fun. Are you too snooty to rub elbows with your own townfolk?"

"Martin, I once heard about a man who joined an organization just to be a good ol' boy. It turned out that as part of the initiation process, he had to arrest his college sweetheart and her entire family. They were guilty of belonging to the wrong church. Sent the entire family to the gas chamber for it."

"What kind of sick joke is that, Norris?" Martin sputtered.

"It's hardly a joke, Martin. The man's fiancée was Jewish. The organization was the Nazi party. I always think about that before I lend my name to any group."

CHAPTER TWENTY

MABEL HAD OFTEN HEARD MARILEE remark how much she thought Clayton resembled the actor Paul Newman. To Mabel the resemblance was not striking. On the other hand, when he was younger, Mabel had thought Clayton looked a little like Nick Nolte. No matter. Now, as she watched him dressing, Mabel had to admit he was still a very attractive man.

"Clayton, you're a damn fine figure of a man," she said, hopefully.

"Huh?" His was an embarrassed grunt more than a response. Clayton Graham knew the signs. Mabel was horny.

"Do you think my breasts need fixing?" She put her hands underneath them and raised them just a bit, so they pointed straight out. "Like this, maybe?"

"Uh, no...nothing wrong with your breasts...I've got things to do..." He turned and fairly dove down the stairs to escape the uncomfortable atmosphere of the bedroom.

Safely inside his study, he closed the heavy oak door and momentarily leaned back against it to collect himself before he moved across the room to where two phones rested on the console at the right arm of the desk chair. His hand went to the blue phone, a private corporate line, which assured complete confidentiality and anonymity.

Before he dialed, he pushed the button on the intercom, "Mose, will you prepare the portable bar and make daiquiris and bring them to the back porch...and have Pansy make sure the guest house is ready for Ms. Moss and Mr. Richards."

He dialed and impatiently drummed his fingers on the edge of the desk.

"Mrs. Guest, please. This is Clayton Graham."

119

"Hello, Mr. Graham."

"Mrs. Guest...just want to confirm. I'll be there tomorrow late...is everything all set?"

"We're ready...will you get here in time to close? Actually, all you have to do is sign. It'll take ten...fifteen minutes, tops. Your Mr. Richards has had his associate make the inspection."

"Yes, that's fine, but I want to make an inspection myself. Can we do it Wednesday morning? The earlier the better. What would be good for you?"

"Would eight be early enough?" she replied, after a slight hesitation.

"Eight is fine. I'll see you then. I'll just meet you at the property. OK?"

"OK. I'll see you then. Have a good trip."

"Thanks again...good-bye." Clayt put the phone back on its cradle.

Glee would be ecstatic when she found out he had bought the house. She hadn't a clue. She was impressed enough that he was getting her a place at the Starfish Cay Club. That was about as far uptown as you can get...more exclusive than Sea Pines or the Landings. In the beginning, he had considered those and Marco, but the small, Graham International, Ltd. steamship offices in Savannah really didn't provide him with enough reason to regularly visit there and the closest major corporate location to Marco was Miami...or Tampa. Anyway, Starfish Cay, with the corporate offices and extensive Graham International, Ltd. holdings around Jacksonville, worked out perfectly. Even before he met Glee, he always had spent a lot of time there.

The house was a better choice than the condo. Even at Starfish, where privacy was prized nearly as much as here on the Drive, condos still meant neighbors...and he was much too visible. The house was isolated...private...safer.

Glee wasn't going to be too happy when Griffin told her about the five-year incremental schedule of ownership. But Griff was as slick as owl shit. His old friend looked out for him. Griff had arranged it so Glee couldn't take title outright for five years, but this would give her some solid sense of security. And, the deal represented an act of good faith on his part. Oh, well, Glee was bright. It was a good deal for her.

Even without the new instant erectile drug, Virecta, he was at the top of his game right now. But he had some Virecta anyway...some of the newer Rigidon, too. He was sixty-two and he knew sooner or later his string was bound to run out...there weren't many men still virile at his age. He was dangling Glee's five-year vested ownership in the house like a carrot. Nobody could say Clayton Massie Graham was a complete fool.

Through the windowed end wall he could see Mose out on the brick terrace arranging the cocktail tray on one of the glass-topped tables. He crossed the room and walked through the French doors, out under the green and white striped awning which partially covered the veranda.

"I can move this if you prefer another table, Mr. Clayton," Mose said anxiously.

"No need. This is fine, Mose."

"Would you like anything else, suh?"

"No, no...just keep an eye on us...we have a few minutes before we have to start for the Club. Thank you."

Mose always waited until Clayton made a cursory examination of the serving arrangement, tasted his drink and released him from further concern. When he saw Clayt's nod of approval, he turned and walked down the steps and around the pool to check on the readiness of the guest house.

Clayton took his drink and walked to the railing at the far end of the terrace. From there, he commanded a southeasterly view of the town, The Tower, and the river beyond. Clayton Massie Graham was well aware that, for now, he ruled it all. It was the role to which he was born. From his earliest remembrance he had tagged along with his father and grandfather to the offices of the corporation. Even though his grandfather, old Clayton Massie Graham, Sr., had died in a pool of bloody puke before Clayton had started high school, the old man had lived to see the Graham Tower rise above the farm plain in the center of the sleepy town.

"It's a boy, Clayton. He'll be Clayton Massie the Third. We'll call him Trip, just like we planned." Mabel had beamed at the plump newborn sucking greedily at her breast. "The Graham legacy will go on forever..."

It had been an empty prophecy.

Trip was a genetic anomaly...a throwback...a skipped generation in the dynastic chain. He had been rebellious, a rogue—a problem from the start. Try as he might, Clayton could find no way to inspire the boy. No one ever thought of Trip as Little Clayton. There had been flashes of talent. He had been a golfer of great early promise...he still played well, but always without inspiration....

"There's a lot of history out there. We helped make our share." From behind him, Griff's voice interrupted Clayt's unhappy reverie.

He turned to see his old friend approaching across the terrace. Griff stopped and picked up a daiquiri and took a sip.

"Griff, am I glad to see you. Where's Nan?"

"On her way to the showers. I let her get a head start...always takes the womenfolk twice as long." Griff nodded across the corner of the pool where Nan was disappearing into the guest house with Pansy carrying her bags. "So, how did the meeting with Trip go?"

Clayton shrugged. "Oh, OK, I guess...I felt a little guilty, but I don't know why. After all, it doesn't really change things for him. Old Massie's trust alone is enough to ensure the next three generations of his family."

"You're right there...there's no end to it. Even with inflation, if all his heirs have ten kids apiece, they'll be taken care of in style for the next century and a half...forever, really." Griff gestured out over the railing. "Don't worry about Trip...at least not his finances. The way Norris is taking the company, Graham International, Ltd. may wind up *Fortune* Numero Uno in ten years. There's enough diversification out there to cover the alphabet. Damn close enough right now. You're making a smart move by protecting Grail for Ivee now. And thank your lucky stars Trip did one thing right...he married Marilee. That's one hell of a woman. When I think Mabel almost ran her off before she even got here...Nan and I were talking about it coming down from Raleigh."

"Yeah, goddamn it, I didn't know about that for a long time...women! Jeezus!" Clayt swirled the tiny island of slush around in his glass and swallowed it. "C'mon let's have another one. Tonight is a big celebration."

Back at the table, they sat down and Clayt finally spoke again, "You know, I was just thinking about Trip before you got here. What went wrong? In high school, he did all right for awhile. But then, when he was sixteen, I gave him a car and a drink of liquor and took him to New York for his first piece of tail, just like my daddy did for me—except old Massie took me to Madie K's outside of Raleigh. I mean, now that was some place...nothing but old money. We had to stop at a gate which had a guard. Then a black man in a tuxedo came down from the house in a big car and took us up to the plantation house. There weren't any cars at the gate, so they must've parked them somewhere away from there. You know something? The great Tex Evans, the famous cowboy star, was there that night. I remember he'd been down to Camp Lejuene that day and was going to Goldsboro to the Army airfield the next day and then to Fort Bragg, making a war movie or some such thing... Boy, he was one big son of a bitch. One of the big shot senators from Arizona was with him...Daddy pointed him out to me. Old Massie paid Madie K a fortune to find me a virgin...wasn't no doubt about that...daughter of one of Madie K's girls...just turned fifteen...and, godawmighty, she was pretty...well, anyway, you know the rest of that....I flat fell in love." Clayt looked off, dreamy-eyed. "You ever go to Madie K's?"

"Never did..." Griff said.

"Oh God, you woulda purely loved it." Clayt reached across and squeezed his forearm.

"That's what you keep telling me." Griff grinned, sheepishly.

"Oh, well, I don't know where I got off the track with Trip. Too late to worry now. I just don't understand any of it. I loved my daddy. Griff, you never really knew him, but I loved him. I would've gladly gone out and killed for him if he'd asked me to. Where the hell did I go wrong? Why doesn't Trip love me?"

"Oh, I think he loves you. We're all different. He does the best he can...I am worried about his drinking...and the life he lives. Something has to be done...soon. You need to talk to him."

"I can't seem to get through to him. Do you think Norris, maybe?..."

"That crossed my mind...but God, how much can we expect from Norris? And anyway, what do you think he could do that you couldn't?"

"Well, Norris got him through the University...it wouldn't hurt to try."

CHAPTER TWENTY-ONE

MARILEE SCOOTED BACK LIKE A CRAB and got up off the bed. Cupping her breasts in her hands, she went into the bathroom and got a drink of water. When she came back to the bed, she searched through the snapshots looking for pictures taken at the beach party.

There! A whole bunch of photos of their table at the Azalea Ball...

Wrong party!

Ah, there...she located the snapshots from that night at the cottage.

God, there had been such a crowd at the cottage...there's Norris on the steps...so beautiful. He makes them all look so ordinary.

It had been a wonderful party. She had felt really alive that night.

As the evening had progressed and alcohol had begun to roll back the custom-convertible tops of Colonial Hall's finest inhibitions, the head of the old devil sex took the driver's seat. Marilee had watched the heretofore dully-predictable tableau of flirtation with new interest. That evening at her beach party, suddenly she'd felt painfully aware. For a long time, her only defense against the maddening one-sidedness of Trip's little legacies of onanism was to deny herself all awareness of her own needs.

Now, flipping through the snapshots, she wriggled slightly to change position on top of the silken surface of the comforter—the sensation of the fabric on her bare nipples was deliciously erotic.

Idly, she glanced through photos of the crowd at the Azalea Ball. Where were the ones of Emma Claire? There! So young...so pretty. Trip had made a fool of himself...hanging on the starlet that night. She looked so embarrassed in the photographs—poor thing. There! Trip again—shortly before Griff and Norris had escorted him to the car.

Pictures don't lie...

Even in the photographs, Trip looked wasted...like an old man.

Look at me looking at Norris, like I could eat him up...anyone could tell!

Recalling her party, from time to time she had stopped to join whichever group Norris happened to occupy at the moment. Once, in reaction to an anecdote in which she was the good-natured pawn, he hugged her to him in a casual display of affection. Norris' hand had seemed to linger for an instant with just the slightest pressure underneath her breast. In her highly sensitized state, it had produced an instant reaction. She remembered feeling conspicuously breathless and flushed. Shaken, she'd moved to the bar and asked Marcellus to pour her another Jack Daniels. She hadn't been able to conceal the slight tremor when she'd lifted the glass.

Marcellus, pretending not to notice, seized the opportunity to make a request.

"Miss Marilee," he had begun tentatively, "I wonder if you could pay me part of what I got coming, tonight? Tomorrow's Sunday. My missus be needin' groceries back at de house."

"I don't know how much cash I have, but I'm sure I can let you have a couple hundred at least. Will that do? I can go ask Mr. Graham if you need more."

"That'll do jus' fine, Miz Marilee." Marcellus beamed.

"My purse is upstairs. Don't let me leave without getting your money. Be sure you remind me if I forget. OK?"

"Yes'm, I will. And, I shorely do 'preciate it."

At that point, Trip had threaded his way unsteadily through the crowd. She had seen by the flush of his face and the vacant smile that he was already more than a little hammered.

"C'mon, we're going to the Azalea Ball. Help me get everybody started." Without waiting for her response, he lurched on past her, moving from group to group passing on the order like some comic strip general.

The scene had quickly become a riot of merry confusion. The asphalt parking court was suddenly jammed with people piling into their cars. The buzz sounded like a cross between Mardi Gras and half time at a Duke–Carolina football game. Marilee knew from experience that the apparently casual and confused mismatching of mates and dates in the helter-skelter rush for the automobiles was not at all the innocent thing everyone worked so hard at making it appear. For years she had observed this petty game of substitution with cynical amusement.

As she went down the steps, she looked for Norris. She was acutely aware of the remarkable changes in her feelings, and she had been thinking wickedly, *Come on Mr. Norris Wrenn, let me introduce you to a very sophisticated game. Until this moment, it has had no name. Indeed, it is such a truly grown-up game and such a magnificently intellectual exercise that one of the rules is not to know...or at least...not to admit you know you are playing. We will be the first to give it a name. We will call it Freudian Cars.*

What a grand name.

Now, just where the hell are you, Mr. Norris Wrenn?

Being one of the last to leave the house, she had been afraid she had missed him. In her anxiety, she had rushed about from car to car until at last, just when she was about to give up hope, she spotted him in the back seat of a black Cadillac with Martin Stowe at the wheel. She stepped recklessly in front of the car to prevent it from starting off and proceeded to the door where Norris was sitting.

She squeezed in beside him. But, hardly before the door was shut she remembered that she had forgotten to pay Marcellus. The car had already eased forward in the slow-moving line.

"Stop! Stop the car, I've got to go back," she had fairly screamed, an edge of despair in her voice.

"What's the matter?" Martin asked, bringing the car to an abrupt stop.

"I have to go back. I promised to pay Marcellus," she wailed above the mounting sounds of protest from the other automobiles. "Go ahead. I'll catch up." Marilee stepped out of the car and started to close the door, but Norris held the door and stepped out beside her.

"Go ahead, Martin, I'll stay and drive Marilee. I need to make a phone call, anyway." He shut the door and stepped back as the long line of cars started to move again.

Big Clayt's car slowed and stopped to see what the trouble was and Trip stuck his head out the rear window.

"What the hell's the matter?" he asked, somewhat belligerently.

"I have to go back and give Marcellus his money," she replied.

"It won't hurt that nigger to wait," Trip snapped back.

"Go on, you're holding up traffic. I'll be along in a minute. Norris is going to drive me. We'll catch up." Marilee turned toward the house.

"OK, but watch out for that guy. He's the intellectual type," Trip shouted drunkenly as the car moved out of the drive.

"Nothing like improving a girl's mind," she had shouted at the disappearing vehicle, immediately feeling sheepish, disbelieving she could have said it.

They had stood there and watched until all the cars had gone. When they moved toward the cottage, Norris' hand slipped casually around her to just beneath her breast. Again, she was jolted by the stimulus, but this time, she welcomed his touch unashamedly. She was taken with an adolescent sense of nervousness and high excitement—that same feeling of inevitability which had prefaced her first sexual experience. Yet, now that she was thirty-one, it was even better than it had been as a girl.

In that instant, she had known quite well what was taking place and she could have stopped it. Instead, she snuggled closer to Norris in a movement well calculated to give him encouragement. She remembered the measured brush of his thigh against hers as they walked toward the house, and a sweetness began welling up in her throat that made her wish she could walk beside him forever.

"Did you think I'd forgotten?" Marilee began. Marcellus was coming out the door when they reached the top of the steps. "I almost did. I would have hated myself if I had."

"Oh no, Miz Marilee, it would have been all right." Marcellus was obviously relieved to see her.

"Hold on, I'll get the money." She ran up the stairs and came back with ten twenty-dollar bills.

"Do you want me to stay and straighten up?" Marcellus asked.

"No. Absolutely not. Get going." Marilee shooed him down the steps to his car.

Now, remembering, she wondered if Marcellus had sensed the urgency with which she had bid him goodnight. She had been so much in a fog she couldn't remember enough of the scene to pass judgement. When she watched the light of his battered old car disappear around the bend in the road, she had turned back to Norris. He stood at the bar, hand outstretched, offering a small snifter of cognac. She paused long enough to switch the main lights off so that the room was lighted by the flickering light of the dying fire.

Sensing Norris was still unsure, she indicated the sofa in front of the fire.

"Let's catch our breath. It's nice without the noise."

As soon as he was seated, she had gone to the fireplace, pretending to concern herself with adding a piece of driftwood to the dying embers. Norris rose at once and took the wood from her and placed it on the fire. When he turned she stood facing him...almost touching.

They were standing very close and she lost all thread of any thought save the preoccupation with the boy's mouth on the man's face. With great deliberation, he had taken her face in his hands and kissed her. Turning her face to meet him, she opened her mouth hungrily. Her arms encircled him, pulling fiercely to get closer. Yet it could never be close enough. They had stood kissing for a long time. Finally, almost unwillingly, in their desperate need for each other they broke apart long enough to negotiate the stairs, arms locked tightly about the other's waist, almost falling in the fierce stumbling gait of the bumping together of their bodies.

On the balcony, she had stood in the bright moonlight streaming in through the window, her arms stretched upward while he undressed her. The pounding of her heart became a roar in her ears.

She had let her legs move apart to welcome his exploration.

Norris fell to his knees and she felt his tongue licking...fingers probing.

Oh!...Oh! Oh my...OH...MY...GOD!

Behind her closed eyelids there had been a flashing of ruby starbursts as if all the fireworks and all the flashbulbs in the world were going off at once...

POP!

Suddenly, all the sweet joy ended with the loud explosion of a conch shell under the tire of Marcellus' car in the drive. The old man had come back for something.

Now, the slamming of the front door and the sound of Trip's voice drifted up to her. The memory of Norris dissolved as Marilee gradually became aware of her surroundings.

Slowly, she swung her legs over the side of her bed and gathered up the photographs and the package of clippings, and took them back to her desk. Looking down at the clippings she thought of her talk with Sadie last evening. Sadie had suggested she come to New York and shop...hide out for a few days.

Why not?

Norris had been spending a lot of time at the Grail New York headquarters lately...maybe she'd find out tonight if he had any plans.

She walked into the bathroom and splashed her face with cold water. Rapidly becoming alert now, she looked at her watch. It was getting late. She slipped on a bra and a raw silk duster and went down to check on Ivee. He would have to be fed before they left for The Club.

Trip was standing at the foot of the stairs sorting through the mail. He looked up as she came down the steps and came forward to embrace her, thrusting his body against her in a coarse, suggestive way. She smiled to cover her aversion to his touch.

"God, you're gorgeous. I think I'll rape you here and now."

"What would Ivee and the kitchen help think?" She tried to laugh as she pushed him away and hurriedly skipped out of his reach toward the door to the kitchen to give instructions to Oleander.

As the door closed behind her, Marilee felt more like gagging than laughing.

CHAPTER TWENTY-TWO

GRIFF PUSHED BACK HIS CHAIR and finished his daiquiri.

"I see Nan waving. I better go get ready. Back in fifteen minutes...what you want to bet we don't still have to wait on the women." Griff moved away shaking his head. "God bless 'em."

Watching his old friend walk around the pool to the guest house to change, Clayt's thoughts returned to his guilt over his failure with Trip. The whole thing about bringing Norris here had been a sham anyway. In the beginning, he'd hoped Norris could turn Trip around in the corporation, the way he'd done in college.

It had been an unreasonable expectation.

Norris Wrenn was a genius, but not God.

With desperate hope, during Norris' first two years at The Tower, Clayt had insisted that Trip participate equally in all functions. He expected Trip's reasonable adherence to normal business hours at the office. Always making sure Trip be given the senior identity, he invented opportunities for Trip to show Norris the ropes with visits to various locations of the complex Grail empire. He still held out faint hope that, under the right conditions, Trip might suddenly blossom.

At first it seemed to work, but the plan was short-lived. Gradually, Trip began finding excuses for getting out of the meetings, deferring to Norris' judgment. Then, more and more, Trip began to transfer his responsibility to Norris' shoulders.

Finally, Clayt had given up. He had had to face the truth. If something should happen to him, steps must be taken to ensure the future of the corporation would remain intact for Ivee.

A few months back, he had gone to Griff. "I want you to work out a new five-year compensation schedule for Norris. Get back to me as soon as possible. Include salary escalations, stock bonuses...the works. I'm going to officially announce Norris' appointment as Chief Executive Officer right away."

Griff had worked out an attractive program.

On a trip to the Atlanta office, Clayton had sprung the surprise on Norris. He handed him the folder outlining the nuts and bolts of the package and spoke to him in a very proprietary voice: "How do you like the looks of that, son?"

Perfunctorily, Norris flipped through the pages, then handed it back.

"I appreciate your confidence in me, but..." Norris hesitated, searching for words. "I'm sorry, but I've been trying for weeks to find the right time to tell you I'm leaving Grail in September."

"September? No...no! I...I don't understand. You've got a real future here, didn't you read that? I want you to be CEO...take control."

"Oh yeah, I understand. But, I'm young. I don't want to spend the rest of my life as just somebody's hired hand. If something happens to you, then Trip would be left in control. I'm not about to invest any more of my life here with the possibility of that happening. I feel like I've contributed some things to the organization and I've learned a lot and increased my credibility in the international business arena, so I think we've both gotten our money's worth. I'm sorry, sir, but there is no way I would even think about it."

Clayt hadn't been able to believe his ears. Right before his eyes, his dream for Ivee was going down the drain.

He refused to give up. Tirelessly, he nagged away at Norris, trying to arrive at a solution.

Norris wasn't afraid to ask for money. He'd asked for a lot. But, the compensation issues were easy. It was far more complicated than that...Norris' future autonomy had to be absolutely guaranteed. And because it would give Norris enormous power if anything did happen to Clayt during the next ten years, it meant trusting Norris' integrity to a frightening degree. It had been the most difficult decision of Clayt's life. After many sleepless nights and much soul-searching, he finally came to terms with himself the last morning of the Azalea weekend at Caswell Beach.

Since then, he had often relived that decisive encounter with

Norris in minute detail.

The night before, he had not slept well, worrying about Trip's drunkenness earlier in the evening. He finally gave up the effort as the first hint of cold grayish-lavender light showed through the cracks in the split bamboo blinds. Quietly, he had slipped into a pair of faded jeans and a hooded sweatshirt. Careful not to disturb Mabel, he picked up his canvas shoes and slipped out of the room and down the stairs.

The light had been on in the kitchen and there was fresh coffee in the automatic coffeemaker. He'd poured himself a cup and walked to the door opening out onto the screened porch overlooking the beach, curious to see who had gotten up before he had. He was not surprised to see Norris standing out on the sun deck at the end of the wooden walkway.

Marilee must have heard him and risen early, too.

She'd hesitated on the balcony at the top of the stairs when she saw him, then had come down the steps and poured a cup of coffee. "Looks like a beautiful day..." she'd offered.

"Yeah...did Griff get Trip back in one piece last night?" Clayt asked.

"That's debatable." She nodded, knowingly. "I doubt he'll be up for awhile."

Ruefully, he'd shaken his head. Momentarily depressed by Trip's behavior, he'd stood there wondering if Norris was coming back in for coffee. Moving nearer the door, he could see the beginning of a pale tracing of pre-dawn color at the eastern horizon.

"I think I'll go out and join Norris...I need to have a word with him..."

Glad that Marilee had not offered to tag along, he had quickly pulled on his shoes and walked down the steps and out across the spidery walkway leading to the beach.

Norris had been less than excited to see him.

"Looks like another perfect day...you can't say we haven't had perfect weather," Clayt had ventured, cheerfully.

"Too bad the others will miss the sunrise, but the diehards were still at it when I went to bed before two," Norris replied, perfunctorily.

"Yeah. I gave up early, even before you did. We got back from Wilmington about half past twelve and I went straight to bed. Experience has taught me to save something for tomorrow," Clayt chuckled.

"I think I'll walk down to the lighthouse…" Norris had turned his back and abruptly started down the steps leading to the beach.

"Wait up! I'd like to talk about your future with the corporation."

"We've been through all that…you're wasting your time."

"Look…I thought we were all right with the salary…isn't the escalation arrangement OK with you, just the way we discussed it? I mean, we don't need to talk salary anymore, do we?" He'd looked anxiously into Norris' face for some indication of agreement.

"Well, the salary is OK. But there's no use in going on with this unless we agree on the stock bonuses and establish a board. Everything hangs on that. I've got to have a significant vested interest before I even consider selling a slice of my life to anyone." Norris' tone had a hard edge.

Clayt was surprised to detect a note of renewed resistance. Yesterday, riding with him in the golf cart, Norris had seemed openly enthusiastic about a future which put him in control of Grail.

"Oh! Yes. Yes, I mean both the bonus and the salary arrangement. Everything we discussed pertaining to that part is OK. I agree to your terms, completely." Clayt had been eager to get the conversation back to a more agreeable footing. "We need to deal with the other aspects you raised. I mean how to ensure your security in the event that…ah…things might arise, which would force me away from control. How can we do that? I mean, I know we could take heroic measures, but short of my making you my heir…ah…leaving the store to you, lock, stock and barrel…short of that, how would you set up an effective mechanism that would protect us both? I draw a blank on that one."

"Simple. First, I would have to have a twelve-year contract." Norris' tone was challenging…negative. The message was unmistakably: *Take it or leave it.*

"Twelve years. Well, now...I hadn't thought much in those terms. I don't know. I've...I mean we've...the board is accustomed to dealing in terms of five years." Clayt searched Norris' face for a clue. He found nothing there to encourage him. "We have to be reasonable. We have to do things for the benefit of the corporation. Tell me what you have in mind. If you can sell it to me, I can sell it to the board."

"I thought the whole idea was to protect the company for Ivee. Twelve years should be as much for your protection as mine. Why don't we just forget it?" Norris increased his pace.

"Wait up. What's the matter? I thought you were optimistic yesterday. What's changing your mind now?" Clayt was on the edge of panic. He could feel the whole thing slipping away. "At least tell me what's on your mind. I didn't say it was impossible. All I want to know is how it would work and if the corporation would be protected for the future generations of Grahams."

"Twelve-year contract or there is no basis for discussion. Don't give me any bullshit about the board. *You* are the bloody board. I don't think you've been listening to a damn word I've said during the three months you've kept pushing this ridiculous exercise. I'm not interested in being a hired hand. If you want a five-year man, there are plenty of bright young protégés out there. Bill Gates was telling me about one on my last trip to Washington. I can call him tomorrow when we get back." Norris stepped up his pace.

"Screw Bill Gates. Wait up. Why are you changing the subject? I want to finish working out a deal for you." Clayton was totally exasperated. "Wait up, goddamn it, Norris."

"I'm tired of this. I told you over three months ago. I'm leaving in September. I gave you eight months to find someone. But instead of getting busy, you've wasted almost half of that time trying to convince me that being your hired hand is the best thing for me. Sorry. I'm tired of this bullshit, Clayt. You want to have your cake and eat it, too. Deal me out."

"Goddamn it, Norris, all I'm trying to do is set you up so you are protected and so is my company. I want *you*. I've been asking you to work out your own deal. What could be fairer than that?"

135

Clayt was almost pleading. "Just tell me what you want."

"But Clayt, I have worked out the deal. Every time I start to tell you, you start to balk. I'm tired of it. You don't listen." Norris slowed slightly to let Clayt draw abreast and impassively looked him square in the eye. "Twelve years. Hell, man, your grandson will just be turning twenty-three."

"Well...that's true..." Clayt nodded. It made sense.

They walked on in silence for about fifty yards. The lighthouse loomed closer now, the light revolving and flashing against the pre-dawn sky.

"Go on. How does the rest work?" Clayt persisted.

"It's simple. And...it's foolproof to the corporation. You will always hold the trump card. When I came here, four years ago, the corporate after-tax profit was running at slightly over three percent. And that represented an all-time high. Now it's five." Norris waited for him to acknowledge his understanding.

"I am in awe of that. Everyone is in awe of that. *Fortune* magazine made that clear to the world in April." He laughed. "They also made it clear it is unreasonable to expect that you can continue the after-tax dollars at that level. I believe they predicted it would probably level out back around four point five. Even so, it's still a miracle. Why else would I be going to all this trouble to keep you? But no one expects you to do miracles all the time, if that's what you're worried about."

"I'm not worried about a goddamn thing. I'm making you a proposal you can't refuse. Suppose the corporation is guaranteed that for ten years the after-tax profit will stay above four percent? If it falls below, the contract can be declared null and void at the discretion of the corporation." Norris slowed ever so slightly to let it sink in.

"You're kidding. You can't do that. Nobody can do that." Clayt didn't have to think hard to make that judgment. "What's the catch?"

"No catch. But there is a payoff for me. Under these terms, you can't get rid of me for any other reason except 'just cause'—that is, outright dishonesty or something like inappropriate behavior...anything that would bring discredit to the corporate image. You won't be able to fire me for any personal whim, like my politics or refusing to kiss a stockholder's baby. The terms can be quite specific. As a matter of fact, I will insist on it for my protection. *Moral turpitude*...nothing else. Like embezzling...or getting caught red-handed with a stockholder's underage daughter. Any other reason and you have to buy out the contract under the terms of the stock bonuses awarded at the five percent level." Norris didn't look back at Clayt. The lighthouse was looming closer now. "Is that clear?"

"Uh, well? And just how much do you propose these bonuses will be? You're currently getting a quarter of one percent of the total corporate stock at the present five percent. If you maintained this impossible profit level you could wind up owning two-and-a-half percent of the entire company at the end of twelve years. My God, that's worth...over...Jesus!...millions."

Clayton had suddenly gone breathless, but it had nothing to do with the brisk walk.

"That's just the point. I'll be forty-nine by then. At that profit rate, just think what Grail...what you...would have realized out of the deal. I only want my fair cut. Of course, I could wind up making nothing, or in the event I can maintain the corporate profit at above the four percent level, I would still make my one-tenth of one percent in stock bonuses. Either way, you're the big winner...even with the built-in escalations for each full percentage point that I will earn if I increase the profit over five percent." Norris shrugged.

"Wait a minute. You mean there will be increases for anything over five? My God, there's got to be a limit." Clayt was overwhelmed now.

"*No! No limit*," Norris said, flatly. "If there was, you'd be screwing yourself. Do you want to limit the corporate profit? The after-tax dollars? The stuff power is made of? That sweet stuff that intimidates presidents and kings?"

"Of course I don't want to limit that! But this is getting grandiose...out of hand. What's the rest of it? How much did you have in mind...for you?"

"My stock bonus increases a tenth of a percent with each full percent of after-tax profit over five."

The wind had come up noticeably and the first red sliver of the sun had just appeared over the horizon. It was lighter now, but there was not yet a hint of warmth in the light. Norris continued to press the pace. Clayt had walked on without comment for perhaps a minute. His head ducked lower against the sting of the wind-blown sand. Finally, without raising his head, he asked, "I'm sure you've worked it out. Tell me for instance. What would your stock bonus be if the net reaches ten percent?'

"Point seven-five." Norris answered without hesitation.

"If the net profit went from five to ten this year, what would that mean in increased net dollars compared to last year?" Clayt asked.

"To me or the corporation?" Norris turned and looked him straight in the eye without breaking stride.

"Both." Clayt struggled, but kept the pace.

"Roughly, the corporation would gain a cool four billion... that's good old American. My stock bonus would increase a half of one percent to a total for the year of three-quarters of a percent of the total corporate issue. If you want that in dollars, just multiply by the current market price. It closed Friday at fifty-nine and a quarter." Norris was still looking squarely into Clayt's face.

"Not bad...Not bad for both of us." He had relaxed and smiled.

Abruptly, Norris stopped walking and looked up. Towering almost straight above them was the lighthouse.

After a moment, Norris looked back to him and smiled a thin, tight-lipped smile; a little of the tension had eased now.

"No...not bad at all," Norris said and turned toward the sea.

A narrow crescent of sun showed above the horizon. The light was turning from lavender to a pinkish glow. Norris bent down and rolled the cuffs of his jeans so they were just below his knees. Without a word, he started moving back in the direction of the cottage, but this time he steered a path which moved them toward the line where the edge of the biggest breakers reached the furthermost point on the hard-packed sand. They walked slower now.

"You've got this whole thing figured out, haven't you?" Clayt's voice betrayed a curious mixture of good humor and respect. "You already know how you're going to bring the corporate profit up. But, frankly, I think anything over five on a sustained basis is unrealistic. In a smaller, less diverse company it might be done for one- or two-year periods, but in our complex situation, I think you've done an impossible job bringing it above five. I think the experts are right. If you continue to do the job, you can probably keep it between four and five."

Norris stopped and picked up an unbroken sand dollar. He examined it carefully and handed it to Clayt.

"I'll take the net to ten. And it will stay there...or above," he said quietly.

Momentarily speechless, Clayt stood silent for a time. "You've really had it figured out for some time, haven't you?"

"I knew how before I took the job."

"What if the board doesn't want to go along with the deal? Twelve-year contract. Stock bonuses in the millions. I mean, this is really hardball you're talking here. What's the alternative?"

"I'm leaving the end of September, remember? You better start looking for a new Chief Counsel...and get in touch with Bill Gates about that hot shot I told you about."

"Be reasonable. Give me a compromise to take to the board, something I can leverage." Clayt looked anxiously to Norris for help.

"Cut the bullshit. *You* are the goddamn board." The hard edge returned to Norris' tone.

"You're pretty sure I'm going to go along with this, aren't you?"

"You're no dummy. I know it's hard for you to take, but if Trip had to take over....well, why discuss it?" Norris shrugged. "I made up my mind it was worth investing five years of my life when I took the job. Any way you look at it, it's been a good investment for me. I can go anywhere I want now...write my own ticket. And you have the healthiest corporate ship on the horizon. I'm leaving us both winners."

Norris deftly raked his bare toes through a pile of shells which had been freshly deposited by the receding tide. He stooped again to pick up another sand dollar. This one was also unbroken. He held it up for to Clayt to see.

"If you believe in foreshadowing and all that crap, maybe this is a good omen. I haven't found a perfect, unbroken sand dollar in years. Now I find two within minutes of each other."

"OK, you said it first. Let's cut the bullshit. You just made me an offer I can't refuse. Why do I get the feeling you've been writing this scenario for four years? You've known all along why I brought you into the corporation...that I needed someone who could fill the gap until my grandson could come into the company. You knew you had me over a barrel, didn't you?"

"Not a bad barrel to be over...if you're trying to achieve corporate immortality." Norris was expressionless.

Clayt extended his hand. "It's a deal, just the way you have outlined it. Get it on paper and bring it to me as soon as you can."

Norris ignored his extended hand.

"Whoa. We still haven't taken care of the main problem. I can't agree until you establish a failsafe to prevent Trip from assuming control in the event you are taken out of the picture."

"The stock will be held in trust until Ivee is twenty-one. That covers ten of your twelve years, perfectly," Clayt answered smugly. "Griffin Richards will manage the trust. He's my personal attorney. You know him. Do you have any problems with Griff?"

"If you mean do I trust him? No, I don't have problems with Griff. Of course I trust Griff—he's the best. But putting it in a single pair of hands won't do. The trust must be managed by a board—Mabel, Trip, Marilee, Griff and me. The grandmother, father, mother, your attorney and me. That way Mabel and Marilee will protect Ivee's interest, Griff will look out for their interest and I'll take care of the corporation," Norris said without hesitation.

"But why Trip?" Clayt was completely puzzled.

"To keep him happy. That way he won't stir up any trouble," Norris replied.

"I don't know. This makes it seem pretty complicated. And it will put you in control. It all comes down to that, doesn't it? How do I?...ah..." he began, but Norris cut him off in mid-sentence.

"Wait a minute. That's what this is all about. You either have to give it to Trip or trust someone. What you put in place now is all you can leave. If you die or become incapacitated, you are gone. When you're gone, you're just gone...and that's the name of that song."

Abruptly, Norris turned and struck out for the cottage.

"Hey, where are you going? Wait up!" Clayt shouted and started after him.

"I bought this beautiful blue and red gingham kite in San Francisco last month. If I'm going to try it out, I need to do it now, while this wind holds." Norris called over his shoulder without breaking stride. "By the way, did you ever fly a kite?"

"No. Not since I was a kid, anyway..." Clayt was dumbfounded by Norris' sudden withdrawal from the conversation.

"Have you ever played ball?"

"No...what the hell kind of ball?"

"Oh, I don't know...hardball maybe," Norris stopped and suddenly wheeled to face him.

"Flying kites...playing ball? How'd we get on this?"

"Maybe you ought to try one or the other." Norris' voice was barely audible over the wind as he turned again and moved rapidly away at a trot.

Clayt stood there for a moment watching him go, letting it all sink in. Finally, it hit him.

"Well, I'll be goddamn! The son of a bitch just had the *cajones* to tell me to either play ball or go fly a kite!" he muttered to himself, half-aloud. In that moment, Clayt knew he had been beaten...and, in defeat, he had become the real winner. God, how he wished he'd had a son like that.

Suddenly he relaxed and let out a little chuckle. The Senator had been right: Norris had at least four balls...all shiny brass.

He really liked that.

That had been six weeks ago. Last week, Griff had finally completed all the documents. Clayt signed the will with the trust arrangement for Ivee. Griff saw to it they were all properly witnessed and executed. Griff left a copy for Norris along with copies of Norris' new contract to be signed by both Clayt and Norris tomorrow morning. There was also a letter signed by Clayt stating that any change in the will or trust would constitute a breach of Norris' contract and the unfulfilled term would be forfeited and Norris would be compensated at the maximum penalty.

Not even in the event of his death would Trip ever suffer. Clayt did not want to cause any spread of the cancerous scourge of envy which he knew Trip held for Norris. Above all, he wanted harmony between the two men. It bothered him when Trip's resentment surfaced this afternoon after he saw the terms of Norris' contract.

But that was the least of it. He didn't really like what Trip had become as a man. And, he felt an admiration for Norris he hadn't felt for any man since his own father. Secretly, he couldn't help but wish Norris might come to look upon him as the father Norris never knew. What was the line about the son being father of the man? Life got pretty complicated sometimes.

"It's a marvelous evening." Mabel's voice startled him out of his reverie. "I'm ready for a party."

CHAPTER TWENTY-THREE

AGNES STOOD FASCINATED, watching the outline of Norris' penis through the light fabric of his cream-colored slacks as he walked across the lawn. Her nipples still tingled from his casual caresses earlier. She liked parties and lately it was getting harder and harder to get Norris out, but watching him now, she suddenly wished this one was already over with.

"I guess we should be going." She indicated for Norris to lead the way. Deliberately walking a half-pace behind him as they crossed the yard and started up the cart path, she enjoyed watching the muscles of his buttocks as they rippled under the light fabric of the slacks.

Her attention was drawn to the figures of Trip and Marilee as they approached. To watch Marilee move effortlessly across the terrace above them filled Agnes' throat with envy. Marilee wore a simple little white dress with sleeves and a high neck. It really should have been against the law.

Looking at Marilee, Agnes felt fat. The stunning white cotton dress she had recently purchased at one of the exclusive boutiques at Charleston Place...the dress which seemed at the time to be made just for her...the dress she had been saving for just such an occasion, now seemed like a rack dress from K-Mart.

It wasn't fair that Marilee was named Mother of the Year. Everybody made over her too much because she was so pretty. And, underneath all that feigned innocence, Marilee was a show-off bitch. Why couldn't people see through it?

How could anyone help but hate her...really?

Norris walked on without slowing his pace, watching as Marilee and Trip approached from their right. Marilee caught his eye and a

143

flicker of recognition passed between them. Norris looked away and slowed to let Agnes catch up. He risked a glance back and Marilee was still staring him straight in the eye. He found it hard to look at her. His earlier resolve to set the record straight was quickly fading.

"Marilee looks stunning, as always," Agnes said, trying to be cheerful. "She was honored at the school today...the Governor is going to name her North Carolina Mother of the Year at a big media event tomorrow in Raleigh. I'm so happy for her."

Yeah...and you'd just love to have a triple root canal, Norris mused wryly. He deliberately slowed his pace so their arrival would lag just behind Trip and Marilee. Still, he felt foolish. He never got nervous at the prospect of meeting world leaders. Kings and movie stars and Pulitzer winners were just people to him, yet here he was now with his palms sweating, afraid he would stammer when he spoke.

Despite Norris' careful maneuvering, Marilee left Trip as he headed for the bar and walked over and gave Agnes an air kiss and a polite embrace.

"Well, I see you brought the invisible man," she said to Agnes.

She turned to Norris and said, "Long time no see."

Lifting up on her toes, she gave him a hug and kissed him on the cheek away from Agnes' view.

Norris stiffened, taken completely by surprise.

"We have unfinished business...we could meet in New York...no one would ever know," Marilee breathed in his ear. Then, before he could blink, she kissed him hard on the mouth.

"Uh...it's good to see you, too...it's been awhile," Norris stammered.

Marilee gave Agnes a brilliant smile and dabbed at the lipstick on Norris' mouth and cheek.

"Agnes...you have just the sweetest man..." she purred.

"I know..." Still burning at how stunning Marilee looked in the dress, Agnes blurted dumbly, totally oblivious of Norris' discomfort.

Much to Norris' relief, Marilee was immediately surrounded by a mob of well-wishing admirers.

"C'mon, Agnes, they're already having last calls for drinks," Norris took her elbow and steered her toward the bar.

"C'mon, everyone—let's eat!" Scarcely twenty minutes elapsed before Mabel started herding everyone though the French doors in the direction of the elegant private dining room where she started a complicated exercise of seeing to it that everyone knew or remembered everyone else.

There were place cards at the table. With the Governor present, everything was arranged as protocol dictated. Mabel officiated as hostess, with the Governor seated at her right. As honoree, Marilee sat to his right. To Mabel's left, Norris was placed as the other person being honored.

When everyone was settled, Mabel stood and began speaking in her quiet way. "It is not often we are so honored as to have the Governor of our fine state and both of its most distinguished senators. And since we are all friends here, there aren't going to be any speeches." Mabel smiled and raised her glass and said, "But, I want to propose a toast. What more can a grandmother ask than to have the mother of her grandson be named Mother of the Year for her home state? Ladies and gentlemen, good friends all, I give you our guest of honor, my daughter-in-law, Marilee Bryant Graham. We are so very proud of you, Marilee."

There was an enthusiastic round of applause and murmurs of, "Here, here..."

Marilee stood and made a shy curtsy and waited for quiet.

"Thank you. I love you all. You're wonderful." She looked straight into Norris' eyes. Blushing prettily, she quickly sat down.

The bitch is such a show-off. Still fuming, Agnes missed Marilee's hungry look at Norris.

"And we are fortunate to have another great occasion to celebrate tonight. For that, I'll let my wonderful husband do the honors." Mabel looked to the other end of the table where Clayt stood up.

"I'm proud of you, daughter. We're a lucky family." Clayt

smiled at Marilee and raised his glass. "And we are a fortunate company, too. The next toast is to a man who has been like a brother to Trip and an adopted son to Mabel and me. And just as importantly, he has, over the past four years in his role as Executive Vice-President and Chief Corporate Counsel, come to be the most valuable executive in one of the most powerful companies in the entire world. In well-deserved recognition of his irreplaceable value to the corporation, tomorrow morning Norris Wrenn will become CEO of Graham International, Ltd. Congratulations, son, you deserve it."

There was polite applause and congratulatory remarks all around the table. When Norris stood, obviously ready to make a few remarks, some of the men groaned good-naturedly.

"The Governor had the good sense to make this an evening among friends...now look who wants to make a speech," Trip's words were slurred. His voice had a nasty undertone.

"I just wanted to propose a toast to our lifelong friendship, Trip...and to your lovely wife whom our Governor has chosen as a role model for all the mothers in our state. To Marilee, whom we all admire for the model of motherhood she brings to all of us here in Colonial Hall and in North Carolina...and the whole damn world." Norris raised his glass. "And to moms, Chevrolets and apple pies everywhere....and to fathers, Cadillacs and bourbon likker...and especially to my old roomie, Trip."

There was another polite ripple of "Here, here" from around the room.

"I'll certainly drink to that, Norris," the Governor said enthusiastically and raised his glass. "And, I'll drink to you. I have long admired you for the excellence and responsibility you represent to our great state and to our great country...and to the world. And now, you'll be directing our most important corporation. The Grahams have brought the attention of the entire world to Colonial Hall and to the great state of North Carolina. This is a great day for us all."

Like magic, the food appeared and everyone began eating. For the moment, the low buzz of conversation became more subdued.

As he ate, Norris' mind wandered off on little fantasies of Marilee showing up at his apartment in New York. Before he could pursue the thought, he felt a touch on his shoulder. When he turned, Ed Stutz, Assistant Manager of The Club, leaned forward and informed him quietly, "You have a call from the White House. You can take it upstairs in the library."

CHAPTER TWENTY-FOUR

THE RANKING PILOT in the elite White House helicopter wing, Colonel Charles Smith, USMC, finished his shower and poured himself a Diet Coke before he went into the living room of his VIP bachelor officer quarters at Quantico Marine Air Station. He picked up the remote control and turned on the TV, idly flipping through the pages of *The Washington Post,* looking for the TV schedule. Up since the crack of dawn, Charlie and his co-pilot had flown a chopper full of Washington bureaucrats down for a whirl-wind inspection of the time-honored boot camp at Parris Island and her sister facility, the Beaufort Marine Air Station.

Politics and politicians had no place in war! A Vietnam veteran with two Distinguished Flying Crosses and less than six months to go on his thirty-year career, Charlie hated them all.

He was just about to flip past CNN World News when the program was interrupted. The photo of a vaguely familiar, extremely attractive young woman appeared on the screen. Charlie's interest quickened and he turned up the sound.

"...JUST IN FROM GREENSBORO, NORTH CAROLI-NA...CNN HAS LEARNED THAT CIRCUMSTANCES SUR-ROUNDING THE DEATH OF ACTRESS EMMA CLAIRE IN A GREENSBORO MOTEL SEEM TO POINT TO A DRUG OVER-DOSE SIMILAR TO THE DEATHS OF THE ACTOR, JOHN BELUSHI, AND MARYLAND BASKETBALL PLAYER..."

Charlie put down the remote, picked up the phone and dialed his co-pilot Major Ambrose "Toots" Miller in nearby Woodbridge. Miller picked up on the first ring.

"Toots...quick...turn on CNN...ah...cable...ah twenty-four..."

"Yeah...I already saw it...I was about to call. She's a dead ringer for the girl we dropped at that fancy waterway estate when we flew the President to Lejeune...April?...right?"

"You think our fearless Christian leader was humping a real movie star and we never had a clue?..."

CHAPTER TWENTY-FIVE

AT THE TOP OF THE STAIRS, Norris could see a soft shaft of light coming from the partially open door of the library. Inside the library, he turned the large knob of the rheostat to soften the light so that the interior was as dim as the corridor. Old habits die hard. It gave him the edge of being able to spot anyone who might climb the stairs and approach the library unexpectedly. He was always sensitive about calls from Washington. From where the telephone was placed, he commanded a clear view of the entire hallway. There would be no surprise eavesdroppers to worry about.

He picked up the phone and pushed the blinking button. "This is Norris Wrenn."

"Chatham Brookes, Norris. Sorry to bother you at your club, but something important has come up...what would you say if I told you you could go ahead with Phoenix...just the way you wrote it?"

"You keep talking, but nothing happens." He had been hearing this for over three months.

"Well...I know, dear boy. Things take time. It finally looks like we may bring it off."

"We? Who's we? I'm tired of silly games. I told you the players I'd need."

"I'm well aware. Charlie Starkweather, Boone Mayfield and Jean Paul Langlois are heading the list. But this time the Swiss and the Japs are in. Ikimoto himself."

"Ikimoto? I don't believe it. It's about time that the Japs took notice of that big 'MADE IN THE U.S.A.' star on the side of the launch platform at Cape Kennedy." Norris chuckled. "What about the British...the Russians...the Chinese?"

"The British are definitely in. Carstairs himself is really respon-

150

sible for getting the idea rolling again." Brookes exuded enthusiasm. "The Russians? Who knows...who cares anymore? The initial response from Beijing is encouraging. Their lackluster response to the war on terrorism hurt their world trade...my guess is that they're anxious to get some good PR."

"Royce Carstairs? Are you putting me on? And, the Chinese— maybe this *is* serious." Norris laughed incredulously, feeling an overpowering tug of sentiment. After all, Phoenix was his baby from his "save-the-world" early days in Washington.

"It's serious, all right. Can you come to New York tomorrow?" Chatham asked abruptly. Norris was unprepared for the question.

New York... Marilee's whisper echoed in his head.

"Come on now, Chatham. Aren't you overreacting?" Now, his heart was beating faster.

"No, I'm quite serious. The President is standing right here. Will you say hello?"

"Well...ah...of course."

"Norris, we miss having you around. I hear great things are happening now that you're down there at Grail. I know this is short notice, but it would be a great favor to me if you'd meet with C.B. Will you do it?" Norris recalled the quiet, strong voice of the President.

"Yes sir, of course I'll meet with Chatham," Norris heard himself saying. "But I can't come to New York tomorrow. I can probably make it Wednesday. Will that be all right?"

"That will have to do, but here's C.B. Work it out. I'm looking forward to seeing you soon. The First Lady sends her regards to Agnes. Here's C.B. now." There were sounds of movement....background whispers told him that they were on a speaker phone.

"This thing is moving fast, Norris. If it's got to be Wednesday, then it will have to do. I'm leaving for New York tonight and will be there the rest of the week. Maybe that's better, anyway. Carstairs is flying in from London Wednesday night. Could you make it early Wednesday? Say mid-morning?" Brookes spoke in short, clipped phrases. There was no nonsense about the man.

"Sure. Tell me where...and when." He located a memo pad

with THE COUNTRY CLUB blind-embossed at the top of the paper and jotted down the address: 125 CARLYSLE–10 A.M.–212.521.1259.

"All right, sir. I'll see you Wednesday," Norris murmured and put down the phone.

As he finished writing, Norris' attention was drawn to a movement at the top of the stairs. His eyes adjusted as he first caught a glimpse of the top of a head. The rest of the figure slowly emerged to full height.

Marilee!

He quickly adjusted the light so it was just a little darker where he sat in the library. She stood for a moment letting her eyes accustom themselves to the darkness before she finally started down the hallway toward him. He could tell by the way she peered intently into the other rooms along the hall that she hadn't seen him yet.

Against the background of the light reflecting up the stairwell from the huge chandelier in the foyer below, he could see her body sharply silhouetted through the thin fabric of her dress. A familiar rush of senses left him at once excited and afraid.

He stood there for a moment before he walked to the door and turned the light control to the full OFF position. Now, he stood in total darkness and watched Marilee as she approached. Then he thought better of it. For an instant he turned the knob and flashed the light brighter so that she saw him. Then he lowered it back to a dimness that was just below that of the hallway.

"Norris, you bastard! Were you going to jump out at me and scare me half to death?" Marilee laughed as she dodged into the room.

"What the hell are you doing up here, Marilee? Have you completely lost your mind?"

"Yes..." She walked directly over to him and took his face between her hands and pulled his mouth down to hers. Her tongue was electric, urgently seeking his.

Helpless to push her away, cupping the underside of her buttocks, Norris pulled her roughly against him. The length of her pushing back drove him to the edge of orgasm.

"Oh, God, I want you..." she breathed into his mouth.

All his anger and good intentions went straight to hell. Senses rocketing toward overload, blood surged into his penis. Almost instantly, he was painfully swollen...begging for release.

Reacting to the swelling, Marilee's hands started to fuss with his zipper.

Norris pushed away with effort, momentarily startled back to reality.

"Goddamnit, Marilee, you've got to stop this."

"Relax. If anybody comes I'll just grab the phone..." She tugged his zipper again.

"Stop, goddamnit! You come sneaking up here in the dark, and the whole world is waiting down there to fall on us." He removed her hand and started out of the room.

"Wait, I know you're right, but I had to know...will you meet me in New York?"

"No...goddammit...N-frigging-O!"

"I'll scream rape..." She moved seductively closer, smiling, licking her lips suggestively. "C'mon. New York...it's safe. You go all the time on business...I go to shop. Who'd be the wiser? What've you got to lose?" She groped his penis again.

"Just every goddamn thing...now stop, goddamnit...we can't..."

"Oh, come on...I won't take no for an answer. Didn't the beach mean anything?"

"It can't mean anything...can't you see how impossible..."

"We can't talk about it here...meet me in New York. Don't just walk away like this...it won't end and you know it...look at you." She reached for him and tweaked the end of his bulging penis before he could move away.

"Quit. How can I go back down there like this?" He gestured helplessly.

"Here let me...I can fix it...." She licked her lips and reached for his zipper again.

Tempted, he looked frantically over her shoulder in the direction of the stairs. Now he was just as crazy as she was. "No...no! Go away...please. Let me get myself under control..."

"If I go now...will you meet me in New York?"

"All right...OK. I have to be there Wednesday morning anyway. But...understand, it's only to end this...this insanity."

"Great! Meet me at Sadie Bailey's place?" She hugged him, tightly.

"No...my place; nobody but Patty has the address...I'm not sure when. I'll call tomorrow. Now, will you please go?"

Marilee leaned up and kissed him again. She squeezed his arm and gave him a loving look before she turned and walked back down the hall and disappeared down the stairwell.

Norris sat down in the nearest chair...weak. He looked down at the bulge in his pants and could see a telltale trace of moisture soaking through. Lowering his trousers, he wiped away the fluid as best as he could with his handkerchief, then redressed himself...tucking his shirttail carefully in. Finally restored to semi-presentability, Norris shrugged and headed toward the stairs. When he took his place back at the dinner table, Agnes glanced up from her plate and smiled. The entree had just been served, and everyone was busily attacking the food, engaged in subdued conversation. The discussion was about *angiostatin* and *endostatin*, Entremed's two new cancer agents. Apparently no one missed him.

He wondered if he looked as guilty as he felt.

Clayton saw Norris come back to the table. He had overheard the assistant manager tell Norris the White House was on the phone, and he resented that Norris had left to take the call. All the calls from the goddamn White House made Clayt angry...and insecure.

Now, suddenly, Clayton's attention was diverted back to Trip who had knocked over his wine glass. On either side of him, guests were pushing back their chairs and scrambling out of the way.

Quietly, Clayton arose and intercepted the assistant manager crossing the room with two servers to help with damage control.

"Ed, will you do me a favor?"

"Of course, Mr. Graham." The young man snapped to attention.

"I'm going to get my son out of here...quietly. Will you see that he makes it safely home?"

"Oh, yessir, I'll drive him myself."

"Come on right now. Let's get it done..." Clayton went over and took Trip's elbow.

Drunk or sober, Trip knew better than to put up a fuss with his father. With Clayt on one side and Ed Stutz solicitously steadying him on the other, they walked him out the side door to the staff parking lot and maneuvered him into Ed's car.

When he returned, Clayton found Norris standing outside the men's room.

"What happened? Where's Trip...?"

"Ed's taking him home."

"Too bad..." Norris murmured and turned to walk with him back to join the others.

"What was the White House calling about just now?" Clayton asked, resentfully.

"Chatham Brookes...and the President...wanted me to come up tomorrow. They want me to revive the Phoenix thing..."

"What the hell...you're not going, are you? We've got a god-damn corporation to run," Clayton snapped, angrily. The White House had called Norris at least once a day when they were down at Marilee's beach house.

"No, of course not tomorrow during the day, but I am going up tomorrow night...I'm meeting Chatham Brookes in New York on Wednesday morning..."

"Goddamn it, Norris, your priorities are fucked up...you need to understand who signs your paycheck." Clayton was livid now.

"I know who signs my paycheck. I think you've forgotten whose idea it was that I stay on here. I know you're upset over Trip. We can talk about all this tomorrow before the signing. Right now, I think we need to join the others...there's been enough excite-ment already tonight...don't you think?" Norris stepped aside and allowed Clayton to enter first.

Walking back in the room, Clayton felt totally castrated. How had he let himself get into such a position? That son of a bitch Trip...now, Norris. Why, all of a sudden, was everything coming apart? If only Norris wouldn't be so goddamn independent. Clayt's gaze drifted to Marilee. Suddenly, it occurred to him that Marilee had disappeared while Norris was out of the room. Now he was getting paranoid; she had merely gone to the powder room. He had to stop this. Since he had started sneaking around with Glee Craige, he was suspicious of everyone.

Still...Norris had dictated all the terms....

Norris was smart. Perhaps the smartest man he'd ever known. Norris had laid out this entire scenario. Could Norris and Marilee wind up in a position where Graham International, Ltd. could be liquidated before Ivee became of legal age?

He looked over at his old friend Griff. Had he really covered his ass?

Griff and Nan were staying the night. He needed to check this out...tonight, after this thing was over.

The party quieted down and lost energy. Within thirty minutes, the group was heading home.

After all the goodnights, Norris and Agnes walked Marilee home. There were little lights along the paths and high in the limbs of the pine trees. Their dark green mushroom-like caps reflected the pale light downward to illuminate the pathways through the woods.

"Goodnight..." Marilee called over her shoulder as she turned into the trees which separated the fairway from their yard.

When Marilee walked in from the terrace, Trip was standing in his robe with a drink in his hand. "Want a little nightcap?" he offered, drunkenly.

"No thanks, I'm going on up." Marilee skipped up the steps to her room and locked the door behind her. Without turning on the light, she went straight to her bedroom window to see if she could catch a glimpse of Norris and Agnes walking up through the yard next door.

Tomorrow she was meeting Norris in New York. She would fly on up...straight from the Governor's press conference. She'd say she wanted to do some Mother's Day shopping. Sadie would simply die when she found out.

Now, a glimpse of movement down through the trees toward the golf course caught her attention. As her eyes adjusted, she could see Agnes and Norris slowly moving up the long slope through the edge of their yard. She watched as Agnes let her hand drop from its easy position at Norris' waist to slide suggestively over his hips and buttocks. Giving his behind little tweaks and squeezes, Agnes urged him up through the lighted path through the trees to the edge of their rose garden.

Norris stopped and turned, and Agnes kissed him and pressed her body hard against him. Then she pulled him urgently through the terrace door into the house.

This open display of lust hit Marilee like an unexpected kick in the stomach.

Once you have me, Norris, you'll never want anyone else again, she vowed.

Moving to the bedside phone she called USAirways to book a first class seat to New York.

CHAPTER TWENTY-SIX

WHEN THE TAILLIGHTS OF THE GOVERNOR'S LIMOUSINE finally disappeared, Clayt took Mabel's arm and walked her back into the entrance foyer of the club where Griff stood waiting with Nan.

"Well, my dear, you did it again. What a delightful evening." Griff beamed at Mabel.

"Let's go home." Mabel checked her watch. "Is my watch right? It's not quite ten?"

"Time passes fast when you're having fun. Forgive the cliché, but it's true," Nan giggled.

They all laughed.

As they made their way from The Club, resentment tightened in Clayton's stomach as Mabel started to squeeze his hand in that familiar knowing way.

The woman never gives up.

He fervently wished he was already in the Lear winging high above the edge of the Atlantic toward Jacksonville. Tomorrow, Trip was going to be hung over. Maybe he could just cancel the golf after the contract ceremony and get an early start.

The thought pulled him sharply back to his concerns about Norris' contract.

"Griff, do you feel like talking for a minute?" he asked, as soon as they were inside the house. Without waiting for an answer, he turned to the women and said, "I'm sure you understand, we need to go over some things, and I'm leaving tomorrow for Jacksonville."

"Don't be too long, dear." Mabel gave Clayt's arm a knowing pat and another little squeeze. She turned and smiled at Nan. "C'mon, Nan, let's see if we can find some coffee."

Without waiting, Clayt turned and walked through the door of his study. Closing it behind them as soon as Griff was inside, he went to the wet bar and reached into the cabinet and removed a bottle of Courvoisier.

"Brandy?"

"Sure." Griff nodded and sank his lanky form into the corner of one of the burgundy leather sofas which sat facing each other in the middle of the richly paneled room.

"I guess I'm a little nervous—about tomorrow, I mean. At dinner I got to wondering what could happen if Mabel and I both should die during the next twelve years. And what about Trip...what if he should die too? Does that leave Marilee in control of Grail? What if somehow Norris and Marilee were making hanky-panky? Is Ivee protected? I know we've been over this...but I need to be sure." Clayt handed Griff the snifter of cognac and took a seat on the other sofa facing him.

"Quit worrying. Ivee is protected all the way," Griff assured him, confidently.

"What about Trip? What if Mabel and I both die? Can Marilee divorce Trip? Can she remarry and as Ivee's mother gain control...sell his stock?"

"No way," Griff stated flatly. "The entire concept of the contract is for Norris to maintain control until Ivee can take over. The family stock cannot be transferred. It's that simple."

"Uhmm..." Clayt settled back and savored the mellow bouquet of the brandy as he swirled the amber liquid in the snifter. "What if Marilee married Norris? What would that do? Norris is smart as hell...maybe the smartest man I've ever seen."

"Nothing...well." Griff fell silent while he mulled it over.

Clayt sipped his brandy. He was still uneasy.

"Could Norris do a stock manipulation and engineer a takeover?"

"No. The majority stock is family held...it's protected by the charter."

"But that's just the point. Marilee is a Graham. I can't help but be nervous. I just want to be sure there's nothing we've overlooked," Clayt persisted.

"Calm down..." Griff was getting a little tired of this. He had seen a change in Clayt lately, and he knew it all stemmed from the guilt he was feeling over the Craige woman he was keeping in Florida.

The woman was out to take Clayt for a ride. Griff was certain of that. He kept hoping that his old friend would come to his senses.

Quite unbeknown to Clayt, two weeks ago he'd asked a trusted colleague in Jacksonville to check the woman out. The preliminary report was that she had a murky past. But it was still too early to confront Clayt. He had to be dead sure. If he was wrong, it would only make Clayton more adamant and cause bad feelings.

As if he could read Griff's mind, Clayt spoke up, "How do we stand with the trust arrangement and house at Starfish? Are we all set? You're still coming down Wednesday to handle the thing personally? I'd feel a lot better. That would give you a couple of days to go back over the contract with Norris. I can call him right now and tell him I want to postpone this until next week. We can't be too sure in a deal this big."

"That contract is solid. I think it's a mistake to delay the thing with Norris any longer than necessary. I think you would be in deep trouble if anything happened to you now. If Norris doesn't have a deal, he would walk out so fast it would make your head swim. That leaves your heirs filthy rich, but Grail would be in deep doo-doo with you incapacitated. If you left Trip to his own devices, you could forget Ivee ever running Graham International, Ltd. With you dead or locked away, the power scavengers would move in and take control sooner or later. As a matter of fact, if Norris were left on the outside, with his inside knowledge he could undoubtedly move right in with you out of the picture. It would be simple; no moral turpitude restrictions. If he weren't already committed to Grail, what could stop him? Without Norris, Graham family control would be history. Ivee would be left with a lot of money, but nothing else but some warm memories of his granddaddy. Go ahead and sign; make certain Ivee's protected."

"No...I want to think about it. Norris is cooking up some deal with Washington—the goddamn White House—I want some time to think this through again. Meanwhile, you check it out...make sure we're protected."

"I am sure...goddamn it. Why don't you get someone else to handle it?" Griff was losing his patience. "They can just handle your arrangement for your little girlfriend's house, too."

"Whoa...back off. I'm sorry, Griff, but, in the mood I'm in, I still don't trust myself to face Norris tomorrow..."

"OK. Just make up some excuse. I'll get Norris to sign tomorrow. Then, I could go over it again before I bring it down there Wednesday morning. That way, all you would have to do is sign it and it would be done." Griff leaned forward and placed the snifter on the low table.

"OK. That makes sense. It's not binding until we both sign. You come down Wednesday, bring the contract with Norris' signature, and handle the new trust for Glee and the house. We can finalize the whole thing down there. That way I'll feel easier. I sure'n shit need to be protected."

"You need to have your Virecta prescription cancelled and your shriveled-up old balls cut off. That woman is making a fool out of you." Griff looked him straight in the eye. "Call Norris now, before he goes to bed, and tell him you have changed your plans. Tell him I'll come over and get the documents signed in the morning. I'll take them to you in Florida Wednesday morning."

Without a word, Clayt picked up the phone. Norris answered on the first ring.

"Norris. Glad I caught you before you went to bed. Something's come up and I'm going to leave early tomorrow for Florida. I'd like to have Griff come by The Tower tomorrow and get your signature on the contracts. He can bring them down to me in Jacksonville Wednesday, and I can sign and have them notarized there."

"No. That won't do. I'll wait. You and I have some unfinished issues about our Washington conversation tonight. I'm in no hurry. I keep wondering why I let myself get involved in this, anyway. Only a couple of months back, I was trying to resign." Norris laughed a tight little laugh, obviously angry. "We can discuss it when you get back. That way I can leave in the morning and meet Tom Bradley before I see Chatham Brookes in New York Wednesday."

Clayt pulled the phone slightly away from his ear. From the other side of the table, Griff flinched visibly when he heard Norris' outburst crackle out of the phone.

"Wait...wait, now. Don't go off half-cocked...I mean why can't you just take a minute to sign the damn thing for Griff tomorrow?" Clayt sputtered. This wasn't going right at all.

"Why can't you sign first? I mean if it's that important?" Norris shot back. "Obviously, you're stalling. Suits me. I'm in no hurry. Maybe we should both think it over."

"Damn it, why do you need to think it over?"

"Same reason you do..." There was silence on the line.

"Norris?..."

"Yeah?..."

"Is there something you're not telling me? Is the White House trying to lure you back?"

"Let me go now. I want to call Tom Bradley before he goes to bed. Have a good trip."

The line went dead.

"Goddamn him." Clayt looked at the phone in frustration and put it down. "Screw the bastard. I'm tired of his arrogance. I'm going to tell him I accept his resignation."

Clayt began dialing the phone.

"Put down the phone, you crazy old fart," Griff said. "Unless you're calling Trip..."

"Trip?..." Clayt stopped dialing and slowly put the phone back into the cradle. "Why the hell would I want to call him?"

"You better start getting your idiot son sober, if you're fixing to fire Norris."

"Well...shit!" Clayt got up and kicked the corner of the table. "Ow...o-oh-whee," he howled and danced around in pain, holding his foot.

Finally, after the pain subsided, he limped gingerly to the window on the far wall and pulled aside the drapes. He stood there looking down on the lights of the town. He looked at Griff and waved his hand at the dark shape of The Tower with the lights at the top blinking a warning to careless aircraft. "You know...there's too much of me out there to let it go now. Poor Trip! It isn't his fault. It's the family curse...but it's too late to worry about the blame. I saw what the booze did to my daddy...and Trip is heading right down the same road. Unofficially, to the last man, alcohol has been the ultimate cause of death of all the Graham men. Beware the family scourge," Clayton said with feeling.

"You should talk to Norris about Trip."

"No..." Clayt pouted.

"OK, then, how about AA?"

"AA! Trip's a Graham."

"Trip's an alcoholic...maybe worse...."

"Oh...shit, Griff, don't go overboard. He's just been hanging around that crowd at Palm Beach. Aren't there places where people go for a week or two to get straightened out? Rancho Mirage...play some golf maybe...."

"Get real...this is serious, he doesn't need a vacation...maybe we could call Ed Scott..."

"Oh...hell no. Let's not get Doc involved. He'll blow it out of proportion. It's not terminal. Norris kept him sober when he first came here...." Clayt caught himself and looked back sheepishly at Griff.

Griff smiled sadly and shrugged.

In the end it was always Norris. He needed Norris...he loved Norris...and he hated the son of a bitch—and he certainly wasn't ready to forgive him for tonight....

"Goddamn Norris, I let him write his own ticket in this. A million men would sell their souls for such a shot. Who does he think he is?" Clayt leaned forward, his face red with anger and frustration.

"Just calm down. You've got a lot on your mind...I know you're worried about Trip...something's got to be done about that...and I mean now. I didn't realize how bad it's gotten until I saw him at Caswell Beach...then tonight...even worse than the beach and that's only a month and a half. I know you won't admit it, but what's really bothering you is all this shady business with your young honey down in Jacksonville. It's called a guilty conscience. If you really want my advice, you'll get out of that before that woman makes real trouble for you." Griff looked Clayt dead in the eye.

"Goddamn it, Griff, quit preaching to me. Just protect my ass legally...and be my friend."

"OK, OK," Griff shrugged. "It's a lousy job, but I guess somebody has to look after you. Your little girlfriend is a very expensive playmate. I hope she's worth it."

"Griff...old friend...you wouldn't believe what's it like...she makes me feel like a young stud again. Imagine...rosy pink flesh, soft and firm. And a total wanton...a sensual animal... absolutely insatiable. Lives only to satisfy her appetites. There's no way to tell you...you wouldn't believe the things she does..." Clayton leaned across and refilled his snifter.

Griff looked at his old friend. They had been through a lot together.

"OK...what the hell. Let's cover our ass. Here's to fast airplanes, old brandy and young pussy." Griff raised his glass.

"That's more like it, you old bastard. The role of a saint doesn't become you." Clayt laughed. "The main thing in the blind trust for Glee is to make sure she understands that she doesn't get the house...or a damn thing...if Mabel finds out. She needs to know she's killing the golden goose if she gets pissed off and tries to threaten me with emotional blackmail."

"Right. Winner take nothing." Griff nodded.

There was a sharp knock on the door and Mabel stuck her head in without waiting for a response. "Are you two going to stay locked up all night? I'm sure Nan and Griff are tired too."

"Yes...you're right. Go on up, I'll be right behind."

Mabel hugged Nan and Griff goodnight. Clayt watched as she moved up the stairs. She really did look good. Unexpectedly, he felt an excitement rising within him.

In the bedroom, Mabel had softened the lights and was lying

with just a sheet over her. When Clayt entered the room she propped herself on her elbow and watched him as he moved direct-ly to her and bent down and kissed her hard on the mouth. Her mouth opened and her tongue betrayed her hunger.

Clayt felt the blood rush to his penis. Goddamn, he was horny as the devil himself.

"I love to look at you. You're huge...so powerful." Mabel reached out and touched his thigh and ran her fingertips up the inside of his leg.

Her fingertips moved up and down, teasing but never quite reaching. It was maddening.

The erotic fantasy of having two women at his disposal fired his desire. What would it be like to have them both in the same bed? He took a little step back and hurriedly undressed.

"Come here. Let me make it wet."

"Uhmm." He moved naked back to the bed.

"Feel good?..."

"Oh, yes...don't stop. Here..." He guided his penis against her tongue. "Oh, yes...."

"Do me, too...." She scooted around.

"Uhmm...turn a little more...."

"Better? Oh, yes...yes...my darling, yees-s-s...."

Immersed in it, her words gave way to moans...then cries...mixed with animal sounds. Their ritual had a language all its own.

"Oh...Clayton...I'm going to...ah...come...oh...yes...oh ...yes...oh, come on...come...uh... oh. OH! OH YES!" He felt her contract and collapse, shuddering with joy.

Afterward, lying there listening to her whispery sounds of sleep, Clayton marveled at how well Mabel knew how to please him. She got inside his head...read his mind.

And, with Mabel he'd never have to pretend he was more of a man than he was.

Still with Glee it was different...wild...exciting. She was so young. Glowing...still in early blossom.

Glee! Oh, shit! He'd forgotten to call.

Taking care not to disturb Mabel, Clayt left the bed and padded quietly downstairs to his study, closed the door and dialed.

"Hello...stop now..." the voice sounded muffled "Hello?..."

"Glee?...that you?...who's there?..."

"Clayt?...Baby, hello. What're you doing calling so late? Something wrong?"

"No. Are you alone?..."

"Of course. You know better than that. You woke me. I guess I was dreaming." She made a little laugh. "What time is it?"

"Well, it's not quite midnight...Sorry, baby, I didn't realize it was so late," he said. "I just wanted to tell you I'll be there earlier tomorrow than I thought. Before five anyway."

He really intended to make it in time for lunch, but he didn't want to promise. If he popped in early, it would be a nice surprise.

"Oh, honey, I'm so glad. I miss you so. Hurry...I wish you were here right now. I don't have anything on...unless you count the air-conditioning," Her laugh had a husky edge.

It brought a sudden rush of desire.

"Uhm...I wish I was there, too. I'll hurry tomorrow. Go back to sleep...goodnight."

"Goodnight, my darling. You're going to need all the rest you can get."

He sat there for a moment before he replaced the phone. Even after Mabel, he still felt charged. Wide awake now, idly he punched up the TV remote. The time display showed 12:01. Hurriedly, he turned down the volume as the sleep-hush of the house was suddenly filled with the blare of laughter from the audience of a late talk show. He quickly flipped through the channels until he found a news program on a local station. The newscaster was speaking into the camera: "....TELEVISION AND MOVIE ACTRESS, EMMA CLAIRE, WHOSE BODY WAS FOUND IN A GREENSBORO MOTEL EARLIER TODAY..."

The TV screen flicked to an exterior of a motel, familiar to Clayt because it was next door to the Massie House, part of Grail's national hotel chain. Pictures of the police milling about the motel while the coroner's crew carried out a stretcher with a body bag dissolved into a close-up studio shot of Emma Claire, followed by a shot of the Town Limit sign of Blowing Rock with a wide-angle exterior of the main street. Then the camera panned upward and across the sweeping vista of the Blue Ridge mountains. Abruptly, the shot cut to a rapidly kaleidoscopic shifting of scenes around the resort clubhouse, which was also a Grail holding, and switched to shots of the Blowing Rock condominiums overlooking the pool and golf course.

The announcer continued, "SOURCES SAY THAT CLAIRE SPENT THE WEEKEND IN THE BLOWING ROCK AREA AT THE CONDOMINIUM OF FRIENDS...."

Clayt turned off the set.

Trip had spent the weekend up there in one of those very same condos.

Claire was the young woman Trip had made such a spectacle over at the Azalea Ball.

He found a snifter and poured himself another ounce of cognac before he resigned himself to bed. Later, it occurred to him that he had no choice...now, more than ever, he had to trust Norris.

Mabel stirred against him and sleep took him as he tried to remember...had there been something peculiar about the way Glee had sounded on the phone?

CHAPTER TWENTY-SEVEN

FIRST MARILEE...NOW AGNES!

The entire evening had taken on a peculiar surrealistic quality for Norris. Nothing seemed real about any of it.

Walking across the yard from The Club, Agnes had pulled him along, playfully pinching him on the ass, and then, urgently, she'd led him through the house and up the steps to the bedroom. Along the way, she was awkwardly trying to loosen her clothing, which resulted in little bumpings into walls and giggly stumblings on the stairs until at last she was naked on the bed.

It had begun as their lovemaking always did, the mindless rutting of two healthy animals. Then, right in the middle of the exercise, the whole thing went crazy again.

He looked down at her inviting him, and strangely, all at once he had felt curiously detached—more the spectator than the participant. Part of him stood apart, passively watching...totally removed from the frantic energy.

In this strange state of detachment, just at the peak of the sexual frenzy, he tried to imagine that Agnes was Marilee, and a wildly inappropriate realization suddenly hit him like a thunderbolt.

How would Marilee find him in New York?

Only Patty, his secretary, had the address of his apartment in the city.

God, what an irony!

His egocentric need for privacy had done him in. He had run afoul of his own paranoia.

Looking down at Agnes, Norris tried to return to the business at hand. But now he had lost the excitement of the erotic fantasy—now, totally detached, he was the impersonal maestro.

Turning and lifting, he urged Agnes to her knees, facing away.

Standing at the edge of the bed he guided them together.

"Come on, baby, give it to your mama. Give it to your girl. Oh, that's it...yes. Come with your baby, come on, honey...give it to your girl...come on, give it...uh...uh, give it to me...let me have it....NOW...OW-O-O-W!..."

"Like this?...huh?...let it come, come on, baby let it come...."

"Oh, my God yes...give it to me, now. Oh yeah, Norris honey...yes...oh, yes-s!"

"Here. Here it is. Is this what you want? Uh...uh all the way in there? All the way...."

"Ahhh...ahhh, OH...MY GOD, NORRIS...YES!"

Ride the wild pony! Sir Norris, The Benevolent—deliverer of thunderbolts.

He let himself remain suspended, distanced...peering over the edge of her pleasure. He held himself, controlled, cavalierly withholding the release. Pulling back from the brink, he stopped short of orgasm.

The lord giveth and the lord taketh...hail the lord of the bedroom.

Agnes never knew...or cared.

"Uh...you killed me, Norris. This time you have finally done it. You ruined me. Oh, God, I mean, really. Was it that good for you, too? Oh, you destroyed me, thank you, thank you...thank you. I love you. Love you...adore you....do you love me?"

"Hhm-m."

"Norris?" Her voice floated over to him a little later.

"Uhm-m?"

"You do love me, don't you?"

"Hm-m."

Beside her, with her back turned away, he thought of Marilee again.

There was only the soft whir of the bedside clock and the whisper of the air-conditioning.

Sleepily, his thoughts drifted back to New York.

Not even Agnes knew the address of his hideaway.

How could he get word to Marilee?

How absurd. It was all so ridiculous. Why had he promised, anyway? An exercise in futility, a postponement of the inevitable...no good could come of it.

Unable to sleep, Norris crept from bed and went down to his study.

The evening's entire *symphonie d'amour*, from the beginning overtures walking from The Club through the woods, through the passionate stacatto passage, bumping up the stairs, and the final clash of cymbals with her climax in their bedroom had been orchestrated to completion in less than a half hour. Agnes was sleeping contentedly when the phone rang with Clayt's call.

The arrogance of Clayt's request made him furious.

If Clayton Graham felt threatened by the calls from the White House...then fine...just let him suffer for awhile—served the bastard right. He had him over a barrel.

Almost without thinking, Norris picked up the phone and dialed a number.

"Tom Bradley..." Unconsciously, Norris listened for any hint of intoxication.

The voice sounded clear. Sober, there wasn't a better man alive.

"Tom, it's Norris. Do you know whatcha got if you have a rattlesnake in one pocket and a rubber with a hole in it in the other pocket?"

"No, but I guess I'm going to find out, right?" Bradley laughed.

"Not from me. I don't know either...but, Tom?..." Norris let it hang for a moment.

"But, Tom, what?..." His old friend waited on cue.

"It's not a good idea to fuck with either one of them."

They both gave way to laughing so loud that Norris got up and moved to the door and closed it softly so as not to awaken Agnes.

"Goddamn it, Norris, it was good seeing you this morning...I've missed having you around," Tom said when he finally stopped laughing. "Are you still coming up tomorrow night...or Wednesday?"

"Something's come up. How about tomorrow morning? Can you make Old Ebbitt...say late middle morning? I've been lusting for some chili...real industrial grade. I haven't been there since the last time with you. God, that's been awhile. I talked to Chatham tonight and I'm meeting him in New York Wednesday. I really need to talk to you, first...before I see him...."

"OK. What time's your flight? I can pick you up."

"No, I'll get a cab. I'll see you at Old Ebbitt. Check United for the flight." He said goodnight and hung up.

Flipping through the Rolodex, he made a note before he picked up the phone again and dialed the 800 number.

"Thank you for calling United. How can I help you?"

"Do you have a bulkhead aisle seat on the early flight from RDU to DCA in the morning?"

"One moment, sir." The line was silent for only a moment. "Yessir...it's on the aisle."

"Book it, please." Norris gave her his credit card information and hung up.

Now...how to pass Marilee the message about his New York address?

What the hell? Just call early in the morning? Must be careful, Trip was home.

Passing notes...secret messages? Difficult in a grownup world....

What do you do when you've never been a child, he mused, heading back to bed.

TUESDAY MORNING

CHAPTER TWENTY-EIGHT

THE DAY HAD GOTTEN OFF TO A SHAKY START FOR CLAYT, but once he had the Learjet airborne, his outlook improved considerably.

Despite leaving an hour and a half later than he had planned, and despite his irritation with himself for not being able to catch up with Norris and get the contract signed before he left for Washington, Griffin had finally restored him to sanity. At Griff's insistence, he had gone ahead and signed Norris' contract. For the moment, at least, he'd done all he could do to rectify last night's hot-headed—potentially disastrous—error in judgment on his part.

Although he knew full well that it was his own damned fault, he was feeling a little better now. Looking down to his left through the scattering of little cotton ball clouds, he watched the patchwork pattern of Carolina farmlands merge with the clear, blue-green of the Atlantic Ocean where sunlight glinted off the water and the slow rhythmic undulations of the frothy surf traced a white feathery line as far as the eye could see.

As he crossed the mouth of the Cape Fear River over Southport, he made a slightly rightward turn, pointing the sleek jet's nose down the beach. Passing directly over the Fort Caswell Light, he could see Marilee's cottage as he took a SSW heading toward Jacksonville.

He had been a nervous wreck when he climbed into the cockpit. Trip's drunkenness, the nagging guilt over his own infidelity to Mabel, and Norris Wrenn's independent attitude—he wanted to forget them all. But, try as he might, he was having a hard time leaving it all back at Colonial Hall where it belonged.

When he'd finally gotten to sleep, he'd had a disturbing, erotic dream. He'd walked into his office suite in The Tower and found Norris fucking Marilee on his desk. When they saw him enter, they

175

had both laughed and taunted him. Then, Norris had picked up the phone and summoned a security guard to escort him to the elevator and put him out of his own building. In the parking lot, Trip, Mabel and Glee Craige had been waiting with a hearse.

The nightmare left him with the same vague paranoia he'd felt when Marilee left the dinner table last night after Norris had been called to the phone. And, as if that nagging anxiety hadn't been enough, sitting on the terrace over coffee while he waited for Griff to return from his morning walk, he'd seen in the *Wall Street Journal* that Colby Stuart had died.

A former classmate and fraternity brother, dear, dear old Colby had been owner/publisher of Colby Press. Colby was a year his junior and had been the picture of health when he'd seen him at the Westminister Kennel Show a few months back.

"Send flowers for Colby Stuart." As he dictated a reminder in his micro-cassette on the seat, it suddenly came home to him with a jolt. *There were no guarantees. Poor devil...only sixty-one.*

Lately, this thing with Trip had him a bundle of nerves. Last night, he'd come perilously close to ruining all the hard work with Norris.

"It's airtight. It protects Ivee...it's really better than that...." At the breakfast table this morning, Griff had put to rest all of last night's sudden anxieties, thank God.

"But what about Marilee? That's another thing that bothers me," he'd asked, still haunted by his bizarre dream. "What if she should divorce Trip? What if she and Norris got together... Would custody of Ivee go...?" The question was left hanging as Griff interrupted.

"Put it out of your mind. Grail is protected. Norris gets his...no more. He built in safeguards just in case something happened to him. You know he's human and not exempt from life's pitfalls. Marilee is personally protected in your will. She is also protected from Trip's whim. That's important. God knows what Trip might do. And speaking of that, you need to do something about Trip. For his sake. Since that night I drove him back to Caswell Beach, I've been worried sick about him. I'm afraid to pick up the papers

176

with him driving that damn car around in the shape he stays in. Something has to be done. You're his father. Somebody needs to have a serious talk with him."

"He won't listen...."

"If you won't, ask Ed Scott...ask Norris," Griff persisted. "What do you think about that?"

"What do I think about Norris? I think I wish that goddamn son of a bitch was right here instead of on his way to Washington. He's just trying to show me that he isn't going to let me jerk him around." Clayt was totally frustrated.

"Well, I think he succeeded in getting his point across...don't you?" Griff had smiled kindly and patted him on the arm as he pushed the sheaf of papers in front of him. "Take it easy. You're running late. Just sign these copies and I'll have Mabel sign—then I'll take care of Norris..."

Clayt had looked at the papers in front of him and hesitated. He looked at his watch. God! It was late!

"OK. But what about tomorrow? Is everything worked out on the transfer of the house? I want you to break the news to Glee about the terms. She's expecting that I'm just going to sign the whole thing over and she'll have complete ownership, free and clear. When she finds out that it's all going to be set up under Graham Properties and that she won't be completely vested for five years, she's going to be madder than a hornet."

"What's her alternative, blackmail?" Griff asked.

"Bite your tongue, goddamn it. You promised that you had us protected against that."

"I have. Calm down; you worry too much. Just arrange not to be there. I'll handle it. Once she understands all that she has to do is behave, she'll quiet down. She won't like it, but she won't make too much fuss. She's too smart for that." Griff had picked up Norris' contract and turned it around for his signature. "The red-eye out of Raleigh gets into Jacksonville around half past nine. I'll pick you up and we can go to Fernandina Beach together. Once you sign the contracts, take off somewhere. I'll meet with Glee and take care of everything," Griff had reassured him.

"Good. I'll see you tomorrow." Clayt had started to leave.

"Come back here and sign this goddamn contract. What if you run that goddamn Lear into the ocean? Do you want to take a chance on blowing everything now?" Griff smiled and patiently tapped his finger on the small stack of legal papers.

So, grudgingly, he'd signed above Trip's signature from the previous afternoon. Mabel and Nan had witnessed it. Now it was up to Griff to track Norris down.

Goddamn it! If Norris backed out now, he had only himself to blame. What was Plan B? There was no goddamn Plan B.

He was stuck. There was only one Norris Wrenn. Try as he might, he could think of no one he would even consider to take over the management of the entire Grail operation.

"Your old granddaddy's doing the best he can, Ivee," he sighed aloud in the sunlit cockpit. He tried to turn his thoughts back to Glee, but, no matter how hard he tried, he couldn't shake the effect of that goddamn dream.

Norris and Marilee...*If those two ever got together....*

Hadn't Marilee said she was going to New York after the Mother of the Year press conference in Raleigh today?

Norris said he was going on to New York from Washington.

The goddamn dream came floating back.

Wouldn't hurt to have someone check them both out.

He'd been meaning to find out where Norris disappeared when he went to New York, anyway. He was tired of trying to keep track of the independent son of a bitch.

Norris didn't fool him. In New York, Norris got his messages at Grail International, but the only time he really stayed there was when Agnes went with him, or when he, himself, was with him in the city on business.

By God, as soon as he hit the ground, he would just call and have Griff get an investigator check the two of 'em out...couldn't be too sure. Even if Ivee was protected, the thought of hanky-panky between Norris and Marilee spelled big trouble.

He snorted and shook his head to free himself of the useless anxiety.

Clayt loved flying. It had been weeks since he had been in the cockpit, and he had been looking forward to that special feeling of freedom he always had up here, away from all the mundane things on the ground. Usually, all his problems vanished almost as soon as he became airborne. But now, no matter how hard he tried to relax, all the doubts and insecurities and...guilt...just kept on spinning around and around in his head.

With the Lear on autopilot, searching through his briefcase he located the Polaroid snap he had taken of Glee in her panties, reaching back to unfasten her bra—sexy as hell.

Thinking of Glee, the erotic dream taunted him. Cursing himself for what was probably the hundredth time since he had started bungling things last night, his attention went to the instrument panel as the needle flipped as the Lear passed over the Charleston omni.

"JAX Center this is Grail Lear six-nine-zero passing over the Charleston VOR on a heading of two-one-one...request descent clearance for landing Jacksonville."

Making love to Mabel last night, when he didn't think he could, had done his conscience...not to mention his ego...a world of good. It had been a good thing all around. Mabel knew all the right things to do, the right places to touch. She loved to see him satisfied. And he knew just what it took for her, too. It was still good...a comfortable thing.

He glanced at the snapshot of Glee again. Glee was a scheming little bitch. But, what the hell, she made him feel like a rogue again.

Mabel had been his first...God, talk about beautiful...only fifteen when she had been his birthday present from old Massie. She would have made Glee hang her head in envy.

Mabel could thank Glee for last night. It always went better with Mabel after he had spent a few days with Glee—or, like last night, when he was planning to.

The photo stared back at him. He loved to watch Glee's round naked ass and pouting breasts bouncing and jiggling as she moved around the place...and now...in the new house, he had ordered a large sunken whirlpool installed in the bath. An eight-foot privacy hedge enclosed a full-sized heated, indoor-outdoor swimming pool. Everything necessary for a first class orgy. All he needed was Glee to peel the grapes.

Idly, he fiddled with the radio.

"....AND THIS IN FROM GREENSBORO, NORTH CAR-OLINA...SOURCES SPECULATE THAT THE YOUNG ACTRESS EMMA CLAIRE MAY HAVE DIED FROM AN OVERDOSE OF COCAINE REMINISCENT OF THE DEATHS OF ACTOR JOHN BELUSHI..."

Quickly, he switched the newscast off.

Greensboro?

Trip?...Drunk again last night...drinking way too much lately....

Lately, he was always reeking of alcohol. Trip was headed for trouble. He'd heard some wild tales about the bunch at Palm Beach. He hoped he knew better than to mess with drugs. What Griff said about Trip driving when he'd had a few was right. He should have a talk with him before he killed himself or someone else. Someone had to take a hand.

Griff said that Trip listened to Norris.

Norris! Always Norris! Where was the bastard now, when he needed him?

That goddamn contract, back there half-completed—he couldn't get it out of his mind.

Norris was a multi-billion dollar investment to Grail—life or death, really.

Goddamn Norris, anyway! And, while he was at it, goddamn himself for being a fool last night!

Enough of daydreams.

It was one hell of a beautiful morning.

He looked at the picture of Glee again—smiling, inviting him. By the time he began making his descent into JAX he was fantasizing in the cloud shapes forms that called up the images of breasts and rounded buttocks and dimpled knees.

At the airport, the rental car was a sporty little white, two-seater BMW convertible. He put the top back before he left the private terminal and made his way out of the maze of airport traffic onto I-95 heading north to the highway connecting with A1A and the northern beaches.

Blaring some kind of unintelligible jungle music, the radio jarred him to the bone. He pushed the SEEK button and the mechanism automatically started searching...

"...GREENSBORO, NORTH CAROLINA SOURCES SPECULATE ACTRESS EMMA CLAIRE DIED OF AN OVERDOSE OF COCAINE REMINISCENT OF THE DEATHS OF JOHN BELUSHI...."

Fear gripped his chest like a cold claw...that goddamn death again! He was tired of hearing about it. He changed the channel.

It bothered him that Trip had been in Blowing Rock over the weekend.

Past Yulee, Clayton dialed his cell phone. When Griff came on the line, he outlined what he wanted done. "I'm tired of wondering where the hell that goddamn Norris hides out. Remember the New York investigator you used for the Metro Securities deal? I want his unpublished number."

"Quit mindfucking yourself...you're getting paranoid!" Griff protested sharply.

"If you won't handle it, I'll do it myself."

"All right, I'll make a call...." Griff grumbled and hung up.

Clayt felt better now. At least Griff hadn't hit him with another guilt trip.

He looked at his watch—almost noon. He could be at the new house at Starfish Cay Club in fifteen minutes. The agent would be waiting to give him a careful walk-through to make certain the work had been satisfactorily completed. Afterwards, he would call Glee from the realtor's office.

Glee was expecting to move into a condominium. He could hardly wait to see her face when she saw the house.

Starfish Cay. A brilliant plan—a moment of perfect inspiration. Unlike Hilton Head Island, Skidaway and neighboring Azalea Trace Plantation, Starfish had no hotels and meeting facilities catering to large corporations for high-level meetings. Along the quiet lanes winding through the bowers of overhanging limbs of the huge, moss-bearded live oaks, the residents behaved responsibly—and their guests behaved like residents, not like tourists.

To ensure total anonymity, he had also purchased a condo nearby in Widow's Walk, an exclusive part of the same development—adjacent to the Cabanas and the Links and Racquet Club.

More importantly, it was only a short walk along the beach and down through the little maze-like paths—almost tunnels—which burrowed in all directions through the thick jungle of yaupon shrub and scrub oak to the house. It was a perfect arrangement. He could come and go as he pleased with perfect privacy.

The entire arrangement had been Griff's idea. Griff worried about him. But Clayt had to admit, it made the whole arrangement very secure.

Clayt was already recognized by the security guards. He had taken ownership of the condo weeks ago and had established a familiar identity as a property owner. His comings and goings were already an accepted thing.

Glee? He had no reason not to trust her, but Glee was young and attractive...and almost insatiable sexually. Knowing she would be living here made him feel more secure. He doubted that she would risk having a casual lover's name recorded on the visitors' log at the gate. Now, she would have to think twice if she were tempted to take a casual fling in his absence.

"That's what you get for loving me..." On the radio, Gordon Lightfoot sang.

Clayt turned up the volume and hummed along.

CHAPTER TWENTY-NINE

THE SUN THROUGH A BRIGHT HAZE WAS BLINDING. Trip blinked hard and rubbed his eyes. A single ray of morning sunlight filtered through the trees into the window.

His T-shirt was soaked. Lately that nameless feeling of dread never left him.

Ooo, shit! Last night! At least he remembered, but that was small comfort now.

Clayton was not going to be happy.

Clayt!...jeez!...

Calendar clock? God bless digital...big red numbers.

Tuesday. May, 7...8:41...A.M.

Clayt? Norris' contract?...

Shit...shit! Late, late, late!

He picked up the phone...hesitated...replaced it.

Not good! First get rid of this head.

He slipped out of bed and pulled himself erect on the bedpost at the foot of the canopied bed. Standing, unsteady, he waited for his head to stop spinning.

Sick...*real sick!*

He stumbled blindly for the bathroom. With no time to spare, he made it to the commode and threw up. Bending low, gagging and heaving, he steadied himself with one hand on the countertop and the other on the top of the toilet tank. When the nausea passed, he opened a drawer in the vanity and pulled out a prescription bottle.

Percodan.

Shit! He struggled with the top of the prescription bottle...everygoddamnthing was childproof nowadays. A fucking conspiracy. Fucking kids could open these things in a heartbeat...it

183

was the adults that had the trouble.

Finally!

Shaking out two pills, he moved to the wet bar in his dressing area.

Vodka? Good ol' Stoli.

And ice...fucking ice...hot vodka won't stay down.

V-8...good old V-8. Careful...just a little now....

There.

He washed down the pills.

Gripping the counter, he shuddered violently as the raw liquor went down.

God!...Awful!...

Come on baby, be nice...stay down there. Ol' Trip needs you. Don't desert me now.

Refilling the glass from the bottle, this time he added more V-8 and let it sit...had to wait and see.

Uhmm...better...easy does it...gonna be OK now.

Maybe.

He gulped the drink without taking the glass from his lips and refilled it before he went to the bedside phone.

"Trip Graham's office, this is Dodie." His secretary picked up on the second ring.

"Dodie, this is Trip. Tell my father I'm running a few minutes late for that contract signing. I let it slip my mind." The vodka was beginning to help, but he was still feeling rough. "Is the old man on the warpath?"

"Your father called in first thing this morning and postponed the entire thing. He took the Lear and headed for Florida...said he would reschedule for the first of next week. He asked me to call The Club and cancel the golf date. I already took care of it."

Thank God!—sweetest fucking words he'd heard in a long time.

"There was a call from the realtor in Palm Beach...want the number?"

"No...I may come in later...but not officially. Don't commit me to anything. Just say I'm 'out' and take the message."

"Oh, I almost forgot. There was a call from the Greensboro police. They want you to call them as soon as possible. I tried to find out what it was about, but they wouldn't say. If they call back, what should I tell 'em?"

His knees went weak. He felt a sudden cramping in his gut.

"Just tell them I'm not in and...ah...take the message." He found it hard to speak.

The nameless fear again.

What the hell was he afraid of? He hadn't done anything.

"Do you want the number?" Dodie asked.

"Uhmmm? Well, yeah, I guess. Let me find something to write with." He located a pencil, wrote it down and read it back.

"Will you call later?" Dodie asked, hopefully.

"Maybe I'll get by there this afternoon. *Ciao.*"

Hanging up, he gulped half of the drink he had brought with him.

Feeling better now. Mucho better.

The call from the Greensboro police? Probably something about his car.

Goddamn!...

The memory of the little scraping of red paint on his car when he was in the parking lot yesterday at Ginger's came flooding back. The knot of fear grabbed again, but at least his head felt better. He wished he could remember more about Sunday night.

Pulling the drapes tightly closed, he finished the rest of the drink.

He went into the bathroom and made another drink and shook two more Percodan out of the bottle and wrapped them in a tissue lying on the counter.

Retracing his steps, he placed the drink and the pills untouched on the bedside table and went back to bed.

Much better now...sleepy though...better take another look at his car before he did anything else today.

CHAPTER THIRTY

SOB! THE RED LETTERS STARED NORRIS RIGHT IN THE FACE.

ESS-OH-BEE?

Son-of-a-bitch?

Norris blinked hard and looked again...5:08...digital numerals...bedside clock....

Instantly alive, he rolled quietly out of bed and went directly to the bathroom. Back in the bedroom, he dropped to the carpeted floor and began doing some crunches and leg drops...had to keep the belly flat.

The brief exercises done, he went into the dressing room. Automatically, he tossed some clean socks and underwear in the soft leather duffel. Selecting a shirt, tie, jacket and slacks, he arranged them all on a wooden hanger and slipped it deftly into a light nylon suit bag. A final look to make certain his toilet kit was inside, he zipped the duffel, slipped into shorts and running shoes and was off. Carrying the two bags, he bounced down the steps and out through the garage.

After he placed the bags on the rear seat of the Riviera, Norris headed around the side of the house and down to the eighteenth fairway. He knew the course by heart. The carefully measured route covered just over two miles up and down the fairways. Rain or shine, it took him about fifteen minutes. Boston, New York, London...it didn't matter; he hadn't missed a day in years. Born of the same careful discipline with which he ordered his life, it separated the men from the boys. It had gotten him here now, alive and kicking, instead of lying in a shallow, water-filled grave in some remote Nicaraguan river delta.

Musing smugly about self-discipline brought him little comfort during his run. If he was so goddamn all-together, how come he had forgotten to tell Marilee his New York address?

Still wrestling with the dilemma, his watch read 5:40 when he stepped out of the shower.

The digital car clock displayed 5:59 as he caught the last view of the guard at the gatehouse in his rearview mirror and settled back for the hour-long drive to the Raleigh-Durham airport.

The problem of getting Marilee his address in New York...he reached for the car phone.

What would he say if Trip answered?

CHAPTER THIRTY-ONE

TRIP CAME AWAKE WITH A START.

Head? Better...much better. Good old Mommie Stoli had kissed her baby and made him well.

Absently, he struggled to a sitting position and took a swallow from the drink he had placed on the bedside table before he'd gone back to bed.

A little relapse prevention...never could be too careful.

Asleep! How long? The clock displayed 9:51.

Idly, he picked up the pad and examined the number Dodie had given him.

Oh shit! The call from the Greensboro cops. Had to see about getting that spot of paint off the 'Vette. And that cocaine paper he'd found...no telling what else was in the car.

He got out of bed and went to the walk-in closet. His bag—still unopened—rested on a folding luggage rack.

He hesitated, afraid.

Hypnotically, he pulled the zipper of the main compartment and, one by one, he began to pull out the items carelessly stuffed inside.

Relax.

Fucking dirty clothes.

He started tossing the garments across the large closet into the wicker clothes hamper. In his rush, he had already removed and discarded two soiled shirts, a pair of stone-washed jeans and a matching denim jacket with fancy embroidery on the breast pockets.

Lipstick?...*Whoa!*

Spotting the tinge of red, he stopped the careless sorting and retrieved the other garments and carefully looked them over.

Lipstick...what else?...

Taking his time now, he began going through the pockets of the clothes. Shirts? Nothing. And—except for some loose change and some grayish green flakes of what was suspiciously suggestive of marijuana leaves—there was nothing in the pockets of the jeans.

Hah! All this worry for nothing.

Whoa!...whoa-ho-ho!

Oh, shit!

The jacket produced a plastic prescription vial with four lumps of a slightly caramel crystalline substance.

Rock. Crack cocaine!

A metallic taste of fear welling in his throat, he placed the vial on top of the chest of drawers.

Now, sweating profusely, he searched more carefully. His hand closed on a plastic card in the other pocket of the jacket. Even before he withdrew his fist, Trip knew the object was a magnetic door key, commonly used by hotels. He had discarded at least a thousand over the years.

MANOR INN...GREENSBORO, NORTH CAROLINA was clearly imprinted on the card.

What the fuck?

His gut was beginning to cramp.

He'd never stayed at the Manor personally, but more than once he had been to post-game parties there during the ACC basketball tournament. Second only to the Massie House, it was one of the most sought-after hotels for the event. Many of his Carolina and Duke buddies stayed there regularly during tournament time.

Racking his brain for a clue to the key, he remembered being at a party there one night during the Greater Greensboro Open in April.

Had he worn this jacket at the GGO?

No way! He'd bought the jacket in Palm Beach two weeks ago—worn it for the first time this weekend in Blowing Rock. The jacket and his jeans had been in the pile of discarded clothing on the floor of his room at the Massie House yesterday morning. He remembered stuffing them into the bag before he changed for his meeting with Clayt that afternoon.

The key...and cocaine...couldn't remember either one.

Oh shit...shit, shit...shit! This was fucking serious...the cop from Greensboro would have a ball with that. One thing for sure, he had to get rid of this shit fast...and take care of that smear of paint.

Fighting an urgency bordering on panic, Trip removed each item from the luggage and made doubly sure he hadn't overlooked anything.

He was shaking badly again and now his head was coming apart. Returning to the bedside, he picked up the unfinished drink and gulped down the pills.

Goddamn sun...blinding....

With great effort he went to the window and started to close the heavy drapes. He caught a glimpse of Marilee's car as it moved down the drive and disappeared through the gateposts.

Where the hell was she going at this hour?

Last night...dinner at the club...the Governor.

The Governor? Marilee...Raleigh? The Mother's Day thing.

There was something about Marilee going off to New York. Was that supposed to be today?

She spent a lot of time with that bitch Sadie. Colonial Hall's prissy Mother of the Fucking Year needed to be at home taking care of her husband and kid.

Well...the kid anyway. He could damn well take care of himself.

What the hell? Let the bitch go. Just one less person to bitch at him.

Mixing another drink, he carried it with him as he headed for the shower.

Out of the shower, he hurriedly slipped on a pair of khakis and a navy golf shirt.

He was down the steps and almost out the door when he stopped dead in his tracks.

Whoa, goddamn it! Just slow the fuck down!

He turned and went back upstairs and carefully wiped the vial with the cocaine and the motel key and wrapped them in thick layers of facial tissue. Stuffing them in his pants pocket, he descended the stairs again. Quietly, he slipped out the door without seeing any of the domestic help.

Within seconds, the Corvette was rolling slowly out of the drive.

Morning traffic was light as he made his way through the back streets, moving southward until he picked up the main highway which crossed the river as he left the city limit.

He knew exactly where he could find the privacy he needed.

CHAPTER THIRTY-TWO

INSIDE THE TERMINAL AT REAGAN NATIONAL, Norris quickly located a phone. On the plane, he'd figured out a possible solution to the problem of getting his New York address to Marilee. Dialing, he hoped he wasn't too late.

"Norris Wrenn's office, this is Patty Smith."

"Good morning Patty, how are you?"

"Hi, boss. Where are you, anyway?"

"I'm in Washington right now, but I'll be going on to New York tonight. Have I had any calls?"

"Yessir. Mr. Richards called twice trying to locate you. He just hung up...said if I heard from you, it was important you call him at Mr. Graham's before ten. Do you want that number?"

"It's OK...I have both numbers. Anything else?"

"Some lady called, but wouldn't leave a number." Patty's voice was noncommittal.

Marilee? He resisted the impulse to ask.

Either Patty hadn't recognized the caller's voice or—knowing Patty—prudently, she didn't want to speculate.

"Can you be reached?"

"Not today...just take the names and numbers on your end. Tonight, you can get me at my private number in New York. I'd rather not let anything of mine come through the New York office. I don't plan to get involved with the troops up there. Chatham Brookes is meeting me tomorrow to discuss something that the President has up his sleeve. Business as usual; I'll be unavailable except through you."

"I know the routine...anything else?"

"No...oh, yeah...I almost forgot." He hoped he sounded off-hand. "Dig out a copy of the Phoenix file. See if you can catch

Marilee Graham at home. Last night at dinner, she said she was coming up for a few days to do some shopping. Ask her if she could bring it to New York with her tonight."

"Should I ask her to leave it at the New York office?"

"Uhmmm..." He pretended to think it over. "No...I really don't want to go by there in the morning before I meet Brookes...that is, unless I have to. Just address the envelope to my private address and make sure she understands that nobody—repeat, nobody—else has that information. Ask her if she'll have it delivered to my place by bonded messenger service when she gets to New York...or better still, give her my unpublished number and tell her to call." Norris tried to be very casual about the instructions. "By the way, you'd better try to get her right now. She's due to be in Raleigh around eleven at the Governor's mansion for the big media event announcing her Mother of the Year award. It already may be too late to catch her. I've got to run."

"What if I can't get Mrs. Graham?" Patty interjected, anxiously.

"Then send it UPS Next Day Air. Better late than never."

"Will do...unless you want me to send it by the corporate courier going this afternoon?"

"No way. I don't want that address to become public knowledge. It's my last refuge. If you do get Marilee Graham, stress my wish for confidentiality to her, please."

"Will do...oh, wait, Boss...you know that movie actress who was found dead in Greensboro...the one who was Azalea Queen?" Patty said.

"Dead actress...what are you talking about?"

"Where have you been? Don't you ever turn on the radio or TV? The actress, Emma Claire, was found dead in a Greensboro motel yesterday morning...she'd been in Blowing Rock over the weekend. She was in Wilmington at the Azalea Ball in April...you were there, remember?"

"Uhmm...oh, yeah. But, I never got to meet her. I was late getting to the Ball. By the time I got there, the whole place was buzzing because she'd left early...just up and disappeared. What about her? What are you getting at?"

"Well...Trip's secretary, Dodie, says he was golfing in Blowing Rock over the weekend and spent Sunday night in Greensboro. And guess what? The Greensboro Chief of Police called this morning early, looking for him."

"Look, Patty, with Trip Graham's driving record, half the cops in North Carolina are wanting to talk to him. It's not like you to gossip...."

"You know better, boss. I just thought you might want to know, just in case the tabloids start calling." Patty sounded hurt.

"Yeah...well, thanks. Have a dynamite day, sweetheart." He did his best Bogart imitation.

"Give me a break, boss. Your Bogie is awful." Patty hung up.

"What kind of fool am I?..." Humming wryly under his breath, Norris hit the street. On the sidewalk in front of the main terminal, the familiar traffic buzz returned his sense of the moment.

Looking for a taxi, Norris stepped back as an official limo pulled up and a sharply dressed driver jumped out and held the door for a distinguished looking man in a gray suit. The driver was no ordinary chauffeur. Both men had a look of importance about them. Just last week a cover article in *Time* said he had that look. What a joke. Ten minutes ago, he hadn't even had the guts to call Marilee at home.

Looking closer at the man in the limo, there was a familiarity.

Norris tried hard to place him.

Brit?

Close.

Aussie?...maybe?

Uhmm...

South African?...

Of course! The man was a longtime fixture in the diplomatic corps.

But...try as he might...Norris couldn't put a name to him. Too long away from this crazy place...too many names...all mostly just faces now. But this one he had known...known him well.

What was his goddamn name?

Damn! He turned away, trying to find a taxi, hoping desperately the unnamed diplomat wouldn't recognize him.

"NORRIS...NORRIS WRENN!..."

Too late! The man's voice rang over the traffic noise, his accent dripping the formal enunciation that comes with an education at the best English schools. When Norris turned, the tall South African was bearing down on him, hand outstretched. Swallowing hard, Norris braced himself and extended his hand with his best quizzical smile of surprise.

"Norris, old sock...Jan Meers...remember?"

Miraculously, Norris' memory came flooding back.

"Of course I remember, Jan. We played with Gary Player at Wintergreen. What a wonderful day that was. How long, five years? How in the world are you?"

"I'm great. And, you're bloody right...it was a wonderful day. As I recall, you and your partner, General Watson, beat us soundly...mainly on the strength of your ball," Meers' clipped English was precise.

"We were lucky...."

"Lucky? Hah! Bloody rot!"Meers guffawed, then asked politely. "Is someone picking you up? Can I have my man drop you anyplace?"

"Well...well, that would be nice of you."

"Not at all. Just let me tell Clive." He walked over to the black man who stood holding his briefcase and spoke to him. In a moment he brought him back to where Norris stood.

"Norris Wrenn, may I present Clive Summers. Clive is with our embassy. Clive has perfect job security—he's our resident expert at finding his way about Pierre-Charles L'Enfant's wretched city with its insane spider web of disrupted streets. Why anyone in his right mind would let a Frenchman design a city is beyond me. Clive will be happy to drop you anywhere you like. I've got to run or I'll miss my plane. Give me a call...don't forget."

He handed Norris a card. Norris fished out one of his own and gave Meers' outstretched hand a firm shake.

"This is quite nice of you. Thank you," Norris barely got the words out before the South African turned and disappeared into the main terminal with a backhanded wave.

"Clive, I need to be dropped at the Old Ebbitt Grill. I'm sure you know it?"

"Yes, sir. In Washington, everybody knows Old Ebbitt."

As the limo moved through the old streets, the feel of the historic city and memories of old times took hold of him. Once you had been a part of it, you were forever touched by the charisma.

"Pull over here, Clive. I'm early. It's such a marvelous morning, I think I'll walk the rest of the way. Thanks, and be sure to give Jan my best. Be seeing you both again soon, I hope." At Lafayette Park, Norris gathered up his briefcase and got out before the limo had hardly stopped moving. He bent over to wave as he carefully closed the door and started to thread his way toward Fifteenth Street through the sea of pedestrians who were moving purposefully in all directions.

Reflexively, Norris looked about, still curious to see if he was being tailed.

Nothing but a boiling sea of people.

He was still a half block away from Old Ebbitt Grill when he spotted Tom's giant frame ambling along ahead of him. A towering hulk of a man, Bradley had been a star forward on the basketball team at Virginia.

Norris quickened his pace and caught up with him just as he was about to enter the restaurant. He reached from behind and firmly clamped his hand over Tom's massive forearm just as he was taking hold of the door.

"Allow me, sir," he said.

"Never mind. I've got it..." Bradley responded impatiently before he caught the voice. He was breaking into laughter as he spun around to face him.

"You haven't changed much, Tom. Always did want to do everything yourself." Norris hugged him affectionately around the shoulder.

"Goddamn, Norris, it's good to see your homely face around here again."

"Good to be back..." Norris gave his arm a squeeze.

"Good morning, gentlemen." The captain recognized them from the old days and gave them a table in a corner, away from the impending midday rush.

"My name is Alfredo. Can I get you something from the bar?" The waiter handed them menus and hovered expectantly to hear their answer.

After last night, Norris was feeling a little ragged around the edges.

"I'll have a Bloody Mary, make it a double. How about it, Tom?"

"Virgin Mary..." Tom shrugged.

"I...ah...forgot. If it bothers you?" Norris said, when the waiter was out of earshot.

"Don't be silly...not at all. The problem's mine, not yours."

"It's nice to know some things don't change." Norris leaned back when the waiter appeared with the oversized old-fashioned glass brimming over with the thick red liquid. "You may well have saved my life, Alfredo, my good man. While there are many—my companion here among them—who will tell you it is not worth saving, I thank you all the same."

Tom laughed. They both ordered chili—industrial grade.

Tom had placed *The Washington Post* on the table. Twin headlines read: PROSECUTOR MUTE ON PIKE SUICIDE and DEAD ACTRESS FORMER KIDDIE PORN STAR. Norris picked up the paper and gave a careful look. "There's something awful familiar about that girl...."

"Sure. Emma Claire...she was the Azalea Queen we talked about yesterday...you saw her when you were at Marilee Graham's beach house," Tom reminded him.

"No. My assistant said the same thing this morning...but that's just it...I never got a chance to meet her in Wilmington. Marilee and I were...ah...a little late getting to the Ball. When we got there, the Queen had taken a powder. Embarrassed the Azalea bigwigs terribly."

"Hmmm...Queenie must have had a hot date...."

"Whatever...I do know Trip Graham had made a complete ass

of himself over her before we got there. But he'd passed out and Griff Richards had taken him back to the beach. This morning, Patty said that Trip..." Norris was interrupted as the waiter brought their chili.

They fell to eating and Norris decided it would be imprudent to mention Patty's news about the Greensboro cop. "Now you're divorced, it must be rough on a single stud in this town. Hell, it was rough on a lot of married ones I knew. Made some of 'em single in a hurry. I guess I should say I'm sorry about your marriage, but I'm not. I never knew Donna well, but I never thought she was much of an asset to your career. Anyway, you sure as hell aren't interested in my approval or disapproval of your women. So, how's single life?"

"Same old me, same old Washington. Speaking of women, tell me—how did it go with you last night...did you get everything straight with Marilee Graham?"

"Uh...well, not really...there was no chance to talk last night...I'm going to meet her in New York tomorrow...just for lunch. It's better that way," Norris lied.

"You got to be fucking crazy? That's like throwing gasoline on a small kitchen fire..." Tom shook his head sadly.

"No...just wait. I know what I'm doing...really...no problem..." Norris avoided Tom's gaze.

"Norris, you are now head of her father-in-law's company. Are you crazy?"

"That's why I need the chance to hash it out away from the corporate flagpole."

"Norris, you've got it made...I can't believe you'd take a chance on messing up."

"Don't worry, I know what I'm doing." He hoped that he sounded more confident than he felt.

"I think you need me for a nanny, if nothing else...." Tom shook his head, obviously disgusted. He changed the subject. "So, what's the latest on this meeting with Brookes?"

"Well, I don't know much more than I told you yesterday, really. Last night, out of the clear blue, he says, 'I'm sitting in here in the

Oval Office with the President. How about coming on up here tomorrow morning and let's revive your ol' Phoenix Project.'" Norris burlesqued the conversation. "They're after something. You know I turned him down both times when he asked me to support his campaign. If you ask me, this interest in Phoenix is a ploy his spin doctors have dreamed up to take the pressure off the fact he's closed down abortion...you know...like that corny trip last week to New York to support the party's campaign to thwart the presidential ambitions of the infamous lady senator from New York. He's sweating bullets...refusing to talk with that *Sixty Minutes* woman. My guess is that they are trying to set me up."

"I called that reporter from *The Post*—the one who said he'd heard Phoenix was a cover for an international spy operation. He tried to dummy up...claimed he'd meant it as a joke."

"Where the hell do they come up with this sick shit? What do you think is going on?"

"Beats me. After giving Roe v. Wade the finger, it's anybody's guess what the White House is up to." Clear-eyed, his hands steady, Tom was animated. "So?...what did you tell the President?"

"I put him off until tomorrow after I meet Brookes in New York. I wanted to talk to you first. Tell me the truth. Do you think Phoenix ever had any real chance of working in the first place? I mean as a practical issue, not some sophomoric dream...." Still feeling a trifle dried-out from last night, Norris ordered another drink.

"Of course it does. But, it would be tricky. You'd have to have complete backing at the highest level without political intervention. The swamp is full of alligators." Tom's voice betrayed excitement.

Nodding reflexively, Norris looked closely at this clear-eyed, steady-handed man. He wondered if he'd ever been like that. Deep in his heart, he wished he could have retained more of his own innocence, but it was a real world. Dreamers like Tom Bradley never made it big financially because they weren't driven by money or hunger for power. They stood aloof from the practicality of things.

Norris knew that in his own career, somewhere along the way, the question "What's the bottom line?" had replaced the dream.

"You've had a night to think it over. Still want the job?"

"Hell, yes!" Tom extended his hand.

"Whoa. I just told you, I don't know yet if they'll give us the go ahead."

"But...you just asked me...." Tom's face fell.

"I know I did. I couldn't even discuss it with Brookes unless I knew that you would go along." Norris shrugged. "I know it isn't fair. But the real thing I wanted to ask is how about going to work for me with Grail—regardless of what we decide about Phoenix?"

Norris could hardly believe it was his voice saying the words. Yesterday, he was wondering if this guy was in an alcoholic crisis and now he was hanging his ass out on the line for him. If Tom Bradley still had problems, they certainly hadn't killed the spark inside him yet. It was a gamble Norris was more than willing to take.

What had suddenly come over him? Last night he'd agreed to meet Marilee. Then the silly fight with Clayt. Now, suddenly he had become the social worker with a budding alcoholic old school-mate. Next thing he knew he'd be off to some Third World slum to pick up the torch for Mother Teresa...was there no end of the role of Norris the Wonderful?

The worst part was that he suddenly realized he had just offered his old friend a job at Grail when, after last night's fiasco, he really wasn't sure he still had one there himself. Was this all some sort of reaffirmation of his own power...or just a symptom of simple insanity?

"Well, I don't know what to say about that...what would I do for you at Grail? Besides, I can't leave the District. You know all about Dad's stroke. He's up and about but he's got a long way to go. It's very hard for him. He's been pretty depressed. I won't...I can't...desert the Chief...not now. I wish you could go see him...or just call him sometime. It would mean a lot to him...."

"OK...do you have your car?"

"You mean right now?" Tom Bradley said with disbelief.

"Well...not until after I've had my fill of chili...."

Bradley stared at him with open-mouthed admiration.

Later, leaving the elder Bradley's townhouse in Georgetown, Norris said, "The job with Grail would keep you right here. I'll want to include your dad as part of the old team. I need two good right-hand men to look after Grail's interests around this crazy town. At any rate, if we decide to do the Phoenix Project, being on Grail's payroll won't interfere. I need to know if you're with me right now."

"The answer is 'yes'...all the way! You can never know what this will mean to the Chief."

"Good. Tell your dad I'll be back again soon. I need his advice on some matters only he can help me with." He shook Tom's hand and got into the Red Top waiting at the curb. Before the cab started off, he rolled down the window. "I'll call tomorrow afternoon and give you a report on my meeting with Brookes."

"Be careful...I feel something in the air...know what I mean?"

"You worry too much..."

"Maybe...by the way, thanks for including Dad. It really did wonders for his morale."

"My pleasure. Tell him I'm putting him on retainer effective as soon as we can do the paperwork. He's forgotten more about patent law than most Harvard professors will ever know. Tell him I'll send a contract with a check to bind the agreement."

"God, you can't imagine how much that will mean to him."

"You just said it all when you agreed to be with me on the Phoenix thing. We're a fine team—a world-class idealist and a world-class cynic, an unmatched pair of jackasses—with a broken-down, rusty Utopian dream for tomorrow...."

"Ta-ta-ta! It's the Norris Wrenn-Tom Bradley Phoenix Show!" Bradley leaped back and spread his arms like a sideshow impresario. "The dynamic duo is back in town."

"You got it, Bubba!" Norris laughed. "And they better not fuck with either one of us."

As Tom stepped back from the cab, Norris' watch showed a little after 2:00 P.M. He wondered if Patty had caught Marilee before she left.

"Reagan National," he told the driver. He'd call Patty when he got to the terminal.

The afternoon traffic was starting to clutter up the streets. Norris instructed the driver to take M Street to Key Bridge onto the Parkway. In no time, they were past the Pentagon and into the circles filtering the traffic into the airport. Glancing back at the traffic, as far as he could ascertain, there'd been no sign of anyone following him all day.

He picked up the *Post* he'd brought with him and looked at the picture of the dead actress. Then it hit him. A year ago, in the spring of 2001, he'd been invited to a reception at the White House trying to woo support for the new administration. Leaving that night, he'd been surprised to see a young girl being delivered by limo at the West Wing...it had been quite late.

Looking at the old photo, he was certain that the girl had been Emma Claire.

With fifteen minutes to boarding time, the gate area was not yet crowded. For once, finding a phone was no problem. He found Tom Bradley's father's number and dialed. The phone rang for quite a long time before it was picked up.

"Bradley residence...this is Polly Meecham..." The old woman's voice had a curious huskiness—almost like she was crying.

"Polly. This is Norris Wrenn, I just left there. Is Tom still there with his father?"

"Oh, my God, Mr. Wrenn, the most awful thing just happened. I still can't believe it. It's just too terrible for words...." Norris' heart sank.

"Polly! What's wrong?" He tried to prepare himself for bad news.

"Mr. Bradley was struck down in the street...right out front. A police car chasing a stolen car. Oh, my God! How could it happen?"

"Why would he go out in the street alone? Was Tom still with him? I didn't think he could maneuver the steps alone just yet." Norris was confused.

"Oh, Mr. Wrenn, you don't hear what I'm saying...it wasn't Mr. Bradley, Senior. By the saints, sir...it was young Mr. Tom."

"Tom? My god...is he?..." Norris couldn't finish the thought.

"Not dead, Mr. Wrenn...but bad off...it's awful. The ambulance just left...they took him to Washington Hospital Center."

"Oh Polly...how?..."

"I just can't talk anymore now, Mr. Wrenn...the doctor is with Mr. Bradley, Senior and the police are here. Could you call back later? I'm sorry, sir, I have to go." The line went dead.

Norris stood there, numbly looking at the phone. He just couldn't comprehend.

Finally, he composed himself and dialed his private number in The Tower.

"Mr. Wrenn's office, this is Patty."

"Patty, I'm ready to board the shuttle. Anything going on I should take care of right now?"

"No, sir. But I did catch Mrs. Graham and she has your package and instructions. Said to tell you she'd take care of it. She's catching an afternoon flight, a little before three. Probably in the air, already."

"Great. You know how to reach me. I won't be calling in the morning. OK, sweetheart, have a dynamite...."

He caught himself in mid-sentence and sobered. "Wait...Patty, before you leave, would you draw a check for ten thousand to Mr. Tom Bradley, Senior, and express it with a standard retainer agreement. We have the address in the computer." He started to say goodbye again, then added, "And enter Tom Bradley, Junior in our files as an employee in good standing with full medical benefits on the corporate insurance. Make absolutely certain it's effective as of *yesterday*."

"Yesterday...like retroactive?..."

"Yes. We're self-insured, remember? Also, send him a letter from me dated yesterday confirming our phone agreement of his employment at a salary of one-hundred-twenty thousand a year and attach another check for ten thousand as an expense advance. Make absolutely certain both the letter and the insurance coverage are dated yesterday."

So, Marilee got the secret address after all. He looked at his watch. She would probably arrive at La Guardia about the same time he did. Maybe she would just send the material by messenger and that would be the end of it. But, after last night, he knew that wasn't likely.

A man wearing a rumpled khaki suit and high-mileage penny loafers came down the steps and took a seat near the window. He stifled a yawn, gave Norris a disinterested look, and pulled out a paperback novel.

Norris was seated and asleep before they finished boarding his flight. When he awoke, they were just touching down at La Guardia.

Ahead, the man in the rumpled suit hurried off the plane.

Inside the terminal, Norris found the nearest phone and finally got through to the ER at Washington Hospital Center.

"Tom Bradley?...Oh...yes sir...traffic accident...closed head injury....still in surgery. Prognosis... guarded...too soon to say." Norris hung up. A feeling of emptiness descended over him like a cloud.

CHAPTER THIRTY-THREE

OVERHEAD, THE 767 FLAGSHIP OF THE GRAIL FLEET glided condor-like under reduced power through the high haze of the morning sky, as it descended on final approach.

"See down there?" Leaning across from the right hand seat, the young first officer nudged Dempsey Gearhart, pointing down to a yellow Corvette. "Isn't that the Yellow Submarine?"

"Oh, shit. What now? I'm sick of that son of a bitch and his spur of the moment trips." Dempsey activated the radio.

"Grail Operations this is Grail Flag...wake up George, can you hear me?"

"That's a Roger, Commander of the Sky...welcome home, oh, fearless warrior," the voice came back immediately. Dempsey resolved to have a private word with George about his inappropriate outbursts. Lately, George was showing signs of getting a little too comfortable in his job. A casual mention of his pre-Grail days when he was going insane working at the Atlanta tower was usually reminder enough.

"George, you don't have any surprises waiting for us, do you?"

"Say again?..."

"Surprises, George...the Yellow Submarine just crossed the bridge, headed out our way. Has Trip Graham scheduled us for anything I don't know about...remember that last minute excursion to Palm Beach a couple weeks back when I got back from Memphis?"

"Nothing...no...nothing that we've been told. Maybe he's headed to the beach."

"Anywhere...but without our help. OK then, I guess it's safe to land?"

"Uh huh, come on in, Great Commander of the Sky."

"Lighten up, George, you're supposed to be a professional. I'm going to burn all your comic books if you don't stop that garbage on the air. There's the minor matter of FAA regs...all that Mickey Mouse, remember? Of course you don't have to worry...I hear Atlanta is always hard up for experienced controllers. I'll put in a good word for you...you can count on that."

"I get the message, Grail Flag, you're cleared on one-eight-zero...wind at five knots from the northeast...."

"Grail Operations, this is Flag again. He ain't going to the beach, George...he's turning in...look alive and straighten your tie."

Trip had traversed about five miles of the narrow, winding road when he braked the Corvette and turned into a brick-paved side road. The entrance was marked with a simple legend blasted into heavy wood:
GRAIL FLIGHT CENTRE
Authorized Access Only
Trip came to a gatehouse with a heavy, steel sentinel arm and a uniformed security guard blocking the way. Pulling up close, he placed his thumb on the electronic fingerprint sensor and the arm automatically swung upward as the guard saluted and watched him pass inside the security fence.

As his car cleared, the heavy sentinel arm dropped into place behind him.

A half-mile ahead, at a cavernous hanger, a group of aircraft were parked. Several were clearly marked with the Grail logo. Others bore the emblems of major corporations. Standing off to the side, clearly away from the rest, were three large, highly-polished jet aircraft marked with the flags and seals of foreign countries. Two large U.S. military jets were also in that same area, guarded by a half-dozen men wearing uniforms.

Beyond the far end of the hanger was a low terminal building, and perhaps a hundred yards beyond that stood a modern control tower with meteorological and electronic paraphernalia sticking out of the roof.

Trip jerked back his head, startled as the sudden shadow of the jet flagship swooped down, seeming to almost brush the car as it settled feather-light on the runway ahead. Feeling a trifle unsettled, he ignored the plane and circled the small terminal. He parked at the rear, near a little annex with separate parking.

The single door marked "Grail—Private" made it clear that the area was not for public use.

As Trip drove by, there were two cars parked on the main side of the terminal building, and less than a dozen parked further back, in the spaces near the hanger. Except for the military personnel guarding the aircraft on the far side of the hanger, there was no one else to be seen.

Trip stooped slightly and positioned his eye in front of the electronic scanner by the door. In a moment, he heard the lock click open. Turning the knob, he stepped inside. The annex was used exclusively as a private waiting lounge for corporate officers, high ranking government and military, and assorted other VIP guests. Though now the suite was deserted, Trip made a thorough inspection of all the rooms.

From his own experience, he knew that the corporate Chief Pilot and several of the key people who ran the facility had optic iris-identity clearance and, on very rare occasions, with extreme discretion, used the privacy of these rooms for steamy little outings with certain ladies of the community who had very good reasons to want to remain anonymous. He also knew that it was not likely this would ever happen in broad daylight on a regular weekday.

Assured that he was alone, Trip removed a plastic bag from the large wastebasket in the ladies room and went back outside and opened the luggage compartment of the Corvette.

Heart pounding, he peeped inside the trunk—almost afraid to look.

Nothing.

He laughed out loud.

Now...where was that goddamn rubbing compound when he needed it?

Grabbing the container and chamois cloth, he sat it on the tarmac near the offending smear of paint. Then, he went back to make a closer inspection.

At first glance the contents of the trunk space appeared quite ordinary. Resting just inside the compartment, flush up against the locking mechanism, his golf bag took up a major portion of the compartment. There were some shoe bags with various club emblems, an emergency kit from The Sharper Image, a little battery operated vacuum cleaner and a bag of practice balls. But these were not the things that caught his attention.

The edges of a plastic hotel laundry bag, half hidden by his golf bag, protruded from among a pile of shoe bags back in the far right corner.

MANOR INN!

The bright red logo caused his heart to skip a beat. The electronic keycard in his pocket bore the same design.

Wiggling it free, the plastic bag was overflowing with part of a towel and a small brown paper bag. From its feel, the plastic bag contained mostly fabric items of some sort.

After he removed the bag, he could see another small canvas USAirways tote bag with a leather luggage tag. Badly shaking, he turned the tag and saw the legend neatly printed in large commercial type:

EMMA LOU CLAIRE
TEN SANDPIPER WAY
NEWPORT BEACH, CALIFORNIA 92501
714/788-9669

Instinctively, he grabbed onto the side of the car to steady himself. Cold sweat popped out on his forehead and his knees almost gave way.

Forcing himself to take a deep breath, he stepped back. Slowly, he walked to the far corner of the building nearer the Terminal Operations entrance, fighting for control.

Trying his best to appear casual, he lit a cigarette and walked a few paces further away from the building to where he could get a view of the hangar area. Carefully, he surveyed the wide paved area which stretched from the hanger all the way across to the terminal and waiting room entrance on the far side of the operations building.

Not a breathing soul, not even a bird in view.

He had intentionally parked the Corvette so that it fairly hugged the side of the terminal building. The rear wall of the terminal was windowless. From that angle, the car was not visible to personnel in the control tower. Perfectly private, screened off from the world.

Feeling foolish, but still unable to shake the uneasy feeling, he crushed the cigarette under his shoe and walked back to the car.

God! He could surely use a drink!

Trying to ignore the shakes, with great effort he forced himself back to the task at hand. Reaching in, he removed both bags and, spreading the opening of the large trash bag from the ladies room, he placed them inside.

One by one he removed the items from the luggage compartment until nothing remained inside.

Nothing left to worry about.

From the pile of items at his feet he retrieved a small battery operated vacuum cleaner and carefully ran it back and forth over the interior of the trunk. When he finished, except for the can of rubbing compound, he neatly replaced the items in the compartment.

The rubbing compound made easy work of the small smear of red paint; as far as he could tell, except for the cloudy film it left, there was no trace of damage. The cloudy film came off with a few swipes of the towel from his golf bag.

Replacing the rubbing compound and towel and his golf equipment back in the trunk, Trip lowered the lid until the automatic closing mechanism took hold and pulled it securely in place.

The entire operation had taken less than thirty minutes.

He looked around again. Except for the cockpit windows of the empty Grail 767 Flagship looming above the corner of the building, there was nothing else in sight.

Picking up the large brown plastic bag, Trip went back inside. Carefully checking the door to make sure it was locked, he secured the night chain in the slot.

Now! Find that fucking drink. Just a little something to steady him.

At the small wet bar, he located a bottle of vodka and poured a plastic airline glass almost full. Without bothering to get any ice from the kitchenette, he opened a mini-can of orange juice, added a splash to kill the raw edge of the hot alcohol, and quickly downed the drink. Now he went to the refrigerator and added two ice cubes. Quickly adding vodka to refill the glass, he went back across to where he had left the plastic bag. Dragging the bag over to a grouping of sofa and chairs, he placed it on the low cocktail table and moved back to pick up the drink before he began to remove the contents to take a closer look.

He opened the small brown paper bag first. Inside were five or six little envelopes filled with what he was sure was cocaine.

The envelopes were identical to the empty he'd found in his car outside Ginger's yesterday.

In a corner of the paper bag was a little square package wrapped in a blue facial tissue. Careful not to touch the plastic bags with his fingertips he took it out and unwrapped it enough to see that it contained a small purse-sized mirror and a single-edged razor blade. He rewrapped it and replaced it all back in the paper bag.

Painstakingly, he made sure there was nothing else in the bag before he rolled the top tightly closed and set the bag carefully aside.

The familiar numb feeling and a certain sloppiness of motor function told him that the vodka was already doing its job.

Perhaps, too good…too fast….

In his haste, he had overestimated…had to back off. Stay straight.

He went into the private office and opened the file drawer. Probing far into the back corner of the deep drawer underneath all the files, his hand closed on a foil strip of pharmaceutical samples. He tore off one of the little segments which held a square pink amphetamine tablet. Punching out the pill, he replaced the strip in its hiding place and allowed the file folders to return to their usual position before he closed the drawer.

A Boy Scout is always prepared!

210

The pill had already started to dissolve on his tongue, and the bitter taste was coming through before he could get back and wash it down with a quick swallow of the drink. Then, he took the glass back to the wet bar, refilled it and returned to the task at hand.

Sitting back down, he placed the hotel laundry bag on the table in front of him. Having no earthly idea what he might find, he gingerly pulled the towel out of the bag and carefully examined it.

The raised letters on the toweling were the logo of the GRAIL MASSIE HOUSE.

Holding his breath, he unrolled the towel, revealing a wispy little black tank suit of the style competitive swimmers use. It was still damp and the label was that of a shop in Palm Beach. He carefully placed it aside while he dumped the rest of the bag's contents onto the cocktail table. When he had turned the bag inside out to make sure that he hadn't overlooked anything, Trip replaced the towel and swimsuit in the bag.

He sorted through the clothing in the small tangle in front of him and found a pair of panties, a soft bra with spaghetti straps and a light fleece sweatsuit in pink and white. The panties had the label of a shop on Rodeo Drive in Beverly Hills and the sweatsuit had the same Palm Beach label as the swimsuit.

He had already folded the collection and stuffed them back into the bag before it occurred to him that he should examine the pockets of the sweatpants and hooded jacket.

Good thinking, he congratulated himself. But he was getting shaky again.

In the right-hand pocket of the sweatsuit jacket he found one of his Grail calling cards with his private number in Colonial Hall scribbled on the back. Underneath, he recognized the number of the beachfront apartment he kept at Palm Beach. The pocket of the sweatpants contained a plastic, electronically coded keycard from the Massie House.

Now, all at once, it came back to him that he had not been able to locate his keycard yesterday morning when he was checking out and he had had to wedge a Gideon Bible in the door to keep from locking himself out when he was putting his stuff in the car.

Carefully wiping each article with the damp towel, he replaced them in the bag before he took the USAirways tote from the trash sack.

Picking up the hotel laundry bag and the brown bag, Trip returned them to the trash bag before he dumped the contents of the tote on the table in front of him.

Methodically, he sorted through the articles, replacing them in the tote after he'd looked them over. In the jumble were a battery operated vibrator and a plastic zipper bag containing some cosmetics and a brush and comb. Also, the pile contained six ready-rolled marijuana cigarettes along with half a carton of some cigarettes of a brand name he didn't recognize.

There was a tiny blue nightie rolled into a loose ball and a little flowered plastic kit, which contained a traveling douche set. He rezipped it and tucked it safely inside the garbage bag.

That left the table clear.

Bending forward to close the larger bag, he caught sight of a blue and silver matchbook cover lying underneath the table.

When he retrieved it, Trip saw the top half of the folder had been torn off, but the bottom half, which really was the back cover when the book was folded shut, had the logo imprint of the Manor Inn.

Shit!

Heart pounding, he got down on his hands and knees and made a careful search underneath the furniture to make sure there was nothing else he had carelessly mishandled.

That was it…nothing else.

Now that he had made certain the area was clean, he carefully put the matchbook cover into the brown trash bag with everything else. Picking up the glass, he thirstily drank about half of it before he returned to the bar and refilled the glass with vodka. He was shaking badly now and his shirt was soaked through with sweat.

Wham!

The amphetamine kicked in with a gentle jolt.

Giving the glass a little motion of the wrist to swirl its contents, Trip held it straight out from him to admire his newfound steadiness. Then he turned and looked about the room to make certain he had left nothing to betray his visit.

When he was sure everything was in order, he freshened his glass and picked up the plastic garbage bag. Locking the door behind him, he stepped out to the parking lot. The amphetamine was doing its work and his vision seemed sharper now as he looked across the corner of the roof to the nose of the big jet.

Silhouetted against the white clouds of the spring sky, the effect of the alcohol and the drug somehow foreshortened his perspective and made the airplane seem closer. With the high sun reflecting off their surface, the little windows of the cockpit loomed high above the top of the terminal building like the beetling eyes of a giant insect from a Japanese monster flick.

CHAPTER THIRTY-FOUR

MARILEE HAD AWAKENED, SHOWERED AND DRESSED with expectancy. It was going to be an incredible day.

Almost out the door, Oleander stopped her and held out the phone with her hand over the receiver, "Miz Graham, it's a Patty Smith, Mr. Wrenn's secretary...wants you to pick up a package and take it to New York...."

Package? New York?

Marilee smiled a 'thank you' and took the phone. "Patty, this is Marilee Graham. What can I do for you?" She was running late. Her first instinct was to tell Patty that she couldn't possibly pick up any package.

"Mrs. Graham, I'm sorry to bother you, but Mr. Wrenn asked me to call...." Marilee listened while Patty explained about Norris' request and his desire for confidentiality. The word *confidentiality* registered instantly. Until that moment, she had not considered the possibility that Norris' New York address was a secret from the world.

Of course. Norris was a fox. This was a game...the package... his unpublished number...how to find him in New York.

By the time she left for Raleigh, Marilee had managed to pick up the fat brown envelope from Patty at The Tower and had arranged for a first-class seat on the mid-afternoon flight to LaGuardia.

In Raleigh, the Governor's ceremony was brief—hardly more than a luncheon and a political photo-op. At the airport bookshop, she picked up the latest copy of *Cosmopolitan*. This new issue had a blurb on its cover featuring three articles on how to be a popular favorite in bed. What to say? What perfume? Which undies? Top or bottom? Oral variations?

Boarding with the first-class passengers on the afternoon flight, Marilee suddenly realized how totally exhausted she was. She was asleep before the coach class passengers finished boarding. She didn't awake until the attendant touched her on the shoulder to make sure her belt was fastened on the descent into La Guardia.

Still half-woozy, she found a cab and was just beginning to come alive again by the time the driver crossed the Queensboro Bridge.

She would never get used to the skyline without the World Trade towers. It seemed incredible that they were still cleaning up the devastation.

The driver finally pulled to the curb across from Central Park near 79th.

She let herself into Sadie's apartment and gave Paulo, the Greek doorman, a twenty-dollar bill for his help. Sadie's apartment had been the first place she had felt she belonged. Paulo always made her feel like she was merely returning from a short vacation and had never actually left.

She pushed him out the door with a hug and went straight to the coffeemaker. The gurgling sounds of the coffee brewing echoed softly through the huge apartment as she headed back to her room.

Wasting no time, she got right to her unpacking. This room had been her home for the year before her marriage. She'd used it often during the intervening years. It was her sanctuary. In almost no time at all, she had put her things away and was running hot water into the tub. From the tub she could see the little Dresden clock on the dressing table. Not yet six. It would still be daylight for two more hours at least.

Visions of Norris at the beach and fantasies of their upcoming rendezvous danced through her head as she toweled dry and dressed.

A wisp of a bra and a pair of the delicate ivory panties underneath. No pantyhose...her legs were a golden tan. A light wraparound cotton skirt and a simple Eileen Fisher flowered silk print top. A pair of white sandals, very comfortable to walk in.

Almost out the door, she was suddenly seized with dismay. She had completely forgotten about her promised meeting with Penny and the cub scout mothers. In her preoccupation with Norris, it was a wonder she could remember anything.

Marilee went quickly to the phone and dialed.

"Penny...oh, I'm so glad I caught you...I had to change my plans. I'm in New York...what can I say, I'm embarrassed...I hope you don't hate me." She stopped and listened. "That sounds fine...you can speak for me. Thank you, Penny...and oh, yes...before I forget, I'd love to play some tennis when I get back. Call me Monday, please?" She hung up the phone.

Now, for the walk while it's light enough. At least, she could locate Norris' secret hideaway. She jotted the address from the envelope on a calling card and started out again.

"Isn't this close by?" Downstairs, she showed Paulo the address.

"Oh, yes, it's just up there...about four blocks, Miss Marilee." He pointed out the way. "See where the tall glass building stands on the corner? The entrance is almost in the middle of the block."

"Is it all right to walk, Paulo? Is it safe, I mean?" She asked, squinting at the fading light. New York could be intimidating after dark.

"Oh, yes, Miss. It's quite safe up here in the daytime. But don't stay too long. It's not safe after dark for a woman...or a man either...alone...anywhere in the city anymore."

Out of fatherly concern, Paulo kept a watchful eye on Marilee as she made her way through the chaotic pedestrian flow of the diminishing early twilight. His attention was momentarily diverted as a well-dressed man crossed over from the park and fell in step a dozen yards behind her, walking casually along. It struck him as odd, because he had a nagging recollection of the same man disembarking from a cab when Marilee arrived from the airport. He glanced ahead, watching her moving blithely along. When he looked back, the man was nowhere in sight.

Paulo shrugged. His old man's imagination was playing tricks on him again.

In less than five minutes, Marilee was standing in front of the non-descript glass tower with greenish-black marble around the entrance facade. The canvas marquee covering the sidewalk out to the curb was striped dark green and white and the shiny brass plate on the wall beside the heavy brass door was inscribed simply with the building number.

So this was the secret hideaway of Norris Wrenn. *Phoenix Rising*. Norris Wrenn, social architect for a new world.

Standing there looking up at the building, Marilee was startled when the doorman suddenly appeared from out of nowhere. Dressed in a tropical poplin suit of suntan khaki, he could have been the head of a brokerage firm. In the best tradition of understatement, the only concession to his function was a modest little brass nameplate on his breast pocket. Under his arm, he carried a leather-bound appointment book.

"Good evening Miss. May I help you?"

"Ah, not really...ah...I was...." she half-stammered, off guard. Nervous. Stupid. Embarrassed, Marilee smiled and turned to walk on by.

"Excuse me, madam. Are you by any chance Ms. Graham?" The question stopped her in mid-stride. She turned back to him, caught completely off guard.

"Ms. Graham?" he asked again, expectantly.

"Yes. I am...I am *Mrs.* Graham."

"Mr. Wrenn is expecting you, but he said he wasn't sure exactly when. He just got in a little over an hour ago. If you'll wait, I'll tell him you're here. Come inside, it's cooler there."

"Well...I don't think Mr. Wrenn is expecting to see me until tomorrow." Marilee hesitated.

"Oh, no, ma'am. He made it very clear you were bringing some material he needed. He'll be delighted to know you're here." He made a little bow. With a sweeping motion of his hand, he invited her to follow. "I'm Wilson, ma'am. Come on inside, I'll just let Mr. Wrenn know you're here."

She wanted to run, but she shrugged and followed him through the heavy glass doors.

The lobby was elegant, all dark green leather, polished brass and marble.

Wilson went directly to the lobby phone and dialed. She could see his face in the mirror on the wall behind the phone table; it was without expression. The surroundings, the decor, the neighborhood—everything about the place exuded respectability.

All at once she was aware that she had not put on any makeup. She was not at all dressed for the big occasion she had dreamed this meeting would be. She caught her breath. She couldn't let Norris see her this way. Praying Norris wouldn't answer, she walked to the door and looked out, unseeing, across the Park.

Hardly before hope welled up inside her, she looked back and saw Wilson was speaking into the phone.

Too late.

From Wilson's smile, she knew that she was doomed.

CHAPTER THIRTY-FIVE

IN THE COCKPIT OF THE SLEEK GRAIL FLAGSHIP, Dempsey Gearhart had just finished making notations in his flight log when Trip Graham emerged from the VIP lounge at the rear of the terminal. Earlier, when he had first seen the bright yellow Corvette turn into the Flight Centre, he had been relieved that Trip apparently was not looking to fly out on another of his unscheduled jaunts.

Taking care of this rich kid was getting to be a world-class pain in the ass.

Still...the job had its compensations...like the little thing he had going with Glee Craige, old man Graham's honey down at Ponte Vedra Beach. He'd just flown out of there this morning after a very pleasant evening drinking the boss' bourbon and porking the boss' concubine. One thing Dempsey knew for certain: with a fifty billion dollar corporation, Clayton Massie Graham, Sr. was not about to be shacking up with some bimbo with AIDS. And, while he believed in giving old man Graham his money's worth, Dempsey also believed all's fair in love and war. Out there on life's real battlefield, it was every man for himself. Still, he knew which side his bread was buttered on; he shuddered to think what would happen if the old codger found out his Chief Pilot was sticking the old joy stick to his young honey on the sly.

Dempsey's attention perked up as he watched the younger Graham open the trunk of his car and begin removing some bags. He wondered if his relief might have been premature. Immediately, the resentment welled up inside him, and he turned on the radio and called the operations office in the terminal below him. "This is Grail Flag, can you hear me, George?"

"That you, Demp? Thought you'd gone home."

"Naw, I had to catch up the flight log. I see the kid going in the

219

back of the building right now. He took some stuff out of the trunk of his car...you sure he isn't planning a trip? Say it ain't so. I got a hell of a headache."

"As far as I know, it ain't. Go on home, Captain Kirk..." Around the company, the 767 Flagship was the Starship Enterprise. "Nothing on the book until the Friday jaunt to Atlanta for the Braves home stand. Don't forget, we got to put down at RDU for the Governor's party both coming and going."

"Roger, the Gov, George. I'm out of here soon as I finish this log." Dempsey maintained high professional standards. He turned his attention back to catching up entries in the Flagship's log.

A half-hour passed before he finally looked up and saw Trip leaving the lounge, lugging a bulging brown trash bag, heading for his car.

Anxious to leave, Dempsey put the leather-bound log book into his flight case and closed and snapped the lid. Sitting there without air-conditioning, the midday sun coming in the cockpit windows, he had become quite uncomfortable. Long experience with the airlines had taught him it was a mistake to hang around airports too long. But, now, all at once, instinctively, there was something about the way Trip Graham was acting that started his adrenaline pumping.

He watched as Trip placed the cup he was carrying on top of the car above the driver's door and moved over to where a trash dumpster was sitting.

Placing the brown bag on the pavement, the younger Graham dug something out of his pocket, opened the dumpster and dropped the object into it.

From this distance it was impossible to identify articles small enough to fit into a man's trouser pocket. Except for a brief glint of sunlight on the object in Trip's hand, Demp couldn't guess what the article might be. At any rate, it seemed Trip had been merely cleaning out some trash from his automobile. Before he picked the bag up again, Trip glanced quickly about him and reached back into his pocket and removed another object and put it in the bag.

Trip picked up the bag, then changed his mind and put it down again. Leaving it sitting in front of the dumpster, he walked back to his car and opened the door and leaned in, obviously examining the car to see if there was anything his tidying up had missed. When he straightened up and stepped back from the car, he had a wad of paper in his fist. Then he closed the door and moved around to the driver's side and took a little sip from the glass he had left there before he opened the door and leaned back in the car to continue his housekeeping chore. When he had finished, he carried the trash back to the bag and placed it inside before he opened the dumpster lid and started to toss in the bag.

But something stopped him.

Trip stood there considering, then withdrew the bag and set it down. He leaned forward and looked inside the large metal bin. Slowly he stepped back and reached up and reclosed the door.

He picked up the bag, moved back to his car and placed it behind the driver's seat. Then he retrieved his drink from the car's roof and got in. Within seconds, he was backing out and moving swiftly away from the building.

Ordinarily, Dempsey would have given this charade little notice, but now his curiosity was aroused by Trip Graham's actions. It seemed so completely out of character that this arrogant, lazy man would be cleaning out his own car.

Almost without thinking, Dempsey left the cockpit and scrambled down the boarding steps. Moving at a half-trot to his car parked in the reserved space next to the operations office, he opened the door and looked back over his shoulder just in time to catch a glimpse of the Corvette disappearing over the last rise beyond the main hanger.

Better hurry, he mused, *something funny's going down.*

CHAPTER THIRTY-SIX

"MR. WRENN IS EXPECTING YOU. Let me help you with the lift, ma'am." Wilson pointed the way. At the elevators, the doorman took a key and inserted it in the mechanism. Once Marilee was safely inside, Wilson reached in and pushed a button marked PH, alone at the top of a double row of buttons with numbers ending with the number forty.

"When the car stops, Ma'am, just go out the other door." He indicated the rear wall of the elevator. "It's private up there. That entire side of the penthouse is Mr. Wrenn's."

Almost before she could nod, the doors closed with a little swishing sound; hardly before she could turn around, the car came to a halt and the doors were opening.

She stood there momentarily speechless. Norris stood in a small foyer facing her.

Sockless in well-worn loafers with jeans and a soft blue button-down oxford shirt, his hair looked damp. In a heartbeat, Marilee's anxiety evaporated.

"What a nice surprise..." Norris was saying. Through the open door behind him, the glass-walled living room revealed a spectacular view across the river into the New Jersey countryside. Smiling, he took her hand. The gesture was so simple, so completely relaxed that she lost all her resistance. Without a thought, she followed him across the threshold.

"I'm a mess..." she protested, looking forlornly down at her clothes.

"Hush. You're lovely. This is the nicest thing that's happened all day. It's really great to find you've done one right thing in your life, just when you were beginning to wonder if anything would go right again."

"I look a bloody wreck and you damn well know it. It's plain for anyone to see I wasn't expecting to find you here. I just wanted to take a little stroll over to find out exactly where you lived...in preparation for tomorrow. I never for a moment intended to have your package brought by messenger," she protested. "And you didn't think for a moment I would, did you?"

"I hoped you would bring it yourself, but I really wasn't all that sure," Norris confessed.

"Oh, my God, the package, Norris!" she exclaimed in exasperation. "I didn't bring the package...but...I can go get it, it's only a few blocks. I really didn't have any idea you would be here tonight."

"Forget the package." He laughed.

"But..." Marilee was confused.

"The package was to make sure you found me...if you wanted to find me," Norris said. "I have the papers with me."

"You fox!" She giggled. "Well, I guess you knew I'd show up, all right. Besides, who do I think I'm fooling? This was all my idea. It's way too late to play coy...for me at least."

"If you hadn't shown up, I would have turned the city upside down...hunted you down and taken you prisoner. Come on in and see the rest of my hideaway." He closed the foyer door and led her into the enormous living room.

"It's fabulous. Do you do much entertaining?" She wondered how many beautiful women had been here before her. And what had they shared of this man? She hated them one and all.

"As a matter of fact, in the eight years I've had this co-op you are one of less than a dozen people who have seen inside." He looked her straight in the eye.

The furniture looked like it was made of packing cases. Big square chairs and a sofa in front of a solid old fireplace with a walnut mantel and friendly squat footstools to put tired feet upon. Made from heavy pine, she had seen the furniture in *The New York Times Magazine*.

Bookshelves on every wall...undeniably, Norris Wrenn.

"Does Agnes come here often?" Her insecurity came down like

a wall between them.

"Agnes? No. Agnes has never been near this place. Except for the decorator and the cleaning woman, you're the first woman to cross the threshold."

"Oh...well...ah...?" She wished she'd never brought Agnes' name into the room...had she ruined the moment?

"I'm with people all day and many evenings. Inside, I'm screaming to be a very private person. You have Caswell Beach. This is one of two places I can come and find myself...if indeed there's any of me left anymore." A cloud seemed to pass behind his eyes, but then he brightened. "So...you are the first. It was worth the wait. Let's celebrate. Sit down and I'll make us a drink. What would you like?"

"I had Wild Turkey on the plane. It's a taste I picked up from you, remember?" She smiled. "What are you having? I'm sure there are other things you could teach me."

He considered her remark. "I wonder who's the pupil and who's the teacher here."

"Oh, come on now, stop teasing." She wandered over to the bookshelves and examined a collection of videotapes. She stopped to take a closer look. Then she looked at him.

"What?" He raised his eyebrows.

"*Caligula*? Isn't that...?"

"Caught me red-handed. Don't report me to Betty Ruth Watts, please." He made a face and rolled his eyes.

Marilee laughed. "Will you show it to me?"

"Well...it's pretty explicit...know what I mean? Have you ever seen hardcore porn?"

"Yes, when I lived here on the park. My secret's out at last. I guess I'm a disgrace to motherhood and the good women of Colonial Hall." She laughed a self-conscious laugh. "It's really hard for me sometimes to go to all those PTA meetings and act like I give a damn about potty training and private schools. And Betty Ruth gets on my nerves with her phony crusades against dirty movies and books."

"I agree. We're victims of people like Betty Ruth. They rob us of our freedom...our right to make our own choices. But then I guess it's my fault I don't do something about it. There's a lot of evil done in the name of good. But inside the hallowed gates of Club Drive...and here high above the mean streets...I don't have to get involved because it doesn't affect me in a direct way. I don't have to abide by ordinary rules. Because of that, I have resigned my responsibility. Money and power have placed me apart from ordinary human status. I just stand by and let the Betty Ruths play their silly games and know it really doesn't have to affect me. That's really the problem. People like me don't want to be responsible anymore. We really don't have to be. Having money and power gives us our own set of rules. So we just let people like Betty Ruth go around messing things up for the good old common folk. But then, maybe it serves us right for letting the Betty Ruths of the world run things for us. Do I have to be responsible for that?"

Norris stopped and looked out the window for a moment before he went on.

"I wish you could meet my old friend Tom Bradley...." his words were barely a whisper.

"Tom Bradley?...would I know him?"

"No...but you two would get along. I'm sorry, it's been a strange day." He turned back and grinned a sheepish little boy grin.

Marilee didn't know what to say. She'd never understand him...but nowhere in the rules did it say she'd have to try.

Last night she had been the woman and he had been like a little boy, shy underneath—afraid to deal with the physical thing between them. But now, all at once, she felt very much the little girl.

"Do I still get that drink?" she asked.

"Oh...oh, of course...be right back." He left the room. She could hear him clinking bottles and glasses and ice. In no time, he was back, putting a drink in her hand.

Norris stood like a fly transfixed in the web as Marilee set her glass down and moved toward him. He tried to say something, but the words wouldn't come. A little strangling sound died deep in his throat as she kissed him softly on the lips. He felt her lips go apart as her tongue probed gently against his lips and slipped inside his mouth.

Urgently, his hands moved against her. A ballet of bendings and unloosenings. Stepping free of his jeans, Norris watched as Marilee knelt before him. His hands moved through her hair, fingers lightly tracing the lines from her ear lobes underneath her jaw, delicately moving to touch the corners of her mouth as she timidly tasted and teased him with her tongue.

All at once, she was devouring him...

"Wait...no more...wait...not yet..." He pulled her gently to her feet. "I can't stand it..."

Now, standing before him trembling with desire, she submitted to his unfastenings.

Contrasted with the warm toast color of her sun-freckled skin, her breasts were milk-white with a delicate lacework of tiny blue veins—swelling and curving from beneath her armpit pointing upward with the large pink umbrella tips.

He bent and—one after the other—took each nipple into his mouth, sucking gently, letting his tongue go around. The nipples grew rock-hard beneath his tongue.

"Do you like me?" she whispered.

"You are perfect. I adore you. Do you like this?"

"Uhmm. Don't ever stop. I love that. You can do anything. Everything. I want you to do everything. Anything you like to do. Do it all."

Stepping free of her skirt and panties, at last she stood naked before him.

"Come on..." Stumbling, they bumped hip-against-hip to the bedroom.

"My God!" Transfixed, she looked at their naked bodies in the mirrored walls and ceiling.

"Do you like to watch?" He smiled at her in the mirror.

"Uhmm?...I've never watched before...."

He lowered her to the edge of the bed and she watched in the ceiling mirror, fascinated as he probed her secrets with his tongue. "Oh, yes...oh, my lovely love...oh yes-s-s, there...ooo NOW!"

Arching violently upward, hips contorting with sudden pleasure, she shuddered little waterfalls of movement against his mouth.

"Did you see me? Oh, my...I...ah...you surprised me. I never was so surprised."

"*La petite mort.* The little death." He laughed. "It's French."

"The French know everything. I think you did kill me, but only a little. Now it's my turn. I'm going to kill you, too. We are going to have a *petite* murder-suicide on our hands. What will the French have to say about that, I wonder." She was already trying to turn him around so she could reach him. "Next time it won't be so quick and so surprising."

"I like to give you surprises. Let's see if I really killed you." He touched her with his tongue again, and she shivered with almost unbearable pleasure.

"Wait. Now, I want to do you."

She pushed him back on the bed and fell to her knees before him and tasted him with her tongue as she had in the living room.

Arching her neck a little, she watched their reflection in the mirror. "See us? We make our own porno movie."

"You talk too much." He gently pulled her mouth back to him.

For a time, Norris floated in warm space, with a slow shifting of bodies, a montage of pink nipples, curving hillocks of ivory flesh, and splashes of fiery red hair. Underneath...overhead...beside.

Yieldings...encasings...enfoldings.

Oh!...

Probings...thrustings....

Oh, MY!...

Flower scents mingled with musky wetness....

OH, YES!...

Maddeningly motionless for delicious moments....

OH!...YES!, again.

Ravenous licking...sucking...OH, OH! YES, YES! Again and, again....

A kaleidoscopic burst of erotic images...

"Oh. My, god, you are awesome....I am drunk with having you. You have killed me. *Petite mort*...is that what you said?" She hugged him tight. "I love you...my little death."

"Love?" Norris laughed and clung to her. "Love?...You've just gotten all your sexual needs taken care of. That's all."

"No. No, that's not all. You are the smartest, surest, most altogether...best...only real man I have ever known. I do love you. Goddamn it, you can't change it. How does that threaten you? Why are you afraid to hear that? Relax, my love, I won't hurt you." She drifted off to sleep, her body hugged tightly against him.

CHAPTER THIRTY-SEVEN

Wasting no time, Demp started the engine and backed the car around. Straining to catch sight of Trip's fancy convertible, he headed down the only road in and out of the airstrip. Although he felt a bit foolish, momentarily he was caught up in the excitement of the chase.

Not much doubt about it, there was something very strange going down—he could feel it in his bones. Thinking back to Trip's furtive act of rubbing something off the yellow Corvette, it seemed likely that the no-good asshole had had another scrape with his fancy car...or...with all the cleaning out of the car, maybe he'd been sneaking around with one of the local ladies and was covering his tracks. Either way, it would be handy information to have.

To get some dirt on old man Graham's snotty little son—what a stroke of luck!

A wise man always kept an eye out for job security.

The old boy was keeping Glee Craige down in Jacksonville, but Demp was powerless to use that info without cutting his own throat. Not that it had stopped him from taking a proprietary interest in helping the sensual Ms. Craige manipulate the old coot to get all fixed up with a fancy condo at Starfish Cay Club. At this very moment, the old boy was flying himself down there to complete that little transaction.

Moreover...if the luscious Ms. Craige listened to ol' Demp, she'd have an income for life.

So far, the little girl had been very grateful for his counsel...hadn't she ever?

Life's a beach, as the saying goes.

When the old boy called last night, he had been in bed sucking on one of Glee's rosy pink nipples. He had to get up at the crack of dawn this morning in order to clear his stuff out of her apartment before the old fart showed up. Remembering that did not improve his mood at the moment. He hated stooping to taking the old boy's leavings, but he smirked inwardly at the old adage: He who laughs last, laughs best.

There was always a way to share the wealth. And, for the moment at least, there was enough of that delectable morsel to go around. Once Glee got the condo in her name, free and clear, then ol' Demp was going to figure out a way to get the gravy and the old boy would foot the bill. Still, that wouldn't really give him control. Everything would still be in Glee's name.

He was sick and tired of kissing rich people's asses.

He'd fucking show 'em, if he ever got some leverage of his own.

By the time he cleared the end of the main hangar, the Corvette had nearly traversed the mile and a half of straight level road which ran parallel to the main runway and was disappearing out of sight down the incline by the embankment at the end of the strip. Dempsey increased his speed, trying to close the distance. Easy though! He knew Trip would have to slow at the security gate, so he slackened slightly, not wanting to risk drawing attention to himself. The trick was to get close enough not to lose him but still keep enough interval so as not to draw attention.

His timing was perfect. Demp smiled a little smile of self-satisfaction when he saw the gleam of yellow disappearing through the trees just before the road reached the main highway.

Now he sped up again. It seemed certain that Graham would head on back to town. Yet, he didn't want to have to guess which way he turned and take a chance on losing him when he reached the main highway. As it turned out, he'd underestimated how long it would take the Corvette to move out of sight on the main road. By the time Demp saluted the security guard and reached the intersection, the Yellow Submarine was nowhere to be seen.

"Shit!" He cursed aloud in the empty car and gave the wheel a hit with the open palm of his hand.

Tentatively, he started the car forward, intending to turn left, north toward town. But, at the last instant a sparkle of sunlight spinning in the road about fifty yards south caught his eye.

The plastic airline glass! Ice cubes already melting in the hot sun.

Why would the asshole be heading south, away from town? This whole thing was starting to go totally weird.

Sheepishly, he was beginning to feel like a regular Mike Hammer.

Concentrating on catching sight of the yellow Corvette should it bob up into view—a frustrating exercise on the roller coaster of subtle little hills and valleys of the rural highway while traveling at that speed—Dempsey almost ran past Trip's car where it had pulled off a little side road at the bottom of one of the long downgrades near a little stream.

About halfway down the hill, a highway sign indicated that there was a trash collection station ahead. All through the redneck South, in an effort to do away with the horrors of roadside trash dumping, it had become a familiar sight to see large dumpster containers conveniently stationed off the sides of the roads for the use of the rural populations. Although Demp had never had any personal occasion to use them, he despaired of the ugliness. Patently neglected, usually poorly serviced by apathetic county sanitation people, inevitably they became eyesores.

Well screened by the heavy woods growing along the small stream which ran through the declivity in the hills, like most city-bred travelers, the urbane pilot ordinarily gave little notice. Moving at eighty miles an hour, he had almost gotten completely by the turn-out when he caught a bright splash of yellow out of the corner of his eye. Instinctively, his foot released a little pressure from the accelerator, but he caught himself and let the car continue on past without slowing enough to draw Trip's attention.

In the rearview mirror, Demp could see a group of three dumpsters as he started up the next hill. The fancy Corvette was parked at the dumpster at the back, nearest the creek. Resisting the urge to stop and turn around, he continued on for about a mile in order to let the sound of his car fade before he started to look for a place to turn. He finally found a place wide enough and returned to the top of the hill where he could see the area. From the reverse angle, the dumpsters were in plain sight below.

He made it back just in time to catch a glimpse of Trip's car disappearing over the rim of the long hill, headed back to town. Slowing, the chief pilot cautiously moved on down and turned into the dumpsite and headed straight back to the spot where he had seen Trip parked.

A thin covering of cinders was well mixed with the soft earth by the constant flow of traffic in and out—it was difficult to find a firm spot on the unpaved unloading area.

There was an unmistakable pair of fresh tire tracks where Trip had spun his wheels in his hasty departure a moment before. It was obvious Trip had had no wish to hang around.

Demp carefully turned his car around so that he was headed out.

All of a sudden he felt very foolish. What did he expect to find, anyway? Goddamn, there must be at least several thousand brown plastic trash can liners lying inside those boxes. How the hell was he supposed to spot the right one?

Oh well...at least he'd spotted which container Trip had thrown the damn thing in.

In the effort to make sure the trash was placed in the dumpsters and not strewn carelessly about, the sanitation people had constructed permanent access ramps leading to narrow platforms running near the top of each of the high-sided containers.

Leaving the door open and the motor running, Demp got out and walked up the wooden incline to the container Trip had used. As he walked up the ramp, Dempsey looked over at the other two dumpsters which were overflowing.

His heart sank.

He saw a sea of anonymous brown garbage bags. Hah! A hundred, at least, had spilled over the sides in careless profusion.

When he looked back into the dumpster Trip had used, Dempsey laughed out loud.

When you're hot, you're hot.

To his amazement, the top of the refuse pile in the dumpster

Trip had used was covered by a solid frosting of white school notebook papers. It was immediately obvious that one of the nearby schools was cleaning house in preparation for the approaching summer vacation.

To his total delight and utter disbelief, plunked down smack-dab in the middle of this white sea of notebook pages was one solitary, wonderfully forlorn, brown plastic trash bag.

TUESDAY EVENING

CHAPTER THIRTY-EIGHT

AFTER LEAVING THE DUMPSITE, TRIP HAD NOT LOOKED BACK. It was not until he had crossed back over the river and was safely inside the town limit that he felt some of his anxiety leave him. Even so, it still bothered him that he had been in such a rush to get rid of the bag of evidence that he hadn't taken the extra ten seconds to climb the ramp by the dumpster to make sure the bag hadn't broken open.

Well, there was really nothing to worry about. He had distinctly heard the swooshy sound of the bag's soft landing.

Besides, the other two trash containers at the site were already overflowing with an anonymous heap of trash. From the look of things, the entire mess would soon be at the county landfill. Bulldozers would cover it over and that would be history.

Now the amphetamine was making him a little jittery. The back of his neck was tense, a sure sign he needed a drink. God, he wished he was back in Palm Beach...away from prying eyes. Even Blowing Rock was better than here. Outside his office, the only place he could get a drink in the middle of the day in Colonial Hall was Ginger's...or home. For the moment, he sure'n'shit didn't want to go to either place.

He didn't have the vaguest notion what time Marilee would be back from Raleigh, and he didn't want her to find him at home in the middle of the day with liquor on his breath...or worse still, a drink in his hand. And lately, every time he showed up home early, Ivee would just start to bug him about playing golf. He'd made up his mind. He was going back to Palm Beach tomorrow and start making plans to build. There was nothing for him to do here anymore—who needed this shitty little one-horse place anyway?

He opted for the Grail Tower. With Clayt out of town, there

was no one there to check on him. By the time he stepped out of the elevator at the top of the Tower, he was really hurting for some booze.

"Oh, Mr. Graham, I'm glad to see you. Those people from the Greensboro police have called back three times. And Sheriff John Henry Galt just called and said it was urgent you get in touch with him." Dodie gathered up a fistful of little message slips and handed them to him.

"OK, thanks. I'll take care of these, but I'm not in to anyone." He took the messages and headed into his office suite. Now, he had the beginning of a severe cramp in his gut.

"Oh, yes...Mrs. Graham said to remind you she is going on to New York for a couple of days. Ivee will be staying with the Harrises until she gets back."

"Hmm-m. Thanks." He closed the door and headed straight for the bar and fixed himself a hefty shooter of vodka with grapefruit over ice. He drank about half before it had time to chill.

The raw booze gave him a violent shudder as it went down. But the shakes had already eased before he had time to refill the large old-fashioned glass to the brim and walk across the room.

The phone calls from Greensboro made him nervous. And now, that local Barney Fife, Sheriff John Henry Galt, had called... and, to compound the misery, his belly was getting worse.

First find a Tagamet, calm his freaking stomach down.

What the fuck could he tell the law? He couldn't even remember checking into the motel—or hardly anything else of Sunday.

Jezus! Saturday was almost a total blank.

God, what could he say?

Thank god he'd had the sense to fix the car and get rid of that bag full of shit.

His brain was scrambled. The amphetamine was already wearing off.

He found a Tagamet and another amphetamine in his desk and took them with a healthy slug of the drink. Better living through chemistry...how did we ever do without it?

Good old booze...and meth. Never let him down.

Maybe he should get out of town tonight. Marilee was heading for New York. He could get a flight out of Raleigh to West Palm tonight. But, first he had to decide what to tell the cops. Ought to talk to Norris. He grabbed the cordless phone on the large cocktail table.

"Dodie, get Norris Wrenn..."

"Sorry, Mr. Graham. Mr. Richards called this morning. Mr. Wrenn has gone to Washington...and then to New York..."

"Shit!...Get me Mr. Richards, then."

"Yessir. But he's gone back to his Raleigh office. I'll have to call you back."

Still carrying the phone, Trip topped off his glass with pure vodka and walked over to the wall of glass. Below, the neat pattern of the little town stretched out below him. Traffic moved lazily through tree-lined streets, crawling in and out of the old residential areas, which eroded into the ill-defined edges of the business district. Beyond, the serpentine red-brick pattern of Club Drive snaked its way between the lush, tree-lined fairways. Mayberry, USA. Clayt had always insisted he uphold the phony standards of the family image.

Fucking place was choking the life out of him.

Fuck 'em all. He was going back to Palm Beach...getting out of Mayberry on the next plane. If it wasn't too late, he'd make a reservation for tonight. He reached forward to touch the intercom but the phone rang before he could find the button.

"Mister Richards is on the line."

"Put him on," Trip snapped.

"Griff. How are you? It's such a great day for golf, I was afraid Dodie couldn't reach you."

"Well, you can thank your daddy for enslaving me here at the office. What's on your mind?" Griff was definitely not in a chatty frame of mind.

"I've had several calls from..." Trip picked up the stack of message slips and read from the one on the top "...D.C. Mills, the Chief of the Greensboro police, this morning, and Dodie says John Henry Galt called a little while ago. I wonder what the hell I've done now? Could you call someone up there and see what you can find out before I call them?"

"Judas Priest, don't you think you'd know if you committed a crime?" Griff made no attempt to hide the fact he was sick and tired of bailing Trip out of traffic tickets and paying off property damages. "You're heading for bad trouble if you don't get your boozing under control."

"Hell, Griff. You know how they're always picking on me," Trip whined. "Can't you just call and see what you can find out?"

He grabbed his belly against a sudden cramp. His gut was giving him a fit.

"Well, OK. I'll see what I can do. I'll get right back to you. But, stand by, I'm not going to spend the rest of the afternoon trying to track you down."

Griff's irritation was obvious. Trip knew better than to say anything. The old curmudgeon was independent as hell. First thing when Clayt got back, he was going to tell his daddy about his attitude.

"Don't worry, I'll stay put." Trip tried to sound contrite. Hanging up, he took a drink.

The booze was helping now. At least he didn't feel like jumping out of his skin. But the cramping in his bowel was raising holy hell. Twenty minutes seemed like an hour. He was rummaging through his desk looking for a Lomotil tablet when the phone finally rang.

"Mr. Richards is on the line," Dodie announced in a flat voice. "Shall I put him on?"

"Hell, yes, put him on," Trip spat back, fighting against the sudden urge to hit the john.

"Well, you probably aren't going to jail today, but the call from the Greensboro police was concerning the death of that actress, Emma Claire, sometime early yesterday morning. They had reports from Blowing Rock that you were at some of the same parties up there over the weekend. And they just wanted to ask you about it. They seem pretty certain her death was drug-related. Cocaine, probably. Did you see her up there? Was she in your crowd?"

"No...I don't recall seeing her. I got pretty wasted. I was pissed

240

from the beginning. The weather turned shitty and we couldn't play golf. I had intended to drive all the way back here Sunday night, but I'd been drinking pretty heavy and had the good sense to check into a motel." He was relieved to hear the police were only concerned with routine questions. "What do you think I should do? What about the call from John Henry?"

"I don't know about John Henry. I assumed the Greensboro chief, D.C. Mills, had probably asked him to track you down. Do you want me to call him, too?"

"No. You think I should go ahead and call Greensboro now?" He wanted to get this over with. He had decided that if he could get a seat on a plane, he definitely was going to go to Palm Beach tonight. He wanted to put as much distance between him and these rednecks as possible.

"Yes, go ahead and tell them you don't know anything and forget it." Griff sounded calmer now. "By the way, I hope to God you're smart enough not to mess with cocaine—you need to back off on all that drinking, too."

"I don't mess with drugs. I'm no junkie. But, I do agree with you...I do need to slow down on my drinking. That crowd I run with is crazy. I'll call D.C. Mills right now...and thanks, Griff." Trip hung up, glad to get Richards off his back.

He debated for a few seconds before he decided the cramping in his belly could wait. He found the message slips with the Greensboro number and dialed.

"Greensboro Police, Sergeant Anderson speaking."

"Sergeant, this is Trip Graham in Colonial Hall. Can I speak to Chief Mills?"

"Oh, Mr. Graham, yessir. Just a minute I'll get him for you."

"Mr. Graham, this is D.C. Mills. How are you?" There was a forced camaraderie in the Chief's voice.

"I'm fine, thank you, Chief. My secretary said you had tried to call me. How can I help you?"

His gut was really killing him now.

"Well, I hate to bother you, Mr. Graham, but you probably read in the papers we have an unfortunate death on our hands up here. I understand you might have had some contact with the deceased—the movie star, Emma Claire—in Blowing Rock over the weekend." The Chief got right to the point.

"I was shocked to hear about her death. I did know her slightly. We met in Wilmington about six weeks ago at the Azalea Festival. Come to think of it, I believe I saw you there. Didn't you go fishing on my daddy's boat?" Trip hedged, congratulating himself that he remembered. The old Chief had gotten pretty drunk and made an all-around ass out of himself. It never hurt to have that kind of personal leverage.

"Well, yessir, matter of fact, I did. We had a great day of it, too. Your daddy really knows how to treat people." His voice took on a friendlier tone. "Please give my best regards to your daddy."

"He's in Florida for a few days. I'm writing myself a note right now to give him your best," he lied.

"Thanks. But, about Blowing Rock, you say you didn't see Miss Claire?".

"I don't think so. I don't remember her being up there. But even if I said I saw her, it wouldn't mean anything. I don't really remember much about the weekend. I got pretty drunk Friday and stayed that way until Sunday. I sobered up Sunday and was feeling kinda' rough, so I got out of that place. It rained out my golfing plans, and it was pretty depressing all around. I wish I'd had the good sense to have left Saturday." All of a sudden, common sense told him it would be better to tell the truth. To plead drunkenness might come in handy later, if other questions came to light. "I was staying alone in one of the corporate condos, but I feel certain there were a lot of the others staying around the Inn who could answer your questions better. Do you want a list? I could give you some names of the golfers who were in my party. The Claire babe certainly wasn't part of our group, but we were all partying around from place to place and somebody might have run into her."

"Well, thanks. I don't think I'll need to bother you for that right now. We have a pretty complete list of who was there and are just trying to get a clear picture of how she left the mountains and got down to Greensboro on Sunday." The Chief was silent for a moment. Trip wondered if he had hung up.

"Oh, one more thing, Mr. Graham. In her purse we found your private number written down on a torn half of a matchbook cover. It wasn't her handwriting. Any idea how she might have gotten that?"

"Not the foggiest..." Trip's gut contracted violently and he started loosening his belt. "When I get that drunk, there's no telling what I do. You know how some of us can be?"

"Anyway, she didn't ride down to Greensboro with you?" It was clearly a question, but Trip ignored it. He'd been jerked around by these hick cops before.

Trip waited. An ominous silence hung between them on the line.

"By the way, Mr. Graham, where did you spend Sunday night?"

His gut was cramping badly now...he needed to get off the goddamn phone.

"The Massie House in Greensboro, Chief."

"Isn't that a tragic coincidence? That hotel is next door to the Manor Inn, where the dead woman was found. Life is full of coincidences, Mr. Graham."

Trip wondered what was coming next. Mills was not just making idle conversation.

"I was just thinking about the Azalea weekend at the beach, Mr. Graham. Don't you drive a yellow sports car...one of those fancy Corvette convertibles?"

"You have a good memory, Mr. Mills. But I guess an officer of the law remembers yellow cars, huh?" As soon as he said it, Trip wished he could bite his tongue. He gave a little laugh.

Where was the Lomotil?...the cramping in his gut was almost unbearable now.

"Yessir, I guess we would remember a car like that. When you get involved in an investigation of a suspicious death, especially one that gets a lot of press, a country cop has to try to cover his ass. You investigate every incident in the neighborhood. There was a report of a little scuffle at the Massie House Sunday night. Someone driving a yellow convertible was bumped by a drunk driving a little red car. When you said you were staying at the Massie, I just couldn't help but remember that fancy car. Did you have words with someone in the parking lot Sunday night, Mr. Graham?"

"Chief, I was trying to get over a bad weekend...I don't remember much of anything. But I certainly think I would know if someone had hit my car. That car doesn't have a mark on it."

Thank God he'd taken care of that.

Jeezie, got to get off the phone or shit my pants.

"Oh, I'm sure you'd know...just asking, Mr. Graham. If you think of anything, give me a call, will you?" The Chief tried hard to sound offhand.

"Certainly. If I think of anything, I will, Mr. Mills."

"OK...and thanks again. Remember now, if you think of anything, give me a call." There was a pause, but the Chief came back on the line before Trip could say goodbye. "By the way, Mr. Graham, I hope you're planning to be around home for a few days?"

"Well, I don't know. Why?" How many times was the son of a bitch gonna say give me a call. He was about to shit in his pants!

"Oh, I was just wondering how to get in touch if we needed you."

"My office usually can reach me. Just call me here. Have a good day, Chief."

"You, the same." The line finally went dead.

Desperately fighting for control, Trip made a dash for the john, dropping his trousers as he went. Just as he was turning to seat himself on the toilet, his control gave way completely.

When the initial rush had passed, Trip looked down to assess the damage and saw he was standing in a sea of bright red blood.

"Oh, God, don't let me die," he cried out in anguish, suddenly cold with fear.

Before the full impact of the horror hit him...blood began spewing from his rectum again.

When the second wave finally subsided, he reached across to the phone on the bathroom wall and weakly pushed the intercom button. "Dodie, get Dr. Scott in here right away."

"What's wrong, Mr. Graham? Are you all right?"

"No...goddamn it, Dodie, NO, I'm not all right. Get Dr. Scott NOW!"

In less than a half-minute, he heard Dodie come into the office. "Mr. Graham, are you OK? Can I come in there?"

"No, stay out! Where's that fucking Ed Scott? Did you get him? Goddamn it, if he's not here call 911...I need help." He started gushing blood again. "Hurry, goddamn it!"

"Dr. Scott is on his way. Oh, Mr. Graham...what can I do? What's wrong?" She peeked around the corner, afraid to come closer. Then he heard her say, "Oh, thank God, Dr. Scott. He's in there."

"Jeezus H. Christ!" Scott exclaimed when he looked in the door. "Dodie, call maintenance and get me all the towels you can find. Hurry! And get Linda Nunnelly up here. Quick, now."

By the time Dodie got back, the violent cramping of his bowel had eased and Ed Scott was helping him step free of his clothes. Trip felt weak all over. When he looked down he was standing in a sea of blood. His clothes and the bathroom floor were a complete disaster.

Please, God, I'm too fucking young to die...

When the bleeding finally stopped, Scott and Nunnelly helped him out of his clothes and cleaned him up. They dressed him in clean clothes from his office closet and moved him to the sofa.

The entire episode had lasted perhaps twenty minutes.

Trip had no more gotten seated than he bolted upright and stumbled into the john and threw up in the sink. It was almost nothing but phlegm and alcohol at first, but he kept retching and the clear liquid quickly gave way to bright red globs mixed with the other material. Soon there was nothing but red blood coming up. When the retching subsided, Scott helped him back to the sofa again.

Trip sat there trembling, soaked with cold sweat.

His granddaddy had bled to death, right here in the fucking Tower.

The housekeeping staff had already begun mopping up, putting the foul-smelling towels in a heavy-duty plastic garbage bag.

Edward Scott had been a combat doctor, so this was pretty much a non-event in his life experience. When the cleaning people left, Scott cleared the room so he could talk to Trip alone.

"Your vital signs are OK. The blood pressure is not too bad considering you lost a little blood."

"Do I need a transfusion?"

"No...no, you didn't lose that much blood. It looked a lot worse than it was." It was a weak effort, but Scott smiled for the first time. "Just the same, I think it would be a good idea to get you in the hospital for a few days. You need some fluids and good food. We need to get you dried out. You look dehydrated. How much are you drinking...I mean on a daily basis? It would probably be a damn good idea to replace your electrolytes I.V."

"No way! If you say I'm basically OK, then to hell with the hospital. I'll go home and go to bed."

Ed Scott ignored him. He went to the door and called the nurse back into the room.

"Call the hospital and get an ambulance. Tell them to prepare the VIP suite on four south." Scott gave crisp instructions to the nurse.

"No, goddamn it, wait." Trip protested weakly, "I don't want to go to the hospital. C'mon, Ed...cut me some slack, for chris-sake."

"My god, man, did you see all that blood? Normal people don't shit and puke an ocean of red blood every day. What the hell's the matter with you? Are you crazy?"

"I won't argue that point. But you just said I need some rest and good food. I can get that at home." Trip was feeling stronger now. He was determined not to go to the hospital. Still, he was badly shaken. "What caused all that? Is it going to happen again?"

"If you don't quit drinking, worse than that is going to happen. I want to get you in the hospital for a few days to do some tests. Your liver appears to be in bad shape. Really bad shape. This is serious." He turned to Linda again and directed her to make the call.

"NO...NO...goddamn it, I'm not going anywhere until I hear

more about what you just said. What about my liver? Just tell me what you're saying. What just happened to me? That was scary as hell." Pleading now, Trip put his hand on the doctor's arm.

Ed Scott relented and pulled the desk chair over and sat down facing Trip, who was lying on the sofa. He had raised himself momentarily on one elbow to protest.

"Well at least you're sober enough to be scared. How much have you had to drink today? You smell like a distillery and it's only...it's not yet three o'clock. Are you drinking every day like this?"

"What kind of tests?" Trip avoided the question.

"All kinds of tests. But mainly I want to draw some blood. I want to see what your liver enzymes look like. From what I can feel of your liver with you lying down, you have some cirrhotic changes. How old are you? Thirty-six...thirty-seven? My god, do you want to die before you're forty? It's all pretty complicated, but what just happened is that your liver was on alcohol overload. It short-circuited its blood supply into the large intestine. It's a common thing in advanced alcoholism." The doctor looked him straight in the eye.

"Are you calling me an alcoholic, for chrissake?"

"Well, how much do you drink every day? I'll bet you can't remember a day when you didn't have a few drinks." Scott was clearly in no mood to kid around.

"Well, I do have a beer or two most days after work and sometimes a cocktail before dinner. Nothing to get excited about..." Trip denied the accusation. "I'm not a heavy drinker."

"Yes, you are. Linda, get a Vacutainer set-up and let's draw a Multi-36, make a slide, and get a lavender top for a CBC with diff and pull a couple of greenstoppers just for the hell of it. Have 'em do a complete liver profile—stat. Let's see where we stand with this thing." He turned back to Trip. "When was the last time you had a good physical?"

"Oh, I don't know exactly. A couple of years, maybe. Look at me, I'm healthy as a horse. I play golf three or four times a week. I feel great." He blustered defensively, but the worry showed through his voice.

"You don't look great. People don't shit a tub full of blood and feel great. Who the hell do you think you're fooling? Open your mouth and say a-a-ahh." The doctor was busy doing things with a little flashlight all the while he was talking. He took Trip's hands, pressed hard on his fingernails and looked at both sides of them intently. Then, without a word he looked at his eyes. "You're a little yellow, how long have you been that way?"

"What the hell are you talking about?" He didn't like all this poking around. It made him feel cornered. He really needed a fucking drink.

The nurse came back and before he could protest she had produced a tourniquet and stuck a needle in his arm and was slipping little tubes in and out of the plastic holder as they filled up with his blood. When she finished, she wiped his arm with a gauze sponge and wrote his name on the tubes before she packed up the little tray and left.

"How're ya feeling?" The doc suddenly softened his tone and showed concern for his patient.

"A little shaky. But otherwise OK, I think." Trip smiled bravely. "Let me rest here for awhile and I'll get dressed and go home and go to bed. I'm sure I'm OK to drive. Let's forget the hospital nonsense. I'll be in good hands at home." Trip earnestly pleaded his case. "What good would come of my being in the hospital?"

"Do you understand you can't drink any more alcohol? None. And I'm afraid you might convulse when you start to withdraw from the alcohol. You could die if someone isn't there who knows what to do. Not many people realize it, but alcohol withdrawal is far more dangerous than any of the other drugs. Contrary to the popular movie versions of withdrawal, heroin and cocaine addicts don't die from withdrawal. They just wish they were dead." The doctor was not being so insistent now. Trip felt like he was winning his plea.

What was all this bullshit about dying from not drinking? Hell's bells, he was about to die to have one.

"What if I found someone to stay with you at home for a couple of days? You're going to feel pretty rocky, and I want to give you some drugs to help you through all this."

"Come on, doc, let's not be so goddamn melodramatic. I'll go home after I rest awhile. I'll go to bed and stay there until I get through the hangover. It's OK, I promise. Maybe you could stop by in the morning?"

"Is Marilee at home?" The doctor reached for the phone.

"No...no, she's in New York. Quit worrying, I feel better now."

"Well, let me think about it. I'll draw these drapes and you can rest here on the couch for awhile and we'll see. I'll check on you in an hour." He went to the wet bar and got a glass of water and handed Trip two little white pills that looked like saccharin tablets. "Here, phenobarb. Take 'em."

Trip watched as Scott drew the drapes and darkened the room and then came back to where he was lying and looked down at him with great concern. "Get a nap. I'll be back in an hour or so. We'll see how you are then."

Trip waited a full five minutes after the doctor left before he got up and slowly made his way over to the wet bar and poured himself a stiff drink of vodka. One wouldn't hurt. The doctor didn't understand. He had cleaned up his act before. He knew how to handle it. A little hair of the dog helped take the edge off. You just didn't quit cold turkey.

Trip drank the straight shot of vodka without taking the glass from his mouth. He fixed another short one and hurriedly drank it down. Carefully putting the bottle back on the shelf, he rinsed the glass and went back to the sofa and sat on the edge for a moment. He was feeling pretty shaky all right, so he just sat there for a few minutes until he could feel the liquor start to hit him.

All that talk about dying? He glanced into the bathroom and remembered the huge pile of bloody towels. Involuntarily, he shuddered.

He wasn't taken in by all the talk about dying. Doctors were a melodramatic lot. One thing for certain, he wasn't going home until Marilee was safely on her way to New York. And his mother had to be kept out of this. She was enough trouble already with her preaching at him all the time. Dodie could be trusted, but Doctor Scott had to be told to keep his mouth shut. There was no way he was going to have a nurse hanging around the house either.

The pills and booze had started to do their work, so he stretched out on the sofa. In his drugged state, he remembered that the Chief had said something about a torn half of a matchbook cover with his phone number on it.

There was a torn matchbook in the articles he had gotten rid of this afternoon.

Did it have the name of his motel on it?

He wished he had dumped that shit individually in separate dumpsters so they would have just been unrelated articles. And he had left his calling card in the damn bag with the rest of the stuff. Dumping them all together in one bag was a pretty dumb thing to do.

The alcohol and pills were making him feel all warm inside. He worried too much. Who the hell went around digging bags out of dumpsters anyway?

And, what the hell, the damn bag was probably six feet under the bulldozers at the landfill by now. But, just to be safe, he might ride out there later and check it out.

He plumped up the pillow and was asleep almost before he closed his eyes.

CHAPTER THIRTY-NINE

DEMPSEY GEARHART SWUNG HIS LEGS CAUTIOUSLY OVER THE WALL of the dumpster and gingerly tested his footing on the blanket of notebook paper before he inched his way across and snatched up the bag.

Making sure he didn't slip on the slick surface of the flat sheets of paper, he slowly retraced his way back to the solid footing of the ramp. Without stopping to check the bag's contents, he fairly ran back down the ramp to his car.

Safely inside the car again, he caught his breath. Sheepishly, he felt a blush creeping up his neck. He'd hate to try and explain a raid on a garbage dump. If he could get out of here now without being spotted, he would give up this Mike Hammer business for good.

Scout's honor.

Now, just to make sure, before he put the car in gear, he paused just long enough to open the bag and catch a glimpse of a fancy bra.

Bingo!

The fine hairs on his neck tingled with excitement.

Feeling less foolish now, the chief pilot relaxed a little. He threw the plastic sack onto the floor behind the driver's seat and slammed the door. In a matter of seconds, he was on the road heading back to town. When he had topped the first rise, he settled back in his seat and turned on the radio.

Frigging hard rock music! He hit the button to change the station...

"...IN WASHINGTON, THE PENTAGON REPORTS NEW MISSILE STRIKES... CONGRESS QUESTIONED THE PRESIDENT'S CRY OF TERRORISM IN THE THREE-MONTH-OLD

ABORTION SHUTDOWN...ELSEWHERE IN THE CAPITAL, THERE IS GROWING SPECULATION ON THE SUICIDE OF FORMER CHIEF OF STAFF COURTLAND PIKE AND CRIES OF FOUL PLAY IN THE MYSTERIOUS DISAPPEARANCE LATE MONDAY NIGHT OF THE TWO PILOTS FROM THE ELITE WHITE HOUSE HELICOPTER UNIT...NOW THE LATEST ON THE MYSTERIOUS DEATH OF MOVIE ACTRESS EMMA CLAIRE AT A GREENSBORO CONVENTION HOTEL EARLY YESTERDAY..."

Absently, Demp switched channels again. The radio gave way to the sound of Gordon Lightfoot lamenting the plight of a poor drunk homeboy, broke and stuck outside a big city airport. *"...this ol' airport's got me down...ain't no earthly good to me...."*

In the Early Morning Rain—Lightfoot must've been reading his mail when he wrote it. Frigging song was the story of his life. Before he became Grail Chief Pilot, he'd been stranded—sometimes drunk and rain-drenched—in more goddamn jerkwater airports than he could count. It had been a long time, but, no doubt about it, he'd played that sorry-ass scene many times before.

Demp had had a harrowing, but lifesaving encounter with Alcoholics Anonymous a dozen years back. Thankfully, in the large cities in his far-flung travels, it had been relatively easy to keep his regular AA meetings away from judgmental company eyes. With Grail, it was still the same.

It had been almost six years since he had taken early retirement from his position as Deputy Chief Pilot with Pan Am and moved here from his New York base to take over the management of the extensive Grail fleet of corporate airplanes. It was a testimonial to his quiet competence as the consummate manager that Dempsey had managed to move into this community without attracting undue attention to himself and his personal life.

Luck had been with him from the outset.

Before he had moved down from New York, he had located and purchased a beautiful old farm just across the river south of town off the road to the Grail air facility. Purposefully, from that first day, he had lived a secluded private life, putting into place all

252

the mechanisms necessary to elude the prying eyes of this judgmental little southern town.

The previous director of the Grail Airfleet had overseen operations from an efficient office on the seventh floor of the Tower. In sharp contrast, Demp almost always flew the most important assignments personally, as captain of the corporate flagship.

To get back in the air and avoid getting bogged down in administrative matters, he had brought with him a crackerjack young executive-type from Pan Am to take over the orderly administration of the fleet. Always a "hands on" manager, this also freed him up to spend most of his non-flying time at the airstrip overseeing day-to-day operations.

Dempsey lived at the predatory level of the jungle, always looking for the edge. He gave little sense of real commitment to his personal relationships. Over the years, he had left behind the wreckages of two marriages, with two children from each. Each woman had been a stewardess with the airline. Before he'd moved here, there had been a trail of other women along the way he had used and discarded in the same cavalier way.

Many men, mostly fellow pilots, were on the list of those he had exploited one way or another in the advancement of his career. Yet, shrewdly, he had managed to make few enemies. He was careful in his dealings with people. Of those he used and left out in the cold, he never rubbed their noses in it. He was always circumspect to leave their dignity intact. That there had been any misuse of friendship was never a thing he left for all to see.

Then, after he had his defining encounter with AA a few years back, he'd tried to make amends to those he could.

Even so, old reputations die hard. Among those who knew him well, it was an unspoken axiom that it was a good idea not to turn one's back on Captain Gearhart. So, over the years, he had built no real resources of personal trust along the way. Nor had he made many close male friends. But, as a professional pilot, and now in the role of corporate executive as well, he enjoyed the reputation of being a no-nonsense guy, and he was fair. He was respected. Dempsey Gearhart was a man no pilot was afraid to fly with.

Above all, Demp was a private person—friendly enough, but he minded his own business.

In Colonial Hall, the Grail Tower rising over the town kept him reminded of the strictest military tradition which dictated that HQ building was always identified by the tallest flagpole. He practiced the one rule his daddy, a career officer in the old army, had taught him with regard to his personal conduct—particularly in the matter of women: *"Never fuck around the flagpole."*

The lyrics of Lightfoot's song ended as he turned into the private lane to his home.

The location of his farmhouse provided the seclusion that made his privacy possible. The farm had a neat little tenant house and barn with an equipment shed in a large cleared parcel about halfway down the road from the highway. Along with his deal for the property, Dempsey had negotiated an agreement with the tenant couple who had managed the farm. They had worked there during the twenty years prior to the previous owner's death, a scant two months before Gearhart had decided to accept the job with Grail.

It was clearly evident from Trip Graham's actions that the bag on the floor behind him was a collection of something the wimpy bastard didn't want anyone to see.

He couldn't get the glimpse of the bra out of his mind. Heart pounding, he could hardly wait to see what other little goodies the bag held. The Graham kid played fast and loose with the society broads around New York and Aspen and lately at Palm Beach. But that was not enough to have any real leverage over him. Hell, everyone knew what happened around that crowd. But around home base, around this uptight little berg, old Clayt would be highly disturbed if his alcoholic little boy was caught screwing a local lady. At the club, Dempsey had seen Betty Ruth Watts rubbing it all over Trip every chance she got. Goddamn...in all his years with the airline, he had seen a lot of women come and go, but he never saw such a horny broad in his life.

By the time he pulled into his garage and closed the door, Demp's curiosity was running wild. Without bothering to put the bag on the kitchen table, he snagged a non-alcoholic beer from the refrigerator and headed straight into his living room. Walking to the coffee table, he carefully stacked and put aside the pile of magazines to clear a space.

Setting the beer on a folded paper towel and taking care not to let the articles be scattered about, Demp dumped the entire contents of the bag onto the wide surface of the table. The swimsuit and the bra and panties were on top.

Pay dirt. The little shit wanted to cover up an affair.

He sat down at the table and took a sip of the non-alky beer before he picked up the bra and examined the label.

Rodeo Drive?

– Sunny California?

Expensive. Certainly not a K-Mart shopper this one.

Placing the bra aside, he picked up the brown paper lunch bag.

Jeezus...heavy shit. Crack cocaine.

He was onto real trouble here...bet on that.

Heart pounding now, Demp refolded the top of the bag and put it with the bra.

Instinctively, he avoided touching any of the articles inside the brown lunch bag. Reading all that Mike Hammer shit had taught him that the brown paper would not hold a print.

Hmmm? Now that he thought about it, Spillane had been a goddamnn fighter pilot.

His attention wandered to the leather luggage tag on the airline tote bag.

Easy...careful.

He took a pencil from the end table beside him and turned the tag.

EMMA CLAIRE! NEWPORT BEACH!

The car radio said she was dead.

His heart did another flip.

Trip Graham and Emma Claire?

Thoughts racing, he took a sip of beer, stood up and walked over to the window and lit a little black cigar. What was he on to?

If he didn't call the police right now, technically he was committing a crime. This could be a real can...or bag...of worms. There would be no excuses for that in a courtroom. But who would know just when...or where he had found this stuff? And...in the final analysis...who besides Trip or the old man would ever need to know? Obviously they wouldn't tell.

Besides, Trip might have a perfectly innocent explanation.

No way, José...he'd bet on that.

The sneaky little shit had gone to far too much trouble to get rid of it.

CHAPTER FORTY

WAITING ALL MORNING FOR CLAYT'S CALL, Glee was not in the best of moods. At the moment she was doing some serious self-recrimination about her latest little adventure with flyboy Dempsey Gearhart.

Men...they'd always been her downfall.

Her appetites were clearly getting out of hand again.

Clayt's call shortly before 10 A.M. telling her he was going to be late was the only good thing that had happened to her so far today.

Up until then, the morning had been a disaster.

The main problem had been getting rid of Dempsey Gearhart. The pilot had taken his own good time in leaving. She had tried her best to get him to go on back last night, so she could have plenty of time to clean up her place and make damn sure there was no telltale evidence of his comings and goings. The awful odor of his goddamn little black cigars was the worse part. She had every window in the place wide open and had already sprayed twice with Lysol disinfectant.

No more! This was it! Studly Doright would never see the inside of the new Widow's Walk condo at Starfish Cay. She'd made up her mind.

She had known all along she would have to break it off with Gearhart sooner or later. Truth was, she should never have let him take her to bed in the first place. Still, she hated to think of losing him. God, the man was a walking, talking, hard-on. Sometimes it was a long time in between Clayt's infrequent trips and a girl had her needs. Might as well admit it, the flying stallion had kept her sane.

She fretted over what she was going to do about the man problem once she moved into the new condo at Widow's Walk. Until the relationship died a natural death, seeing Dempsey now at her new address would be impossible. They had around-the-clock security at Starfish Cay Club. Every person coming and going who wasn't a registered property owner was logged in and out and had to be OK'd by a resident owner.

From now on, they would probably have to meet at a local hotel. That, in itself, would probably cause him to lose interest. No matter how independent the Lone Eagle pretended to be, she knew he loved his nice cushy job with Grail. He didn't want to do anything to jeopardize that. He had almost as much to lose as she did. At least she had that as leverage.

She sighed. As much as she hated to think about it, the flying stallion's days were definitely numbered. It wasn't going to be easy, though. She didn't want to think about those lonely nights. She certainly didn't want him pissed at her; he could wreck everything.

By early afternoon, Glee's outlook improved.

Tomorrow, she would be moving.

Quarter 'til two. Clayt would probably be landing about now. He might already be heading into town to his business meeting.

The movers had already packed her belongings. She looked around at the stacks of cartons. They'd promised her they would be here tomorrow no later than eight. And they assured her it would take no more than an hour to load.

She wasn't taking much more than her clothes, her books and tapes and CDs and other personal things. The furnishings stayed.

She was shucking this place like a bad habit.

If she played her cards right, the new condo was only the tip of the iceberg. There was a lot more where that came from. She had come a long way from that morning she had shown up late for the interview with the powerful Mr. G. Not bad for a little more than a year's work. She was moving right along.

The phone rang at a minute before two. She was disappointed when it turned out to be Dory Wannamaker.

"What are you going to do when you move out to snob heaven? Don't you have to have clearance from a property owner to get in and out of the place? How are you going to sneak the Daredevilof-the-Airways in and out? The trunk of your car maybe? Now that's an idea. But I warn you, if Daddy Warbucks finds out, you better be sure there are no escape clauses in the title to that condo...or you'll be out on the street." Best friend Dory was the High Priestess of Doom.

"C'mon Dory, be nice, now. Your claws are showing." Glee was used to Dory's brusque honesty. She had come to regard it as a very valuable asset. "Besides, if Clayton ever even considers dumping me, I'm sure he'll know enough to think twice before he risks having someone spill the beans to ol' Mabel honey, back in Heavenly Hall, Nawth Kalina."

"Better be careful. Men who have that kind of power don't intimidate easily by anyone, much less women like us. They hire and fire a hundred women like us every day. We're a dime a dozen, babe. We have just been a little smarter...a lot more practical...a lot less starry-eyed, infinitely more cold-blooded and a lot luckier than most. But just think about it. How'd ya' like to start over and find another Clayt? Honeychile, there ain't another Clayt in your future. You're twenty-eight and right now you look twenty. But one morning soon, you're going to wake up and look in the mirror and reach for the phone to call the Greenbrier Spa to book a makeover. It happens. What then? Can you really hack it as a real estate agent?"

"Well...come on now, Dory, ease off of me. I was having a good day. I'm about to become the legal owner of a condominium in Widow's Walk at Starfish Cay Club, Florida. Donald Trump is rumored to have tried to buy the whole damn island. Remember, it was featured in *Town and Country* last year, and they did a feature in *Coastal Living* not long ago. To sum it up, I'm finally about to become somebody. Glee Law-Craige, daughter of the famous, or infamous, Jim Garth Law, TV evangelist and faith healer of Granger's Corner, Kansas, is about to become somebody. Some-frigging-body. Understand? Don't rain on my parade, Dory. As for Dempsey Gearhart, I've thought about all that. I've got to clean up my act. I know it."

"OK, baby, I didn't mean to be a wet blanket. It's just that you worry me. I'm serious. You need to forget the flying ace. I don't care how good he is in the sack. He ain't worth it. Cut him loose. He's trouble. Listen, Glee, I'm your best friend...you need to play this as straight as you can. Do you hear me?" More a statement than a question, Dory's tone was one of concern, not admonition. "I wouldn't be pushing my luck with Daddy Warbucks...you wouldn't want to back him into a corner. Just be real nice and take what you can get. You ain't never gonna be the next Mrs. Graham, you know that, don't you?"

"Well, stranger things could happen. Suppose ol' Mabel honey should just up and die? That might change things," Glee said without conviction.

"If Mabel-honey dropped dead today, Clayton Massie Graham still wouldn't marry you. He couldn't take you back to Clone-yall Hawl, Nawth Kalina, for godsake. Men like Clayton Graham don't marry their mistresses, Glee. Why should they?"

"He loves me, Dory. He really does." Glee wanted desperately to believe that. "How many men buy their mistresses a condominium worth a cool half-a-million? Does that sound like he would just trade me in on someone else?"

"Don't kid yourself, kiddo. For him, a half-mil is just the number five followed by five zeroes written by his lawyer on a check transferring money from one business account to another. What do you want to bet he doesn't even sign the check?" Dory asked smugly. "For him, love is something you feel for a yacht, or a custom-made car...or one of his fast airplanes."

"Dory, you're wrong. Clayt's a fine man who has never known anyone who really cared about him before. Not like I do. I'm really special. He loves me, Dory. He really does. You don't understand...." A beeping signal indicated another call was coming in on the line. "Uh oh, I've got a call...got to go. I'll call tomorrow when I get a chance. Bye...."

Glee depressed the phone button. "Hello?..."

"Hi, baby...I'm at the realtor's office...I'll be there in about an hour...don't start without me." Clayton Graham laughed.

"I will, if you don't hurry...."

"OK...see you in an hour." Clayt made a kissing sound and hung up.

Glee got up and started to undress. She wanted to shower again and shampoo her hair. She wasn't sure it wasn't her imagination playing tricks, but she couldn't get the odor of Dempsey's cigars out of her nostrils.

The phone rang again. Clayton must have forgotten to tell her something.

"Hello?..."

"Obviously, you can talk or you wouldn't have picked up," Dempsey said with a little snort. "Have you heard from Daddy Warbucks yet?"

"Yes, he just called from Starfish. He's on his way. Why did you call? I don't want you to call like this anymore. It's too dangerous and I'll be goddamn if I'm going to blow this set-up. You know you have a lot to lose yourself, Dempsey."

Suddenly, she was angry...and afraid...scared to death, really.

"OK. I know. But wait 'til you hear what I just stumbled onto...then maybe you won't worry so much. I think Trip Graham just presented us both with a nice little insurance policy. He would shit pure blood if he knew what I just found out." He paused to let the words sink in.

"What're you talking about? Quit playing games...I don't have much time." She was in no mood for nonsense.

"Listen. You're not going to believe this. Did you hear about that movie star being found dead in a Greensboro motel?" Dempsey sounded excited.

"Huh? Oh yeah...Emma Claire...been on the news all morning...overdose, like Belushi, they said. What about it?"

"Well, I am sitting here looking at two bags full of evidence that links Mr. Trip Graham with the Claire woman...clothes with her labels, her hotel key...about six thousand bucks worth of cocaine...the whole nine yards," Dempsey gloated, smugly.

"Oh? Well...so what? Trip Graham is a notorious womanizer."

"Listen goddamnit...this puts him with Emma Claire in Greensboro. Don't ya' get it?"

"Well...Jeezuschrist....my god! I don't know...." Glee stammered, confused. "Are you sure? I mean sometimes things aren't what they seem...."

"Sure? I'm positive. He tried to get rid of all of it. Only I saw him and followed him and got it after he dumped it and took off. Sugarbritches, unless I miss my guess, we got the whole Graham family by the balls." Dempsey crowed like a barnyard rooster.

"Oh, Demp, baby! Do you really think so? That would really be something." Her mind raced ahead. Clayton would never let anything happen to Trip—the Graham name. Still, this was danger-ous. "What about the law? I mean isn't it illegal to conceal evi-dence? Remember Belushi...didn't they convict that poor woman of...of murder...." The word stuck in her throat.

"Well no...probably not murder, but bad enough...felony drug death...some such nonsense. Who knows? Certainly a messy situa-tion at best. Something the Grahams would do almost anything to conceal, I'll bet my ass on that." His tone was triumphant. "Looks like after you get your condo tomorrow, you'll have an ace in the hole if the old fart decides to dump you later."

"Judas, this is really scary. Please be careful. Wha'cha gonna do?" It was all too sudden for Glee to comprehend.

"Well, I'm not going to do anything for the moment. Just wait and see what develops in the investigation and then maybe the next step will be easier to figure out. Try to follow the news on TV and that way you'll know as much as I do. Give me a call after you get moved and know how you can be reached. Maybe you can feel a little better about seeing little ol' me, now...huh, baby? Well, have a good evening." He hung up before she could say anything else.

Heart racing, Glee tried to let it all sink in. God, what would it be like to have power over a man like Clayton Graham? She would never have to worry about anything again.

Whoa, Glee, she thought, this is *déjà vu*. A few years back she'd made the same mistake in Richmond with the FFV Craige clan. Be careful. Dory was right. You don't ever have complete power over a man like Clayton Graham. Still, a little leverage was a nice thing to think about.

She had the condo in the bag now. Who could tell what the future would hold. It looked like she was going to have a very relaxed evening.

All of a sudden, the phantom smell of Dempsey's cigar smoke had vanished. If she put her mind to it, she was sure she could figure out some way to keep the flyboy on beck and call.

The Lone Eagle really might prove to be a handy man to have around.

CHAPTER FORTY-ONE

THE MEDICAL DIRECTOR OF GRAIL CORPORATION WAS CONCERNED—
gravely concerned. Edward O. Scott, M.D. sat in the Doctor's
Library and studied the computer printout of Trip's lab results.

The situation was worse than he had suspected...

Far worse!

The rather lengthy data was neatly printed on a sheaf of three
identically formatted forms, all clearly laid out with little spaces
blocked off and appropriately labeled to report the results for the
multiplicity of thirty-five sophisticated diagnostic laboratory tests
on human blood, urine and other specimens taken from the human
body.

The results of all the routine chemistries, the electrolytes, some
of the routine enzymes and the CBC and urinalysis were all completed and reported in their proper boxes on the first page.

On the following two pages—in the blank space which comprised the middle third of the form and was reserved for the free-
form reporting of the less routine, more exotic tests—there
appeared a seemingly endless list of results from the exhaustive battery of tests Doctor Scott had ordered on Trip Graham following
his rectal hemorrhage at The Tower earlier in the day.

Although many of these special tests were reported as RESULTS
PENDING or TO FOLLOW or—if the test was exotic and had to
be referred to an outside laboratory—SENT TO REFERENCE, it
made no real difference at the moment. There was no doubt about
the primary diagnosis—no doubt at all.

Trip was suffering from full-blown acute alcoholic hepatitis,
most likely with permanent liver damage.

The final assessment of the far-reaching effects of Trip's
advanced alcoholism would be better assessed later, of course,

when the complete results were available...but for the time being, that was a matter of only secondary consideration. The immediate course of action was clear. It was essential that Trip Graham be admitted to a hospital for intensive treatment without delay.

After he had gone over the pages for perhaps the third time, Ed Scott sighed, picked up the phone and dialed the code for an outside line. Then he dialed in an eleven-digit number.

"Psychiatry, Miss Rowe. May I help you?"

"This is Doctor Scott, the medical director at Graham International, Ltd. in Colonial Hall. Is Doctor Curtis in?" He tapped his pencil on the table and waited.

After talking to what seemed the entire roster of secretarial and administrative staff at the large university medical school, Ed finally heard the familiar sound of Ewing Curtis' voice. Their friendship went way back. "Ed, is that you? What the hell are you up to, my boy? Besides getting rich and lowering your goddamn golf handicap? Some of us have to work for a living...heal the sick and all that bullshit...you know about that, do you boy?..."

"Don't give me that 'great healer' feces, Ewing...I can't stand it. I need help with a capital 'H'."

Ed quickly sketched Trip's history, then asked, "Can we get him admitted at Holly Hall, I mean like right now, in the next twenty-four hours?"

"No problem...I'll make the call. It's not quite seven...can you get him there tonight? We'll take him anytime...just call and let 'em know when you leave Colonial Hall so they'll be expecting you. You know the routine."

"Well, tonight is probably an unreasonable expectation...still, I can try. What do I need to do? Tonight...or tomorrow...whenever...I'll be coming along with him ASAP."

Ed Scott listened carefully, jotted some notes, hung up and headed out.

No use in putting it off. Trip was going to put up a fight.

Trip paced the floor and counted the chimes of the grandfather clock.

Seven.

Ed Scott would be snooping around here any minute, no doubt. Time for just another short one...just a quickie?

Only had two...well...maybe three...since this afternoon at The Tower.

One more little shooter couldn't hurt.

Trip quickly downed the shooter of vodka and a diet pill when he heard the doorbell ring.

There is no substitute for experience. Before he was halfway across the room, Ed Scott suspected Trip had been drinking. He seemed hyper...agitated...just a tad too bright...edgy, maybe? *Something?*

"Well, well, Ed. How do I look? Lots better huh? Took a good nap and Mrs. Sanford made me eat a bowl of soup...thinks chicken soup can fix the world."

"Well, you seem to be in good spirits, anyway." Ed Scott wondered just how much alcohol the younger Graham had had since this afternoon.

"Can I get you anything? I mean just because I can't have a drink doesn't mean you can't. Doesn't bother me...not at all...I'm serious. I mean it. Go ahead if you feel like it."

"I'll fix myself a glass of that tonic water...can I get you a Coke or anything?" the physician asked politely as he moved to the wet bar.

"Naah, I'm fine. Be right as rain in a day or two. Too much life in the fast lane lately. Just nature's way of telling me to slow down, eh, Ed?"

"Well, it's nature's way of saying you've got to do more than just slow down. You've got to quit drinking...and smoking pot and...oh, yeah...no more amphetamines and cocaine..."

"Come on, cut out the bullshit, Ed. You know goddamn well I don't do dope. What're you trying to pull here?"

The doctor took the folded lab report from his inside jacket pocket. Without a word, he handed it to Trip. He fixed a glass of tonic with some ice and took a seat on the sofa facing him across the coffee table. Sipping silently on the tonic water, he watched

Trip's face for a reaction.

"Well, what a crock of shit! Positive for cannabis...and cocaine, for chrissake. Where would I get any cocaine? Somebody either made this up or the reports got switched."

"Would you care to volunteer to have the police doctor repeat this just to get to a point of honesty between us? That way we can start this conversation where it belongs, on the footing of stark reality. There's no mistake in anything. You've been using drugs. But that's not the issue here." The physician leaned forward and set his glass on the coffee table.

"Wha-a...what do you mean?" The bluster was gone from Trip's manner now.

"I mean, look on the second page where it says Liver Profile. Look at the list of tests...the results are marked 'H' or 'L' to indicate HIGH or LOW. There's not a single normal in the whole list. Your enzymes are off the scale. No wonder you appeared slightly jaundiced this afternoon. You're in bad shape, Trip. We've got to get you in treatment...it's like a hospital."

"Oh shit, give me a break. I'll just stop drinking and take vitamins and...what'll they do in a hospital anyway? Is there a cure for the liver problem?" Trip knew about treatment...he'd heard all the horror stories from his idle friends. Betty Ford graduates, a lot of 'em.

"Treatment, but no cure...it's not that simple. Withdrawal's dangerous in your condition. Even if you could go white knuckle, no telling what would happen if you go cold turkey. And afterward, you're gonna need a lot of help just to stay clean. Grail sends employees to treatment all the time. I've got it all set up...as a matter of fact, if we can get in touch with Dempsey Gearhart we could fly you to Pinehurst tonight. Anyway, tonight or not, you've got to go no later than the first thing tomorrow morning. I'll go along and keep you company while you're admitted."

"Whoa, hold on, I ain't gone anywhere yet...you can't just bulldoze me."

Ed stood up immediately and shrugged, "OK, suit yourself. I'll call your father and let him handle it. You're a big boy. If you want to die before you're forty, I can't stop you. But I'm serious. You can't ever have another drink of alcohol as long as you live. And if you don't stop now, you're not going to have a lot of time to reconsider. How many drinks have you had since I left you this afternoon...just four short hours ago?"

"None...nada...zero...you know you told me not to..." Trip looked back at the lab report to avoid having to look the doctor in the eye.

"Oh, cut the bullshit, Trip. You're only kidding yourself. How about it? Want me to call Dempsey Gearhart and see if he can fly us up in the chopper? It's not far. Take maybe a half-hour after we leave the pad?"

"Look, I'm not going to some hick joint. If I go, I'm going to Betty Ford...or the place in California where those actors Robert Downey, Jr. and Ben Affleck went."

"Oh, sure. The tabloid media camps on the doorsteps of places like that. Do you want your name...and Grail...all over the front page of the *Wall Street Journal*...ever see the shit they run on poor Liz Taylor in the *Enquirer*? Holly Hall is one of the best...and it's private...quite discreet. It's right near Pinehurst. I know the people well. It's already set up...they're expecting us."

"Well, maybe...but hell no, no way...not tonight...maybe in a couple of days. I've got a lot of things I have to take care of before I can do it. You understand."

"Suit yourself...I'm going over to the big house and talk to Clayt." Ed had coerced a few people to seek medical treatment in his day, and he knew better than to give in, or let up on the pressure. Dealing with addicts was different from dealing with a diabetic or someone who had heart disease. With addicts, the denial was like a stone wall. The very nature of their disease kept telling them they would be OK...that they could do it without help. He reached out and took the report from Trip's hand and turned and walked for the door.

"Wait just a goddamn minute...don't go over there now. Besides...Clayt's not there...he's gone to Jacksonville. Come on, let's talk this over." Trip followed him into the hall.

"There's nothing to talk about until you give me a definite time to leave for the hospital." Ed took out his cell phone. "I'll tell Mabel I'm coming over. She'll tell me how to reach Clayton."

"Goddamn it, Ed, stop. What do want me to do? Where is this place? How long do I have to be there? Come on back here and tell me what I'm up against." Trip grabbed the doctor by the upper arm and turned him around. "Be reasonable, ol' buddy, give me a chance...you'll see."

A half-hour later, Trip was still stalling around, trying to con him that he should at least be given a chance to do it on his own.

A total waste of time, Ed Scott mused, driving away. He should have known better.

Trip watched Ed's car move away before he went back in and closed the door.

What Ed said was mostly bullshit anyway...Ed Scott was just trying to scare him...well, maybe...that lab report did look bad. But he wasn't buying all that bull...Ed Scott didn't scare him.

Well...maybe...upset him a little.

Not about the drinking though. What the hell...he could quit...who needed it anyway?

Thank God his daddy was out of town or he'd already be on the way to that fucking hospital! The call from the Greensboro cop kept nagging away at him. It bothered him to remember he'd left his calling card in the pocket of the Claire bitch's jogging suit. And the hick cop's remark about the matchbook cover—that bag of evidence was damning. With Ed Scott out of his hair, it just might be a good idea to drive out to that dumpster and see if he could find that bag...he'd been in too big a hurry this afternoon.

But first just a little drink...just one couldn't hurt.

All this liver bullshit was really getting on his nerves.

CHAPTER FORTY-TWO

Norris lay beside Marilee, quietly musing.

"*Be the giver*" had always been his credo. That way you didn't owe anybody any damn thing.

Things...give only things. A rule to live by?

It had always worked for him.

Never give yourself. That part belonged to you.

Take it or leave it. If you gave nothing of yourself then there would be nothing to go back for, if either party walked away.

Was it different now?...it all felt different somehow.

Vulnerable! Made him very uneasy.

Uneasy?...about what?

He lay there pondering.

What did he have to lose? That one was easy.

Just about every-goddamn-thing.

Anyway, it was too late now; he couldn't help himself. He wanted this strong, intelligent, sensitive—not to mention, beautiful—woman. She was really the only glimpse of a real woman he had ever had. Maybe would ever have.

And, besides, she thought he was just about goddamn perfect.

He drifted off again.

Finally, when he woke, it was nearly ten and dark outside. On the bed beside him, Marilee was still sleeping quietly. The soft glow of the hall light filtered into the room, glinting tiny filaments of a tropic sunset in her hair. Quietly, he slipped into a raw silk robe, went into the kitchen and dialed the phone. There was a crackle of static before the ringing started.

"Information. What city please?"

"District of Columbia...Washington Hospital Center..." He jotted the number. There was a tiny popping sound as he was hanging up.

270

Norris unscrewed the phone's mouthpiece. It had been a long time since his covert ops training, but everything looked on the up and up. He shrugged self-consciously. He'd been reading too many spy novels lately.

He replaced the mechanism, dialed the number and requested Patient Information.

"Mr. Bradley's out of surgery...in ICU...still unconscious but stable...condition guarded."

Hang on, Tom ol' sport...hang on.

He hung up, considered a minute then dialed again.

"Tobias Bradley..." a ragged edge of stress tinged Tom's father's voice.

"This is Norris, sir...I just called the hospital...they say, 'so far, so good'."

"Yeah...damn surgery went OK...but it's still touch and go...."

"How about you, sir?...you all right?"

"Yeah...considering. The whole thing has gone weird...I guess you heard."

"No...I don't understand...."

"The District Police have denied they were engaged in a high-speed chase...."

"Oh, well...they just don't want to admit there's egg on their face...." Before he could finish, the Chief stopped him.

"No, no...more'n that...all the witnesses have vanished into thin air."

"Hmmm..." He really didn't know what to say. This was coming at him too fast.

"And that's not all. When I got home from the hospital, there was a message on Tom's machine to call a reporter for the *Post*— apparently Tom had asked about a Colonel Charles Smith, that chopper pilot for the White House—something to do with the crazy rumors going around up here about Marilee Graham's beach party down in North Carolina in April. Tom told me you had talked about it Monday at DCA...Do you have any idea why Tom was interested in a White House helicopter pilot?"

"Uhmm?...Tom mentioned something about the President flying down to Lejeune to go marlin fishing that week...but I wouldn't give it any sort of significance."

"Don't you think that's weird?"

"What? The President fishing? He better *fish—or cut bait!* His offshore drilling tycoon buddy was hauled back before the Grand Jury today. The Court will frown on the Oval Office's claim of executive immunity. He better watch out...war or not, Congress can still impeach his ass."

"No...no...I'm not talking about his marlin fishing. Haven't you been watching the news? That White House chopper pilot and his first officer just disappeared off the face of the earth."

CHAPTER FORTY-THREE

As soon as Ed Scott left Trip, he called Mabel on the car phone.

Mabel had decided to retire early and was reading in her bedroom when the phone rang. Still in her robe, she ushered Ed into the keeping room. A young black girl was setting the coffee service on the antique sideboard.

"How do like your coffee, Ed?"

"Black for me."

The girl quickly poured the coffee and brought the cups. "Will there be anything else, ma'am?"

"Not for the moment, Pansy...unless Dr. Scott would like something to eat." Mabel looked to Ed Scott.

"No thanks, I'm fine."

Mabel turned to Ed as soon as they were alone. "What's this all about? You scared me half to death on the phone."

"I'm sorry I frightened you, but this is damned serious. If we don't do something right away, it's going to be too late. Where's Clayton? He needs to hear this."

"He's in Florida. Flew down this morning. He won't be back until Saturday," Mabel replied. "I don't even know how to call him right at the moment...I'm sure Griff knows...he's flying down there tomorrow on some business deal." She looked absently at her watch, trying to focus on what was happening.

"Well, you really need to get him on the phone tonight. He needs to come back up here, right away." Ed was obviously trying to impress her with the urgency of the matter. But to Mabel, the entire thing seemed a bit farfetched.

"Aren't you overreacting?...really, Ed? Trip, an alcoholic...I mean, come on now? Sure, I know he's been drinking way too

273

much lately...Clayt and I talked about it last night. And, what's all this about a hemorrhage this afternoon? That certainly sounds serious...but then it certainly couldn't have been too serious. You said on the phone he was home. That doesn't sound like an emergency. He looks healthy as a horse." Mabel struggled to understand.

"To look at him you'd never believe it. But in all my years of practice, I've never seen anyone his age any worse. Who would think a man in his thirties could be that far gone...his liver is severely damaged already. Trip can't ever drink again. We need to get him to a treatment center as soon as possible...tomorrow morning at the latest. Look at this. See where it says GGT? Gammaglutamyltransaminase. It's an enzyme. Normal is zero. A healthy liver doesn't make GGT. The liver only puts out this enzyme when it's being insulted by heavy doses of alcohol...or other hepatotoxins. And when it's severely damaged...like in cirrhosis...which is what Trip has—Alcoholic Cirrhosis. To give you a frame of reference: a value of twenty-five or maybe fifty would be what a physician experienced in treating alcoholics and addicts would call a 'one-martini GGT.' Do you see what Trip's GGT is?" Ed held the report steady right in front of her nose.

"Eight hundred and thirty-five!" Mabel said in a whisper. She definitely got the point.

As the impact of what Ed was saying finally sank in, Mabel sat down. Suddenly dizzy, she tightly gripped the arm of the chair.

Ed Scott stepped immediately to her side and put his hand on her shoulder. "Are you OK?"

"Well, no...I'm not exactly what you'd call OK." Absently, she reached up and patted his hand. "Sit down and explain all this to me again. I don't understand about the hemorrhage? Couldn't that just be an ulcer?"

Ed Scott took a sip of coffee, obviously trying to decide how to begin.

Finally, he said, "No, the hemorrhage isn't an ulcer...although I wouldn't be at all surprised if he probably turned up with one, considering the way he insults his stomach. The hemorrhage this afternoon was from his rectum and it was bright red blood. This is a common occurrence in advanced alcoholism. It's sort of complicated, but it means the liver is on overload and is refusing to accept any more of the alcohol-loaded blood to detoxify. It's like a short circuit. The portal vein conveys alcohol-loaded blood into the liver. An overload sometimes causes the liver to rebel and dump the blood directly into the large intestine and bingo...the patient starts to shoot blood out his rectum. Scary as hell when it happens to you. It's caused many a drunk to clean up his act...but it usually doesn't last. Alcoholics have a hard time admitting drinking is a problem...for them it's a solution."

"I'm sure you had a nice talk with him? At least you didn't have to put him in the hospital." Mabel still refused to grasp what the doctor was saying. "It would have been a disaster if he went to Graham Memorial drunk...we'd never live it down."

"Huh?" Ed couldn't believe Mabel was more concerned about her reputation than her son's health. "Well, now listen, just because I didn't send him to the hospital doesn't change anything...his condition is quite grave. When I checked his vital signs, it was obvious he hadn't lost enough blood to really affect his blood pressure. More often than not, this is just an early warning or is the result of an isolated episode of heavy drinking. But he did look slightly yellow...jaundiced. That made me suspicious. So, I drew some specimens of his blood and had the lab run them stat...you know?...rush them. Look at the rest of the lab report...see, right here." He took the papers from his coat again and handed them across to her. "Not only does his lab work indicate serious, acute...and chronic liver damage...but it also shows he's using other drugs...Trip can never take a drink again. Or use drugs either."

"Drugs...what kind of drugs? I told you...Trip doesn't use drugs." Mabel was adamant.

"The lab tests showed he had recently used cocaine. Recent because cocaine doesn't hang around in the blood too long in high concentrations...the marijuana level was high enough to indicate recent use, too. And he was loaded with amphetamine. This isn't something you'd find every day in the blood of most young male executives. Trip is definitely an alcoholic and certainly has used an entire pharmacopoeia of other drugs recently...the amphetamine and cocaine were almost certainly used today. Something has to be done." Ed Scott left no room for doubt in his judgment. "I just talked to him and he's stalling me...I've arranged for treatment. He could go tonight if he would agree. Will you talk to him?"

"Drugs. I refuse to believe you. I'd know if he did. I'm sure this is just an isolated thing...he just got back from a weekend in Blowing Rock yesterday...he's just been in a bad crowd and over-done things. He'll stop this. I know he will. Trip's a good boy...we just always let him have his way too much. He had a little trouble in college, but Norris Wrenn helped us get him all straightened out." Mabel was not convinced.

"I told him this afternoon he had to lay off of the booze. I cer-tainly thought when I let him talk me out of going into the hospital for a few days that spewing all that blood out of his rectum would have scared him sober for awhile at least. But when I went by the house just now, he was up and obviously had been drinking quite a bit before I got there. He denied it, of course. They usually do. I've seen the signs before. Trip is an alcoholic. He can't help it. He's going to keep on drinking unless we get him into a hospital and get him treated. He keeps trying to con me. I've got it all arranged for him to be admitted to Holly Hall...it's private...I mean super-pri-vate. So damn private nobody ever hears of it...not like some of the other treatment places where the reporters hang around looking for Liz or some pro baseball player to show up with their latest relapse." The doctor spoke with intensity. "You have to get Clayt back here from Jacksonville... can you reach him now, tonight? There's no time to lose. If something isn't done, God only knows what'll happen...nothing good, I can promise you."

"Do you really think we should bother Clayt?"

"Goddamn it, Mabel...have you heard a word...?"

"Well, yes, but...it's late. Clayton took the Learjet...you know, flew it himself. I'm sure he's dog-tired. He was up, going over some contracts with Griff at the crack of dawn. I really don't like the idea of him flying back at night. I don't even know if I can get hold of Griff to find out where he is. I'll try, but I'd rather this waited until morning. Not much can be done tonight anyway, can it?" Mabel was overwhelmed.

"Yes, damnit, everything can be done. We're wasting time. Trip's gonna fight this thing, but he won't fight Clayt. Where's Marilee? Trip raised hell when I asked him how to reach her. She has to be told right away."

"Wait a minute, Ed, not so fast. I need time to think about this," Mabel protested.

"Do you have Marilee's number in New York? I should be the one to talk to her, anyway." The doctor ignored her hesitation.

"Well...I have it somewhere. I think it's upstairs...it's unpublished. She stays with the movie actress, Sadie Bailey, when she's in New York." Mabel placed her cup down and got up. "I'll go see if I can find it."

"Where's Norris? Everyone seems to think Norris is the miracle man around here. Do you have his number handy?" the doctor asked.

"Norris...oh, you can dial him on that phone. Just push the top button. But he's in Washington...I think. Clayton was upset he went up there. He was supposed to be here to sign a contract this morning."

"OK, you go see if you can find Marilee's number and I'll try to get Agnes and see if I can get Norris while you're looking." He put his arm around Mabel's shoulder and walked her to the door. He watched until she started up the curving stairs. Then he went to the phone and listened as the automatic equipment dialed in the number. The phone picked up on the third ring.

"Wrenn residence." The voice on the other end was unmistakably black and female.

"This is Dr. Scott. May I speak to Mrs. Wrenn?"

"Just a minute please, I'll see if Miz Wrenn is here." The maid put the line on hold without waiting for his answer.

After perhaps a minute, the line came open again. "This is Agnes, Ed, how are you?"

"I'm fine, Agnes. I hope you are." He really wasn't in the mood for polite conversation. "I hate to bother you at home, but I need to get in touch with Norris. Do you know how he can be reached?"

"Well, no...he left to go to Washington this morning and then he was going on to New York, but he wasn't sure whether or not that would be tonight or tomorrow. He usually checks in with his secretary when he's out of town. If I need him and I don't know how to reach him, I call her. Do you want me to call and see if she heard from him this afternoon? Is there a problem?" Agnes was curious now.

"Uhm...no. Nothing that can't wait until tomorrow. I...it's a corporate matter I needed his help on." He dismissed the subject as if it were of no importance. "Thanks, anyway. I really shouldn't have bothered you. Hope you have a good evening."

"Are you sure? I mean it's no trouble, really." Now, Agnes didn't want to let him go.

"No, please, I shouldn't have bothered you. Thanks...and goodnight," he tried to sound as pleasant as possible as he hung up the phone.

Agnes was embarrassed. She really hadn't thought much about it before, but she usually had to go through Norris' secretary to find out where he was when he was out of town. It was downright humiliating not to know how to reach your own husband. Damn Norris! He seldom left her a number, particularly when he was in New York. On the rare occasions she had needed to reach him, she usually wound up leaving a message at Grail International where the corporation maintained a block of suites for visiting Grail executives. She had stayed there many times herself when she went to New York.

Now that she thought about it, Norris had been spending a lot of time out of town recently.

Lately, she had been thinking a lot about taking the girls up to her father's place in Virginia for the summer. Norris was gone most of the time and the girls were still young enough not to have to worry about regular school schedules. She could leave them with her mother and Tina, her brother's wife, and slip off for some shopping in Washington for a few days with Georgianna Cummings, her old classmate from Randolph-Macon.

What the hell? Why not go? What was stopping her? A few days with Georgie would be fun and it was Mother's Day, wasn't it? Norris wouldn't even notice she was gone—he really didn't relate very well to the girls, anyway. Spent more time with Marilee's son than he did with his own daughters.

There were moments when she wished she had given Norris a son. But since she'd had her tubes tied, it was too late for that now, thank God. Besides, he hardly made love to her anymore, anyway. She hardly saw him long enough to say hello anymore. Before last night, they really hadn't been to bed in...weeks, a month maybe. Might as well be the Virgin Mary...could have saved herself the operation. She hated this place. There wasn't much to do when Norris was away.

All at once, Agnes decided. She would just pack up and go tomorrow. Where was the number of the New York Grail International? She found the number and dialed without hesitation.

"Grail International. May I help you?"

"Mr. Norris Wrenn, please. He's staying in the Grail Executive Suite." Agnes spoke slowly so the clerk would understand the importance of the call. She knew how to deal with these people.

The room phone began to ring immediately. Agnes waited—no answer. After about ten rings the operator came back on the line. "I'm sorry, ma'am, Mr. Wrenn doesn't answer. Would you like his voice mail...or may I take a message?"

May I? Very good...take two goddamn giant steps.

"Please have him call his wife...at home. It's important," she replied imperiously.

"I'll turn his message light on now, ma'am. We'll relay the message as soon as he calls," the operator assured her.

"Thank you." It was all she could do to keep from slamming down the phone.

Goddamn Norris, anyway. And goddamn this place. She went to her dressing room and hauled out her suitcases and started to pack.

To hell with him. *He* could find *her* if he ever decided he wanted her.

"Is Mr. Wrenn here tonight?" the hotel operator asked the desk clerk after Agnes rang off. "I never know. Grail corporate just keeps that room open all the time for him, and the only way I know when he's in town is when he checks his messages."

"Well, your guess is as good as mine. All I do is work here and take the messages. You understand you should call the Grail Corporate Message Center and leave the message there just in case he doesn't call here," the pretty clerk reminded him.

"Oh, yes. I was just going to do that. The rich and famous have it rough, don't they?" the operator said, enviously. "We hardly ever see the famous Mr. Wrenn, but judging from his calls, he stays somewhere in this city quite a lot...wonder if he has a little something on the side?"

The young clerk gave him a wink. "Teddy, boy, don't forget who signs your paycheck."

"Huh? Oh...yeah." He smiled as he dialed the corporate message center.

Ed Scott had just hung up the phone and was helping himself to a generous serving of Wild Turkey when Mabel walked back into the room.

"Did you find the number?" he asked.

"Yes, here. I wrote it down." She held out a little slip.

"Good, let me try to get Marilee right now. Then you need to find Griff and find out how to reach Clayt." He went back to the phone and dialed in the number Mabel had given him.

The phone on the other end picked up on the first ring and Sadie's recording began, "Hello, this is me. I'm sorry I'm not here...."

Ed listened intently until he heard the recording end and waited for the little beep before he spoke. "This is Dr. Edward Scott in Colonial Hall. I'm anxious to reach Marilee Graham." Ed left the number of his cell phone and hung up.

CHAPTER FORTY-FOUR

AFTER HE TALKED TO THE HOSPITAL, Norris tried to make sense out of what Tom Bradley's father had told him. Thinking back over lunch with Tom at Old Ebbitt Grill, he couldn't shake the feeling that he'd missed something important. He finally shook his head in dismay and dialed the phone again.

"Doug Reed..." The static cleared. The voice on the other end was crisp.

"This is Norris, Doug. How are you, old sport?"

"Great, just great. Where the hell you been lately? I've missed you...and your business. What's up?"

Having Doug Reed's charter air service on a retainer to use when he didn't want his travels to become common knowledge throughout the company was a handy arrangement. Norris was frequently scouting out acquisitions and making confidential deals. Whenever possible, Doug flew him personally. They had become good friends and managed to sneak in a round of golf together on the layover trips where time was not an important factor. It had become a comfortable thing.

"I'm sorry to be so late, but I wonder if you can fly me up to Sheepshead Light tomorrow around noon? It's important. You can just drop me...and my party...and come right back. Maybe take the small jet?...we don't need to see the sights." Norris held his breath, hoping there wouldn't be a conflict. But then, Doug had never failed him.

"Well...ah...I'll have to juggle some things, but sure thing...count on me. I'll be all set and waiting. A little before noon, OK?"

"Yeah. And if I'm a little late, don't worry. I have one other thing I have to take care of in the morning and then I'll be out of here." Norris breathed a sigh of relief. He felt like a schoolboy.

"Anything special I can do?" Doug asked.

"Get someone to pack us a lunch...and just be ready. And, Doug, I'd appreciate your standing by early morning Friday to get us back," Norris added, "...and thanks, old sport."

Old sport, he mused. I haven't called anyone that since college. What's happening to me?

Was that static on the line just after Doug hung up? Norris struggled to shake off his nagging feeling of free-floating anxiety.

He consulted his little black book and dialed again.

Although this time he listened carefully, he couldn't be really sure if he heard the hum again when he picked up. The little breaks in tone could be merely static. He was used to that when he called Sheepshead. He paid no attention when it took longer for the connection.

The ring at the other end had a peculiar flat sound Norris had come to recognize as belonging to those remote, independent phone systems which were not under the aegis of all the Johnny-come-lately phone carrriers. Since Congress self-destructed the telephone system by splitting AT&T into literally hundreds of little piss-ant companies, poor innocent people couldn't sit down to dinner without some airhead telemarketer offering a cruise on the QEII while trying to hustle a better long distance deal.

"Robbie Douglas hyar." The voice on the other end had a thick burr.

"Robbie, this is Norris. I'm sorry to be so late. I hope I didn't wake you." The digital clock on the VCR under the television showed almost eleven.

"Oh, gud ev'ning, sur. No, sur, not at all. I was expecting your call. I was just reading a bit. What time will we be seeing ya?" The Scottish inflection was more obvious now.

"Hopefully around three...earlier if possible. Have the Rover at the strip, like always."

"I'll take care of it myself. Will there be anathun eelse you be wantin' done?"

"No...that's all, I'll see you tomorrow. Goodnight and

thanks..."

"Ga' night, sur." The phone clicked dead. Norris listened...nothing unusual now.

The thought of whisking Marilee off to Sheepshead was intoxicating. He could hardly wait to see her face.

Suddenly, he was starving.

"Today while the blossoms still cling to the vine..." He began humming softly. Taking a container of frozen homemade chili from the freezer, he placed it in the microwave to thaw as he busied himself stirring up cornbread batter and a six-egg omelet.

When he had flipped the chili-laden omelet, Norris took the heavy iron skillet of steaming cornbread from the oven. Its golden brown crust was cracked slightly open. Lifting the heavy pan to his nose, he savored the aroma.

While he cooked, he had set two plates and silverware on the counter in front of the stools. When he turned to place the steaming pone on the waiting trivet, Marilee was standing before him, rubbing her eyes, smiling sleepily from across the counter. His heavy white terry robe virtually swallowed her whole. Even with the sleeves turned up, she had to lift her arms to let her hands poke out. But not even the formless folds of the oversize robe could conceal the woman underneath.

Norris felt himself react immediately.

"Hungry?" he asked.

"Ravenous. Smells delicious. What is it?"

"An omelet filled with homemade chili and corn bread. Whatever you want to drink. I have fresh coffee for later...or now if you prefer."

"I'm a country girl. I wish I had some buttermilk. Not many people drink it...not in our set...and certainly not any women. I ordered it in Sardi's once and almost got laughed out of the place."

Grinning from ear to ear, Norris went to the refrigerator and produced an old-fashioned glass dairy bottle and sat it in front of her. "*Voilà!* Ice-cold, country-fresh buttermilk...any other requests?"

"You're a miracle. Is there anything I want that you don't have?

Don't answer that until you've eaten. You're going to need your strength." She blushed and turned to her food.

When they had eaten and cleared the dishes in the dishwasher, they sat drinking coffee in the study in front of the window looking out at the lights of passing tugboats on the Hudson.

"It's hard for me to believe I'm the first woman who has been here like this. But if it's a little lie, just let me go on believing it forever."

"Are you free to disappear for two...maybe three days...'til Friday? There's somewhere else I want to take you," he asked, quite unexpectedly.

"Tomorrow's Wednesday...well, I guess I could..."

This woman can destroy you. Norris shivered as he heard her agree. Too late to worry now...he knew he would do anything to hold on to what they'd just had for another day.

He shook his head. He had to get a grip on this pubescent insanity.

"Where are you taking me?" The question brought him back.

"Curiosity killed a cat. Can you leave around noon?"

"Yes. Is this the place you told me about? Your secret paradise?..."

"Don't ask questions...just trust me, OK?"

"I trust you, but I'm dying with curiosity," She looked at her watch and yawned. "It's been a long day. Can you at least tell me what I should pack?"

"Pack just like you would if you were going to Caswell for the weekend." He stood and pulled her erect and held her close. "C'mon, I'm sleepy too."

"If I'm going to go back to Sadie's tonight, I really should arrange for a cab."

"Don't go. You'll have plenty of time to pack in the morning while I go to my meeting. I want you here with me." Funny! He couldn't remember the last time he wanted a woman to stay the night, but now he couldn't bear the thought of her leaving. "Don't you want to stay?"

"Oh, yes, yes...I didn't know if you wanted me." She smiled

shyly. "What do you sleep in, anyway? Will you lend me something?"

"I've just the thing." Norris ducked into the closet and came out holding a white dress shirt.

He caught his breath as she dropped the robe and stood before him naked. Tossing aside the shirt she pulled him down, lifting her knees and spreading her legs to open herself.

"*La petite mort! Encore...encore!*" she whispered in his ear.

Afterwards with the lights out, lying close, feeling her measured warm breaths against his throat, he was reminded of a dimly-remembered time when he had still believed in perfection.

For this moment at least, it was good to remember.

CHAPTER FORTY-FIVE

THE PHONE RANG AT LEAST A HALF-DOZEN TIMES before Griff groped in the dark and picked up.

"Griffin Richards...." He fumbled sleepily for the light. Blinking hard...it was barely nine.

"Griff? This is Ed Scott. Did I wake you?"

"Well, as a matter of fact you did. I'd hardly gotten to bed, I'm dog-tired...have to catch a plane at seven-thirty in the morning. So...what's up, Doc?" Instantly alert, Griff snorted disgust at his inadvertent pun.

"Trip Graham had a bad episode this afternoon at the office. The short of it is we need to get him to a hospital...Holly Hall...it's a center for treating alcoholics...and addicts. Clayt needs to get back here right away. If not tonight...then first thing in the morning." Ed wanted to get the point across without complicating the issue.

"Hmm. Clayt and I discussed Trip's drinking over breakfast this morning. Inexcusable. We thought we'd get Norris involved as soon as he gets back from New York. I have important business in Jacksonville with Clayton tomorrow morning. Can't you put this off...tomorrow afternoon at least? This is nothing new. What the hell makes this such an emergency, Ed?"

"Goddamn it, Griff, is business all this family thinks about? We're talking about Clayton's son's life. Doesn't anybody care what happens to the people in this family? Let me explain this in plain language." Ed quickly recounted the events of the afternoon and the lab confirmation.

"Jeez...I'm sorry, Ed, alcohol is one thing, but drugs? I had no idea it was this bad." Griff was suddenly serious.

"Well, the truth is that right now drugs are probably the least of Trip's worries. Even after all that blood and my warning him he couldn't drink again, the scariest thing about all this is that when I looked in on him less than an hour ago, he's still drinking. From the looks of him, I'd say he'd had more than one or two. Of course he denies it. Trip's in deep shit. Understand? Judging from the lab results, this has been at a precarious point for some time. We have a life-or-death situation on our hands. Clayt should remember that Old Massie died in a pool of his own goddamn blood—it ain't a pretty picture. I reserved Trip a room at Holly Hall, but he keeps stalling. If he doesn't get help, he's going to die...Clayt has to convince him...we've got to get him to Holly Hall."

"Clayt isn't going to like it when he hears you're putting him in that drying out place. But, OK...take him, if you think you should."

"Goddamnit, Griff, haven't you heard a thing I said? Trip won't listen to me. He refuses to go. If Clayt won't do something, his only son's going to die. I can't...I will not be responsible."

"Well...OK, OK...maybe Clayt could call him...but we've been working up this Florida thing for quite awhile."

"Jeezuschrist, Griff, this isn't like you...I always thought you were the one with some sense. Where's Clayton? Give me his number; I'll call him myself."

"No! No...I'll try to reach him. I'll have to track him down. He had a lot to do. I'm not sure where he finally wound up. I'll have him call you if I can find him. Where are you?" Griff asked.

"With Mabel. I'll stay here for awhile. If I have to leave, call my cell phone or at home."

"OK, I'll get back to you in a little bit. Goodnight..." Griff hung up.

While he was talking to the doctor, Griff was already flipping through his address book and had located Glee's number. He began dialing as soon as the line was clear. The phone rang for what seemed like forever. He was about to give up when Glee answered.

"Glee, this is Griff. This is an emergency. Get him to the phone."

"But, Griff..." Glee started to protest, but the urgency in his voice stopped her. "OK...hold on, I'll get him, he's in the shower...Clayton, honey, it's Griff...." Griff heard her shout and put down the phone.

"He wants to know if it can't wait until morning?" Glee came back on the line.

"Tell him it can't wait for anything. We have to talk now." Griff left no room for argument.

"All right, hold on...." Griff heard her call him again.

"Did the old coot say what he wanted?" Griff heard Clayt as he approached the phone.

"No...I told you, honey...." Glee tried to calm him down.

"Griff? What's so goddamn important?..." Clayt blustered when he came on the line.

"Just be still and listen...." Griff interrupted. "Ed Scott just called. Trip's sick. Ed wants to talk to you. He's waiting with Mabel. I might as well warn you. Ed thinks you should come home first thing in the morning."

"What do you mean, sick? Is it a virus?...I mean...it's nothing like his heart...is it? Is he in the hospital?" Now Clayt sounded a bit more subdued.

"No, not his heart and not in a hospital...but...that's just it. Ed thinks he ought to be and Trip won't go. Trip hemorrhaged this afternoon and he's drinking...Ed's waiting with Mabel...he's at your place right now. Call him. He can explain better than I can." Griff wanted desperately to turn this over to the doctor.

"Hemorrhaged...what do you mean?...where?" Clayton sounded a trifle worried now.

"He shit and vomited bright red blood all over his office this afternoon at The Tower and Ed is very concerned. Says that it's the same thing that killed Old Massie, and Trip won't quit drinking. He's still just plain drunk, hard to deal with. Just call Ed, goddamnit, Clayt, and call me back. Then we can decide what to do. OK?" Griff was totally exasperated.

"Well, OK. I'll call you right back." Clayt hung up.

"Get me a drink of that Wild Turkey, will ya' honey?" Clayt took a deep breath before he dialed his home number.

"Ed Scott," the doctor answered on the first ring.

"Ed, this is Clayton. I just talked to Griff. Besides just being drunk and an all-around pain in the ass, what's wrong with Trip? Griff said he was bleeding from the asshole? Is it like an ulcer? Where is he now? What's going on?" Clayt demanded.

"Well, he hemorrhaged from the rectum and also the esophagus...he's home at the moment...drunk. I can't get him to go into the hospital. I can't reason with him. You need to come back here. We've got to get him in the hospital. He has to quit drinking. His blood alcohol was three times the legal limit...and the hospital lab report showed up positive for illegal drugs...and what's worse...his liver's gone. We've got to get him away from the booze. This is serious. He could die, goddamnit!" Ed was getting tired, trying to convince everyone of the gravity of Trip's condition.

"Lab report? At the hospital? Christ Ed, if that gets out...didn't you think about that?"

"Clayton, Trip was standing in a pool of his own bloody shit...don't tell me how to practice medicine...I've already talked to the lab director. He's destroyed all the copies. But this is too serious to worry about that now." Ed was sick of dealing with fools. "If we don't get him in Holly Hall right away, I won't be responsible."

"OK. Calm down...but Holly Hall? That place is for alkies...I think you're overreacting."

"Did you hear what I said? Your son's got alcoholic hepatitis...it's killing him...."

"Well, I know...but Holly Hall?...it's a goddamn disgrace. Think of the corporation...the family. Can't you just give him something to knock him out...and then get him out of town and get him dried out? Maybe Richmond or Atlanta...under no circumstances put him in Duke or Chapel Hill...word would be all over the media. This is downright embarrassing." Clayt was indignant.

"Clayton, Trip's seriously ill. It's urgent that you come home as soon as possible. It's probably way too late to think about flying back tonight, but first thing in the morning, without fail," Ed persisted.

"Oh, come on Ed...I've got business...." Clayt was losing

patience. Trip was a pain in the ass.

"Goddamn it Clayton...what's the matter with you?...haven't you heard a word...?"

Clayton struggled to control his temper. Ed was making a goddamn mountain out of a molehill. Ed Scott was a highly-paid professional. Why couldn't he handle such a trivial, isolated incident? What was wrong with these people, anyway? Son or no son, this was hardly serious enough to fly back to Colonial Hall just to try to talk some sense into a drunk. The important thing was to be sure it was handled with discretion. He didn't want the Graham name dragged through the dirt.

"Where's Marilee? Can't she do anything with him?"

"Marilee is in New York. We have a call in for her now. But you're the one who needs to be here. He'll listen to you. Clayton, this is not just a case of getting him sober now...this is serious. Trip is sick, very sick. He has advanced liver disease, and there are other complications which are life-threatening if he doesn't stop drinking. His alcohol level was three times the legal limit this afternoon and he won't quit. He also was loaded with amphetamine...and marijuana...and cocaine. He won't listen to me. I need...no, by God, *Trip* needs your help."

"Drugs. Oh, come on...I don't believe it...."

"Well, you better...the lab report looks like the evidence inventory from a major drug bust...."

"Jesus...drugs... who the fuck knows about this? Just make goddamn sure this whole thing is kept quiet. If those hospital lab people talk, they're fired...I built that fucking hospital. They'll never work in North Carolina again. Do you understand? And tell Trip to forget that fucking house in Palm Beach. I'll personally see he goes to live in Bumfuck, Alaska...or someplace worse. He's not going to act like this in Colonial Hall. Where's Ivee? Who's keeping the boy? Let me talk to Mabel, Ed."

Ed couldn't believe he still hadn't gotten through to him.

"Listen Clayton, I'm sick of arguing with you. Your son is in grave danger. He's jaundiced...yellow as a pumpkin and still drinking. Don't you remember the way your daddy died? Trip could die the same way. Tonight. We have to get him to a hospital as soon as possible. Now, do you care about that or not? If you don't agree to come home right away, I'm going to wash my hands of this. If you don't want to accept my judgment, Mabel can just get another physician."

"Well, by God, why don't you just do that? I think you are making a lot of trouble over nothing. He's just drunk. You're a doctor. If you can't get him into the hospital, what good are you?" Clayton was not about to be threatened this way.

"OK, Clayton. Here's Mabel; you work it out it with her...I've had it with both of you." Ed was tired of arguing with the pigheaded bastard. He turned to hand Mabel the phone.

"Goddamnit, Ed, wait a minute!" Ed heard Clayton protest and waited for him to continue. "OK, Ed, maybe I don't understand. Tell me again...go slow—the Tower...the bleeding, all that. What happened?"

"Clayton, Trip gushed bright red blood all over the bathroom in his office. He vomited blood. He was standing ankle-deep in his own blood. His lab work shows he had been using cocaine and pot and he was loaded with amphetamine...speed. He's in deep shit, Clayton. You need to get back here just as fast as you can. This isn't a matter of just getting him into a hospital for a few days. We have to get him into a treatment hospital for a month at least...probably longer. Do you understand?" Struggling to maintain his composure, Ed resolved to look into retirement first thing in the morning. He'd had enough of these idiots. It was time he played some golf and spent some time at Wrightsville Beach on his boat.

He couldn't remember the last time he'd gone fishing.

"Clayton, your son needs you, your wife needs you...most of all, I need you back here...if not tonight, tomorrow morning. Are you coming or not?"

"Well, yes...OK. I'll see what I can do. I'll call Griff and try to make arrangements for the business to get handled here," Clayton hedged—obviously, he still thought the doctor was being melodramatic. "Has anyone heard from Norris? He needs to be there.

Norris can handle Trip. See if you can reach Norris. He went to Washington this morning, goddamn him. Why is he always gone when I need him? Remember now, I don't want the word out on this. We have to think of Grail—the family image. Now just go tell that goddamn sorry Trip Graham you talked to me and if he gives you any shit, he'll never see Palm Beach again...."

Edward Scott slowly placed the phone back on the cradle. What was the matter with these people? If the stock market was having a crisis, they wouldn't have any trouble understanding the urgency of the situation.

When Clayton hung up, Glee was standing in front of him wearing only a silk robe. From feet to chin, she was the personification of sexual ecstasy, but now her face had twisted into a harpy mask. The narrowing of her eyes as she took a step closer warned him she was not one bit happy about the idea of his having to go back to Colonial Hall in the morning.

"Clayton, you're not going back tomorrow, are you?" she began. "What's this all about, anyway?"

"Well, I hope not. It's Trip...he had a hemorrhage today. The doc says he refuses to get help. Marilee's out of town, and Mabel just can't do a thing with him. Mabel's useless. All she's ever done is spoil him. The boy might have turned out OK if she hadn't babied him so much. She says I was too hard on him when he was little. Truth is, I'm not hard enough. I've let things slide with him too long. Anyway, I think he's just drunk and has everybody buffaloed. Let's don't ask for trouble just yet, all right? Things will calm down by the time morning rolls around."

He reached up and took her hand and pulled her over to him and buried his face between her breasts. Glee pushed the breasts against his face, turning herself slowly so the nipple of her right breast brushed hard against his lips, insisting he take it in his mouth. He could feel her nipple respond as he sucked hard and let his tongue run over the surface.

"Wait..." Before she could finish turning her body the other way, Clayt pulled back and picked up the phone and punched in

Griff's number. "Let me get all this all out of the way right now, so we don't have to think about it anymore tonight."

Griff answered on the first ring, listening while Clayt filled him in.

"I don't know what to say, Griff. Ed Scott insists on my coming back there in the morning, but my guess is Trip will sleep this thing off and then the good doctor can get him into the hospital tomorrow. I'll call Trip in the morning when he's sobered up. Once I put the fear of God in him, I'm sure he'll go quietly. I'll be damned if I can see any reason for us to change our plans tomorrow, can you?" Clayton was asking for a vote of confidence. "How accurate are those tests, anyway? Do you think all this could be a mistake?"

"A mistake? No. I'm sure everything Ed says is true...let's see what happens." Griff was tired of this useless, self-serving rationalizing.

"Well, get Norris back there. Did you call that investigator like I asked you?" Clayton demanded.

"Yes, but, my God, that was only this afternoon. You can't expect miracles. He was going to try to pick up Norris when his shuttle got into LaGuardia. But there was no way to tell when he would be leaving Washington." Griff was losing patience. Right now, he felt like telling Clayt to get fucked.

"OK, OK...personally I think we're all overreacting. Unless something else happens, then I'll still see you down here in the morning. If I have to go back there later, then I will. You won't need me down here anyway. I've already signed the papers and Mrs. Guest notarized them like you said. She'll bring everything and meet you and Glee at the courthouse in Fernandina Beach around ten-thirty. I'll look for you at lunch at the Starfish Cay Club tomorrow, OK?" Clayton was about to say goodbye.

"Do you want me to call before I leave in the morning...just in case?"

"No, why bother? Just come on down. We'll probably have this real estate business cleaned up long before Trip wakes up with a hell of a hangover."

"Well...oh...by the way, if Mabel asks where you're staying, what should I tell her?" Griff asked, anxiously.

"Oh, jeez! I forgot. Tell her...and anyone else...I'm at the Grail Beachside here. Mabel has the number. I'll check my messages out there, like always. Don't worry. I'll take care of this end."

Clayton breathed a heavy sigh of relief. Ready to hang up the phone, he reached up with his left hand and rolled Glee's rosy, hardened nipple between his fingers. He could feel himself becoming almost painfully erect underneath the towel he had wrapped around him. Virecta was a wonder. His hand moved and unfastened the loosely tied sash of her robe and let it fall open as he began to explore the juicy crevice between her legs. He murmured goodnight and replaced the phone.

Glee reached across and turned off both the ringer and the answering machine before she knelt before him and took his penis in her mouth.

After he hung up, Griff sat and stared at the wall across the room. He had debated telling Clayt about Trip's call from the Greensboro cops, but why make matters worse? All at once he was feeling a lot of guilt for being party to Clayton's sordid little infidelity. He was certainly no prude, but he didn't like the way he was feeling about himself lately. He was tired of lying...keeping secrets. He really loved Clayton and didn't want to judge him harshly. But this whole mess was getting out of hand. He hated what this cheap dishonesty was doing to them both.

He sighed and turned out the light.

He'd barely nodded off when the phone woke him again.

"Shit...shit. Shit!" he cursed in the dark, fully expecting it was Clayton again. "Yeah?" he growled, reluctantly reaching across to turn on the light before he sat up on the side of the bed.

The voice on the line took him completely by surprise.

"Hate to bother you, Mr. Richards, but this is D.C. Mills in Greensboro. Something has come up about that matter we discussed this afternoon, and I knew you'd want to be aware of it."

"No bother, Chief. What's going on?" Griff's stomach did a little flip. He'd already had enough surprises for one day.

"Well, I don't want to alarm you unduly, but it looks like we might have to...ah...ask Trip Graham some more questions about that movie star. Looks a whole lot like he may have been with her at some point Sunday night before she died."

"Well...I don't know. When I talked to him this afternoon, he said he told you as far as he could remember, he hadn't seen her. What makes you think he can help?" Griff tried to sound unconcerned.

"The thing has gotten out of hand. We have reporters and TV crews coming through the cracks in the floor...CNN, *Time* and *People* magazines...the whole nine yards. You know how these show-biz folks attract attention. Worst of all, someone leaked the information she died from an overdose. Goddamn it, if I find out who, his ass is grass," the Chief complained.

"My god, Chief, I hope you aren't going to turn the media loose on the Graham family." Griff's heart skipped a beat. "You know what those jackals would do with that. It wouldn't matter if he was home with his mother and wife studying his Sunday school lesson, the press would have him tried and convicted before you could drop the charges."

"Oh, no...you know I wouldn't let that happen, Mr. Richards. But I certainly need to talk to Mr. Graham again...off the record of course. I just thought you ought to know, being his daddy's attorney...and friend."

"Are you suggesting Mr. Graham should have an attorney present when you question him, Chief?" Griff tried to catch a warning in the statement, but he couldn't be sure it was any more than a very politically wise law officer trying to cover his ass.

"Oh, not at all, Mr. Richards, not at all. But it would be helpful to us all if you talked to him in the morning and told him what I told you and asked him to try to remember all he can about Sunday. I just don't want any of those smartass media people coming up with any surprises for any of us." D.C. seemed eager to express his loyalty to the Grahams.

"Well, I thank you for looking out for us, Chief. I can promise

I'll make a point to tell Trip Graham's daddy what a good friend you've been." Griff was relieved. If he stalled for time, Ed could get Trip in the hospital and locked away from all this until the whole thing blew over.

"Thanks, Mr. Richards. Hope I didn't wake you. Y'all take care now." The Chief hung up.

Damn Trip, damn Clayt...goddamn 'em all! Griff muttered and slammed down the phone.

What a mess. What was he going to do now? This changed everything. Clayton needed to be back here now. And Norris, he certainly needed to be back here, too. No telling what could happen if the press got wind of this. Griff pulled on his robe again and went downstairs and turned on the light in his study. He moved to his desk and started flipping through the Rolodex until he found the number for the Grail International in New York.

"Good Evening, Grail International, may I help you?" The operator picked up immediately.

"Norris Wrenn...he'll be staying in the Grail Executive Suites," Griff said and was connected immediately. The phone rang perhaps a dozen times. Finally, the operator came back.

"I'm sorry, Mr. Wrenn doesn't answer," she said and asked, "would you like his voice mail or perhaps I could take a message, sir?"

"Yes. Leave a note on his door...have him call Mr. Griffin Richards, no matter what time he comes in. It's important." He left his number and thanked her.

Debating for a moment, Griff located Glee's number and dialed again.

It rang and rang...no answer.

Finally, Griff hung up and looked at his watch. Not quite ten. In his present condition, it was quite possible he had misdialed the first time. After a minute he dialed the number again, this time more carefully. Now he counted the rings. After the twentieth he gave up. Where the hell could they possibly have gone this time of night?

Goddamn them both to hell.

CHAPTER FORTY-SIX

ED SCOTT HAD HARDLY FINISHED TALKING to the hotel operator when the phone rang again.

"This is Dr. Scott...." he began, then stopped and listened.

"HE WHAT?....ARE YOU SURE?..."

When she heard Ed's outburst, Mabel walked back to where he stood and waited anxiously at his elbow, hoping for some indication for the cause of his alarm.

"Yes...well, sure...I'll make arrangements immediately...can you call me right back when the EMS crew shows up? I'll try to have a chopper ready at the Flight Centre. Don't worry. I'll take it from here. Tell the ambulance crew I'll meet them there. Check his breathing...be sure he doesn't have any real physical problem...." The doctor listened, nodded and seemed to brighten considerably. "All right, good job. Now, let me get busy about getting that helicopter."

"Is it Trip?...Oh, Ed, it's...it's not a car wreck...my God, where would he be going in a car?...what happened? I thought he was home when you left...." Mabel pleaded as soon as he broke the connection.

"Calm down...it's not a car wreck...and he's not injured. That was Sheriff John Henry Galt. His deputy found Trip passed out in his car at one of those roadside dumpsites, out beyond the entrance to the Grail Flight Centre. I think I have Dempsey Gearhart's home number somewhere...." He was already thumbing his little notebook. "The good Lord works in mysterious ways. Now's our chance to get him to treatment...." Ed located the number and picked up the phone.

What goes around comes around. Dempsey Gearhart gloated as he

297

approached the hangar at the Air Centre. For the first time in a long time, he was grateful he could fly helicopters. It had been a skill that had gotten him a lot of unwanted extra work from time to time, but tonight he had good reason to be glad. A scant half-hour ago, when old Doc Scott called out of the clear blue, wanting to take Trip Graham to a hospital somewhere near Pinehurst, for the first time Demp could remember he was happy to have the opportunity to fly that asshole somewhere.

Even before he could make out the shape of Mabel's car parked on the taxi apron, when he topped the rise at the end of the runway, Demp could see the flashing red lights atop the ambulance.

When he pulled up to the hangar, he was happy to see the night crew already had the chopper warmed up, its rotors slowly revolving against the night sky.

On the way over, he had heard on his CB radio the Sheriff's deputy laughingly tell the dispatcher, "Funny place for someone to pull off and pass-out drunk. When I found him he was lying halfway out on the ground on top of a whole mess of white notebook paper...looked like he had taken it out of the dumpster and scattered it all around."

Hearing that, Demp laughed out loud. The stupid asshole must've gotten real nervous thinking about that Claire woman's jogging suit...and the other stuff. Took a real fool...or a drunk...to leave his personal calling card with a stash of illegal cocaine.

On the radio, the deputy said that when he found him, Trip also had an envelope full of Norris Wrenn's press clippings. Demp didn't know quite what to make of that, but there was no telling what a drunk would do next.

When Demp got out of the car, Mabel was reading the doctor the riot act.

"Remember, you're positively not to admit Trip to the alcohol or psychiatric unit. I won't have him put in with a bunch of crazy people or drunks," Mabel addressed Dr. Scott, sharply. "I don't want it a matter of record he has a problem with alcohol...and certainly there's to be no mention of the drugs. You do understand that, don't you?"

"Look, Mabel. If Trip dies from this, it won't matter what the diagnosis was. Do you understand? This is your son's life we're talking about." Ed looked across the car and waved when he saw the chief pilot approaching. "Dempsey, thank god you finally got here," he called.

"I hope you'll handle this with sensitivity, Ed. I don't think you understand. It's important," Mabel persisted.

Incredible, Demp mused wryly. He wondered if Mabel Graham had heard anything the doc had said. Trip was her only offspring. Didn't his life mean anything?

"OK, we're off. Give him a kiss, Mabel." The doctor obviously wanted out of here.

"Well...OK...." She leaned into the EMS vehicle and pecked Trip on the cheek. When she straightened, she asked Ed Scott, "Do you have any breath mints? He smells awful...there's a very sour odor about him. I'd be embarrassed for anyone to smell him like that."

"I think I have some mouthwash...now let me get him on the way," he urged, impatiently. "Don't worry. He's in good hands." The doctor helped Trip out of the vehicle.

Mabel caught his arm and leaned in close.

"Don't forget, leave alcohol out of your diagnosis," she whispered and squeezed his arm.

"Just pray that we're talking about a diagnosis, not the cause of death."

"What?..." Mabel gave him a blank look.

"Never mind. Don't forget, call Griff?" Ed patted her arm. "Tell him to call Clayton."

"Oh, yes. Yes, I'll do it now." Mabel obviously seemed in shock.

"Good girl. By the way..." Ed handed her a brown envelope. "...Trip had this in his hand when they found him."

Mabel took the envelope without looking and turned toward the terminal to call Griff.

When she finished talking to Griff, Mabel stood alone inside the operations building. The police and Air Centre personnel were still milling aimlessly about. Absently, she opened the envelope Ed Scott had handed her and extracted a yellowing photograph.

Mabel stiffened when she read the notation scrawled on the back: MADIE K'S - JUNE 30, 1959.

Hypnotically, she turned the photo over. The faces of the pretty young girls standing on the steps of the stately old manor house were forever etched in her memory. Time had been kind to one of them. Even after all the years, almost anyone would be able to pick her out of a crowd.

Returning the photo to the envelope and fighting back her tears, Mabel headed for the car.

WEDNESDAY

CHAPTER FORTY-SEVEN

IN THE DARKNESS, THE RED NUMBERS on the bedside clock glowed 5:21. Reaching behind him, Norris could feel Marilee's naked, quite pleasingly-rounded bottom pressing against him.

He gave it a little squeeze and a tender pat. Stirring against his hand, she sighed contentedly.

Rolling quietly out of bed, Norris gathered up his shorts and running shoes.

Where was that damned sweatshirt?...

Ah-hah!...

Groping his way, he moved into the kitchen and turned on the small light over the stove.

Starting the coffeemaker, he went into the sitting room and called Washington Hospital Center and asked for Intensive Care.

"Mr. Bradley?...still critical, I'm afraid, Mr. Wrenn. Prognosis? Ah...guarded...but he seems to be holding his own, for the moment at least...." The nurse was professional, but not unkind.

Hang on Tom. After Nicaragua, don't die on me now, old friend...please?

He finished dressing. Still heavy with sleep, automatically Norris moved through the morning ritual. Gathering yesterday's newspapers from the coffee table in the living room, he put them in the recycle container and removed the plastic garbage liner in the can under the kitchen sink. He closed the bag securely with a tie and replaced it with a fresh one.

His granny once told him, "Neatness is the hallmark of an orderly mind."

He hadn't had a lot of reassurance of that lately.

He dropped the recycle container and the garbage bag down the chute in the foyer. Slipping silently out of the apartment, the sound of the gurgling coffee dripping into the thermos carafe followed him out the door.

Sprinting now across to the Park—no traffic at this hour—he loped straight down the path toward the lake. In the gray pre-dawn light, here and there he encountered other runners. Some were long familiar to him and he nodded a friendly recognition as they passed. Since the World Trade Center tragedy, some familiar faces had gone missing.

Norris looked furtively about for suspicious company as he tried to turn his mind to the business at hand.

Suppose Tom didn't make it?

In just a few hours, he would be face to face with Chatham Brookes. Good old Chatham...couldn't help but like the man. Totally apolitical, Chatham was a genuine statesman—if such a dinosaur existed anymore. It brought a curious sense of comfort to think about him now.

Was Chatham really serious about offering the opportunity to resurrect Phoenix?

And this sophomoric notion about saving the world? Did he really believe it anymore?

Right? Wrong? Good? Bad? Empty words—black holes in a modern vocabulary.

It was all so corny...or was it?

Did anybody really believe in anything of value anymore?

Money? Power? Now there's the ticket...

Cynical?

Perhaps.

One thing for sure: without money or power you couldn't do a goddamn thing...good or bad.

"The White House calling again? What's all this Phoenix shit about, anyway?" Clayton had asked him impatiently, one evening during the Azalea Week down at Marilee's cottage, after he'd been on the phone for the second time that day with Chatham Brookes.

"Oh, just an idea I had a few years back," he'd replied.

"Oh, yeah. That fairy tale about a search for 'superbrains.'

Mining gold from the ghetto, eh?" Clayton had snorted. The senior Graham hadn't been in too good a mood because Norris had steadfastly refused to talk to him about staying on at Grail under the terms Clayton offered.

"Something like that," he had answered Clayton, not wanting to pursue the conversation.

"So what do you do when you find the superior-of-the-superior...what was that magic number?...IQ's of one-forty-two or over? What do you do with all these diamonds in the rough? What happens to 'em when they're cleaned up and educated and shoved out the door of your friendly neighborhood major university? What happens then? Huh? Where do they go? Who decides? Do we get our shot? Do we get our choice of the choicest?"

"Who decides? They decide, Clayton. Freedom in a free world. Or doesn't anybody believe in that anymore?"

"Freedom?...Well, shit on that. Nothing's free. You want that we—the big boys—should foot the bill. If we pay, we should have our say, right? I mean if we pay, then there should be a payoff...a bottom line. Doesn't that make sense to you?" Clayton asked, clearly looking for a fight.

"But there is a bottom line."

"What? What's the bottom line?"

"A better world to live in. For everybody...not just those of us who are lucky enough to have our little green sticker on the windshield that permits passage through the gate to Club Drive."

"Whatever happened to the old-fashioned idea you only have one right: Root hog or die? God bless them that gets their own. I'm sick and tired of giving these ne'er-do-wells a free ride. And I'm not at all sure you're right about all these paternalistic policies you're putting in at Grail, either. OK...I know...I know; so far they're paying off, but the jury's still out as far as I'm concerned. This thing of the corporation playing 'big daddy' just doesn't cut it with me."

"Who gave you a free ride, Clayton? Did you have a paper route to pay your way through the university? Did you work your way up in the corporation? Did you just wake up one day and, like God, in six days part the rivers and the seas and create Grail before

305

you took the seventh day to head for the Bahamas?"

"Oh, now you're getting ridiculous...my father and his father and grandfather worked for everything we have. Don't forget where your paycheck is coming from."

"I already told you, I'm going to change that. In August, remember?" Norris had gotten angry. It was a futile exercise. "I earn my goddamn paycheck. Going on fifteen billion at the bottom line from four years ago when I got here. If you want, I can leave right now...anytime you say."

"Wait, now. Hold on..." Clayton had suddenly remembered he was trying to keep him from leaving. "We're just talking philosophically...can't you take a joke?"

Take a joke? Maybe the joke was on him. But somebody had to show them before they took, took, took and left nothing to replace the wasted resources.

So much waste.

The loss of our best resource, the human mind—the nobility of spirit, the dream.

Still? Maybe Clayton was right. There has to be a bottom line. The problem was making them see it. Where was Norris Wrenn the dreamer, the believer? Where was that Norris now? Had he gotten lost somewhere on the way to the bank?

Well?...what was so wrong with the idea of money, anyway?

Was money really such a dirty word? After all, everything was about resources.

Resources were the heart of Phoenix...the heart of everything...money made the world go around.

Freedom?

Ironic. He had always thought money and power represented true freedom...now he wasn't sure. Perhaps it was all an illusion. He wondered if in the end money and power wasn't enslavement in disguise.

What about that one, Tom? Hang in there, Tommy. Don't desert me now. I need you with me, old friend. Now more than ever...

Phoenix?

Funny how it started...how he'd come to give it a name.

He hadn't really been thinking of the mythical Phoenix, the bird rising from the ashes, when he tagged the idea with the name *Phoenix*. It all related to a thirteen-year-old black boy, the son of a family who worked on the Senator's farm in Virginia. Norris had found him in the tack room of the stable reading a book on Greek philosophy.

"Do you like that stuff? Understand it, I mean?" he had asked the lad, surprised.

"Yessir. I read a lot of things. It's my lunch time...I'm not goofing off."

"Oh, I didn't think you were. Anyway, stuff like that is important. What else do you read?" Norris had asked, amazed.

"Well, I like stuff about medicine, you know, anatomy...all about the body...I wish...I...." The boy's eyes went out of focus, as if he didn't dare speak the thought out loud.

"You want to be a doctor...I betcha. Well, by Godfrey, you should be one!" Norris had caught the hunger in the boy's voice.

"Oh, I can't be a doctor. My pa is already talking about me dropping out of school when I'm sixteen, so I can help train horses for the Senator," the boy had replied.

"I'm Norris Wrenn. What's your name?"

"Phoenix Collins...I'm pleased to meet you, Mr. Wrenn. I know who you are, sir. I saw you on television the other day. You're working for the President." Without the heavy slur that was the charming rhythm of the South, Collins' speech was carefully enunciated. Crisply spoken, it had a charm all its own, out of time...away from this place and the history it represented.

"Do you really want to go to college, Mr. Phoenix Collins?"

"Oh, yessir I do, but we all have to know our place. My daddy's a famous trainer. I'm pretty lucky to have a chance to work with the Senator's horses. I'm not complaining, sir."

Obsessed with the tragic waste, after he left that day, Norris hadn't been able to shake the thought of the boy. A human throwaway...a discard. How many more?

Quietly, he had gone to the boy's teachers and confirmed that his tests showed him to be clearly in the genius range. Then he went to the Senator and started a campaign to educate the boy. He kept on bugging his father-in-law until he shamed him into paying for the boy's schooling. When Norris handpicked the school and the Senator found out, he had been livid.

"Fork Union Academy! Goddamn it, Norris, have you lost your cottonpicking mind? What's the matter with the local high school?" the Senator had fairly shouted.

"The boy has an IQ of one-forty-nine, Senator. About one out of every one thousand have that kind of brain power. In this whole state there are less than six thousand minds of that caliber. We can't afford to waste a resource of such dimension."

"But...he's...just a...." the Senator had begun, but didn't dare finish the thought.

"Just one of God's children...is that what you were you about to say, Senator? Or maybe, just an American? The Chinese seek out and nurture their best young minds. If we don't take some steps, they'll blow us away some day. Besides, I've already given out a press release that you have established a permanent annual scholarship competition in your good ol' Old Dominion...The Phoenix Foundation...has a nice ring, don't you think, sir?"

"Goddamn it, Norris just who the hell do you think you are? That's my money," the Senator had sputtered.

"Just a political expedient, sir. I just knew you'd want to do it. Besides, it's set up as a foundation and I've solicited support... response is overwhelming in the old home state, sir. Virginians are always out for a good cause."

"Political expedient, you say?" the Senator sputtered, clearly interested in anything political.

"An election year, remember? It's all deductible."

"Well...ah...in that case...all right...but Norris, not even you can single-handedly save the whole goddamn world." The Senator was a practical man.

Phoenix Collins had not disappointed him.

Undergraduate work completed in three years at the University, then on to grad school.

Just last week Norris had gotten the invitation. In a week, on May 15, he would be going to Phoenix Collins' graduation exercises at Harvard School of Medicine.

Phoenix Collins, M.D. A Jonas Salk, a Jenner or a Pasteur...a Walter Reed? A young physician for the ages....

A young boy reading Plato in a horse barn, how long ago now?...ten years?

Maybe Phoenix Collins would want to become involved with Phoenix. Poetic. Yes...so absolutely perfect.

Phoenix Collins...Phoenix Collins, M.D., by God, why hadn't he thought about it before?

Suddenly, Norris was overcome and tears spilled down his face as he sobbed silently with joy for the young man's struggle and achievement.

Norris spread his arms and raised his hands high and did a halfback pirouette.

Some of the runners in the park stopped and smiled.

Of course! Doctor Phoenix Collins must be consulted immediately.

He could hardly wait to tell Tom....

Don't desert me, Tommy.

Embarrassed at a sudden flow of tears, wiping his cheeks on his sleeve, he looked across at the inquiring face of an approaching pretty, long-legged young runner, all jiggle and bounce in her flimsy tank top and skimpy satiny jogging shorts, nodding good day and smiling sympathetically.

"Nothing like a good sweat." She returned his smile, as he gave his cheeks another swipe of his sweatshirt.

The sudden rush of tears...what was happening to him lately? Marilee Graham had him on the verge of blithering sentimental idiothood. Nervously anticipating the prospect of whisking her off to his New England hideaway as soon as he was done with Chatham Brookes this morning, he'd planned everything but an orchid in a florist's box. He couldn't wait to see her face and walk her down the docks to watch the lobstermen come in. To stand on the high flat plateau above the village with the wind blowing in their faces—the chaotic splash of wildflowers would delight her. It was a fantasy he'd entertained since the morning down at Caswell when he'd told her about Sheepshead.

Wasn't this all something on the order of a machismo victory lap? The gold trophy? Adolescent fantasy fulfillment? So what?

So what next? Act Two?...Three? The curtain call?

But Friday this act would be over. What would he do about Agnes?

In the cold light of reason, Norris tried to examine the events of the past two days as he ran along the edge of the lake.

With the memory of Marilee still burning his flesh, it was impossible to deal with things in an objective way.

In his own cold, honest way of looking at things, he understood he was flirting with disaster.

A casual fling with Marilee Graham? Impossible? Well, too late to change that now.

Was he sorry?

Not at all.

A goddamn mess, really. But he'd take that mess over any success he ever had. What now?

On the one hand he was about to take over the helm of one of the world's most powerful corporations and on the other he had just bedded down the mother of the boss' grandson and the wife of his old college roommate—the corporate heir apparent.

Now, Norris stopped dead in his tracks to watch a pair of mating ducks, honking and noisily flapping, happily oblivious of his presence.

His self-satisfied exercise finished, the mallard drake waddled up the bank, quacking proudly of his accomplishment. Then, suddenly, the drake veered and went back into the water, purposefully swimming for yet another attractive mallard hen, smugly waiting her turn.

That's the ticket, old sport.

Inside he should be crowing like a rooster over last night's triumph in the bedroom.

Crowing?

Well...maybe inside he *was* crowing just a bit at that.

The hat trick? *The Girl, the Gold Watch and Everything*...he smiled as he recalled a title from an old John D. MacDonald novel. In his insanity, he was trying to figure out how to have it all.

Poetry, guitars, birds, musty sweetness, silky textures. Pinks and freckle-tans and cornsilk hair.

Perfumes and soapy smells. And slightly minty tastes served on the tip of a tiny little hummingbird tongue, darting and probing.

Flower-petal openings. Clingings and strainings and pressings and urgings.

Warm dividings and unfoldings, devilish resistings ...yieldings...soft adhesive enveloping.

Closer, closer, but...never, never close enough...

So much for cold, honest viewpoints!

Tom's accident suddenly left him with a colder eye for tomorrows. A new perspective...a legacy of a contracted future. Forget tomorrow. Today is all any man can hope to deal with.

Sheepshead Light?

Maybe he'd just stay out there in the middle of the ocean with her forever—there was money enough. He'd write all those books filled with soaring thunderheads of dreams of a better world. He'd give them all a noble plan, and then let them dig their way out of their own excrement. No more riding around on spavined horses looking for broken-down windmills...who needed windmills any more, anyway? Cadillacs, and Mercedes and Jags...a Rolls or a Bentley or two...who wanted broken-down nags to ride?

Who cared about any of it?

What would Tom Bradley say?

"Fuck 'em all but six, and save them for the pallbearers." That's what Tom would say.

Hang on, Tom...hang on!

The thought of showing Marilee his private Shangri-la this afternoon gave his heart a tug.

Damn the consequences, full speed ahead! Norris laughed out loud and resumed his run. Nothing could stop him. Norris the invincible. He could fucking run forever!

Worry about tomorrow later. He raised his arms again and looked to the sky.

He really felt alive, for the first time in recent history.

Run finished, Norris slipped quietly back into the apartment. He showered in the hall bathroom and tiptoed quietly about so he would not awaken Marilee. Toweled dry, he put on his robe and took a cup of coffee to the living room and located the copy of the Phoenix file he had brought with him. Shuffling through the thick compendium of clippings, articles and memos, at first he felt embarrassed.

A synthesis of naive idealism and his insatiable ego-driven ambition, Phoenix had been his brainchild.

Here in front of him were the clippings from *Esquire* and the covers from *Time* and *Newsweek*—in the year of our lord, nineteen hundred and ninety, "Man of the Year" in all the magazines and papers.

Save the world? Had he really been such a Pollyanna? Now, it was as if he were looking at the work of a stranger...and all over a high school sophomore reading Plato. Such idealism. Now, slowly, as he leafed through the material he became immersed in the work. Norris was amazed. This was truly fascinating. Somehow along the way he had forgotten that he had once believed in such a simple set of values. These were truly noble ideas—nothing here to be ashamed of.

What had happened to all that passion?

Did he even believe in himself anymore? He wasn't sure.

In front of him was a picture of the original gang: Tom Bradley standing beside him shaking hands with the new President. He had picked his winners all right. All the right moves. Another clipping from *Forbes*, this one with a photograph of the members of the "International Moneytrust"...his team: Charlie Starkweather, Chicago philanthropist; Boone Mayfield, Harvard School of Business; Jean-Paul Langlois, French industrialist; and the key player, Royce Carstairs, British aviation pioneer. In the background was the Jap before Ikimoto—dead now, killed in a car wreck—standing with the Chinaman, Lee, right beside Tom Bradley.

It was a goddamn dirty shame.

What was he going to do without Tom? In a few hours, Chatham would be pushing him to commit to some sort of action. He would have to stall...play it by ear.

Certainly not even Chatham Brookes would expect him to resurrect the project overnight.

What was he going to say to Chatham Brookes? When he left home yesterday, he had counted on turning the main thrust of Phoenix over to Tom.

Tom. Together, we survived a war.

How could it be? One minute laughing and talking excitedly about the future and then, in less time than it took for a person to travel to the airport...struck down. But not dead yet....

All at once he remembered what Tom's dad had said last night about police denial and vanished witnesses...and that reporter from the *Post* asking Tom questions about Phoenix.

Tom's accident? Some sort of plot?

Involuntarily, he shook his head to chase his paranoia.

The very suggestion that Phoenix could be made a cover for some team of government spooks left him suddenly angry and depressed.

International politics...a sick joke.

Without Tom's help, he'd be a fool to take it on, anyway.

The sound of running water from the bedroom bath roused Norris from his reverie.

He straightened the disarray of papers in their folders and placed them in his briefcase. Quickly, he located the folder with the Phoenix summary paper and put it on top, to scan in the limo on the way downtown. Still feeling frustrated, he closed the briefcase and set it by the door.

Refilling his coffee mug, he poured a mug for Marilee and took them back to the bedroom.

The bathroom door was closed so he went to the sitting alcove.

313

Placing Marilee's mug on the table between the two chairs, he turned the lamp on low and settled comfortably to wait.

In less than a minute she emerged, rubbing her eyes sleepily, wearing only the oxford shirt he had given her to sleep in. As she walked toward him, the fabric clung and released, revealing and concealing...sensually modeling her figure as she moved. Norris set down his cup, leaned forward and took her hands, pulling her onto his lap with her legs astride his, facing him.

"Good morning. That shirt has never looked so good," he breathed into the hollow of her throat.

"Uhmm...good morning. Where have you been?" Then she saw the little pile of sweat-sodden running clothes on the floor and said, "I should have known. You went for your run. Back home I watch you from my window."

"You do?"

"Uhmm. What time is it?" Twisting his wrist, she tried to see his watch.

"Almost eight. I have a limo coming at nine-fifteen. Why don't I just drop you at your place? That way you can pack while I go meet with Chatham. I should be back by noon. I'll pack a few things here before I leave and we'll be off. We're having lunch on the plane. It's arranged. How's that sound for a game plan?"

"I still don't have a clue as to what to take." Marilee pouted and kissed him on the chin.

"It would be a good idea to take a sweater and some warm pants...if we wanted to walk, it might get chilly in the evenings."

"Oh...I'd love to walk...remember that first morning at Caswell when we walked on the beach? It all started between us then."

"Uhmm. We'll take lots of walks."

"I can hardly wait...but first things first..." She moved her hands across his chest and tweaked his nipples.

"Goddamn! Don't do that!" He almost jumped out of the chair at her touch.

"Don't you like it? Did it hurt?"

"Well...no. But god, it made my toes curl. I never expected to be so sensitive there."

"Uhmm...I'll remember that." She smiled an enigmatic smile.

"I'll bet you will...." Norris looked at her mischievously. "Two can play those games, remember that."

"I was counting on it."

"There's some fruit and cereal in the kitchen. I never eat breakfast myself. I had Wilson send for it yesterday...just in case you showed up." He blushed.

"You knew damn well I would." Marilee laid the tip of her finger on his nose and then bent and kissed him hungrily. "God, I love you. I can't let you go away from me. What will we do? Can you just keep me in your pocket?"

"I wish. Go away! We don't have time for this now..." He kissed her nose and gently pushed her to a standing position. "Get us some coffee while I pack and dress. In a few hours, we'll have all the time we want."

CHAPTER FORTY-EIGHT

GRIFF'S ALARM WENT OFF AT 5:00 A.M. Even before he put on his slippers and went to the bathroom, he tried to call Clayton again. Still no answer.

He had the operator check the line. As far as she could determine, there was no trouble with the phone.

Wearily, he called the Grail Beachside and left another message. That done, he decided he'd waste no more time with that. Just out of bed and tired already...might as well get it over with. After all, what could he do about any of it anyway? Alcohol. The Graham curse killed old Massie. That it had caught up to Trip had only been a matter of time.

Grudgingly, he showered and dressed and went to get his brief-case and overnight bag, which he had packed last evening after all the craziness started. But, even after he had taken the bags to the car, Griff dawdled a moment, reluctant to leave. In his bones, he knew it was a mistake for him to go to Jacksonville with things the way they were here with Trip. It made no sense at all.

And even worse than him going down there, Clayton needed to be back here.

The calls from that Greensboro police chief made him very uneasy.

Ballsy behavior for a redneck cop.

For a politically-wise "homeboy cop" like D.C. Mills to dare question the moves or motives of a Graham in North Carolina was in and of itself a symptom of something ominous. Only the threat of a breaking scandal in the national...or international...media could bring a good ol' boy cop like Mills to even call—much less, inquire—about anything—not even a missing Graham hunting dog.

Still reluctant to leave, Griff went back into the house and poured himself a cup of leftover coffee and dialed Glee's number again.

Listening to the ringing noises on the other end, Griff put his cup in the microwave and philosophically considered his responsibility in all this. He was not happy with himself.

And he was downright disgusted with Clayton.

How could his old friend let that woman take precedence over the health of his only son? Did the son of a bitch have no conscience? The answer to that was easy. Clayton Massie Graham, Sr. never stopped to question his motives about anything. The Grahams—the Grail mystique—didn't really have anything to do with people. It had nothing to do with good, bad...right, wrong... sorrow, joy...love, hate...not in the sense the Grahams had emotions like regular people, or reacted like regular people or cared like regular people. They only looked like regular people. Grail was a fabrication—the glorious Graham tapestry. What was Grail made of anyway? Things...places... goods...raw materials...machines...buildings...certificates of ownership... memberships and all the other things that don't endure.

But certainly not compassion....

A Graham was brought up never to feel anything but good about anything he did.

It was simple. If the motives were Clayton or Mabel Graham's they were right. Who dared dispute it?

To the Clayton Massie Grahams, people were just people. You looked at them...you examined their family tree, what clubs they belonged to and what schools their children attended and what use you might make of any of all that—then you filed them in their proper pigeon hole.

Graham values? They respected people and things with a dollar sign attached. Even their own? At the moment, to Clayton, Trip was nothing more than a bitter disappointment, a problem...a liability.

Mabel and Clayton both were more concerned with the theater of their lives.

The Grail mystique?

317

Sadly, the Grail mystique had no real substance of its own. A theatrical production. Cosmetics...a dab of grease paint, good lighting and...of course...money.

Even a worn-out old play and a tired, second-rate cast can be revived...afforded a veneer of ever-fresh perfection. New supporting cast, new writing, new director and new players. Set design? A regal drawing room papered with genuine U. S. Treasury bills.

What about the actors? You can't cover up bad casting forever. Upon close inspection, the flaws show through the cosmetics. Now everyone was frantically trying to keep the Grail show from getting bad reviews. It was easy when the imperfections were scattered at random among the spear-bearers, but now one of the main actors was threatening to mess up the entire production.

Where was Norris?

Like some Woody Allen film, this called for the *wunderkind* writer/director/actor to come rushing in to save it just when it looked as if the script was without substance and the young male lead was suddenly taken too seriously drunk to continue.

Griff couldn't deny that he had let himself become a star player. He felt soiled, dishonest.

It was all suddenly getting him down. He was looking too much out from under a rock lately. It was an unfamiliar perspective.

It would all blow over as soon as Norris got back.

"*Come on, Clayton, answer...goddamn you.*" Griff kicked the edge of the kitchen counter in frustration. Finally, he placed the phone back on the cradle. He removed his cup from the microwave and took a sip of the steaming coffee.

Reluctantly, he closed the microwave and turned out the lights before he headed toward the front door again. In the darkened hallway, the unexpected jangle of the phone startled him in the stillness.

"Griffin Richards, here..." he answered, half-holding his breath.

"Griff, I was afraid I'd missed you. I just discovered Glee had turned off the ringer on the phone and the answering machine last night. What's going on up there?" Clayt asked. "What time's your plane?"

"Clayton, I've been desperate to reach you." Griff ignored the question about the plane. "Ed Scott took Trip to Holly Hall last night. But something else has come up. I didn't want to worry you earlier, but now I'm concerned. D.C. Mills, the Greensboro Police Chief, called. I'm afraid there may be trouble with the police...or, worse really...the news people, the media...TV and magazines...the whole nine yards."

"Slow down. Police? What'n'hell are you talking about? Media? What's this all about?"

"You need to get back here, now." Griff took a deep breath, then patiently recounted the details of the police chief's call. "That Barney Fife says Trip had that Claire woman in the car with him. Mills seems pretty sure of that..." Griff emphasized the words, *pretty sure.*

"Pretty sure, my ass," Clayton picked up on it. "Dead certain, huh?"

"That's the way I see it. Anyway, the bottom line is that I stalled Mills last night because Trip was sick. But Mills is going to call back to talk to Trip this morning. I definitely need to talk to the Doc, and I think I need to go to Holly Hall and talk to Trip before the cops do. You need to get back here in a hurry. The Chief swore he'd keep it under wraps for now, until he talked to Trip, but all the TV and news people in the whole world are in Greensboro circling like vultures. If there isn't a break soon, then there's probably going to be real trouble." Then Griff remembered. "Trip told me yesterday he doesn't remember anything much that happened Sunday."

"That's bullshit, how can you not remember a whole day? Trip's trying to cover up something. Why didn't you tell me this last night? Goddamn it, man, what do I pay you for?" Clayton exploded.

"I tried all night, goddamn it. Call the frigging Beachside and check your messages. Get your sorry ass up here and handle your own messes."

"Oh, shit, Griff, calm down! We can't just walk away from this real estate transfer. Glee has her heart set on it. The movers are coming in about two hours." Clayt didn't apologize, but he softened. "Goddamn Trip. Anyway, he's in the hospital, isn't he? Can't you have Doc Scott stall that cop? Fly down here on the red-eye now...we can fly the Lear back there this afternoon. Hell's bells, we'll be home by three at the latest. No sense making a mountain out of a molehill. What's wrong with you, anyway? We have a real estate deal awaiting transfer, and the movers...everybody...including Glee, expecting to get on with it. There's only a matter of nearly a half-a-million bucks involved...more... much more, if you included the trust," Clayton protested.

"Goddamn it, Clayton. Think about it. Sure, Trip's in the hospital and we can most likely keep him under wraps for a day...maybe two. D.C. Mills and just about the whole state is in our pocket...including the Attorney General and the Governor. But the Feds are surely in this now...it's drug related. And that's just the point. Your son was a walking drug raid. Trip's lab report showed he was doing cocaine yesterday and had smoked pot and was loaded with amphetamines, too. Not to mention the fact his blood alcohol was three times the limit for conviction as being too drunk to drive. *Time*, *People*, CNN are all camped on Mills' doorstep in Greensboro. If the national media gets a whiff that Trip is in any way involved, then the *Enquirer* is going to be camping in your front yard for the next ten years...talk about a nightmare." Griff paused for a breath. "We need to be talking to Ed Scott and arranging for that lab report to get lost and make sure Trip isn't given any blood tests at Holly Hall. If you want to stay down there, then stay. But, think about it...the media just might get curious enough to try to track you down. If the trail leads down there, what then?"

"Oh, jeezus..." Clayton said, suddenly aware the situation was reaching critical mass. "Do you think they could...?"

"If this blows up...count on it. If the whole goddamn world comes raining down on your ass like a million miles of bad Dow-Jones ticker tape, don't blame me."

"Maybe you're right...if I beat rush-hour traffic to the airport I could be there in about two...maybe three...hours...."

Griff let the silence lie between them like a disconnected circuit.

Finally, Clayton asked, "You still there?..."

"Yeah. I'm here. Listen hard and don't argue. Pack your stuff and sneak in through the pool entrance of the Grail Beachside. Take the elevator up to the Executive Suite and get the messages off the door. Then stroll nonchalantly by the desk. Make damn sure someone notices you. Cover your ass. As soon as you get to your car, haul your ass to the airport. I need to get busy. Call me, soon as you get back. I got my cell phone. I'll keep Ed Scott informed. We have to trust the Doc. He's the only one who can cover our tracks. Take care and don't panic."

"Where the hell is Norris? Have you tried to reach the independent asshole? What about the investigator you called yesterday?"

"I'll try him as soon as I hang up. But I've left messages at the Grail International, and I'll call Patty, his secretary, as soon as she gets in. Today is Wednesday, right? Norris had an appointment in New York this morning." Griff moved with the cordless phone to where he could see the calendar hanging at the end of the counter. "God...it seems like Friday, at least...what a week. Let me go now, so I can stay on top of this mess. Get a move on. You need to be back here. No telling when we can get Norris back. See ya' soon. Take care."

"Wait. When will you come down and finish the deal? Goddamn, Glee's going to raise hell when she finds out I'm leaving." Clearly Clayton's voice was filled with dread. "Oh, shit! Now she can't move today. Everything's all packed up here. There are boxes everywhere. She's going to kill me. What should I tell her?"

"Tell her I'll get down there...tell her...tomorrow...tell her anything. Now let me get off this phone and see if I can catch the Doc. Take care." He hung up without waiting to hear any more.

CHAPTER FORTY-NINE

WHEN HE HANDED MARILEE TO THE DOORMAN AT SADIE'S PLACE, Norris said, "I'll be back as soon as I can. Before noon if I can make it."

"Hurry. I hate to let you go." She leaned in and gave him a peck on the mouth.

Through light morning traffic, the limo driver made good time getting to the address Chatham had given him. In a very respectable Manhattan neighborhood of brick and brownstone houses, the street reminded him of the Georgetown section of Washington. About halfway down the block, the house was of neo-Colonial architecture, circa late 1800s. The shutters were painted that rich, almost black, shade of Williamsburg green and the woodwork was elegantly embellished with molding painted a deep-pewter shade of gray.

He was not at all surprised when Chatham Brookes, himself, answered the door.

"Chatham. Good to see you." Norris gave Brookes' outstretched hand a firm shake and followed him into the house.

"Can I get you coffee...or tea, perhaps?" Chatham hesitated after he had escorted Norris along a paneled hallway.

"Coffee...black...would be fine." Norris preceded him into the room and placed his briefcase on the floor beside a chair facing the door. Still standing, Norris quickly looked around. A nervous reflex held over from his undercover days in Central America.

He turned to Chatham and took the cup of coffee his host had poured from a pewter service on the sideboard.

"Uhmm...thanks. Well...how are you, Chatham? It's been quite some time since we were face to face. I must admit the President's call the other night caught me quite off guard. To be brutally honest, until you called last month, I really hadn't thought seriously about Phoenix for quite some time."

"Well, you may have given up, but I can assure you your concept has never been dead. It's been making ripples and waves and undercurrents around the world ever since it was published. It just keeps coming up. The idea is so simple and so sound. You are indeed a man of noble dreams." Chatham gestured at the chair. "Well...don't just stand there...relax...sit down."

Norris sat. "I'm not sure about dreams anymore. These days find me very much the cynic."

"Norris Wrenn a cynic?...you're hardly that." Chatham laughed.

"People change. Grow up. Phoenix was all a long time ago." Norris shrugged.

"Oh, c'mon Norris, you don't fool me. Quit playing the role of a hardboiled captain of industry. I've known you since the day you came to Dabney Farnsworth's office, still starry-eyed and wet behind the ears. Since you've been with Grail you've instituted corporate personnel policies that have redefined the word *paternalism* and reduced employee turnover to an all-time low. I know that the *Harvard Business Review* is doing a feature article on just that for the end of the year. Another first for Norris Wrenn. You're a man of...and by...and for...the people. If you're such a hardass, how come people always benefit when you're around?" Chatham leaned forward and looked Norris dead in the eye.

"Well...it's just good business to take care of your people." Norris shrugged. "It has nothing to do with giving a rat's ass about the poor dumb bastards. They probably aren't worth it. They always disappoint you...but then, just when you least expect it, they make you a hero in the end. Anyway, what's that got to do with Phoenix?"

"Well, nothing and everything really...and it has something to do with what I want to talk about after I bring you up-to-date." Chatham got up and crossed the room. He brought back a small stack of manila file folders. He shuffled them, found the one he was looking for and sat the others on the lamp table beside his chair.

Without preamble, he opened the folder and removed a single sheet of paper that was on top of a file of what looked to be twenty or thirty sheets of paper and handed it to Norris. It was a letter to the President from Royce Carstairs dated almost two months ago. It stated simply that, after careful thought, he—Carstairs—had come to realize the value of the Phoenix concept in a world struggling to find a common denominator for peaceful coexistence. It said he had already been in contact with the members of Norris' old team—"the moneytrust boys"—and there was solid agreement between them that Norris Wrenn should be persuaded to revive the Phoenix concept.

Norris was surprised that Carstairs, or even the President, could contact all those people without his getting wind of it. But, when he thought about it, he realized that in his effort to hide from Marilee over the past six weeks, he had definitely been out of the loop.

Norris handed the paper back to Chatham. "Well, it certainly does look like Carstairs has gotten serious about Phoenix again. But why? He was the reason it never got off the ground in the first place."

"Probably because he wants to be knighted by the Queen...he thinks he can be Prime Minister. And the President thinks that would be a good thing," Chatham stated simply. "It's good politics...translate that: *Good economics*."

"Uhmm. Yes, I tend to agree." Norris thought it over and added, "And apparently so do the 'moneytrust gang.' How about the Chinese...and the Russians? Hell, the Russians have subsidized their brightest and best for years. Economically, they're going down the tube, but in some ways they've always been smarter than anybody. You said there was a gathering of support from the minor players. How far has Carstairs gone?"

"Actually, he's been quite busy. He's flying in today. Can you meet with him tonight?" Chatham leaned back, confident Norris would agree.

"No, I can't meet with Carstairs before next week. It wouldn't do any good anyway. Did you hear about Tom Bradley?"

"Yes, we know all about it. Quite tragic. After you spent most of the day with him...and then your going to visit with his father...it must have come as a bad shock to you. I'm sorry, I always liked Tom...and had a lot of respect for him. But come on, man, he came through the surgery...he isn't dead yet...why can't you meet with Royce?" Chatham leaned forward, not believing Norris was refusing. He stopped in mid-sentence when he saw Norris' expression.

"How did you know I was with Tom? You had me followed? What on earth for? How long has this been going on?" Now that it was in the open, Norris was too unbelieving to consider whether he was angry or not.

"Oh, only for yesterday, from the time you arrived in Washington. Let's say it was merely a precautionary measure for your own protection. You're a public figure, and now we feel we have a vested interest in your well-being." Chatham tried to shrug the whole thing off as being unimportant.

"Why don't I believe you? Is that asshole out there in the fucking baby-shit-brown shoes assigned to me? Are you keeping watch over me now?" Norris was highly agitated. They knew he had just spent the night with the boss' wife. They had no reason to invade his privacy like this. No right. And here he was, getting ready to take off on a carefree escapade...like some sex-crazed jet-setter...he simply wouldn't allow it. "Goddamn it, Brookes, get me the President. I won't stand for this adolescent cloak-and-dagger shit."

Norris stood up and started for the phone.

Chatham just sat there. He said, in a very controlled voice, "Sit down, we're not tailing you now. The man outside is assigned to me. There's always someone assigned to me. It has to be that way. Jeezus man, don't you read the papers...or watch TV? The total body count from the WTC is still uncertain. Remember our Embassy in Beruit...the warship Cole? The al-Qaeda and God knows how many other crazies are plotting to blow up an airplane or a train...or storm an embassy right at this very moment. What do you think those people in that little village in Scotland thought when those bodies and pieces of airplane came raining down from heaven like some grotesque thundershower? And, what about

Oklahoma City? We're not talking cloak and dagger here. Like it or not, that's life in our time." Brookes didn't blink an eye. His voice carried an intensity Norris hadn't heard before.

"Don't bullshit me. I won't have my privacy tampered with. This street runs both ways." Norris stood glowering down at him. "I swear if I have the slightest hint I'm being followed, I'll forget I ever heard of Phoenix...and I just may drop some very juicy hearsay to the media about our current Commander-in-Chief's private life."

"Calm down. You're talking like a schoolboy. Don't you know who you are? Norris Wrenn isn't just the guy next door. You've been on the cover of every major magazine in the damn world. This country has a vital interest in your well-being. Circumstances could change that might demand we protect you. Certainly, after all your time in Washington you must be aware of that. Let's face it, your life isn't your own," Chatham spoke, calmly. "Now sit back down and let's talk. Why can't you meet with Royce?"

"First of all, I'm not ready to meet with him. I haven't made up my mind if I want to get involved again. Secondly, I don't know if I can find someone who will be my designated hitter in this. Tom Bradley was going to do it, but now he had the bad taste to get rundown about mid-afternoon yesterday...that leaves me in a very independent mood. Frankly, I don't know who else that might be. It's all too sudden. I hadn't taken this very seriously until night before last...and finally, I have personal plans for the next few days that I'm not about to change for anyone." Norris was tired of feeling manipulated. He turned, ready to leave. "Tell Carstairs I'll call him the first of next week."

"Wait, come back here. I have something more important to talk about." Chatham stood and put his hand on Norris' forearm.

"What do you mean?" Norris stopped; there was an increased urgency in Chatham's tone.

"Please. Sit down a minute and hear me out."

Reluctantly, Norris turned and went back to his chair. "OK, show and tell...what's this really all about?"

"How would you like to be Chief of Staff at the White House?"

Chatham asked, without blinking an eye.

"Why would anyone want to be anything at that crazy place? What am I supposed to say?"

"Just don't say, 'No,'" Chatham gave a nervous little laugh. "I'm sorry at the way I dropped it on you, but you're a tough man to talk to this morning. What's bothering you anyway...the little surveillance thing yesterday? Or maybe Tom Bradley's accident. Anyway, will you think about it?"

Norris looked Chatham in the eye. "Has all this Phoenix talk just been a smokescreen to get me to Washington?"

"No! Oh, hell no. That's serious. We...some individuals and I...thought Phoenix would be something you could do just as well if you were at the White House...but the two things are completely unrelated. The Chief of Staff thing has been in the works for some time now. It's part of a long-range plan by some people who care about this country's future. Off and on your name has been coming up. You were still a little young, but you were a popular considera- tion for a future Cabinet position in the last administration...you'd make a great Attorney General, for sure...but now I might as well put all the cards on the table. There's a strong move afoot to groom you for Secretary of State. Certainly, you must know you represent a powerful persona in the international arena. Eventually, you could wind up as President, you know. It must have crossed your mind."

"Are you kidding? Me? Chief of Staff?...Secretary of State...President? Why the hell would I...or anyone in his right mind...want to be President? Do you have any idea what my income will be at Grail under my new contract? In ten years I'll be worth tens of millions. More than that, really. Why the hell would I...?" Norris saw the look of concern on Chatham's face and stopped in mid-thought and took a deep breath. "Look, this is very flattering, but you're barking up the wrong tree. In case you've for- gotten, I did not endorse him...or his opponent...or their predeces- sor. I don't want my name mentioned in the same breath. Until the al-Qaeda brought the WTC down, he'd been a joke—flying around in Air Force One mouthing empty rhetoric. In California and Texas he promised to banish racial prejudice...in Mississippi he assured us he'd put an end to poverty...in North Dakota he vowed to stamp out alcoholism in Native Americans." Norris paused for breath. "In Africa he apologized for slavery but humbly pointed out it produced our great black leaders. To hear his Press Secretary, he single-handedly orchestrated peace between the Irish and the Brits. He says he'll put an end to teenage smoking, but promised the tobacco farmers they will not suffer...he guaranteed the baby boomers that Social Security is alive and well. And, now he's closed down abortion. Enrollments are up in Public Relations courses at colleges across the nation...there aren't enough spin doctors in the universe to cover up this jerk's past, present and future. What really scares me is that the people elected this drooling idiot. Why can't they see through this garbage? As long as we're winning the war on terrorism and the stock market is up and unemployment down, Jack the Ripper could be in the White House and the voters wouldn't give a shit. Count me out...politics is not something I want to be part of...."

"But you already are. You control a lot of power. Why not bring it to bear from the inside? Spin doctors or not, Congress is looking askance at the closing down of abortion. The country needs you, desperately. I don't represent the administration. To the men I represent, your political affiliation means nothing. Think about it...won't you?" Chatham pleaded. "Don't just walk away. In the end, you would regret it. Take a few days. We'll talk again," Chatham urged, quietly.

Norris knew there was nothing to be gained by just saying "no, thanks" and walking away. But he couldn't see any reason to give Chatham hope either.

"Well...I know this is too important to just dismiss out of hand, but I really think you'd better be prepared for plan B. As for Phoenix, if I can come up with someone to do the footwork, I'd really like to see that fly again. Anyway, I'm late and I need time to think. I'll call you...say Monday?"

"Well, I'd like it to be sooner...." Chatham said hopefully. "How about day after tomorrow... just to touch base? You might have some questions."

"Well, if I do, I'll call, but right now, don't plan on hearing from me until Monday." Norris' thoughts turned to Marilee. He was itching to get away.

"Well, all right...this is my cell phone. Call me anytime...this is important, but I don't have to tell you that." Chatham handed him a card.

"To tell the truth, I'm too overwhelmed at the moment to let all of this sink in, but I do understand it's important." Norris laughed and stuck out his hand. "I will be in touch."

"No later than Monday. Is there a number where we can reach you?..."

"No chance. If it's life or death, call Grail Corporate in Colonial Hall. Talk to my assistant, Patty Smith. She can always reach me. Goodbye, Chatham. I can't say this was dull." Norris started out before the other man could protest. Then, as an after-thought, he stopped and turned. "Chatham, I'm not kidding. Call off your dogs. I won't stand for having a tail."

"What do you have to worry about, Mr. Perfect?" Chatham winked. "But...don't forget the eleventh commandment: Thou shall not get caught."

Norris dismissed him with a wave and turned quickly away.

CHAPTER FIFTY

As HE PUT THE PHONE BACK ON THE HOOK, Clayton heard Glee behind him. When he looked up, the scowl on her face told him that she had heard.

"What the hell's going on?" she snarled, standing there, her face a harpy mask and her arms crossed just under her bosom.

"You're beautiful when you're angry." Clayton smiled, disarmingly.

"Cut the bullshit. What the hell's going on? Isn't Griff coming down?" She was in no mood for games. "And why are you leaving? What the hell do you think I am...." she couldn't finish the thought. She just stood there livid, obviously on the verge of tears.

"Don't take on so, it's just something that's come up. I can't help it. This thing with Trip's...ah...his illness...the situation has gotten complicated...there are some things that might have to be handled. Don't panic. Griff said he'd be down tomorrow...maybe even later today. Just as soon as this is taken care of," Clayton lied smoothly. He reached out to her and took her hands and pulled her toward him. She resisted slightly at first and then she collapsed on his lap astraddle him and buried her face in the hollow of his neck and shoulder. He could feel her sobbing softly, the wetness of her tears running down his neck and onto his chest. He reached up and gently smoothed her hair. He didn't try to speak...anyway, what could he really say? Besides, the silky texture of her pubic hair was rubbing low on his belly where both their loosely belted robes were open and he marveled that he was becoming hard again.

When Glee felt his erection, her sobbing diminished. Finally, she stopped crying altogether as she wiggled to spread her legs. Without saying anything, he let his hand slip between her widely-straddling thighs. Her sex-swollen labia parted at his touch.

Slippery wet again, the erotic scent of her wafted up to him and suddenly Clayt was overcome with need.

Without a word, Glee moved to welcome him. Almost before he was completely inside her, she let go a sharp cry of release and began to ride him fiercely, shuddering over and over in almost continuous waterfalls of ecstasy.

Clayton could feel his own release beginning to build, rumbling inside him like an approaching locomotive until the roar inside his brain deafened him and the blunt force of the flow gushed out, flooding into the sticky-sweet velvet cavity.

It was over in a matter of a minute.

"Oh, my, oh my God," Clayton finally gasped.

"That was outrageous. That was the best...the all-time best." Glee slumped forward and let her face nestle in the hollow of his neck again. She fell silent now, but Clayt could feel her gathering energy. Finally, she straightened and looked down at him. "Can't you and I just run up to Fernandina and take care of the papers? Then, I could still get the moving done today," she pouted.

"It's too complicated. Griff has to set it all up. After all, you do want everything to be done right, don't you? It's your future. It's going to be your property...and your business. That's what it's all about. I hate you have to be disappointed, but a day or so won't matter." He pulled her chin forward and kissed her lightly on the nose. "Now...let me up. I've got to call the airport and make sure the Lear is serviced. Then I've got to shower...*again*." He laughed and winked. "You make me more of a man than I knew I was."

"All right...but I hate it. Can't you just call? Ask them to let me go ahead and let me have the movers move my things...they'll trust you...there isn't any furniture or stuff like that, come on, why not?" she whined. "I could rent a condo down the road at Amelia for a day or two...."

"Nope, there's insurance and things I don't know enough about to discuss...that's what lawyers are for. Let me up, now." Clayt was losing his patience. "I'm wasting time...that goddamn airport will be a zoo by the time I get there."

"Well, I think it just plain sucks. An all-around shitty deal. A lot you care about me," she said. Reluctantly, she moved aside and headed for the bathroom as Clayton dialed the airport.

When he hung up, she appeared in the doorway again.

"What would Mabel do if she suddenly had to move out of her house and...."

"Stop, goddamn it! Look...Glee honey, Griff's a very careful man, believe me. And, to be cold-blooded, one of the reasons he has to be here is we had to be very careful none of this would cause a mess in the event of my death. It's all set. Now all you have to do is be patient for another day or two. God knows, I certainly don't like having to go back there and clean up Trip's mess." He stopped in front of her as he went through the door and kissed her on the forehead. "Now, don't you think it would be a good idea to call the movers and tell them it's all off for today? Griffin promised he'd be down tomorrow."

"But..." Glee started to protest, then something clicked in her head. Last night she had overheard enough of Clayton's phone conversation to figure out Trip was sick...and drunk...and had taken some drugs...and generally was giving everyone a hard time. But this thing this morning was different. When she was still half-asleep, she was sure she'd heard Clayton mention the word 'police' when he was talking on the phone.

All that stuff Dempsey had found yesterday. Maybe he was right. Maybe they had the Grahams by the balls. As soon as Clayton left, she'd call Demp and see what was going on. Glee flashed Clayt a phony little smile and headed into the bedroom to call the movers.

She was just putting down the phone as Clayton emerged, carrying his bags.

"Well, I'm out of here." He shrugged.

"Can I walk down with you, at least?" She reached for one of the bags.

"No...I'm sorry, hon. I'll call you later...sometime after dinner. Anyway, just be patient. I'll be back as soon as I can...a couple of days at the most."

"I'll probably start my period next Monday...Tuesday at the latest. If you could come back tomorrow...that's only Thursday...then we could get moved and have the weekend all to ourselves. Almost like we planned." Glee smiled and kissed him with her mouth open.

"Uhmm..." He recoiled slightly from the kiss and pulled away.

"Do I have bad breath or something?" Feeling rejected and abandoned, suddenly she felt a strong wave of hatred for the old bastard. She fought back the urge to brush her teeth.

"Don't start anything we can't finish." He laughed and headed for the door. "Sunday's Mother's Day. I'd have to be back home for that. But, if things work out OK, I might be back here tomorrow afternoon. We'll see...just let's keep our fingers crossed. I'll call you later," he said and was gone before she could blink an eye.

"I hope your goddamn rotten son bleeds to death...while he's in jail...waiting to go to the electric chair," she muttered under her breath. Feeling badly used, she went into the bathroom and brushed her teeth and stepped into the shower for the second time.

She was tired of being jerked around. She didn't want to start any trouble, but she would if she had to. Nobody...but nobody was going to take her condominium away from her. After she got that, she really didn't care what any of them did. If there was some leverage, some way she could obtain power over Clayton Graham, she wanted to know more about that. Goddamn Clayton Graham...she would show him he couldn't treat her like this.

Now, with the warm water running over her she began to put some order to the confusing sequence of events that had begun last evening with all the calls. Trip was sick...a hemorrhage. Booze. And there were drugs involved. Cocaine...a lot. What had Dempsey said? Trip was trying to destroy evidence that linked him with the Claire woman. Not murder...what did he say? Felony drug death? That was serious, she knew that.

She had to call Demp.

Out of the shower, she looked at her watch. Not yet 7:00. She poured herself a cup of coffee and on impulse went into the living room and dialed Dempsey's number. It rang once before she realized she hadn't called collect so she hung up and placed the call again. The phone rang for a long time before she heard him answer.

His voice was heavy with sleep as the operator cleared the charge.

"Uh...ah...Glee? Uh...what's up, hon?" Demp struggled to sound awake.

"Demp...sorry to wake you, but I just needed to talk. Do you want to grab a cup of coffee and wash your face and call me back?" It was best to wait until he was alert before she started a serious conversation.

"Well...uh...what's on your mind?" He still sounded like a zombie.

"Look, I've got news...will you get some coffee in you and call me back as soon as you're awake? Say, ten minutes...or fifteen? Whatever?" Now, all at once, she was itching to know more about what he'd told her yesterday. Every time it appeared she was going to wind up the winner, everything turned to shit again.

Silence.

"Demp? Are you there?"

"Huh? Oh...yeah. Yeah...what time is it? Seven? Judaspriest, I've only been to bed about four hours. I was flying that Doctor Scott and a nurse and Trip Graham around the country all night. We didn't get back here until almost two. By the time I got home, it was nearly three. Hold on, while I warm up the coffee pot, will ya?" He sounded more alert now. "Where the hell is Old Moneybags? I thought he was there with you."

"Well, he was. I mean he was here last night. He got called from back there last night about Trip drinking too much and getting real sick, a hemorrhage. Anyway, Clayton was talking on the phone when I woke up about an hour ago and I heard him say something about 'the cops'. The next thing I know he hangs up the phone and said he had to go back right away. Then he just packed up his things and left. I remembered what you told me yesterday, and I want to know what the hell is going on? Look, why don't you just call me back here in a few minutes? I'm sure as shit not going anywhere. OK?" Glee waited for a reply.

334

"Cops? Goddamn! Yeah, I'll call you right back...soon as I can get the coffee on. I want to turn on the TV and see what's on the news about that Emma Claire case. This is getting very interesting. Give me a few minutes." Demp hung up without waiting for her reply.

On the floor near her feet, where Clayton had dropped it, the headline of the morning paper fairly jumped off the page:

DID ACTRESS DIE OF OVERDOSE?

She picked up the newspaper, located the remote, turned on the TV and switched to CNN. As the weather girl was finishing the forecast, she turned the volume up to a barely audible level and quickly scanned the paper about the actress' death.

Nothing...some new hoopla about the disappearance of some White House chopper pilots.

Her coffee cold, she poured it into the sink and refilled the cup. Wandering aimlessly about, she looked at the boxes stacked against the walls and her resentment boiled up again.

She glanced at her watch. What was taking so long? Had Demp gone back to sleep?

The sudden jangle of the phone startled her back to reality.

"Glee?" Dempsey sounded better now. "What's going on down there?"

"You first...what's going on up there?"

"All hell broke lose. Trip Graham fucked up. C'mon, tell me what happened down there."

"Well, last night the phone started ringing and...like I told you...there was all this excitement about Trip having a hemorrhage and being drunk and drugs were mentioned...still...when we went to sleep, Clayton seemed to think it was all a lot of fuss over nothing. Then this morning Clayton got up early and, the next thing I know, he's telling Griffin Richards he'll fly back there this morning. I heard the word 'cops'. That seemed to trigger all the sudden change in plans. Anyway, the worst part is Griffin isn't coming down here to close the deal on the condo at Starfish and I'm mad as hell..." Now, she was on the verge of tears again.

"Well, well, well...very interesting. The plot thickens,"

Dempsey said. "I just checked the Raleigh paper and the TV and they don't really have anything new to say about the Emma Claire death except that it's probably a cocaine overdose. I've got that cocaine...powder and crack...and all the other stuff right here that Trip thought he got rid of yesterday. Listen babe, I kid you not, this ties him in absolutely tight with Emma Claire. Goddamn, I'm talking underwear...and other stuff...some with her name in it. It was all in a motel bag from the place she was staying and another bag with her bathing suit from the Massie House in Greensboro where Trip was staying, I'm sure. His calling card was in the pocket of her jogging outfit...Jeez, have we latched on to dynamite here. I'm telling you, babe, we got 'em between the rock and the hard place." Dempsey paused. "And the old boy said 'cops' to Richards, huh? That does it. They called me to fly Trip out of town late last night. He really was sick though...I'm talking sick as shit."

"Got him out of town? Where? What do you mean?" Glee was having a hard time trying to figure it all out. What did Trip being sick and the Claire girl's death have to do with each other? They kept getting mixed together in some way she didn't understand. She asked, "Did Trip Graham overdose too?"

"Uhmm...you might say that...some deputy sheriff found him out by the same dumpsite where he threw away this bag of evidence yesterday. Passed out cold. I'm sure the dumb asshole went back out there to make sure all this evidence was better disposed of." Demp gloated.

"Wait, slow down...go back...." Glee was really confused now.

"Well, they...I mean Doctor Scott, the Grail medical director, called me around nine...maybe a little later...and asked me if I could get a company helicopter and a pilot ready to fly Trip to Holly Hall—it's a very exclusive, very fancy and highly confidential drying out hospital near Pinehurst. Turned out to be quite a night. Relax, babe, we got 'em by the balls," Demp crowed, happily.

"Well...I don't know...but they're sure'n'shit scared of something. They don't care about anything except their precious family—the sacred Graham name...fucking Grail. Fuck 'em all. I hope they put the darling bastard in jail and spread it over the newspapers all the way to...all the way to the goddamn Shangri-La-la land," Glee snorted, angrily.

"Don't be too quick to wish that. If the cops are looking for a person or persons unknown, then we really hold all the cards. Remember what happened to that woman involved in the Belushi thing. She ended up shit creek without a paddle. The Grahams would do almost anything to prevent that kind of publicity...I am goddamn positive of that." Demp's tone left no doubt.

"Well...what happens now? I'm sitting down here waiting until god knows when...Clayton said maybe tomorrow...but he probably was just trying to calm me down. As soon as I get that condo, they can stick it right up their ass anytime they want to. They won't fuck with me. Clayton wouldn't want his precious Mabel-honey to find out about us. So what's the plan, Flyboy?" Glee was still uncertain how they could use the information. "Blackmail is a dangerous business."

"Well...all we can do for the moment is sit tight and see what comes next. Did you say Clayt is flying the Learjet back here now? I'll call the tower and see if they've heard from him. Then, I think I'll just mosey over to the airstrip and hang out for awhile. I'll call you later and give you a report. If you need me, call me at my office. Keep smiling...looks like things are coming up roses, babe," Dempsey said. "Stay cool and *ciao*."

"Call me later, anyway. Just to see if I'm sane, OK?" She was still feeling quite insecure.

"OK. Don't worry so much. I'll call maybe late-middle-afternoon...if I don't have anything to report before. Bye." Again, the phone went dead before she could respond.

Sitting there, Glee stared out over the balcony rail at the warm early morning glint of sun shimmering low across the glassy surface of the sea. Now the mists had cleared, to the north she imagined she could see the faint finger of land which was Starfish Cay. Why did everything always have to turn to shit for her, she wondered. What had she done to deserve such a raw deal from men?

She got up, padded back to the bedroom, got into bed and pulled the cover over her head.

CHAPTER FIFTY-ONE

IT WAS NOT QUITE HALF-PAST ELEVEN by the time Norris' limo made its way back across town. His head was still buzzing from the encounter with Chatham.

It had all been so unexpected.

He had hardly been prepared to be offered one of the most powerful political jobs in the country. And a future cabinet post...Secretary of State...maybe even President of the United States of America? Who were they fooling? What a joke. But, no doubt, they were dead serious. Nobody kids about a thing like that. They were just trying to use him. He had to put an end to all this nonsense. He was about to become a very rich CEO of a *Fortune*-13 corporation...that was the only full-time job he wanted.

President?...what a soap opera. He didn't care about being president...did he?

Well?...did he?

Of course not. Contemptuously, he shook his head.

Still...if he wanted to run, he was pretty sure he had a good chance to win.

He was as big as Lee Iacocca had ever been—more charismatic really...and certainly more popular than Bill Gates. Lee Iacocca could've been president...no contest. Gates, never.

Enough of this nonsense...he shook his head again. He had better things to think about.

When he arrived at Sadie's building, Marilee, dressed in an old sweatshirt, thin cotton jeans and sandals was waiting upstairs, her door wide open. Trimmed with mellow saddle leather, her expensive duffel with the name of the famous designer woven discreetly into the fabric, sat just inside the foyer.

Norris took her in his arms and kissed her.

"All set?" he asked.

She nodded, breathlessly.

He bent and picked up the duffel.

"Then let's get the hell out of here."

The phone rang and Marilee hesitated. She looked at him.

Norris shook his head.

The answering machine clicked on as they headed out—thankfully, the sound was off.

In the limo, Norris called Washington Hospital Center.

"Mr. Bradley has been rushed back to surgery...some bleeding in the abdominal cavity...." Norris' knuckles went white against the tiny cellular instrument.

Don't quit now, Tom....

When he hung up, he squeezed Marilee's hand.

On the way across town, he was helpless not to look back to see if he could catch a glimpse of a suspicious car.

Everything looked OK...as far as he could tell....

At LaGuardia, he directed the driver down a little side road between two of the major airline terminals and through a gate in the high chain-link fence which separated the taxiways and runways from outside traffic.

A sleek, private jet sat waiting on the parking strip outside a large hangar housing planes of several commercial charter services and corporations.

Before the limo had fully stopped, Doug Reed—leather flight case in hand—emerged from a door marked Operations and started toward them at a brisk pace.

Within minutes they had boarded and Norris was helping Marilee fasten her seat belt as they taxied out to take their place behind a line of large commercial jets.

After the aircraft had quietly lifted into the sunlit sky, cleared the cluttered New York air traffic pattern and finally reached altitude over Long Island Sound, Doug Reed leaned back and told Norris where he'd stowed their lunch.

"Thanks, pal. When we get within sight of Bar Harbor, let me know. How long, do you think?" Norris asked as he went to the compact little galley and started to put ice in two tall glasses.

"An hour...maybe a little less. I'll let you know. If you need anything, holler." The good-natured pilot smiled through the cockpit door and winked.

"Bar Harbor?...so that's your secret hideaway?" Marilee asked.

Norris smiled and shook his head. He put down his sandwich, opened his briefcase and took out an official marine navigation chart. He loosened his tie and folded it carefully and placed it in the briefcase before he unfolded the chart.

"Maine...yes. But not Bar Harbor." He traced the ragged shoreline with his finger. "That's Bar Harbor...but...we're going *here*." His finger pointed out a tiny, but well-defined, dot of land a little removed from a maze of islands off the coastline. By comparison with the other dots around it, the island was not overly large. There was a small semi-circle of water on the leeward side where an almost round little harbor was neatly sculpted out of the land mass. The basin was so landlocked it was almost completely enclosed by the encircling fingers of the island.

The legend *Sheepshead Light* was printed next to a small dot by the harbor.

"That little village is right out of a history book. Except for electricity and a really good local satellite-linked microwave telephone system—both installed and maintained by the Coast Guard—Sheepshead Light remains virtually unchanged over the past several hundred years."

Doug stuck his head out of the cockpit. "Norris, Isle Au Haut is just off our port side."

Norris nodded.

"Come on, let's have a look." He took Marilee's hand and moved to the long, deeply-padded bench along the left-hand side of the aircraft. When he looked out, there was nothing but open sea directly underneath the plane and, up ahead, as far as the eye could see through the cloudless sky, there was only the rugged island-dotted coast below. Disappointed, Norris looked to the rear and barely caught sight of a populated area on the northern end of a large island sliding quickly underneath the rear of the plane, already almost out of view.

"Look." He pointed. "We're already past Isle Au Haut. We're running a little ahead of schedule." He pointed out the island on the chart.

Marilee watched fascinated as the ragged coastline passed underneath, and almost before Norris had the words out of his mouth, she felt the aircraft slow perceptibly and start into a long, downward glide.

"Come over here now; Sheepshead Light will be coming up soon. It's almost thirty miles off the mainland. Keep your eyes looking in that direction, out to sea. We'll be approaching from the southwest." Norris pointed ahead and about forty-five degrees to the right.

Marilee had followed him to the starboard side of the compartment and crouched in a kneeling position beside him. She peered impatiently northeastward out across the shimmering sea below. Catching his scent and feeling his breath upon her neck, her thoughts drifted back to the ecstasy of last night. Now she wanted only to be on the ground, alone with him again.

"Look, there it is! Watch and you'll see the glint of the sun off the lighthouse prisms. There, see it?" Norris pointed ahead, but at first Marilee could see nothing. Suddenly she caught a blinding sparkle across the distance through the bright, mid-afternoon haze. The island began taking shape as the jet rocketed down ever closer to the sea. Almost before she could get her bearings, the village became clearly defined across the nearly landlocked little bay, and the airstrip loomed up at them beyond the lone church steeple near the top of the steep, almost cliff-like terraces leading down to the harbor. At the water's edge, across the narrow little street from where the fishing boats were tied up, there was a grayish-blue wooden structure with dark shutters at the windows.

Norris pointed it out. "See the large building on the waterfront? That's the Lion and Thistle. It's the only inn on the island. That's where we're staying. See the three windows across the top right-hand corner? The view of the sunset is lovely from there."

"It looks like something right off the pages of a storybook. There are certainly a lot of boats. Are there many tourists this time of year?" Marilee didn't like the prospect of a lot of people all over the place. Both of them were far too recognizable to the public.

"No tourists on Sheepshead. Just local lobstermen and shopkeepers—the realest people you'll ever meet," he assured her.

There was a warning bell, and the seatbelt sign came on overhead. After Norris had helped her get securely fastened in, Marilee looked out the window just in time to see the town suddenly rushing underneath. They passed so close she felt she could almost reach out and touch the gull perched on the cross crowning the church steeple. From where the church stood, the street dropped sharply down the steep hill to the waterfront. The church was the uppermost structure on the short, steep little street which rose to the flat, treeless plain stretching across the upper plateau of the island to the lighthouse on the point of land to the eastward side.

As the impossibly small landing strip loomed closer and closer, Marilee's tummy flipped apprehensively. It became apparent that the pilot had overshot the runway. Instinctively, she reached across and grasped Norris, momentarily frozen with terror.

"Relax. When you're landing a hot airplane on a small strip you don't need any surprises. Doug is making a pass to check out the wind direction and to make sure there's no large debris on the runway...and sometimes you flush out a flock of birds feeding in the grass." Norris pointed below. "See the windsock. The wind is light today...from the ocean. We'll make a wide turn and come back over the harbor to land into it. It's just routine. This strip is maintained by the government only as an emergency strip. It's rarely used except by me and the people who maintain the light. See that little cottage by the lighthouse? The lightkeeper, Moe Greenberg, lives there. Hey, look! There he is standing out by our car waving...Moe's a young intellectual. Writing a book. Perfect place for it. You'll like Moe."

A fleeting glimpse of a young man, a house, the light and the Land Rover...then whoosh! Before Marilee could get her breath, the island passed underneath in a blinding rush. She felt as if she was sitting in a Cinerama theater, watching the roller coaster tracks whizzing beneath her seat.

Dear God, she thought, *don't kill me now. Not when I've just found my reason for living.*

"My god, is that runway long enough to land on?" she gasped.

"Of course it is...relax. We'll be on the ground in five minutes now." Norris chuckled and squeezed her arm. "The Lion and Thistle is a homey little place. It has about three fishing boat captains and a couple of schoolteachers who live there year round. It's locally glamorous because—according to the townspeople—JFK once brought Marilyn here for a weekend one summer. Some of the older folks won't talk about it, but if you'll listen, the younger gossipy types will tell all the fascinating details..."

Pondering his meeting with Chatham Brookes, Norris studied her profile as Marilee looked out the window. Such an amazing mind...such quiet maturity...and the enthusiasm of a schoolgirl. What a First Lady she would make. Those snobs in Washington would take notice—forget Jacqueline or Nancy Reagan.

JFK had been how old when he had taken office?...forty-three...forty-four?

If he should run in 2004, he would be only forty-two. Retired as President of the United States at forty-six or fifty...now that was certainly something to think about.

If the brown-shoed company boys found out, he wondered what Chatham and his unnamed secret associates would have to say about his sneaking around with a married woman?

Too late to wonder now...most likely, the bastards already knew.

Why should he care? The spooks might as well forget about taking notes on his sex life. Did they think he would give up his deal with Grail to go throw Frisbees and hunt Easter eggs on the White House lawn? What did he care about being Chief of Staff...or even Secretary of State...if that's what it turned out to be.

And...president? Who the hell were presidents anyway? In most cases, it was their great-grandfathers who had gotten into politics and left them with a family tradition. The family fortunes had dwindled over the spread of political generations, so now politicians were easy to buy with consultation fees and any sort of under-the-table money you offered them. Like the incumbent Ivy redneck, mostly they were people who had never done a real day's work in their lives. People who couldn't make it in law practice and got into politics to keep the kids in school. Men like that were the property of men like himself. Why would he want to lower himself to that level? As soon as Clayt got back from Jacksonville, he would be his own man forever.

Nobody would ever own him again.

Presidents and power...that myth was so much bullshit! Being CEO of Grail was where the real power was. He would be a fool to give up the right to be left alone. No jerks in ill-fitting suits and GI shoes lurking about.

He stole another glance at Marilee.

God, just looking at this woman sitting across from him made him forget everything. Her strength and grace filled him up.

The well-scrubbed scent of her made him dizzy. He could still taste her kiss. And the memory of last night's orgasms. For Hemingway's heroes only the earth moved. What did Hemingway know? What did anyone know? Last night she had introduced him to blinding starbursts flashing through a milky way.

There are some things that are so rare you didn't even dare believe they exist...you lived and died...sleepwalking through life...never suspecting that they are there all the time, never to be known by you. Then through some sort of divine intervention...or call it blind luck...you walk out on a pre-dawn beach and it changes your whole value system—your whole goddamn life!

The wheels of the plane made a sharp squeaking sound as the rubber contacted the runway and the plane touched lightly down.

The plane came to a halt and Norris leaned across and kissed Marilee on the ear lobe.

"Welcome to Paradise...."

As soon as they stopped rolling, Moe Greenberg stuck his head

344

inside, and, in less than two minutes, the three of them had off-loaded the luggage into the Land Rover parked a few steps from the plane. Norris shook hands with Doug. In less than five minutes from the moment of touchdown, the plane was airborne again.

"Well...Norris, long time no see," Moe began...then he looked at Marilee and said, "it's about time he brought you up here, Mrs. Wrenn."

Norris didn't say anything...what was there to say to that? He hadn't thought about any of this. It wasn't at all like him to be doing things without thinking them through. He always had things carefully worked out. He wondered what poor Tom Bradley would have to say about being careful now, lying unconscious back there in the hospital?

Too late for either one of them to worry about that now.

CHAPTER FIFTY-TWO

WHEN CLAYTON GRAHAM PULLED THE RENTAL CAR out of the parking deck beneath Glee's high-rise apartments, he was still debating whether or not to take Griff's advice and go through the little charade of stopping by the Grail Beachside to establish at least a surface case for having been in residence there last evening.

Basically, Griff was right. If he took the messages from the door of the Presidential Suite and went by the hotel desk on the way out, then who could say he hadn't been there at least all or part of the evening? The hotel was the most popular place on the beach and always full. There were perhaps four hundred registered guests there right at the moment. And, if this thing turned out to be a nasty matter with the law, then it couldn't hurt to cover his ass.

He shrugged. What could he lose?

Of course, the idea of the cops didn't bother him as much as he feared the media. He could handle the law. Even the Feds. But the media was tricky.

It was Clayt's experience that journalists were much more inventive with the truth than the cops...and certainly much more ruthless and less bound by the rules of conduct than the law. But in this instance, as in most similar cases, the law was being controlled by the threat of the press looking over their shoulders and under their carpets and poking in their closets. The law had their own asses to look out for.

The North Carolina media he could manage. Even nationally, his people at Grail could usually handle an isolated paper or magazine. But when it became a matter of a feeding frenzy like the death of this actress, Emma...ah...Whatsherface, which had already attracted a regular shitstorm of lurid national attention, then, cops or media, it made no difference, there would be no stopping anything...or anybody.

Without further deliberation, Clayt turned south and made his way up A1A to the hotel. He was in luck. He found a parking space on the street at the north side of the building. Now, he didn't have to pull into the parking deck. From there, carrying his jacket carelessly swung across his shoulders, the perfect picture of a Yankee vacationer out for an early morning stroll, he quickly made his way across the dunes toward the swimmer's entrance. Except for a handful of early-morning risers, at this hour the beach was still nearly deserted. When he casually strolled up the steps leading to the large hotel's pool and beach entrance, a few people nodded but none took special notice.

Inside he took the elevator and got off at the fifteenth floor. From there, he moved just around the corner and took the coded plastic card from his card case and inserted it into the mechanism to the door to the private lobby accessing the stairs and a special elevator to the corporate executive suites occupying the Penthouse level. He ignored the elevator and took the stairs, swiftly traversing the two flights up to the Penthouse. Again he accessed the electronic mechanism to obtain entry. The entire Penthouse was reserved for Grail executives and their guests. At the south end was a large suite reserved for the Graham family, and two smaller suites on the end overlooking the beach were in the control of top executives from The Tower in Colonial Hall.

One quick glance revealed no one in sight. He made his way without incident to the door of the Presidential Suite, inserted the card and slipped inside. Lying on the floor just inside the door were the message slips from Griff's calls the night before. He checked through them and found the one from Griff earlier this morning. He gathered them up and stuffed them into his jacket just to make sure he had evidence of his presence. Just as he was about to retreat and make his exit downstairs for all to see, he was suddenly struck by an inspiration. He went to the wall phone in the kitchen and dialed his unpublished number in Colonial Hall. The answering machine picked up on the second ring, which meant he had other messages already on the machine. Clayt listened patiently until he heard himself finish the recorded message and heard the tone. Then he punched in the code and listened to the messages. There was only one: Curtis Strange had called from Williamsburg, Virginia about an invitation to play in the celebrity Pro-Am in Monterey, California in January. Clayt pushed in the code to save the message so he didn't have to make a note and congratulated himself for establishing a record of a phone call from this phone. Now he moved quickly to the bedroom and pulled back the covers and tossed the pillows in disarray. On the way back out, he stopped in the bathroom and unwrapped a bar of soap and dropped it on the floor of the shower and ran the water.

After a moment, he looked around and tossed the bath mat carelessly on the floor and dropped two bath towels casually on the counter beside the sink. One of them slipped to the floor and he didn't bother to pick it up.

Now, it became a game.

Unwrapping a glass, he ran in some water and carefully sprinkled the bath mat and then the towels just enough to dampen them. As an afterthought, he took a wash cloth, soaked it under the faucet and tossed it into the tub. For a final touch of theater, he unzipped his trousers and urinated in the commode.

He did not flush.

Feeling like some character out of a TV movie, he left and took the elevator down to the lobby.

"Good morning, Mr. Graham. I just sent a message up to your room, did you get it?" At the desk, the Night Manager recognized him immediately.

"Yes, thanks. I was out for a walk. If anyone else calls, tell them I'm on my way to the airport. I'm flying directly back to Colonial Hall. My ETA will be no later than noon. I may be back later in the week. Thanks." He waved as he turned and moved across the lobby out the door.

Back in the car, he retreated directly back down A1A to where J. Turner Butler Parkway headed west to connect with I-95. It was not yet 8:00, but the Jacksonville traffic was already stacked up. He considered himself lucky. Basically, he was traveling against the heaviest flow...still...at the moment, it was hard to tell the difference.

When he finally made the airport, he bypassed the parking lot at the private hangar and went around the building and pulled directly up beside the Lear. Without turning off the engine, he transferred his gear into the airplane before he moved the car back to the other side of the hangar and parked it.

It was still early. With almost no activity going on in Operations, Clayton was able to quickly clear all the pre-flight paperwork. Within fifteen minutes, he had strapped himself into the left seat of the Lear cockpit.

"Jacksonville Ground, this is Grail Lear six-zero-six-niner-zero, request taxi with alpha."

"Roger, Grail Lear six-zero-six-niner-zero, with alpha, clear to taxi, follow the Delta 757 off to your left to runway zero-nine as you come off the hanger line."

Now, waiting not too patiently for the line of large commercial jets ahead of him, he vowed for perhaps the tenth time in as many recent trips in and out of Jacksonville to check into using the smaller private field north of here. It was located closer to Fernandina Beach and Starfish anyway. That way he could avoid contact with the other, mostly larger, planes in the Grail corporate fleet which were limited to using the larger, commercial fields. Using the smaller, more convenient field would avoid the possibility of running into Grail people when he wasn't scheduled here—that always meant making up silly excuses to explain his presence in the area.

More than once, he had to go spend an entire day at the local offices just to cover his ass.

He was going to be freer now that Norris was taking control. He could just disappear from time to time and not have to make any excuses to anyone...except to cover his butt at home. That part was easy. To Mabel his travel was a way of life. She was used to his being gone. She hardly took notice anymore.

A few years back, Jacksonville had grown like a mushroom—in square miles, the largest city in the country. But that was about ninety-nine percent Chamber of Commerce bullshit—it included countless square miles of useless salt marsh. Still, the city was thriving again. Already the early morning buildup of heavy commercial air traffic was mute evidence of new prosperity of the area.

Thinking of Mabel, he wondered if he shouldn't have called her from the Operations office before he took off. Well, it was too late for that. He hoped Griffin would be able to head off that cop from calling Mabel. Goddamn, he didn't want her any more upset than she probably was already from the craziness of last night.

What the hell had happened lately? The whole fucking world had gone insane around him.

Goddamn Trip...what could he do with him now? Clayton had seen his father fight and lose the battle with the bottle. If Trip really was an alky like Ed Scott said, then it was going to be a major problem to keep him out of the public eye. He vaguely remembered that Norris had instituted some sort of corporate treatment program to handle alcohol and drug problems for employees. He remembered because he had fought it tooth and nail as being too goddamn expensive. The entire plan had raised the cost of the benefits package by millions. But then Norris had bought out an insurance company, and Grail became its own provider.

That goddamn Norris was a genius. He'd figure out what to do with Trip, no sweat.

Was Trip really involved in Emma Claire's death? How do you get involved in an overdose anyway? In that Maryland basketball player's death, they had finally let off the roommates, or friends...whomever—the others who had taken part in the thing. In that case, it seemed more a matter of trying to establish where the cocaine came from, not a matter of anyone giving him a needle...or was it that way in the Belushi thing? He couldn't remember. It was impossible to believe Trip could shoot something into someone's arm. And he still couldn't believe Trip had used all those drugs Ed Scott said showed up in the lab report.

Goddamn that lab test, anyway. It would be a disaster to have that lab report floating around. He hoped Griff had been able to take care of that detail. He'd have to have Norris have a talk with Ed Scott. This whole thing sounded like poor judgment on the doctor's part. Scott had obviously overreacted.

Why?

Oh yes...that thing about the hemorrhage...Clayton sobered momentarily when he remembered his own father lying in the boardroom in a pool of blood. Well, he had to admit Trip's hemorrhage was certainly cause for concern. Somehow though, he couldn't believe Trip's condition was that serious...after all, he was only thirty-seven.

But for Ed Scott to order a drug test on a member of the Grail hierarchy...and a Graham at that? Ed had handled that badly. The doc should have exercised more professional discretion.

Clayton taxied the Lear to the run-up block behind the big Delta jet.

"Grail Lear six-ninety, stand by for the tower on frequency one-eighteen point three...good flying, Grail," the familiar voice from the ground controller crackled in his headset.

"Roger, Jax Ground, Grail six-niner-zero changing frequency... have a good day," he acknowledged.

And Norris. A genius, no doubt about it, but a streak of stubbornness a mile wide...and where was the bastard when he needed him?...he went running off to Washington every time the phone rang. Lately, it seemed the White House was calling every day.

Sitting there, watching the USAirways 767 rolling down the runway, Clayt resolved to have a heart-to-heart with Norris before he got too big for his britches. As soon as the private investigator got busy, at least he'd know where the bastard holed up when he was in New York...why was Norris so secretive, anyway?

"Jax Tower, this is USAir two-niner climbing through a thousand...there are a blue-million seagulls on the lake due east, off the end of the runway. I never saw anything like it..." Now, the transmissions between the tower and the traffic came over the earphones.

"Roger, USAir, this is seagull country," the tower said happily.

Maybe he should have called Griffin from back at Grail Operations...no, Griff knew he was coming...he'd call Grail Air Centre and give 'em his ETA...Griff would be calling there.

"Jax Tower to all aircraft on this frequency, there is a large flock of seabirds on the lake off the take-off end of zero-niner."

He hated to leave Glee all pissed off like that...but well-fucked nonetheless. She couldn't complain on that score. He'd get Griff back down here by early next week for the house deal....

"To all the girls I've loved before...." he hummed the Willie Nelson number to himself.

"Grail six-ninety, you're number two for takeoff."

"Roger, Jax. Grail six-niner-zero is number two."

Clayton busied himself with a final check of the cockpit and moved ahead in the run-up block when the big Delta jet swung into position and began running up its engines. The wind was out of the east and the pattern was back over the northern edge of the city toward the ocean.

"Delta seven-two, after takeoff turn left to three-six-zero degrees passing through five hundred...you're cleared for takeoff." Clayton listened automatically to the tower as he moved the Lear forward in the run-up block.

Clayton watched as the Delta began to lumber slowly down the runway and gather speed. Then, suddenly freed from the bonds of earth, it soared sharply skyward and banked gracefully to the north.

"Jax Tower, USAir is right about the birds on that lake; I never saw so many. Looks like something has scared 'em up and they're getting airborne...there's a regular cloud of 'em. They could be a hazard to traffic," the Delta pilot observed.

"Not likely Delta, not if they're below you at five hundred...the pattern is turning away from 'em. Anyway, seagulls are notoriously low-flyers," the tower chuckled. "They get airsick above one hundred feet."

Clayt knew the tower allowed a routine interval of two minutes between a heavy jet and a plane the size of the Lear, but he was getting antsy now. He checked his watch...almost half-past-nine. He would be pushing it to make it to his house by eleven-thirty at this rate.

"Grail Lear six-ninety, left turn to three-six-zero degrees out of a thousand, watch for wake turbulence departing Delta heavy jet, you're cleared for takeoff."

"Roger, Jax, Grail six-niner-zero is history..." Clayton gave it throttle and started the Lear rolling down the runway.

Squinting against the bright glare of the morning sun, Clayton observed the Delta had already started its left turnout, almost out of his vision. He caught a glimpse of a shadow directly off the end of the runway, much lower than the Delta. Those goddamn seabirds, he guessed. The Delta was right...there seemed to be a regular cloud of them. The tower had said seagulls weren't high flyers, though.

Clayt laughed aloud at the line about the birds getting airsick. That controller ought to be in show biz.

About halfway down the runway, the voice of the controller popped in his phones. "GRAIL LEAR DELAY...REPEAT!...DELAY LEFT TURNOUT UNTIL REACHING TWO THOUSAND. WE'VE GOT A MILITARY WITH AN EMERGENCY COMING IN...ACKNOWLEDGE IF YOU COPY," an edge of tension crackled in the controller's voice.

"Roger, I read you, Jax. I'll hold my heading." Clayton felt the aircraft lift off and he held his heading east. When he glanced up from his instruments, he was suddenly aware of an ominous darkening on the bright morning sun-glare off the windshield. Instinctively, he raised his eyes in alarm. In front of him, the cloud of birds was blotting out the sun. He tried to pull the airplane sharply up and to the left, but the cloud of seabirds rained on the airplane like an avalanche.

"Jax, I'm taking birds all over...jeezus god!...I'm buried in fucking birds..."

He felt a sickening lurch of the plane. But he could no longer see for the splattered blood and feathers. All at once, the right hand windshield exploded into the empty seat. At the same moment he felt the aircraft losing power. The controls went soft, unresponsive....

"Lear, do you wish to declare an emergency?..." Clayt heard the controller ask.

He was falling now...tumbling really.

"Fuck your emergency, you silly asshole..."

CHAPTER FIFTY-THREE

LIKE OTHERS IN THE MYRIAD OF ISLANDS which abound off the New England coastline, Sheepshead Light was nothing more than a mountain peak. The vestigial island was an eloquent reminder that Maine was situated astride the ancient Appalachian mountain chain. The highest and easternmost of the peaks rising submerged from the seaward edge of the old mountain system, Sheepshead jutted stoically out of the sea.

The runway was the only semblance of a road running from the lighthouse to the top of the street leading down from the white-steepled church to the harborside. Where the airstrip ended, there was a well-rutted vehicle track leading across the remaining quarter-mile of rocky plateau directly to the church.

Underneath a thin surface of sandy topsoil, the island was a monolith of granite. The elevated upper plain was virtually treeless and, except for the well-maintained runway pavement and the isolated areas where the smooth surface of base rock had eroded through, the pebbled, coarse sandy earth was rooted with thickly-matted, tall coastal grasses and a kaleidoscopic profusion of white, pink, blue, gold and crimson wildflowers.

As they approached the rim of the upper plateau, a mass of wind-twisted, low-growing shrubs sprang up along the upper rim, raggedly screening the roofs of the houses on the topmost street just beneath the plateau's periphery. The uppermost row of houses were nestled so that their chimney tops were almost precisely on a level with the thick, hedge-like growth. This afforded a modicum of protection when the northeasterly winds blew from the sea. Only the slender top third of the solitary church steeple was exposed to the full force of the elements.

"See the church steeple? It was built originally around 1790 and was intended to be a homing needle—visible from just beyond the horizon's curve. It was a full twenty feet higher when it was first raised. The spire was blown down by a monster storm that first winter, so the local lore has it. The entire structure was reconstructed to be lower to resist the wind, and the lighthouse was built to provide a steering beacon. These are a hardy, practical people. Many of them are sixth and seventh generation...we have three newborn inhabitants who are the eighth generation of the original settlers. Sheepshead has always been mainly a fishing village. In early days, some whalers were here, but now the main harvest is lobsters. The best come from these waters and are highly prized. Only the most discriminating restaurants are able to command Sheepshead Light Lobsters for their clientele..." Norris chuckled, self-consciously. "Do I sound like the local Chamber of Commerce?"

"A little..." Marilee squeezed his arm in delight and nuzzled her head beneath his chin.

The trip down the steep street from the church to the waterfront made Marilee's stomach drop, much the same as taking an unexpected step down in the dark. The slope was much steeper and more abrupt than it had appeared from the low-angled perspective of the airplane. As they descended the two abbreviated blocks of quaint wooden houses neatly painted in weathered shades of olive and bluish-gray, she got an occasional glimpse of townspeople about. Most were women, some hanging out clothes or sweeping porches. Several walking up the hill had market baskets woven from local sea grasses.

For the most part, the women wore faded jeans or khaki wash pants with man-tailored shirts, but here and there Marilee saw a plain wool skirt with a blouse. Deferring to the rapidly fading warmth of the midday, late-spring sun, some of the women already wore light jackets and others carried sweaters, the sleeves knotted loosely around their necks against the constant breezes which came off the vast expanse of water stretching in every direction as far as the eye could see.

"This all gives me an eerie feeling we're on the set of some

English spy movie...do you recall the quaint seaside village with the long stone quay at the harbor in the Meryl Streep film, *The French Lieutenant's Woman?* I remember it, partly because Sadie Bailey auditioned for a supporting role. Sadie's come a long way since then...." she bubbled, completely charmed.

Almost before she knew it, Moe was making a sharp left turn southward at the bottom of the hill, where the street abruptly ended at the harbor side.

Mounted on the wall above the door, the sign was charming.

THE LION AND THISTLE.

The old building was a delight. Right off the streets of a Cornwall village.

The entrance was set obliquely into the corner of the building. The wide, heavily paneled double doors of the inn were painted a bright burnt orange.

The corner entrance opened onto a small asymmetrical pentangular foyer, with a wide stairway leading directly to the upper floors. There was no registration desk or, for that matter, anything else to indicate the place was in any way commercial. Once inside, there was no hint of being in a public house.

To her right, glimpsed through double doors standing partially ajar, was a large pleasant sitting room with heavy, time-honored furniture covered in brightly-flowered chintz of mostly blues and orange hues. There were book-laden shelves and tables with magazines neatly arranged in layered rows. A chessboard rested on a little table in the far corner.

The interior walls throughout the building were wainscoted with wood paneling. Above the wainscoting, wallpaper printed in a small colonial pineapple pattern, echoing the oranges and blues of the chintz, ran to the ceiling.

"Yummm..." Marilee sniffed the spicy cooking smells.

"Look lively now, mates." A tall slender, gray-bearded Scotsman appeared as if by magic. His skin was browned a ruddy color Marilee thought of as being typically Scottish, and although she could see that, unshorn, his head would still have sported a healthy fringe of hair, he kept it cut so close it was nearly shiny bald.

"Tha las' time I sa' sich a displa' of pursnol property was when the gud Queen hersel' cam to Edinburgh."

He pronounced the last "Addnabera."

With a friendly smile, a twinkle in his eye and an approving nod her way, the wry Scotsman paid no mind to the fact they were as yet not formally introduced. Marilee watched as Robbie Douglas wrestled their bulky duffels up the two flights of wide, banistered stairs.

Norris explained that the two apartments along the hall to the left at the top of the uppermost flight of stairs served as the long-standing residences for both Robbie and Donald and Bridie Dunn, the elderly couple who prepared the food and oversaw the domestic order of the inn.

Turning to his right, Norris unlocked the single door.

His apartment occupied the entire other half of the top floor.

Indelibly stamped with the same deeply personal imprint that was reflected in his place in New York, the flat was at once recognizably: "Norris Wrenn."

"If you'll excuse me, ma'am." The rangy Scotsman apologized politely, pushing by them and vanishing into the apartment.

Norris took his laptop briefcase from Moe and placed it down.

Robbie reappeared like magic in front of Marilee and extended his hand with a little bow, "Robbie Douglas, yur humble survant, ma'am."

"I..." Marilee began but Norris interrupted.

"This is Marilee, Robbie."

"I'm pleased to meet you, Robbie. Thank you for your help."

"No trouble atall, ma'am." The dour Scotsman's face suddenly beamed.

"Thanks Moe, see ya around," Norris turned and shook the young man's hand. "Maybe we'll walk out to the lighthouse tomorrow morning. You can bring me up to date on the book."

"Oh, yes...yes! I want to hear all about your book. What's it about?" Marilee approved.

"Illicit sex and big business." Moe laughed.

"Ah...umm...sounds exciting...." Marilee felt herself blush.

"Long live hanky-panky! There's always a sequel to that." Norris laughed.

"Great. Come early and I'll give you breakfast," the young man enthused. "Just name the time, I'm up around four or five."

"Four or five...in the morning?" Marilee couldn't help it. The question just popped right out.

"Well, yes...but you can come anytime you like. Morning is my best time to work. I try to get my thousand words before I take a break around nine or ten...can't write books lying in bed."

"How about if we came over later, say mid-morning...and have some coffee?" Norris smiled and extended his hand. "How's around ten o'clock...give or take an hour?"

"Anytime's OK with me. See ya. Nice meeting you, Mrs. Wrenn." Just before his head disappeared from Norris' view he looked back and gave an AOK sign to Norris with a circled thumb and forefinger of his right hand. Marilee saw the resounding sign of approval. Secretly, she couldn't remember when she had been so pleased to know she had been given a vote of confidence.

"Thanks, Robbie, I'll see you later after we unpack. It's good to be back." Norris turned and moved inside. Without another word, he closed the door behind him.

The sexual tension that had been building all day swept over Norris like a hot wind as he took Marilee in his arms. After a toe-curling kiss, she pulled back. "Show me the bathroom, my love; I'm about to die to pee. Aren't you?" she asked seriously.

"Well, now you mention it, I could do with a go at the necessary, myself, old girl." Norris affected a passable British accent. "But then we do have two of them, you know?"

"Quick...show me..." She grabbed his hand and gave him a tug.

"Straight back...off to the left in the bedroom." He slapped her on the backside.

It pleased Norris to watch her go bouncing back through the wide hall. Her panties showed clearly through the thin cotton slacks, outlining the classic roundness of her bottom. Resisting the urge to follow her into the bathroom and take her on the spot, he went into the bedroom and undressed.

CHAPTER FIFTY-FOUR

THE DISTINGUISHED LOOKING MAN ENTERED the quiet little Soho tea-room and, pleasantly waving aside the matronly hostess, walked directly to the small booth in the furthest corner where a plain, but oddly attractive and elegantly dressed women stood and held out her hand.

"Well, how did it go with the eight-hundred-pound gorilla?" she asked and poured him a cup of tea.

"With him, it's hard to say...but I'll bet my farm in Virginia and the house on Abaco he dreams of ravishing the supermodel in the Oval Office tonight."

"Hmmm..." She sipped. "So?...you think he's human after all?"

"Oh...he's human right enough." He frowned when his cell phone rang. "I told them not to call unless it was..." He put the tiny instrument to his ear.

Listening intently, a flicker of emotion passed behind his eyes. Then he hung up.

"What is it?" Sensing his tension, she touched his arm.

"Clayton Massie Graham crashed his Lear at JAX this morning."

"Oh...shit..." the woman said. "Is that the end of our plans for Wrenn?"

He took a thoughtful sip of tea.

"Not at all. Rather the beginning, I should think."

CHAPTER FIFTY-FIVE

Completely sated, Norris dozed.

"Will you walk with me? I want to see this place before the light is gone. We have a little time before dinner yet," he heard her saying.

"Uhmmm...I'd love to...walk with you, I mean. You finished me...this time you really did me in. I'll never be able to have sex again," he murmured contentedly.

"Oh, poo!" Marilee had already dressed, standing beside the bed running a brush through the tangle of flaming red hair. She stopped still and looked at him longingly, "Anytime you're ready, I'll gladly let you kill me again! *Vive la petite mort!*"

"Long live the little death? That's an oxymoron!" He laughed.

"Don't be such a smartaleck." She pretended to be offended.

"Hussy. Keep acting like that and I'll cut you off."

"Oh, no! Anything but that. Come on and show me the island." She pulled the cover off of him.

"OK," he said, and rolled out of bed. "I'll only be a minute. Time's a-wastin'."

When they reached the street, Norris steered her to the left where a crowd of perhaps thirty people were gathered at a boat down near the southernmost of the harborside docks.

"Looks like some excitement," he said and quickened his stride.

As they neared the crowd, he could see the captain and the mate were displaying to the crowd two of the largest lobsters Norris had ever seen. The mate turned and carefully placed the one he held back into the holding tank and took out another just as big...perhaps even larger.

"We found 'em last week. At first we thought it was just a freak. But they're there in numbers, all right. We're sure of it now," the captain was saying.

There was a murmuring of "ooohs" and "aaahs" among the dockside crowd. Here and there, some of the locals broke away and started to find their way back toward the center of the village. As they passed, they nodded and smiled at Norris and gave Marilee a curious, but generally pleasant, stare. Norris greeted them simply and warmly, but made no attempt at introductions. Marilee did not sense he was avoiding having to introduce her. She understood that, for this moment, it was simply not necessary.

They were almost all the way to the land's end now. When she looked back, the town spread out before them across the harbor. The sun was getting low, and the entire dockside and lower part of the village was in shadow, but the light still caught the tops of the houses on the uppermost streets, and most of the white steeple glinted bright in the afternoon sun.

When Norris looked back out to the sea, a big sportsfisherman was approaching the mouth of the harbor, and the late sun caught the top of the flybridge. There was a vague military sweep to her hull that reminded him of several other small naval boats he had seen refitted for covert security surveillance off the coast of Central America…it gave him a sudden twinge of uneasiness.

He tried hard to shake the feeling. Remembering the morning meeting, all at once he felt resentful that he'd let Chatham Brookes shadow him under a cloud of vague suspicions.

Now, his attention wandered from the boat as he watched a small, single-engine plane approach, circle twice and disappear over the steeple above the rim of lighthouse plateau.

Norris looked at his watch. "C'mon, let's hurry, I want to walk up to the rim above the church while the light is good. The view from there is magnificent."

By the time they'd climbed to see the view and started back to the inn, the sun was down.

Passing the big general store near the inn, Marilee stopped to admire a ceramic figure of a cherubic angel posed lying on its stomach with its wings at rest. She pulled Norris into the store and bought the angel. The shopkeeper handed her the boxed figurine in a little plastic bag. Marilee hugged it to her breast. "Oh Norris...now we have our own angel to watch over us..."

He looked away to hide his smile.

At dinner, Mrs. Dunn served them personally. Beginning with steaming bowls of chowder, she overburdened the table with dishes of succulent food—two huge dolphin filets, broiled with butter and sprinkled with cracked lemon pepper and paprika, and dishes of small whole potatoes and green beans and broccoli. Finally, even though Marilee protested, Mrs. Dunn placed in front of them steaming wedges of blueberry pie with a scoop of ice cream melting over the sides.

Heavenly.

As they were leaving, Robbie Douglas tugged at Norris' sleeve. "Did the gentleman find you, sur?"

"Who was that?" Norris tried not to overreact.

"Moe brought him down from the strip about an hour ago. He didn't speak to me, but I heard your name when he was talking with Moe...I thought he might be looking for you."

"We saw the plane and when we were walking back, Moe waved at us when they went by in the jeep," Norris shrugged. "I'm sure he wasn't looking for me...probably just curious." Norris smiled to dismiss his irritation that Moe would talk about him to strangers.

When they walked outside, there were lights on in the new sportsfisherman, which had tied up just across from the Thistle. They strolled over to get a better look.

The afterdeck had been converted into a salon with an elaborate arrangement of zippered canvas and clear vinyl curtains. Two men were seated inside on comfortable, padded chairs. Feeling self-conscious standing so close to them, Norris guided Marilee back to the Inn. At the door, Marilee suddenly stopped and turned, "Did you see that? I never saw such a tacky thing."

"What are you talking about?" he asked, preoccupied with the need to get her back upstairs.

"Those two men sitting inside that new boat...they had on Bermuda shorts and both were wearing black, knee-length dress socks and those awful English light-brown, wing-tip shoes."

Norris stiffened. The airport in Washington Monday…earlier today in New York…all at once the whole world was brimming with brown shoes. And then there was Tom's mysterious accident…Chatham Brookes' talk of a White House appointment…suddenly everything was getting far too weird for him.

Inside the apartment, Marilee said, "It's too late tonight, but I'll need to phone tomorrow morning and check on Ivee. We didn't talk about it, but I simply have to go back Friday. That's two more days, at least. I hate it, but Sunday is Mother's Day, and I'm sort of in the spotlight, you know."

He kissed her and took her in his arms.

In bed again, there was a delicate familiarity now…the loveliest of proprietorships.

"I've never felt so wantonly ravished…" Marilee sighed, sleepily.

"Uhmmm…" Norris languished in a twilight state.

Chiding himself for overreacting, his tension melted like a morning mist.

It was not quite half-past nine, when Norris came awake again and looked at his watch. He felt relieved that he'd only dozed off for a few minutes.

Beside him, Marilee was sound asleep. Resting there collecting his thoughts, finally it occurred to him that he should call Patty.

He went into the kitchen and started the coffeemaker before he went into the hall bath and splashed his face with cold water. When he returned, he took the coffeemaker carafe into the study and closed the door so as not to disturb Marilee.

Looking out the window, the light was still on in the salon of the sportfisherman just below. His apprehension returned.

Finally, he dialed the Washington Hospital Center. "Mr. Bradley is out of surgery…blood pressure stable, pulse good…but not fully conscious. Condition improved but still guarded."

"*Guarded*…."

Norris was beginning to hate the word.

"Come on, Tommy-boy, we've got miles to go and promises to

keep," he breathed aloud to the empty room as he dialed Patty's unlisted number at home.

"Hello," she answered on the first ring.

"Patty, I just realized I hadn't checked in since yesterday in Washington. How're things, love?" Norris felt the best he'd felt in ages.

"Oh, my god, boss, where on earth are you? I've been worried half-crazy! I've been trying to reach you all afternoon. Haven't you heard the news?" Instinctively, Norris steeled himself.

"No. What's happened?" He held his breath.

"It's awful, boss. Big Clayt was killed in an airplane crash this morning. You've got to get back here, as soon as possible...the whole crazy world is looking for you. You have to get back here tonight?"

Momentarily, Norris was speechless. "Clayton...dead?...jeezus, Patty, how did it happen?"

He listened while she told him the sketchy details about the seagulls. "Can you get back tonight? I'm serious. Everyone here is crazy. The staff at the Tower is lost without you."

The island airstrip had runway lights, but asking Doug to make a night flight seemed a bit heroic even under these circumstances.

"I'm sorry, babe, there's no way...I'm so freaking far out in the boonies, I might as well be in outer space. I can't possibly make it back until early tomorrow. Just hold tight and I'll be back there in the morning." Norris was deadly calm. In his mind, he'd already begun working out a plan to get them off the island.

"Oh, boss..." The disappointment in her voice let him know that he had let her down.

"Clayton...I still can't believe it...how's Mabel? How's Trip?" Norris ignored his guilt.

"Oh shit, Boss, that's another story all its own. Everything's a mess. Trip had a hemorrhage in the Tower suite yesterday. I don't know the whole story but they...Dr. Scott...put him in a private hospital somewhere near Durham late last night—some sort of snooty, ultra-private clinic. Frankly, I think it's for alkys. He was smelling like a distillery when he left here yesterday and he had uh... defecated and puked up blood all over the bathroom in his office. Griffin Richards was calling all over, trying to get you to come back last night. He said he called and left messages at the Grail International."

"I'm sorry babe, I just got busy...I guess you heard Tom Bradley was nearly killed yesterday. I had just left him and was on the way to Reagan National when it happened. So, after I had my meeting with Chatham Brookes this morning, I decided to get off to myself to think...it just hasn't been a very good week." Norris played for sympathy. Patty always looked out for him. He sure as hell needed her on his side now.

"I'm sorry about Mr. Bradley, but my God, the news of the crash has been on all the networks all afternoon. When you decide to get lost, you really get lost," she said in utter frustration. "The phone's been ringing off the hook. All the papers, *The Wall Street Journal, Time, Newsweek, The New York Times...The Post,* all of 'em. The networks, all of them, too. Are you sure you can't get back tonight? I could get Demp Gearhart to pick you up. Where are you, anyway?"

"Patty, just trust me, I'm up in the...the boonies. I decided to take a day off for chrissake...there's no way I can get back there until tomorrow morning. Listen to me. Call Griffin Richards and tell him I'm on my way back there and will try to arrive before noon tomorrow. OK?" He paused, but before she could answer, he remembered he didn't even know when they planned to have the funeral. "When do they plan to bury Clayton? Have they made the arrangements yet?"

"Well, I think they're planning on ten o'clock Friday. Mr. Richards wanted you to approve the final arrangements."

"Well, when you call him, tell him I think Friday morning is perfect. If we waited any longer, it would turn into a circus. Can you call Gus Poe tonight in New York and tell him...if he hasn't already...to make sure to use our special list. Gus will know what I'm talking about. It's a list we prepared for just such an emergency...includes all the key players...he'll know what I mean."

Gathered...back in charge...suddenly, Norris was himself again.

There really wasn't much he could do anyway until he got back to New York.

"Oh, yes...tell Gus Poe just to release the prepared obit to the press and send out the Yousuf Karsh photo. Tell him I cleared it. Have you got all that?"

"Yeah...I gotcha...tell Gus about the list and the obit. And I'll call Mr. Richards about the funeral." Patty was sounding more like herself now.

"OK? We straight now? I'll be unavailable by phone until tomorrow morning. I'll call you from somewhere. Can you handle it?"

"So, all you want me to do now is call Gus and Griffin Richards? What about your wife? Are you going to call her?" Patty seemed almost afraid to ask.

Judas!...he'd completely forgotten Agnes.

"Oh, Jeezus, I didn't think about that. Call Agnes and tell her you talked to me. Just tell her I was...tell her I'm OK and...well, that's all you need to say. I'll see her tomorrow morning. I need to get moving now. I've a lot of traveling to do."

"OK, boss. By the way, before I let you go, do you have any idea how to get in touch with Marilee Graham? They can't locate her either. She picked up your package and went off to New York Tuesday after the Governor's press conference, and nobody has been able to reach her. She's supposed to be staying with that movie actress friend."

As far as he could discern, there was no hint of suspicion in Patty's question.

"No...the messenger brought the envelope all right...as soon as I get to New York, I'll look into it. I'll talk to you tomorrow morning. And, Patty, thanks, you're the best." Just as he was about to hang up, he had an inspiration. "Patty, call Demp and have a plane standing by at the New York Grail terminal...no later than seven, I have no idea exactly what time I'll get there. Get a number where Marilee Graham can be reached and just have him tell her to go to the Grail hangar at LaGuardia and wait 'til I show up. I'll check back with you when I get to New York in the morning. Can you handle it now? Just relax and try to get some sleep. The next few days are going to be a roller coaster ride for both of us. I'll talk to you in the morning. Take care, babe."

"Don't worry, I'll take care of this end, boss...and be careful...there's no discount on double funerals. I'll be waiting to hear from you." She hung up.

As soon as he put the phone down, the irony hit him. The very thing Clayt had feared most had happened.

His death blew the whole ballgame into a cocked hat.

And all day long he had been congratulating himself on his cleverness. This morning, when he was being so high and mighty with Chatham Brookes about the Phoenix thing—and the heady overtures from the White House—in his mind he was already the head honcho at Grail.

But with that contract still unsigned, was he back to being just a caddie for Trip Graham again?

And what about Marilee? You can hardly work for a guy and play footsie with his wife.

No matter now how it worked out with Marilee, he was very likely history at Grail. If Clayt had only signed, he might have wound up with the girl, the gold watch and everygoddamnthing.

This was his second lesson in two days. Norris didn't have to wonder what Tom Bradley would have to say about that now. In the end, did it matter? You just did the best you could and got on with it.

Standing now, Norris looked out the window at the lights in the snug little houses across the harbor. Even in this unspoiled place, there was always work to be done by someone tomorrow. Off to the southwest there was just the faintest glow at the horizon.

Was any of it worth it? He really didn't want to think about it now.

Now, he'd just have to go with plan "B". The problem of the moment was that he had no plan "B". At the thought, he couldn't help but laugh out loud.

Marilee had asked him if he was going to do the Phoenix thing...would he go back to Washington?

Maybe....

Providing the "brown shoes" didn't tie a can on his tail.

Save the world? He needed to quit this maudlin speculation and start thinking about saving his ass.

Of course, there were a number of options open. In the real world he played hardball. He could write his own ticket. Yet in the final analysis, they were all just like the job he had now. It would be like trading staterooms on the Titanic. In the end, he would still be on a dead-end ride. Under Clayton, the Grail deal would have really made him more than just rich...he would have been free, really free...powerful in his own right.

He suddenly straightened and shook his head.

By god, right now he'd best stop all this wallowing in self-pity. The world hadn't stopped spinning for Norris Wrenn just yet. There would be time enough to sweat out the small stuff when the dust settled. Norris collected himself. Right now he had to figure out how to get them out of here.

He called Moe at the lighthouse.

"Moe, something has come up. I've got to get off the island. What time does it get light enough to see around here nowadays?"

"Well, it's probably light enough for a plane to land VFR by six, I think." Moe said.

"OK, I wonder if you could turn on the landing lights at 4:30 and bring the jeep and come pick us up around four forty-five in the morning?"

"Well, sure..." Moe was curious but reluctant to pry.

"Thanks, Moe. We'll be waiting downstairs."

Norris moved to his desk and found Doug Reed's home phone number in New York. When he told Doug what he needed, the young pilot said without a stammer, "No sweat. I'll see ya around five."

Norris debated about waking Marilee and decided against it.

She would need all the rest she could get.

Now that the shock was wearing off, it occurred to him that Clayton Massie Graham was a legend. The TV news would be full of news about his death. Norris picked up the TV remote and turned the sound off before the picture came into focus—he didn't want Marilee awake.

Flipping down the channels, Clayt's image was everywhere. Fascinated, he watched a rapid montage of pictures from the various networks...a long shot of the Grail Tower...Clayt waving from the door of the Learjet...changing channels, abruptly Norris paused at a change of scene.

There was a seductive pose of the actress Emma Claire. It was followed by a quick cut to the exterior of The Manor Inn in Greensboro. Surprised to find the actress's death was still an item, Norris's thoughts wandered idly back to that late night when he'd seen Emma Claire being delivered to the White House's West Wing portico. Someone had stepped out of the shadows and escorted her from the limo.

Who?

Try as he might—with all the other things he had to think about at the moment—he couldn't put a name to the phantom figure.

Now the screen switched to a picture of the two missing White House helicopter pilots...then to a shot of a gang of reporters swarming to interview the senior senator in charge of the abortion hearings...back to Clayton Massie Graham again.

Too tired to care, he pushed the OFF button, and Clayton was sucked into a tiny dot of light.

Norris got up and closed the door and absently took his guitar out of the case.

Sitting back down, looking out over the rippling little striations of light from the houses reflected on the peaceful harbor, he strummed and sang softly to himself: *"Freedom's just another word for nothin' left to lose...and nothin' ain't worth nothin' but it's free. Feeling good was easy, lord...good enough for me, good enough for me and Mar-eye-lee..."*

THURSDAY

CHAPTER FIFTY-SIX

AT 7:30 A.M., A VERY GROGGY, VERY UNHAPPY TRIP GRAHAM was still struggling to emerge from his detoxifying—but nonetheless drug-fogged—state when the nurse approached him at the breakfast table in the cafeteria.

"Mr. Graham, I'm Belle Cheskis. There's someone to see you in the conference room off of the Director's office. If you'll follow me, I'll take you there."

Trip left the table and dutifully followed behind. In the day and most of two nights he had been at Holly Hall, he had no idea where the fucking Director's office might be. In fact, breakfast had been his first trip to the dining room since he had arrived.

Most of yesterday he had stayed in his room. He remembered getting some shots in his hip when he arrived Tuesday night and again yesterday morning. And the nurse had given him several capsules and tablets every so often yesterday. When he inquired what she was giving him, she said, "Phenobarb and some vitamins and stuff to help you stop shaking and help you come down from all that other junk."

He hadn't been overly impressed with her fucking professionalism.

He really hadn't been too happy about any-fucking-thing. He didn't like the cheerful fucking color of the fucking carpet or the fucking cheerful wallpaper either. And the fucking furniture in his room sucked. In fact, the whole fucking place sucked. The people sucked. The fucking trees around that fucking cheerful pond sucked...and the ducks...and the goddamn pond itself—he didn't want to leave that out—was kinda shitty, too.

Still, he had behaved himself. He really hadn't felt well enough to muster up a good aggression...besides, he was afraid they might restrain him. True, he hadn't seen anyone in straitjackets, but he was afraid—he really didn't know what to expect. What he really wanted was to get the fuck out of here and hit the nearest fucking liquor store...or bar...or even a six-pack at the Seven-Eleven...just a drink of homemade wine...just a fucking drink...of fucking anything.

Even cough syrup or a good mouthwash would do. In the day room, he'd heard a patient say he'd drunk hair tonic...but he'd never get that fucking hard up.

He wasn't a fucking alky—that was what alkys did.

But he did have the fucking shakes.

Bad...fucking...bad.

Around noon yesterday they had taken him into the fucking doctors' offices and, even though he had weakly protested, they had checked all the same goddamn things, poked him in the same fucking places and stuck their fucking scopes into the same bloody holes they had ultra-violated when he came in the night before.

"Mr. Graham, how much alcohol do you drink in a normal day?" They had asked a bunch of fucking dumb questions—most of them not so cleverly disguised—to explore how much fucking booze he had been drinking and for how fucking long. And how much fucking dope he had smoked and how much fucking cocaine...and had he ever shot up...or smoked rock...on and on.

Very fucking cute.

Very fucking boring...and now he really felt fucking bad.

That bad.

Anyway, when they were through, he had been too tired to go to lunch, and he gratefully accepted a glass of orange juice and a little beaker of honey.

"Take this...to help the shakes," the nurse had assured him.

Except for being awakened several times to take some more orange juice and honey and a handful of pills, he had slept the night through and had awakened early this morning, hungry as a bear. But when he sat down to eat breakfast, his stomach began cramping again and his fear of shitting his pants and running the risk of bleeding to death made him break out in a cold sweat.

So, he accepted some more orange juice and took some honey

and it did make him feel a little better...maybe?

If every fucking thing around here was supposed to help the fucking shakes, then why was it he still had the fucking shakes, he wondered, sitting at the breakfast table.

Then he promptly sloshed his coffee all over himself.

"Oh, fuck!" he despaired.

Hell's bells, he thought, watching his spastic hands as he tried to set the cup down without spilling any more. If they knew so fucking much, they would know what he really needed was a goddamn drink...just one itsy-bitsy little smoothereeno...or two...and he'd be fine as fucking wine. It didn't mean he had to get drunk again...or even have two...for that matter...one stiff one would do nicely. Then he'd just lay around by the pool for a day or two at the club, eat good and hit some golf balls and he'd be good as new. He wanted out of this fucking place. He wondered if they could keep him. There weren't any fucking bars on the windows. He resolved to ask his buddy, the lady-doctor-patient, as soon as he could get her aside.

But then the fucking big-titted nurse showed up.

The nurse ushered him into a conference room and he stopped cold in his tracks. In front of him stood Griff Richards and a man whom he immediately recognized as that redneck policeman, D.C. Mills. Even though he knew Mills was not here on a social call, Trip still felt greatly relieved it was not his father he had to face.

"You remember the Chief, don't you, son?" Griff shook hands and nodded toward Mills. "Chief found out I was coming down here, and he thought you might shed some more light on this damn thing about the movie star's death that's been aggravating folks up his way."

"Hello, Chief," Trip murmured, "I don't know if I'll be any more help than I was yesterday...Tuesday...I guess it was, now. I guess you can see from this place, I wasn't lying when I said I didn't remember much about Sunday." Sheepishly, he indicated the framed licenses on the wall, which gave mute evidence that Holly Hall Treatment Center was a JCAHO- and CARF-certified hospital to treat Alcoholism and Chemical Dependency.

"Uh...yeah. Well, uh...ahh...." the Chief began and cleared his throat. Then he spread his hands and looked at his feet as if he had suddenly found something of great interest on his shoe tops. "...hell, son, but for the grace of God, I could be right here in your shoes...lord knows I like to take a drink now and again. Anyway, I just wanted to say hello before you and Mr. Richards have your chat. Find me when you've finished." He looked to Griff and turned to leave.

"Well, thanks, Chief, stick close. We won't be long. Doctor said we shouldn't take too much of Trip's time. He's lost some blood and isn't strong yet," Griff said, as the old lawman left almost on tiptoe and pulled the door quietly closed behind him.

Funny way for a cop to behave...but then people acted funny in hospitals...or when they were in front of lawyers or preachers.

As soon as Mills left, Griff indicated for him to have a seat across from him at the polished conference table.

"Sit down and get a good grip on yourself, son. This a rotten way to treat you, and I tried my best to stall the Chief...I kept him out of here all day yesterday. As a matter of fact, I wouldn't even tell him where you were. He got real upset with me...and I really don't think you have too much to worry about from him...it looks like that Claire woman, she just up and OD-ed on crack cocaine and that's probably that...at least I hope so. The main thing he's worried about is keeping you, the family...and Grail...out of the papers and that's the truth...but there's something else I have to talk to you about first." The older man mopped his brow with his pocket hanky and took a deep breath. "There's no easy way to do this...I hate to have to add to your troubles, but there's no way to keep it a secret and I certainly didn't want you to see it on TV or all over the front page of the paper...."

Richards paused again to gather himself.

Why didn't the old fart just get on with it?

"What the fuck's going on?" Trip waved, angrily.

Griff looked away and then bowed his head before he turned and looked him in the eye again. Then, it hit him. Something was different. He really had better get a grip on himself.

"Your daddy was killed in a plane crash yesterday in Jacksonville...."

"Huh?..." His breath rushed out of him as Richards' words hit him like a fist.

Griff kept talking, but the words seemed hollow...white noise...sound without meaning. Lear crashed...Jax...Trip heard them, and he knew what they meant, but it was as if he were in a theater and it was all happening to someone else. The words were just a jumble.

The scene went by so fast. Then he watched numbly as Griff went to the door and the balding, pot-bellied, red-faced law officer returned.

One thing was real enough. At that moment, he had no doubt that he needed a stiff drink more than ever before in his entire life.

"Maybe I'd better be present for this," Griff was speaking formally now, obviously in his role as an attorney.

"Well, I don't know...Mr. Graham's not being accused...well, I mean, beyond finding a...a quantity of illegal drugs, we haven't even established a crime. Mainly I've got my hands full, trying to deal with the press. There seems to be some evidence Mr. Graham might have spent some time with the woman before her death, and I want to make sure that's not picked up by the newsboys...it could be a big mess...I...er, I just want to try to get it all straight in my head. I don't like surprises," Mills stammered. The old cop clearly didn't relish the idea of Graham International, Ltd.'s corporate attorney hovering about.

"Don't worry, Griff...it's OK. I'll call if I need you," Trip croaked, hoarsely. The fear was clearing his head now. The adrenaline rush left him feeling better, in control.

"Well, all right, but just take it easy, Chief...the boy's just been told his daddy's dead."

"Don't worry, Mr. Richards...I understand. This has hit us all pretty hard." The chief bowed his head.

Griff squeezed Trip's shoulder affectionately and left the room.

"Well, I don't know where to start...this is so awful about your daddy. You know the last time I saw him...two months ago down at Caswell the day of Miss Marilee's big 'doings'...he asked me if I'd be interested in coming to work for him. You know...as Director of Corporate Security...work right out of the Tower in Colonial Hall." The Chief's expression was open...inscrutable. "Funny, I told him I'd think it over and we'd talk more about it. Too bad. I've been thinking about that a lot since then...been meaning to call him."

Trip's nerves were still raw. He felt like he was flying apart. To hell with this fucking small talk. What was really on the baldheaded bastard's mind?

"Too bad...well...ah...now, just what was it you wanted to ask me? I told you everything the other day." He shrugged.

"Remember when I told you on the phone there was this report of a ruckus in the motel parking lot involving a red car and a yellow Corvette? Well, later an officer who was off duty that night came to me and told me he'd stopped your yellow Corvette in the parking lot at the Steak Barn and you had a woman with you. He thought she might have been that actress. Were you with a woman that night, Mr. Graham...maybe your wife...or a family friend? In the event the coroner finds this thing is drug-related...I mean if...well, it could become messy. That Claire woman certainly had at least one visitor in her room that night. If you're covered, it would certainly simplify things." The chief leaned forward now, anxiously.

"Chief, I already told you, I don't remember anything much about that day after I left Blowing Rock...and I sure don't want this fucking gossip out I was seen with some woman in Greensboro. My wife was home in bed...and I don't have any cousins there. This whole thing sounds pretty irresponsible. What the hell was an off-duty cop...officer...doing stopping a car on Sunday night in the parking lot of a public place...is that what your men do off-hours? Go around making citizen's arrests just to stay in practice? Looks like you guys up in that neck of the woods would have learned your lesson after you fucked up that case involving that crazy doctor's son and his society cousin. That writer Bledsoe put you at the top of the bestseller list with that one—made quite a mini-series on

378

primetime TV...and just how the fuck did this Barney Fife of yours know it was me? Did he run a make on my car?" At the moment, he was in no mood for this shit.

"Now, don't get upset, Mr. Graham. My officer thought he recognized you when you were leaving the Steak Barn in front of him. He thought you might need some assistance getting home. You showed him your license and, after talking to you, he felt you were OK to drive...there was no official communication...no report. He was just trying to be helpful. And if you're not involved, you don't have to worry. I made sure he kept this confidential."

The chief remained calm. He hardly batted an eye. "My concern is to protect the Grahams from the press if that coroner's report comes back with the verdict of death by overdose. There was a syringe that is almost certain to show traces of a speedball. She wasn't a regular junkie...no tracks...nothing like that, but that syringe had a smudged print, enough to make a positive ID. Off the cuff, it ain't hers. So, someone either shot up with her or helped her do hers. Cases like this get messy. Personally, remembering the Maryland basketball player and that poor gal who took a bad rap in the Belushi thing, I think some innocent bystanders got left holding the bag...well...anyway, we don't even know the cause of death yet. Probably get the report tomorrow. I just don't want any surprises. It would be too late to help you much, if it all came crashing down on your doorstep. If the press gets into this...and the fucking State or Feds...excuse me, Mr. Graham...but that case with Judge Sharpe's niece you were referring to, it wasn't us that screwed it up...except for an unsuspecting uniformed officer called in the chase on the radio...we weren't even involved. But this Claire woman's death is already threatening to get out of hand. I've had *Time, Newsweek, CNN...Sixty Minutes...*godawmighty, you name it...even heard through the grapevine that *The Washington Post* and *The New York Times* had reporters digging around...but your name has not come up. I've got a tight lid on that...count on it."

"Well, I...er...I wish I could be of more help. I can tell you one thing. I'm not involved. I just got drunk and passed out...in my own room." Trip spread his hands and looked around the room.

"I'm going to change my way of living when I get out of this place. And, Chief, I sure do appreciate you trying to help. I just don't know what to tell you, except I got blitzed, but it was on booze, not cocaine...and I never shot up anything. Not in my whole life." Even before he finished speaking, he wondered if the cop was dumb enough to swallow that.

"Well, again, let me tell you how torn up I am 'bout yo' daddy's death. Yessir, I wish I'd taken him up on his offer to come to work in Colonial Hall. I would sure have liked working for your family...you Grahams practically built this state." Mills got up to leave and extended his hand. When Trip took it, the chief clasped his other hand warmly around it—a real fucking corny move!

"If there's anything I can do...you'll let me hear from you... promise now?"

"Uh, yeah...well thanks. My daddy always thought a lot of you...when this is all over come see me, Chief..." Trip stammered, very uncomfortable now, wondering what the hell was going on behind the sly old bastard's eyes.

Trip watched warily as he moved toward the door. When the Chief had almost left the room, he stuck his head back in like that fucking TV detective, Columbo.

What a freaking ham-bone move.

"You don't recall seeing the torn half of a matchbook cover in your suitcase, or car...or perhaps in the pockets of the clothes you were wearing Sunday in Greensboro, do you, Mr. Graham?"

"No,...I...ah...." He almost blurted, "Why?" Thank god, the question stuck in his throat.

"You know," the chief continued almost without a pause, "We found traces of some cocaine and some marijuana in that room you were staying in."

"Uh...well..."

"Oh, I know, you could probably find the same stuff in every damn motel room in the whole U.S. of A...huh?"

"Oh...uhmmm...sure...." He tried to muster a grin.

The Chief gave him a long hard look and nodded. "Well, thanks again...I can't tell you how sorry I am to hear about your daddy. Clayton Graham was a special man...but I'm sure he died proud to know he'd have a fine son like you to carry on. You'll make a fine President for Grail, Mr. Graham..ah, Trip. Well?...See you at the services tomorrow morning. You get back on your feet right soon." He could have sworn the old fart had started to wink and caught himself.

Trip followed him out.

Griff was waiting in the hall. "I'm coming back in the chopper after lunch. Doc says, after rounds, he'll officially release you on a funeral pass."

Watching the two of them walk around the lake to where the pilot was already starting to wind up the chopper's rotors, it struck him that the old Chief had some sort of fixation about Clayton offering him a job.

Watching them climb in the chopper...the news of his daddy's death...the raw nerve the Chief had exposed at the mention of the torn matchbook cover...it had all been a very effective piece of work. The foxy old bastard caught him off guard...kicked him right in the nuts.

Was he ever glad now that he had trashed all that stuff he'd found in his car.

Still?....he couldn't figure out what happened to that fucking bag. Pretty sure it was safely in the dumpster underneath all those goddamn notebook papers. Had to be! By now it was all covered up...buried by the 'dozers. Couple of years, it would be under some housing development.

Jeezus, what he wouldn't give for a drink right now.

He watched the chopper rise above the big oak trees. In six hours he would get out of here and go home and get a goddamn drink and put back together all these millions of fragments of him that were threatening to fly off into space at any given moment.

Goddamn Dempsey Gearhart was flying the fucking chopper...bastard had flown him down here Tuesday night. It was humiliating to have had that fucking worn-out airline pilot see him that way. But he'd straighten Gearhart out, now he was going to be boss. There were a lot of people who'd have to show him more respect.

Fucking Norris Wrenn was right at the top of the fucking list.

The clock on the wall over the nurse's station showed half-past eight.

He smiled at the nurses—had to look fucking cheerful. He didn't want that damn doc holding up his release. Griff Richards said he would be back around one. Took maybe an hour back to Colonial Hall. Be about six hours tops—before he would be able to find a drink.

They would fly directly home...The Club had a heliport. He reckoned it wouldn't take more than thirty minutes at the outside. He would have that drink by three at the very latest.

Unless, of course, Marilee was at home when he got there. She might fuck up the deal. What if the bitch decided to become his babysitter?...fucking hovering over him. He really didn't have to worry too much about his mother. Mabel would be at the big house receiving the hundreds of people who would be thronging to the funeral like vultures.

Marilee? He wondered about those goddamn clippings he'd found...what the hell was she doing with a whole fucking envelope of clippings about Norris Wrenn?

Could be that Ivee *was* starting a scrapbook...fucking Norris was his own kid's hero. Sucking up to his kid—making him look bad. Every time he turned around there was a new reason to hate the bastard.

When he got home he'd get a drink...one little smoothereno would get him squared away. He had liquor stashed in his room. Nobody could bother him there...and if Marilee took babysitting him too seriously, he could always go down to the Tower. There was plenty of booze in his office.

Not even goodytwoshoes Norris could invade his space down there.

First thing he was going to do was burn that goddamn contract Clayton had been about to sign which would make Norris a tin god. Yes, by God! That bastard had been sucking off the Grahams for too long...and most of the time his own daddy had thought more of that son of a bitch than he had of his own son. From now

382

on, good ol' Norris Wrenn was just a hired hand.

First thing after the funeral, he'd deal with his mother...and his wife...and his precious son. And Norris—mustn't forget Norris. He'd deal with 'em all, just like a good son and a good husband and a good father...and a good Graham and...all that other fucking good stuff...should.

But right now he needed a fucking drink. Just let him out of here. He'd get a drink somewhere.

CHAPTER FIFTY-SEVEN

IT WAS NOT YET TEN and the hot Carolina sun was already high in the sky when the sleek Grail aircraft settled onto the landing strip in Colonial Hall. As the plane taxied directly up to the low terminal building, Norris could see a very solemn-faced Patty waiting anxiously on the parking apron as the pilot maneuvered the plane into place and killed the high whine of the powerful jet engines.

Patty broke into a bright smile and ran swiftly to the plane when Norris, smartly dressed in his business suit and carrying his briefcase, emerged from the door of the aircraft. "Oh, Norris, am I ever more glad to see you!"

"Hi, love. I know it's been rough on you." Norris gave her a hug, then turned back to help Marilee out of the plane.

"Marilee, I think you know my assistant, Patty Smith," he said, and took the small overnight bag she carried and handed it to the young chauffeur who stood waiting.

"Hello, Patty. It's nice to see you again," Marilee said, warmly. Then she added, "I'm sorry it has to be under these circumstances."

"Oh, Mrs. Graham," Patty wailed, "I'm so sorry, isn't it just awful?"

The driver went into the plane and emerged with the rest of Marilee's luggage and they followed him to the ostentatiously long limousine Patty had waiting adjacent to the parking apron.

Patty caught Norris' look of disapproval of the limo and shrugged. "It was the best I could do, boss. Everything is utter chaos at the Tower. All the regular corporate vehicles were checked out. When I learned Mrs. Graham was coming with you, I had to take what was available. There's just no way three people could squeeze into my little 'Z'."

"No sweat...don't know what I'd ever do without you." Norris gave her arm a squeeze.

After Marilee and Norris were seated inside, Patty leaned in the limo and pulled down the jump seat and took the seat facing them.

Once they started moving, she said to Norris, "I told the driver to go to the big house. I thought you'd want to stop by to see Mrs. Graham first thing...I thought perhaps you'd want to see her too, Mrs. Graham." Patty turned tentatively to Marilee.

"Uhmm, well, yes, of course. But I have a dilemma. I've got to get over to Jaynie Harris' place and see Ivee...poor darling. I spoke to him this morning, before we left New York. He's being very brave, but I'm sure he's overwhelmed. Ivee adored his granddaddy. Clayt was away a lot the past few months, but they have always been virtually inseparable. This is the first time anyone close to Ivee has died. He's going to miss Clayton...I'll miss him too. I need to go home and see about a car. Mine's in Raleigh at the airport," Marilee's voice trailed off. She was really thinking out loud more than speaking to the others. "But I'll see Mabel first. Poor thing. Then I can walk home and use Trip's car to go pick up Ivee."

"We have to meet a number of outside people flying into the Raleigh-Durham airport today, Mrs. Graham. I've already arranged for Dempsey Gearhart to ferry a driver to pick up Norris' car. If you'll give me your keys, I'll have Demp take an extra driver with him on the helicopter and we can get your car to you this afternoon," Patty offered. She was used to handling such things.

"Oh, Patty, that would be a lifesaver." Marilee smiled gratefully. She located her car keys and handed them to Patty. "And...please...won't you just call me Marilee?"

When they finally pulled up in front of the big house, the drive was clogged with cars. Most were large and expensive and some were chauffeured. Cavalierly blocking the main steps leading up to the portico was the Governor's black limousine. Norris directed the driver to pull around the official car and wait. Then he escorted the two women into the house.

Inside, Patty headed straight to the phone in the foyer to call Dempsey Gearhart at the Air Centre and make the arrangements about returning Marilee's car.

"Oh, thank God, you're here at last! Mabel's been asking for you both every five minutes since she heard the awful news yesterday afternoon." Rushing forward, Nan Moss greeted Norris and Marilee. She hugged them both and turned and led them toward the rear of the house to see Mabel. "Come along, the poor thing's back in the keeping room."

"Wait, let me find a tissue," Marilee tugged at Nan's elbow and pulled her to a stop just outside the large sitting room. Inside there was a low murmur from a group of perhaps fifty assorted men and women standing around in little groups.

"Oh, Norris...Marilee, thank God you're here at last...we were so worried. Griffin called everywhere," Mabel exclaimed when she saw them. She looked exhausted. Lost.

Mabel took Norris' hand. "Griffin said he spoke to your secretary, and you agreed we should have the funeral...the services... tomorrow morning at ten. I think he's made all the arrangements, but I really don't know what all he's done. Do you suppose you could call him and see? Trip's in a...the hospital...poor thing. I haven't talked to him. I know he's devastated by his father's death. Griffin was going to see him this morning...to see if he was well enough to come to the...ah...services. I hope he's strong enough to come. Oh, Norris, I don't have anyone else now...I have to depend on you...and Griff...and you dear...God bless you both." Mabel barely glanced at Marilee. Her voice was a flat, measured monotone. Clearly, she was operating on nervous energy—in shock.

"Don't worry about any of that now." Norris bent forward and kissed Mabel on the cheek.

"He thought so much of you, Norris. He was depending on you to take over...he really considered you a second son, you know—of course you knew that. He hoped to live to see Ivee step in."

"Well, yes, he was like a father to me in many ways..." Norris told Mabel, automatically.

Norris looked around the room. *Had it all been for nothing?*

For the second time in as many days, he was sharply reminded of his grandmother's warning about wishing too hard for things.

Four nights ago, he'd had this all in his grasp. Now Clayt was dead and the contract unsigned.

Had Fate stepped in and pulled him up short?

If they thought he'd hang around here, kissing Trip's ass, then they had another think coming. With Trip in charge, no matter how much they offered him, they could kiss him goodbye.

Thanks, but no thanks; back to the old drawing board.

What was plan B? The White House was begging...but that left him strangely unmoved.

One thing for sure...he wasn't broke. He knew he could always hire out as a consultant... even if he never turned another hair, he'd never really have to worry about money again.

Maybe he'd just go to Sheepshead Light and write again.

Big Random...Doubleday, too and Simon and Schuster and Putnam...one time or another, they'd all offered him book deals.

Would Agnes fight a divorce?

Would Marilee live with him at Sheepshead in the summers, Caswell in the spring and fall?...winters in Key West, maybe?...he'd seen some property near his mother's place on Sanibel Island....

Marilee would divorce Trip now, all right...but there was still Ivee. He knew Clayt had already changed his will...contract or not, he, Norris Wrenn, was part of the board. He'd seen to that himself as a preliminary requirement to the deal. If he wanted to, even with Grail under Trip's control he could probably do a takeover after about a year—it was a thought he'd had before. But he wasn't all that certain control of Grail was what he wanted anyway...

He was certain of one thing—*he didn't like winding up the loser.*

The disappointment of the unsigned contract left a taste of sour grapes in his mouth.

And he hadn't heard the last from Washington...not by a long shot.

But...he really couldn't see himself hanging around the White House. His jaws ached, just thinking about all the smiling he'd have to do. And spooks taking notes on his sex life?...not this old boy. He shook his head.

He needed to be out of here.

"Don't trouble yourself over anything, Mabel. I'll help Griffin with all the details. You look a little peaked. Have you eaten anything? How much rest did you get last night?" Norris patted her hand. He knew the drill by heart—he had done it better than anyone when he was first moving up in the rarefied air around Pennsylvania Avenue.

Norris the wonderful...knew everygoddamnthing...he made himself sick.

Norris suffered patiently through a brief discussion of the funeral, then excused himself. "I'll be at the Tower looking after things. Call me if you need anything, Mabel dear."

He bent forward and gave Mabel a final peck on the cheek.

Right now, he needed to get the hell out of here and make sure the corporation suffered as little as possible until this blew over. After all, even if his contract was left unsigned...that was all spilled milk now. Clayton Massie Graham was history.

And he still had a sizable stake in all this.

He intended to look after his own ass, now more than ever.

He'd asked the Grail corporate media chief, Gus Poe, to call a press conference this afternoon in the big room at the top of the Tower. He knew with his presence, and staged in that spectacular setting, it would produce a boomerang effect on tomorrow's opening market.

It was too late to stop any confusion on Wall Street for today and he knew Grail would probably lose at least five points by closing. But Norris also knew the value of good theater...in the financial world, he was the expert.

He planned to have his broker buy Grail heavily just before closing today when the sell-off took the stock to its lowest. A hundred-and-a-quarter invested just before closing...by ten o'clock tomorrow morning, he felt certain his blind account would have made a nice profit on paper.

He turned back to Nan. "Don't forget, have Griff give me a call as soon as he gets a chance. And call me if you need anything...anything at all." He smiled and patted her arm...again.

Looking for the easiest path back through the crowd to the door, Norris took Marilee's elbow, urging her toward the front hall.

"You're on your own, kid. Go find Ivee before you're trapped," he whispered in Marilee's ear. "Call me at The Tower as soon as you're free. I'm history here. *Ciao*."

"You really do love me, don't you?" Marilee whispered in quiet desperation.

He squeezed her elbow. "More than you can imagine...don't forget to call."

Before Marilee could protest, Norris collected Patty and headed for the car.

CHAPTER FIFTY-EIGHT

AT THE FLIGHT CENTRE, Dempsey Gearhart was not at all vexed at having to wait while Patty sent the driver back with Marilee's keys.

Ordinarily, the fleet management was well organized and ran rather routinely, but with the suddenness of Clayton's death, the excrement had hit the proverbial propeller and all routine plans went out the window. It seemed as if every big-shot politician and every Grail VIP, including their wives and second cousins, wanted to be flown into Colonial Hall for the funeral.

During the past twenty-four hours, since word of Clayton's death reached him, he had managed to get only a few hours sleep. To this point, he hadn't chosen to do much of the flying himself, but the corporate fleet consisted of over fifty aircraft of various sizes and uses, and management of their scheduling was his responsibility. To make matters worse, he had to arrange for all their ground transportation.

And now, as if that wasn't bad enough, he had Glee Law-Craige to deal with. She was in the middle of a real fire-snorting snit-fit. The crazy bitch would be arriving in Raleigh on the noon Delta and she was out for Graham blood.

Until Patty called, Dempsey had felt a little nervous about sneaking off to meet Glee. Now he had an excuse to personally fly drivers up to RDU to pick up both Norris Wrenn's and Marilee Graham's cars. Norris Wrenn's assistant had set him free. The way he saw it, Patty's call personally released him from the standby orders he'd received from Griff Richards earlier that morning and presented him with the opportunity to personally fly the chopper with the shuttle drivers to Raleigh-Durham airport and pick up Glee and sneak her back to his place, away from prying eyes.

"If that goddamn Griffin Richards doesn't talk nice to me, I'll walk to the front of that goddamn church and deliver a few historic words about Mr. Clayton Massie Graham, Sr. that will peel the varnish right off the pews," Glee had fumed on the phone late last night.

"Calm down...don't get yourself worked up over nothing," Dempsey had tried to reason with her. "After all, remember what Griff Richards told you when you talked to him this afternoon? Clayton had the real estate deal all nailed down before the crash."

"*Calm down, my ass,*" Glee snorted. "Richards didn't want to explain the particulars over the phone...all the old coot really said was that as soon as the arrangements could be finalized, he would come down and explain the particulars and settle with me. *Explain the particulars? Settle with me? Shit!* Who the fuck does he think he is? If there's any goddamn settling to do, then I'll have something to say about that. What really pisses me off is he told me he didn't think it was a good idea I come to the goddamn funeral. Says if Mabel even gets a breath of scandal, all bets are off. Well, that's what lawyers are for. He's scared to death I'll show up. Fuck him...fuck 'em all. I'm not going to be left sucking hind tit! I have a ticket on the 9:05 Delta out of Jax into RDU. Can you meet me at high noon? Can I stay with you? Or are you afraid of being embarrassed, too?"

"I'll meet you, or I'll have someone meet you...and yes, certainly you can stay here." Dempsey felt very uneasy about Glee. He really didn't trust her, but together, with the leverage she had, and with the stuff he had that tied Trip into the death of the movie star, Demp felt sure they could get their hands on a nice little piece of the Graham's loot. All of a sudden there were going to be billions of dollars shifting hands, just because some confused seagulls decided to fly higher than was their usual habit.

The Emma Claire death was strictly page two in this morning's *Observer*. But, that really didn't mean anything. Congress was asking questions about Chief of Staff Courtland Pike's suicide and they were still looking for those two White House chopper pilots...the big headline proclaimed:

CLAYTON MASSIE GRAHAM DEAD IN CRASH!

The Graham fortune...the money and power involved...had eclipsed the media's interest in some minor drug scandal in a minor movie star's death.

Besides, when he read the Claire article carefully, he could read between the lines that her death was far from closed as being a simple overdose. As long as the case was under investigation, he knew Trip and the Grahams had their ass in a crack...and if they tried to quietly close it, what was to keep him from going to Trip and threatening to have it reopened? In a way, Clayt's death made the future look even rosier. Without his daddy beside him, Trip would fold like a pussycat under the pressure.

And the good news was that right out of the clear blue, Demp had been dealt another winning hole card when Griffin Richards had called this morning at the crack of dawn, requesting a hush-hush hop in the chopper. Skimming over the early morning fog, he had flown Griffin Richards in the chopper to Raleigh where they had picked up D.C. Mills, the Chief of the Greensboro Police. He was sure Richards thought he wouldn't recognize the passenger. But Dempsey had flown Mills to Nags Head to the Marlin Tournament last year. Anyway, his two passengers had been very grim and businesslike. He had not been surprised at their destination...and they had only spent about thirty minutes down at that cozy little clinic near Pinehurst where he had flown Dr. Scott and Trip late Tuesday night. Then he had dropped the Chief back at the police hangar at RDU. When they got back here, Griff's instructions had been to remain on standby for a return trip in the chopper, back to Durham later this afternoon.

It smelled like a cover-up to Demp. Things were really looking better for the home team. All he had to do was sit tight and just keep quiet for awhile.

Glee made him very nervous. He never knew what to expect out of her. Now, to make matters worse, she was in a rotten mood.

A very dicey situation.

And...Clayton's death had raised some other interesting questions.

Demp had been there in the terminal this morning when the

small executive jet had deposited Norris Wrenn and Marilee Graham at the gate. The thought occurred to him at the time that they made an interesting...and very charismatic...couple. He couldn't help but be struck by the coincidence that they were both in New York when this happened. Marilee Graham was a real beauty. Norris and Marilee both went to New York a lot. Thinking back now, he remembered word had it Marilee Graham was big buddies with the Hollywood actress, Sadie Bailey, and spent a lot of time visiting her in the Big Apple. He made a note to take Ruby, that chick at his Grail Tower office, out to lunch. Ruby booked all the corporate travel arrangements on commercial flights...she just might know some things that would prove interesting.

Now more than ever, he knew Norris Wrenn was a force to be reckoned with. In Dempsey's book, Norris Wrenn stood alone at the top of the list of men he never wanted to fuck with.

Demp Gearhart didn't take a back seat to many men, but he was a careful observer of the people who held the power over his paycheck. He had made a decision the first time he had personally flown Norris on an extended tour of the Grail main branches, scattered among major cities coast to coast—he would try to stay on the good side of this dude.

All the same, he made a mental note to run a computer check on Norris Wrenn's trips and also see if Marilee Graham ever used the corporate planes except when she was with her husband. He couldn't remember that she had...still. It just might be interesting to find out how often she'd been in New York when Norris had.

Anyway, he owed Patty Smith a debt because he couldn't very well refuse a request from Norris Wrenn's assistant to get Mrs. Graham's car back to her...now, could he? Certainly Mr. Griffin Richards would have to agree with that. He grinned as he saw the limo pull up to the hanger near where the helicopter was parked. The driver came toward him tossing a set of keys in the air.

Well, just look out Colonial Hall...here comes Ms. Glee Law-Craige.

CHAPTER FIFTY-NINE

WHEN SHE DROVE TRIP'S YELLOW CORVETTE over to Jaynie Harris' to pick up Ivee, Marilee stopped on the way back home and put the top down.

It had torn the heart out of her, the way Ivee stoically played the role of a brave little soldier. Laughing and pretending to be in good spirits—stiff upper lip and all that. But when they were safely home and the door had closed behind them, he had suddenly gotten quiet. Hand in hand, without a word, they had walked back to the large keeping room, and Marilee had taken him in her arms and they both had sobbed their hearts out.

Ivee had loved his granddaddy, and Marilee had really loved him, too. Clayton had his faults, but as both the supportive father-in-law and doting grandfather, what he may have lacked in warmth, he made up for with his generosity.

"Where did they take daddy?" Marilee was unprepared for Ivee's question. She was still trying to deal with the news of Clayton's death. In her shock and sense of loss, she had almost forgotten Trip was in that hospital for alcoholics. She found it hard to believe Trip had slipped that far. She knew he drank too much sometimes, but she hadn't really noticed he drank that much more than most of their crowd. For Ivee's sake, Marilee was hopeful the entire thing had just gotten blown out of proportion.

But the other news Griffin had given her this morning was even more disturbing.

"Marilee, I know you've got a lot on your mind but I think you should know that when he crashed, Clayton was on his way back here yesterday because the Greensboro cops have questioned Trip about the drug death of that movie actress, Emma Claire," Griffin had begun, hesitantly, trying to chose his words carefully. "When she died, Trip was in Greensboro, registered next door at The Massie House..."

"But what does that prove?" she had snapped back defensively before he could go further. After all, Trip was Ivee's father, and all this had an ugly ring to it. Marilee knew Trip played around...she really hadn't cared as long as he didn't rub her nose—and his son's nose—in it.

"Well, nothing...but there's more. They're pretty sure now she died from an overdose of cocaine. They suspect Trip was with her that night...and they're afraid it will leak out. You know how the media is. They're already making idle comparisons with the John Belushi thing. An off-duty cop pulled Trip Sunday night to give him a warning, and Trip had a woman with him...it's hard to tell you this, but it's better you hear it from me. Anyway, I've managed to keep the Chief from asking Trip any more questions because he was in Holly Hall, but I'm in a box on this. I've got to take the Chief in the chopper to see Trip this morning at the clinic. As a matter of fact I'm on my way to the airport right now. And, we haven't told Trip about Clayton's death yet. We need to get up there before he hears it on the TV. Anyway, I think the cop's interest is pretty routine...most likely it will help remove Trip from suspicion." Griff wasn't making much sense.

"I don't understand. If it's routine, why does the Chief want to talk to Trip?"

"Well, he just doesn't want to wind up with egg on his face. If the media uncovers a link with Trip, God help us all!" Griffin said, fervently. "But I can assure you Mills is on our side. The Chief knows which side of his bread gets the butter."

"Make damned sure he does. My God! We can't let that happen...it would kill Ivee...." Marilee's heart sank at the thought.

"Don't worry, the Chief certainly doesn't want any more grief than he's got already," Griffin had assured her.

Now, Marilee looked at Ivee and didn't know what to say. She thought about it for a moment and patted him on the hand, "I don't know much about it either, darling. I need to call Dr. Scott and find out right this minute, before we do another thing."

Before she dialed the number, she asked him, "Would you like to go to The Club? We can have lunch out by the pool." She knew it would be better if Ivee couldn't hear her end of the conversation. She had a lot of questions to ask Ed Scott. There was no way to be delicate about most of them.

"Oh yeah, mom. That would be fun. I think Jody and his mom may be there. Could we ask 'em to join us?" Ivee had just spent two and a half days with the Harrises and still couldn't get enough of his friend's company; those two were inseparable.

"Well, if you don't think they're sick of you." She winked at him. Actually, she really liked Jaynie Harris and had meant to see more of her. The more she thought about it, the better the idea sounded. "Go up and change your clothes...on second thought, jump in the shower and get the top layer of dirt off. And hurry! I'm starved." She waited until he left the room on the dead run before she picked up the phone.

When the receptionist answered, Marilee asked to speak to Dr. Scott.

"Marilee?..."

"Ed...I hear there's been some excitement since I left for New York Tuesday...." Suddenly embarrassed, she searched for the right way to begin.

"Yes...ah...yes indeed. I...I'm sure you know I had to take Trip to Holly Hall?" he said. "I'm sorry we couldn't get in touch with you. God knows we tried."

"Well, that's nobody's fault really. It was just one of those things. Can you tell me what's happened to Trip...everyone's so vague. I'm quite confused."

Marilee listened without interruption as the physician described what had happened to Trip and how he had taken him by helicopter. He was careful to point out the seriousness of it all...and how, with the personal escort of Dr. Ewing Curtis, who was an expert in the field of addiction...they had taken Trip directly to Holly Hall, one of the most exclusive treatment clinics in the country.

"The clientele there reads like Who's Who. When it comes to

privacy, it makes Betty Ford's place look like the Atlanta airport," Ed Scott concluded with professional pride.

"But do you think this is really all that serious? I mean, if he was using drugs, I think I would have known...after all, I'm his wife," Marilee protested lamely.

"Marilee, it's deadly serious...serious as a heart attack. Those lab tests don't lie. Trip's liver is absolutely on tilt. If Trip doesn't quit drinking for good, he won't see another birthday...certainly not two..." Scott's tone left no room to doubt his concern.

"My God...How long will he have to be there? What can we do? Can I see him? Should Ivee go with me? How...?" the questions spilled out. She still found it hard to believe.

"Well, he'll probably be there about four weeks...and of course you can visit...we'll have to check on the rules. As a matter of fact, Dr. Curtis' staff will suggest you come to the Family Therapy group...be in residence for a week..."

"You mean I would have to go there and...and...."

"Yes...it's the therapeutic standard nowadays...alcoholism is a family illness...."

"Wait just a minute...I hardly drink at all, Ed...."

"Oh...no...no. Not that way...the therapy team at Holly Hall will explain it...you have to understand how to live with an alcoholic...know about the disease...."

"God, I could teach 'em all a thing or two...I...." Marilee stopped herself before she went into the sordid tale about her father.

"Well then, I don't have to tell you...first thing is you should try to help him stay away from the sauce...I mean, it would be a good idea if you quit drinking yourself...at least around him. He'll have to go to AA. And there's an organization called Al-Anon. It's like AA, but it's for the wives and er...ah...family members and loved ones of recovering alcoholics. You can take Ivee. They have a group called Alateen for kids Ivee's age. You definitely need to go to that. There are several groups right here in Colonial Hall...." Ed began.

Marilee reacted immediately to such a preposterous idea.

"You mean I should go to AA? And Ivee...why he's just a boy. Be serious. Trip's the one that's got the problem. Ed, don't you know that we...none of us...can go. The Grahams don't belong in AA. Frankly Ed, I think you're overreacting...." Marilee couldn't believe the man was serious. "Trip would never go...besides Mabel wouldn't hear of it anyway. Surely it isn't necessary. Why can't he just stop drinking? It's just a matter of a little willpower...."

"Well, I hope he can, but I've seen a lot of cases and I doubt it. Not Trip. He's going to need all the help he can get. In Trip's case I can assure you I'm not overreacting. When you see him, take a close look...his eyeballs and skin are slightly jaundiced from his liver disease. People die every day from that, Mrs. Graham." Suddenly on the defensive, the doctor reverted to a more formal form of address—but Ed Scott wasn't about to give in.

"Where is this Holly Hall place? When can I go up there?" she asked again. "When can I see Trip...and this Dr. Curtis?"

"Well, you don't need to go anywhere to see Trip today...he's coming home. I don't like it, but under the circumstances, both Dr. Curtis and I had to relent and agree to let him have a brief pass to come to the services for his father. We feel in cases like this, the unresolved grief which would result from keeping him away would probably be more detrimental to the recovery process than having him up there in a controlled environment, but with his thoughts off somewhere else." Quite unnecessarily, Ed Scott tried to justify the decision. "Let's see...it's about a quarter to twelve now...Trip should be leaving Holly Hall in another hour and be home by two at the latest. Griffin Richards is picking him up and bringing him here in the helicopter. When he gets home, Marilee, please take every precaution he doesn't get near any booze. For godsake, keep him away from that bunch of drunks in his father's study."

"Well, I don't know what I can do to stop him if he wants a drink, but I'll do my best to help him, Ed. And, Ed, stay close...I got a feeling we're going to need you, for moral support, I mean." Marilee wasn't so sure about the last part. She didn't like the sound of any of it. Yesterday all this had seemed far away.

The very idea of her taking Ivee to a bunch of meetings with a group of drunks...fat chance!

Marilee was standing in the front hall flipping through the mail when Trip walked in, followed by Griff carrying Trip's duffel in one hand and his hanging bag draped over his other arm.

Griff was obviously upset, and Trip had an unhappy look about him.

"You were out of line with Dempsey back there...you talked to him like some flunky. Dempsey Gearhart is the best—a real asset. He was chief pilot for one of the biggies in New York...he does a hell of a job for us. *People* just did a short piece praising him and spotlighting our corporate fleet operation. We're lucky to have him. Dempsey has had his hands full today. VIP's have been pouring into Raleigh since last night...he had to route the executive jet to New York this morning before dawn to pick up Norris and Marilee...just ask Norris what he thinks of him..." Griff was saying when Trip interrupted.

"I don't give a good goddamn if he was head of American, TWA and Pan Am combined, and I sure as hell don't care what Norris Wrenn thinks about him. I've had it with that cocky flyboy. He's too big for his britches. Why did that son of a bitch keep me waiting just so he could deliver a driver to Raleigh to pick up some hicks from out of town? Did you see that insolent look on his face when I told him he needed to get his priorities straight? I want to see the son of a bitch tomorrow afternoon at the Tower, after the services. I intend to shape up this casual attitude we have around here toward the corporate executives. And, as for Norris, I blame Norris Wrenn for most of it...him with his fucking democratic management. I'll bet the 'Flying Ace' didn't keep the famous Mr. Wrenn waiting in New York."

Trip stopped his tirade when he looked up and saw Marilee.

"Well, hello, Trip. How are you feeling?" she said automatically, but she made no move to go to him.

"Hello, yourself," Trip mumbled. "I see you finally made it back. Hope it didn't spoil your shopping." He was obviously looking for a fight.

"I'm glad to be back. I'm so sorry about Clayton. We all loved him so. Ivee just doesn't know exactly how to react. He's so young; it hasn't hit him yet." Marilee ignored Trip. She wasn't going to get into a fight.

She turned to Griff. "Griff, how are you? I don't know what we'd do without you."

"No better than the rest of us under these circumstances. Where can I put these?" Griff asked, indicating the luggage. "I need to go see about the arrangements."

"Just put them down over there. I'll get someone to take them up." She indicated a little love seat in the foyer by the door. "By the way, Griff, are you going to the Tower? I rode down on the corporate plane from New York with Norris this morning. He said tell you he is anxious to see you...."

"Thanks, I'll call him. I'm certainly glad he's back. I feel a lot better now he's here to take care of things. Grail can't do without him," Griff said, and started out the door. "Take care, Trip. The doctor said you should get plenty of rest...ah...well, take care...."

"Yeah...I know all about that. And, while I'm thinking about it, tell Norris Wrenn I want to see him tomorrow after the funeral...at the Tower. We need to have a serious understanding about who's running things now." Trip glared at Griffin, daring him to take exception.

Griff ignored him. "Take it easy, folks. See ya later."

"I guess Mr. High-and-Mighty-Wrenn was acting like a big shot on the plane coming down." Trip looked at Marilee.

"Well, he had a lot on his mind. He has a lot of responsibility now Clayton's gone. He must be pretty smart—the White House keeps calling him. I think Grail...the family...we're all pretty lucky to have him, if you ask me." Marilee looked for his reaction.

"Washington? What the fuck do I care about that? If he wants to stay on, he's gonna have to learn who's boss now. I was his roommate. He can't fool me like he did my father. As far as I'm concerned, I'm going to tear up that fucking contract."

"I'd better find someone to take your things up to your room." Marilee turned to go back through the dining room into the

400

kitchen. "Then maybe we can have a glass of tea or a coke and talk. I want to hear all about your trouble. I'm worried about you."

"Don't bother. I'll take 'em up. I want to go lie down. The chopper kinda wore me out. It's not exactly the executive jet, you know?" He picked up the bags and started up the steps.

"OK, do you want me to bring you anything? Are you hungry?"

"No, thanks. I just want to lie down for awhile."

Marilee watched him climb the stairs and disappear before she went over to the wet bar at the far corner of the room and found a bottle of Stoli. She held it up to the light.

Did Ed Scott actually think she could hide all the booze?

She poured the vodka over two ice cubes to almost three-quarters full in an old-fashioned glass.

Listening guiltily for a minute to see if she heard Trip, she quickly looked in the refrigerator for something to mix it with.

As for Ed Scott's little speech, Marilee knew alcoholics made the whole family sick. Just look at her, already guiltily sneaking drinks herself. She savored her drink and looked out over the terrace at the unspoiled, sun-dappled view of the golf course and the gables of The Country Club. Wryly, she wondered if this was the way things were going to be around here from now on.

Not for long...not if she had anything at all to say about it.

She guessed she'd have to go to that Family Program...if she just walked out on Trip now, people would talk. She knew when she looked at Trip everything Ed Scott said was true. Not only was he yellow, but he had light bruises all over him. That looked like something really serious. She made a note to ask the doctor about it.

She wondered about the will. Somehow, Marilee felt certain she was taken care of...after all, she *was* Ivee's mother...that had meant everything to Clayton.

It bothered her now, what Trip said about Norris' contract. Norris owned the condo in New York and the Thistle, but she wondered if Norris had any real money of his own. She knew Trip was serious about showing Norris who was boss. Norris wouldn't put up with that for a second.

Well, where did that leave her now?

Marilee walked back in and poured herself another drink and carried it with her up the staircase. Safely inside her room she went straight to her little white desk and located her bank book.

"Every girl should have some mad money!" Sadie Bailey had told her before she'd even graduated from Miami—before she'd started making some serious money in New York.

After the funeral, she'd like to pack up Ivee and just run away to Caswell...or Sheepshead... anywhere as long as it was with Norris. She'd never look back.

She'd keep up appearances for a month or so. But one thing for sure, she was going to see a good divorce lawyer about her options first thing Monday...the day after Mother's Day...

FRIDAY

CHAPTER SIXTY

THE ONE STIFF DRINK Trip had hoped would see him through the morning was wearing off and he was feeling shaky again.

Marilee had lingered at the door of the church and said something to Norris.

Watching them, Trip remembered he'd meant to ask her about the bulky package of newspaper and magazine clippings about Norris he'd found in her bedroom while she was in New York. He was sick of Norris being the Graham family hero...particularly with his own wife and son. The ungrateful bitch better have a good explanation about those clippings. He was top dog now.

As the driver held the door of the long black funeral limousine for Mabel and the others, Trip abruptly stepped in front of Dempsey Gearhart and grabbed him by the arm as he came off the church steps. "Did Griffin Richards tell you I want to see you this afternoon at the Tower?"

"I haven't spoken with Mr. Richards." Dempsey struggled to hide his contempt for Trip. The recollection of the shabby way the drunken bastard had treated him yesterday when he and Griff Richards had showed up ten minutes late to rescue him from that fancy drying-out place was still fresh in his mind. Not that he really gave a shit. He'd had about all of Mister Trip Graham he could take. This afternoon sounded like a perfect time for "show and tell."

Well..."tell," at least.

There'd be time enough later for "show." He'd keep Trip's two little bags of goodies...the hard evidence...safely in its hiding place for now. No use to make a scene about it...not yet, anyway. And right here, right now, was hardly the time and place. Still, Dempsey had no intention of spending the rest of his life taking Trip

Graham's shit. He was looking forward to the opportunity to get things straight between them for once and for all.

"What time did you want me there?"

"Call me later," Trip snapped rudely.

"Sure thing...." Dempsey stared noncommittally into Trip's yellow, bloodshot eyes. The asshole reeked of booze. At the moment, Trip Graham didn't look too tough to him.

Trip turned and followed Ivee and Marilee and his mother into the limousine.

Glee had told Dempsey that Big Clayt had made a deal with Norris Wrenn to run Grail—to get Trip out of the executive penthouse. What the hell. Norris ran the outfit anyway; everybody knew that. Still, right now, more than ever, Dempsey hoped the rumor was true.

Dempsey liked his job. He wasn't about to give it up because of this comic-strip version of Clayton Graham. He could really enjoy working for a guy like Norris Wrenn. Dempsey didn't have to take a second look at Trip Graham's sorry ass as it disappeared inside the limo to know that he hated the sight of it. He was tempted to just call the police and turn the bastard in. But then, he didn't like the way that high and mighty Griffin Richards had been treating Glee either.

And, for that matter, he wasn't at all happy Glee had come. Glee was an all-around sticky wicket...squirrelly as they get. Involuntarily, he turned to look for her. With Glee you never knew what was coming next.

Now he saw Griffin Richards bearing down on her. The usually unflappable attorney didn't look too happy at the moment.

Dempsey moved to intervene.

Griffin Richards had spotted Glee in front of the church just before the services. All through the eulogies, Dempsey could sense that Richards was smoldering with anger at her arrogant disregard of his explicit admonition not to come. Immediately following the eulogy, as everyone was filing out of the church and those going to the graveside were being quietly herded toward their cars, Richards

406

headed straight for Glee with blood in his eye. Barely able to control his anger, he growled through tightly-clenched teeth, "I thought I told you to stay put, young lady. You have no business here. You're skating on thin ice with me. If you know what's good for you, you'll get on the first plane back to Jacksonville and wait until I call you."

Richards scowled at Dempsey who had now moved to Glee's elbow. He started to say something and then decided against it. Without waiting for a reply from Glee, Richards turned and walked back to where the limo carrying Mabel, Nan, Trip, Marilee and Ivee was pulled up to the curb just behind the hearse for the trip to the graveside.

"Well, fuck you, too, Jack!" Seething with rage, Glee muttered at Richard's back.

Dempsey nervously looked about, and, taking her firmly by the elbow, steered Glee toward his car. By the time he had maneuvered through the side streets and evaded the confused jumble of the funeral traffic, Glee had fallen silent and Demp turned on the radio looking for some music to help defuse his anger at them all. "...TO ALL THE GIRLS I'VE LOVED BEFORE...WILLIE AND JULIO COMING TO YOU FROM K-A-I-R:...THE STATION THAT CARES...IT'S TEN THIRTY-ONE, FRIDAY, THE EIGHTH OF MAY, TWO DAYS TO SHOP BEFORE MOTHER'S DAY AND IT'S A BEAUTIFUL DAY IN RALEIGH...NOW, LET'S TAKE A BRIEF LOOK AT THE HEADLINES...AN INFORMED SOURCE IN GREENSBORO SAYS THERE MAY HAVE BEEN A PERSON OR PERSONS UNKNOWN WITH MOVIE ACTRESS EMMA CLAIRE AT THE TIME OF HER DEATH...GREENSBORO CHIEF OF POLICE, D.C. MILLS, REFUSED COMMENT...IN COLONIAL HALL THE GOVERNOR EULOGIZED THE PASSING OF CLAYTON MASSIE GRAHAM..."

Glee reached forward and turned the volume down. "Did you hear that? The Greensboro cops are looking for persons unknown. I think it's time we gave Mr. Trip Graham a call...."

Dempsey looked at her and nodded, "I just spoke to Trip...he wants to see me at the Tower this afternoon. I've had enough of his shit. I'll hit him with it then."

"Will that high-and-mighty bastard, Griff Richards, be there, you think? Did you hear what he said to me back there? I feel like giving 'em all a piece of my mind."

"I doubt Trip'll have Richards there. Besides, we can't afford to make a scene...it would spoil everything...." Dempsey had no intention of putting up with Glee. There was no telling what she might do.

CHAPTER SIXTY-ONE

MAIRLEE'S WATCH DISPLAYED 10:30. Thanks to Norris, things were moving ahead of schedule.

She'd overheard Norris speak to Lonnie Reynolds just before the services began. "I'm glad you're doing the service, Governor. The worst thing at a time like this is for some long-winded politician to get up at a funeral and make a bloody boor of himself."

"Uh? Oh, yes!...I agree wholeheartedly...." Lonnie had stammered.

Marilee saw the Governor take out a thick pack of three-by-five cards, encircle them with a rubber band and put them back in his inside breast pocket. Then he furtively jotted a few quick notes on the back of an official calling card. Marilee breathed a sigh of relief. Thank god! For once in his life, Lonnie Reynolds had had the good sense to know when to shut up.

Earlier, before they left for the church, Marilee was sure that Trip had already been drinking. All through the services, she had nervously watched for signs that it was affecting his behavior. But as far as she could tell, he was not yet seriously impaired. Nevertheless, she still detected an unmistakable aromatic essence to his breath. Disregarding the air-conditioning, she leaned across and touched the button to crack the window and let in some fresh air. Thankfully, Mabel seemed to remain oblivious to the telltale odor. If Griffin and Nan were aware of it, they made no outward sign.

Ivee was subdued. He rode quietly beside Marilee on the jump seat facing his father and his grandmother. It was painful to see him so dark and brooding. To an eleven-year-old, all of this had to be overwhelming.

At the graveside, everything went off in good time. Afterward, Marilee had given Ivee a hug and a kiss and turned him over to

Jaynie Harris. Then she got into the limo to return with the others.

They had hardly been at the big house five minutes when Trip looked at his watch and asked Griff, "Did you tell Norris I wanted to see him at the Tower this afternoon?"

Griff nodded. "Norris said he'd be there. He and I have a lot of things to talk over."

It infuriated Trip that Griff seemed to condescend to him. Well, this afternoon, he would put the high'n'mighty Griffin Richards in his place. He'd let 'em all know he intended to take over Monday.

When Governor Reynolds and Martin Stowe and their wives came into the house, the ladies murmured politely and brushed quickly past Trip and Marilee toward the rear of the house.

"There's a mountain of food in the dining room. Beth, would you or Ora Mae see if you can get Mabel to eat something? I'll fix her a plate if she'll tell me what she'd like," Marilee called to the wives as they passed her heading back through the hallway.

The door to the study was open. Trip noted enviously that the domestic staff had cleaned up the disarray of dirty glasses and empty bottles. There were fresh bottles of mixes and trays with sparkling clean glasses. Ice buckets had been refilled and were sitting on a serving cart by the wet bar.

Marilee caught Trip glancing nervously her way as he eyed the liquor.

Not much doubt about it, Marilee noted, Trip was dying for a drink. Remembering her hopelessly alcoholic father, she felt only contempt. She had lost all feeling for common drunks a long time ago.

The Governor shook hands with Griff and Trip. "Well, I'm not much of a drinking man...rarely ever touch the stuff, but I think Clayton would kind of like it if we all sort of stepped into his study there and had a drink to his memory."

Griffin cleared his throat and looked sternly at Trip who had already taken a step toward the door. Trip pulled up short, mindful that virtually the entire world was watching him like a hawk.

"I hope you'll all excuse me. My stomach's been bothering me. I have to go to the office this afternoon, and I'm feeling pretty stressed all of a sudden. I think I'll walk over to the house and lie down for awhile. Thank you for coming, Lonnie. You mean a lot to our family." Trip quickly shook hands, accepted embarrassed condolences all around, and turned and started back out the front door.

"Wait up, Trip, won't you let me fix you a plate?" Marilee called after him. "You should eat something..."

"Nah, I'm just tired. A little rest will make me good as new," he called over his shoulder and kept on walking.

Marilee was certain that he was going home to get a drink.

Incredible. But she was helpless to stop him. His eyes were yellow as a pumpkin. He couldn't go on like this for long—it would kill him. Dr. Scott had only agreed to let him come home for a couple of days...he was supposed to go back to Holly Hall Sunday. Well, what did she care, anyway? If he made her a widow, what would be the difference?

But she didn't wish him dead...she really didn't.

She tossed her head to dismiss the thought. Why think about it? There was enough gloom around without asking for more.

"I think I'll grab a sandwich and head down to the Tower. Norris will be headed down there soon, I'm sure." Griff turned toward the dining room. Marilee wanted to ask him about Norris' contract, but she thought better of it. Griff was no dummy. If they weren't careful, sooner or later he'd start to notice things and put two and two together.

Her heart sank at the prospect of the weekend. It was going to be an eternity until Sunday.

She watched with wry disdain as the mourners edged in the direction of the study to pay their last respects to Clayton's first-class stock of booze; then she headed back to locate Norris. She desperately needed a moment with him alone.

Trip felt he was disintegrating molecule by molecule...simply flying apart.

Once he had sauntered nonchalantly down the brick drive and out of sight, past the brick gateposts, he broke into a sort of a dogtrot beyond the entrance to the Club parking lot, taking a

411

shortcut through the trees into his own side yard.

Safely inside, he was shaking so badly he could hardly get the top off of the bottle of Stoli. He spilled more than he poured as he tried to fill the glass.

"Whew!...godamighty...just in time..." he breathed aloud as he finally got the drink down.

Without hesitation, he quickly poured another.

"All right! Hang tight a minute, baby..." he muttered at his reflection in the mirror as he knocked back the second drink, this time without spilling quite so much.

"Oooh, yeah!...work your magic, baby. Come to papa...Daddy needs you," he crooned to the Stoli bottle. The booze washed down his gut, spilling a reassuring warmth. Recapping the bottle, he put it back under the sink. He wasn't going to get hammered this time. He'd show 'em he could handle it.

Fuck 'em anyway.

"Got that loving feeling...." he hummed. *Top Gun...that old Tom Cruise movie.*

Trip Graham...Top Gun...yeah! That was him all right.

"Whoa-oh-oh-ho-oh!...." he crooned.

Fucking magic!...feeling mellow, already.

He eyed the bed. A little nap would be just the ticket. Then he'd go down to the Tower and get it straight with Norris and Griff Richards...and Dempsey Whatshisface...the arrogant flyboy.

Hmmm? Was that the downstairs phone?

"Mistah Graham?..." Someone at his door? Goddamn!

"Mr. Graham, it's Mr. Gayheart, suh. He says you was 'spectin' him to call."

"Uhmm...tell him to call my secretary. Wait!...never mind, I'll take it up here." He closed the door and went to the phone at the bedside table. His hand was growing steadier, and his mind was clearing already. Good old Stoli was doing its work. Might as well get this out of the way. He really didn't want to fire this guy. Everyone said Gearhart was good. He just wanted to make god-damn sure everyone knew who the new boss was.

"This is Trip Graham...." It suddenly occurred to him that it might be a good idea to start referring to himself as Clayton Graham, III, now that he was the head of Grail. Or maybe just Clayton would do it...or?...technically...was he a *Senior* now? He wasn't sure how it all worked. He made a mental note to check it out.

"Mister Graham, this is Dempsey Gearhart. I think you were anxious to see me?"

Was that an edge of insolence in the pilot's voice?

"Well, yes...uh...but as I recall, I asked you to call my secretary...I was specific about that, I'm sure." Trip let his voice go flat.

"Oh yes, you made that very clear, *Mister* Graham, but I think what we have to talk about would be best discussed some place else. Say, my office out here at the airstrip. We'd be all alone."

There was a sudden tightening in Trip's gut. What kind of shit was this man talking? Was he drunk?...on something funny, maybe?

"Why the hell would I want to come out there? What I have to talk to you about, I'll do in my own office...and if I were you, Gearhart, I'd be careful how I talked. I'm losing patience with you." He was feeling better by the second now. The magic elixer always worked. He held up his right hand.

Steady as a fucking rock.

"Mister Graham, I don't think you understand. Perhaps if I gave you a clue?" Dempsey waited for a reaction.

"Have you been drinking, Gearhart? If you have, I'm warning you, I'll...I'll suspend you on the spot. We should see about your license...there are federal regulations, I believe." Trip didn't like the way this thing was going at all. He really hadn't intended for it to turn into an unpleasant, drunken confrontation. He had expected better from the man. All he wanted was for these people to know who was running the show. Still, he guessed if there was a problem, then it was better to find out now. But he couldn't reason with the man over the phone, and now he certainly didn't feel up to dealing with him if he was drunk.

Trip didn't feel up to an ugly scene. And he still had to deal with Norris. Norris was more important anyway. This one could wait.

"If you've been drinking, Gearhart, I think we had better wait until you can get a grip on yourself. After all, I believe Mr.

Richards said that you've been working pretty hard lately...and then there's my father's death. That's got us all under a strain, I guess. Under the circumstances, we'll just put off our meeting. Take the weekend to get yourself straightened out. How's that sound to you? Fair enough?"

"But you don't seem to understand, Mister Graham. I want to talk about that actress Emma Claire and two bags full of stuff that you took out of your car and threw in a dumpster out past the Air Centre Tuesday just after lunchtime. Does that ring a bell, Mister Graham?"

Oooh, Shit!

Trip grabbed the bedpost to steady himself, suddenly speechless. He thought his heart would jump right out of his chest. Were his ears playing tricks? A hallucination?

He tried to clear his head.

Slowly, Trip pulled himself erect. Taking the cordless phone, he started toward the dressing room...goddamn...he needed another drink. How did this guy know about the bags? No one could possibly have seen him. He'd made sure about that.

He'd been so careful—he struggled to remember.

Maybe the asshole was bluffing.

"Mister Graham, are you still there? You didn't hang up, did you? I wouldn't want to take this stuff to that nice policeman Mr. Richards brought down to Holly Hall on the chopper with him yesterday. What did you tell him about all that Emma Claire business, Mister Graham?" Dempsey waited.

"Goddamn it, Gearhart, I'm not up to this. I just got out of the hospital. I don't know what you're trying to do...or what you think you know...but I...I'll see to it that you'll never fly for anybody again. I...I'm going to call the Chief and report this if you....if...." Trip's mind went blank. He was so scared he could hardly think. Did this bastard have him cold? "Are you trying to blackmail me, Gearhart? If you are, you are in deep shit."

"Mister Graham, I'm just trying to be a loyal Grail employee. I don't feel like you're very appreciative of that. But like you just said, you've been sick in the hospital...do you call that snobby drunk tank a hospital, Mister Graham? If you want, I'll wait right here while you come down and let's see how I can help you with your problem...the corporate problem, now that you're the boss, huh?...Mister Graham? According to what they're saying on the radio now, they're getting real curious about that actress' death. What's it going to be, Mister Graham?" Dempsey was tiring of the game now. "Cut the shit and get your drunken ass down here to the airstrip, pronto. Do you hear me? Maybe I should call your mama, do think she should be in on this? Or perhaps Mr. Wrenn? What's it going to be? You coming or not?"

"Uh...well, yeah, sure...don't mess your pants. I'll come talk to you...what is it you want?...I...er...." Trip couldn't get the top off the Stoli. "Just hold on, I'll be there in thirty minutes. Let's say...around noon, a few minutes past...your office...at the field...right?"

"Hurry, Mister Graham. I get upset when I have to wait." Dempsey hung up.

Glee slammed down the phone in the outer office and came in clasping her hands over her head. "Do you think we got him?" She asked nervously.

"By the goddamn balls, babe! By the goddamn balls!" Dempsey extended his open palm upward and she whacked it with a resounding smack. They hugged and danced around.

"What're you gonna tell him you want? Don't forget that I want to get that deal on the condo at Starfish finished...and maybe some kind of lifetime income...that goddamn real estate business idea sucks. I sure's hell don't want to be selling real estate in my old age." Glee looked anxiously at Demp.

"Well...I don't know what I'm going to push him for. We gotta be careful...he's right, this is blackmail. Pure and simple. But we do have him by the balls. I'm just going to wait and see what happens...see if he makes me an offer. What do you think?" Dempsey took a seat.

"I think I'd like to have a drink. He'll be here in a little bit. I need to keep my nerve up." She reached for the bottle on Dempsey's desk.

CHAPTER SIXTY-TWO

When he put down the phone, Trip's gut was cramping badly.

What to do? Goddamn! What had been in those bags anyway? All he could think about was the grass and the joints and the bag with the cocaine rocks and powder. He'd wiped it all clean, he knew that...he'd been real careful. The key...jeezusgod! His room key...the magnetic plastic thing with the holes in it. Couldn't think straight. Shit! Shit! Shit!

And her clothes...and the matchbook...the Chief asked him about that yesterday?

His personal calling card!...Oo-o-o-h, double shit!

Need a drink...get a grip. He took a pull straight from the bottle and shuddered violently at the burn of the warm raw vodka in his throat.

Go easy, he admonished his reflection in the mirror. *No time to get shitfaced. Just get smoothed out, that's all.*

Heart pounding, he wrapped an unopened bottle in a sweater and headed down the steps.

Need some for later, he was goddamn sure of that.

Starting his car, Trip decided to go back by Mabel's. He needed to find Griffin Richards. If this flyboy got unreasonable, he'd need Richards' help. Not exactly sure what he'd tell him now, but he needed to make sure that Griff didn't run off and leave this afternoon before he got back. Griff was always a good man to have in your corner.

Might not hurt to find Norris, too. Got to keep the old head screwed on straight.

Hitting the release, he let the top go down. Fresh air would probably do him good. He took the rolled sweater with the bottle wrapped inside and slipped it behind the seat on the passenger side

416

before he let the car roll forward. Just beyond The Club he pulled up short. The driveway to Clayton's house was jam-packed with cars.

His heart sank—a car with a Public Use tag and the unmistakable look of an unmarked law enforcement car was parked right behind the Governor's limo. It gave him a sinking feeling.

That fucking hayseed cop? That redneck Mills had promised he'd be at the funeral.

Backing quickly around, he headed back out toward The Club. He was almost sure that the Governor would be in the study off the front hall, drinking with the boys. High society funerals were a great place to do some politicking. Where the Governor was, the Chief was sure to be. Griffin Richards was almost certain to be in the back sitting room where Mabel and Nan were receiving the crowd of people. Two cars passed him and waved and smiled those phony little self-conscious sympathetic smiles as they cautiously moved the occupants along the wide drive looking for places to park.

Mutherfucking vultures, still coming in. It would go on late into the evening. He looked at the clock on the dash...got to get a move on. Pulling sharply to the curb, Trip parked on the cul-de-sac outside the gateposts.

When he got out, his knees almost buckled. A drop of cold sweat trickled down his back. Skirting the gate, he stumbled cautiously through the thicket of trees and azaleas which separated the grounds of The Club from the Graham manor house. As he drew even with the side where the wide brick terrace wrapped around the house, he looked cautiously about.

No one in view. So far, so good...had to avoid people....

Avoid that fucking cop at all costs.

One little peek through the French doors of the rear terrace to see if he could spot Griff. One quick word, then head for Grail Flight Centre.

Can't keep Gearhart waiting. The man was in an ugly mood.

Picking his way quickly through the trees, he made it to where the French doors of the library opened out onto the brick terrace.

417

Just as he was going to peep inside he heard a voice coming through the door, which was standing slightly ajar.

Marilee!

Flattening himself against the wall, he froze. Jesus, he couldn't afford to get trapped here. All he wanted was a quick word with Griff. Griff would stand by him if it came to that. Fuck this. Go back. Call from the car.

He turned and started to back off the terrace, away from the house.

"Have you talked to Griff about the contract yet, honey?"

Marilee all right, clear as a bell, speaking to someone in the room.

Honey? Honey, who? Trip stopped. *And, contract?...what did she care about the contract? What did she know about the contract, anyway?*

"Well, not yet. Clayton had Griff change his will. I'll know more this afternoon after I talk to Griff. I guess...it won't matter...it'll work out for us one way or another, won't it?"

Norris?

Honey?

Change the will? His heart sank. What were they saying?

Trip leaned forward. He could just glimpse their reflection in the round Federal mirror over the mantel. Unbelieving, he watched the distorted image in the convex magnifying mirror as Norris leaned forward and gave Marilee a proprietary peck on the mouth.

Trip felt his knees go weak.

Norris and Marilee!

Frozen with disbelief, Trip sagged against the wall, struggling to keep his feet.

Jeezus, why hadn't Griffin Richards told him about the will? Was Griff in on it, too! Was there no one left that he could trust? What now?

Fucking traitor, Norris! What a friend he'd turned out to be. He should've known not to trust him. He'd tried to warn his daddy. Well, goddamn 'em all.

He still had money...his granddaddy's money would see him

through...nobody could touch old Massie's trust. What the fuck did he care about the rest of it, anyway?

His attention wandered to his watch. Dempsey! Had to get his ass outta here. Granddaddy's money no good in jail. Had to go get Dempsey off his back. Stall him anyway—make him think that he'd go along. Then find a lawyer he could trust. But who? His mind was blank.

He leaned out from the wall and peeked through the French window at the mirror again. He could see Marilee and Norris leaving the room. Norris had his hand resting lightly on her waist, then let it slide sensually down over the curve of her buttocks just before they went out through the door. Trip watched numbly as Marilee looked up and smiled at Norris.

They turned the corner and were gone.

Backing off the porch, Trip ran blindly for the car.

CHAPTER SIXTY-THREE

"THIS IS THE OPERATOR, WHAT CITY PLEASE?"

"Southport, operator..."

"One moment, sir. I'll connect you."

When the Southport operator came on the line, Trip said, "Operator, please get me the office of Samuel Peyton Merritt, Jr.; he'll be listed under Attorneys-at-Law. Make it person-to-person, please." He looked at his watch.

Late...almost 11:45. As soon as he got off the line, he had to call Dempsey and explain he had been delayed. He certainly didn't want the flyboy to do anything rash.

He listened impatiently to the operator talking to Chip Merritt's prissy secretary, "Operator...if your party will leave their number, I'm sure Mr. Merritt will call them back as soon as he's free."

"Operator, tell Mr. Merritt that this is *Clayton Massie Graham calling from Colonial Hall.* I'm sure Chip wants to talk to me...*Now!*" He had very little patience with secretaries...or operators either...for that matter. He wished that drink would do its work...shitfire, he felt he was going to explode any second.

"Oh. I'm sorry, Mr. Graham? Can you hold, sir...I'll go tell Mr. Merritt." Without waiting for his answer, the secretary left the line. In a few seconds she was back. "Operator, I'll connect you now,"

"Trip, ol' son...." Merritt's deep, slow drawl came over the line. "My God, it sure took the wind out of me to hear about your daddy...what can I say, ol' son?"

"Well, thanks. Look...ah...Chip, I need to see you...right away. Will you be there later on, later this afternoon....or this evening?..." Desperately, he tried to clear his brain. "It's important!"

"Sure...either way, ol' son. I'll be here 'til five-thirty or six...maybe you could join Carol and me for supper. Is Marilee gonna be along?" the young lawyer asked, genially.

"Uh...ah...no...and don't count on me for supper. What I have to talk about is er...very personal and I...er...well private." Trip thought about Dempsey and asked, "Can I call you back around...around...ah...say three...or a little later...when I'm more certain of my plans?"

"Oh, sure...just play it by ear? Three's fine. Looking forward to seeing ya, ol' son. Just let me know." He hung up.

When Trip put down the phone, he couldn't remember the number for Dempsey's office...the airstrip...he was drawing a complete blank...instinctively he started to search his pockets for his address book. Suddenly, he realized that he still had on his suit from the funeral. Momentarily Trip considered and dismissed the idea of changing before he left...it would be better for the drive to the beach...but no! He was already late...goddamn it, where was that fucking number? He looked in the glove box and found the little Grail directory...how would it be listed?

Trip looked at the number and promptly misdialed the first time he tried. *Goddamn!...Slow down!*...he took a deep breath and dialed again. Gearhart answered on the first ring.

"Gearhart, this is Trip Graham...I'm running a little late...but I'm leaving right now. Just hold on. OK?" Trip pleaded.

"Well, OK, but be careful. We certainly wouldn't want you arrested or anything, would we?" Sounded like the bastard was laughing when he hung up.

As he crossed the bridge heading east toward the flight center, Trip turned on the radio and it blared out the dying sounds of a hard rock band, which he was hardly in the mood to hear. Before he could change the station, the announcer came on with the station's identification letters and then announced: "IT'S ELEVEN FIFTY-FIVE. A LATE FLASH JUST IN FROM GREENSBORO. CHIEF D.C. MILLS OF THE GREENSBORO POLICE HAS ANNOUNCED A PRESS CONFERENCE FOR 1:30 THIS AFTERNOON...SOURCES SAY THERE HAS BEEN A BREAK IN THE CASE SURROUNDING THE MYSTERIOUS DEATH OF

MOVIE ACTRESS EMMA CLAIRE...STAY TUNED FOR A BULLETIN AT 1:35...IN COLONIAL HALL, THE ENTIRE STATE MOURNED THE DEATH OF CLAYTON MASSIE GRAHAM, SR. THIS MORNING...IN WASHINGTON THE PRESIDENT'S PROBLEMS..."

Trip braked the car and slowed as he approached the traffic light at the intersection ahead...then he edged the car into the right-hand lane and turned south on the highway to Wilmington and Southport. The road went right by the flight center. He reached up and adjusted his radar detector...with a little luck, he could see Gearhart and still be at Chip's office before three o'clock. By then, he'd have heard that goddamn bulletin and know what the cops had on him.

It was going to be a bad afternoon. He would need some ice and cups. Pulling into the lot of a roadside convenience market, he left the motor running as he opened the car door.

In his rush, Trip almost knocked Chief D.C. Mills flat on his big fat ass.

CHAPTER SIXTY-FOUR

"WHOA, MR. GRAHAM..SLOW DOWN...ARE YOU HURT?" The Chief grabbed Trip by the shoulders and steadied him.

"Uh...no, I'm OK. Goddamn, Chief, where did you come from?" Trip looked around. The unmarked car he'd seen earlier at his daddy's was parked right up against his bumper, completely cutting him off from escape. The chief had left his motor running, too. "I didn't see you at the services...I...I looked for you at the big house ah-uh-afterwards," Trip stammered. This was fucking serious. Never rains but it pours...lately, the whole goddamn world had started raining down on him.

"Well, yeah, I know. I was late...they said you'd just left when I finally showed up." The Chief looked Trip in the eye, then averted his gaze downward. "I called your house, but I missed you there."

"So, how'd you find me, anyway?" *God, now, he had to have that drink for sure.*

"I tried to call you at home and just missed you. Then I called back and the maid told me you took the key to the beach house. I was lucky. The town's practically deserted...everything closed down for your daddy's funeral. I spotted you a few blocks up ahead when I got even with the Tower...just now caught up to you, when you hit the light back there at the bridge."

"Well? So what's on your mind?" He really didn't want to know, but it was all coming down now anyway.

The Chief looked down, kicked at an empty beer can and sent it rolling across to the curb by the front of Trip's convertible. It made a raucous rattle in the hot noonday silence. There was an awkward moment before he lifted his gaze again.

Finally, he said, "Mr. Graham, we need to talk. Right now. All hell is about to break loose on this Claire woman's death and I'm

423

afraid you're right in the middle of it. C'mon, I don't like standing here like this. People will notice. Turn off your engine and let's get in my car and just drive around and talk."

Trip nodded. Without a word, he squinted up at the sky. Not a cloud in sight—might as well just leave the 'Vette with the top down. Reaching across the doorframe, he switched off the ignition. When he turned, the Chief stood waiting beside his car.

Feeling as if he was going to come completely unglued if he didn't have a drink, Trip weighed the consequences.

What the hell? What did he have to lose now, anyway?

"Chief, I've had a rough time the past few days. I want a drink...I got some vodka in the boot of my car. Can I fix you one?"

"I'm over twenty-one. Why not?"

"Be right back." Trip turned and walked into the convenience market. In a few minutes, he came back with a small cooler, cans of grapefruit juice, a sleeve of plastic glasses and a bag of ice. When he opened the trunk of the car, he went to work and put the ice in the cooler and opened one of the cans of grapefruit juice and made a pair of stiff drinks. Shielded from view, he turned his own up and downed it in a gulp and quickly poured more vodka to the rim, without adding any juice this time. Then he closed the trunk lid and carried the cups over to where the Chief waited.

"Thanks." The Chief nodded. Without changing his expression, he said, "It's hot as hell out here. C'mon, let's ride."

When they left the lot, the Chief turned back toward town and took the truck route along the river, driving slowly west.

"OK, let's get on with it," Trip said. The liquor was already doing its work. "What's up?"

"Well, if you haven't heard on the radio, I've set up a press conference for the medical examiner at one-thirty in Greensboro." The Chief consulted his watch. "That's in about an hour and fifteen minutes. The tests on the actress came back from the lab in Chapel Hill this morning."

"So...?" Trip was tired of playing footsie.

"So...it's pretty sad. The woman had enough booze and cocaine in her to kill a horse. We knew she had those needle marks in her arm and, of course, I have that syringe with the thumbprint on it. I haven't put that syringe into evidence...it's right there in my glove box...but, as a matter of personal interest, I had someone look at it privately." He looked across at Trip with an unwavering stare. "That fingerprint ain't hers, Mr. Graham."

"OK, goddamn it, quit dancing around, did she die of the speedball injection? Is that what the report says? I already told you Chief, I draw a blank on the whole thing." Trip was fed up with this cat and mouse. Why were they bringing it down on him?

"Well, with cocaine it's not ever a clear call. Even with the stuff in her blood sample, the actual cause of death in these cases is usually listed as respiratory failure or cardiac arrest—the chicken or the egg. Technically that's actually what happens." The Chief shrugged. "Except for the evidence of drugs, it could have been natural causes...the medical examiner will say that, but you know what that pack of vultures from the TV and newspapers are going to say. With them it's cut and dried. And when they find out *you* were with her..." his voice trailed off.

"You think someone shot it up for her, and you're saying it was me? Is that my fingerprint? Is that it? If that syringe isn't in evidence, who knows about all this, except you?"

"Well, no one...not yet at least...."

"The coroner?..."

"Not him either...nobody...not yet."

"Well, I'll just be goddamned! You're going to make a disclosure that I was seen with her...throw me to the goddamned wolves just to cover your sorry ass." Trip was furious, his voice an icy sneer. He took a small sip of the straight vodka and stared directly into the Chief's face, unwavering. "And you said my daddy offered a piece of shit like you the job of Chief of Grail Security. You gotta be pulling my goddamn leg."

"Well, I'm not insulated from responsibility by having unlimited money, Mr. Graham. I live in a glass house. The public is just looking for an excuse to burn a cop. You know, Mr. Graham, I have to live in this world, too. But for people like me, the rules are different. You might just say people like me *have* rules...people like you don't. Sometimes I have to just let the chips fall where they may. Up to now, I've gone way out on a limb to keep you and your family completely out of it. Shit, I'm guilty of suppressing evidence right now...if anybody knew I had that syringe...and that torn matchbook with your address in that girl's handwriting...then there's her cosmetic case...c'mon, Mr. Graham, give me a break. When I told you in the hospital the other day that I went to your room at the Massie House and found cocaine and some reefer...there were some pills on the bathroom floor, too. I wasn't just talking leftover traces from the last Grateful Dead concert at the Coliseum. That stuff was yours, Mr. Graham. A young woman is dead, and it's been page one in every newspaper in the world for four days. You're still sitting here, and only you and I know that you were involved. I kept hoping the autopsy would let us both off the hook. My whole sorry-ass life's in there," he nodded toward the glove box again. "I've been in law enforcement all my life, Mr. Graham...I've worked hard to get where I am. Everybody respects me...I'm not sixty yet, and if I keep my nose clean and don't step on the wrong toes, I'll retire in another six years. That's all I have to look forward to. With my pension, I'll have to wind up moonlighting as a fucking bank guard or a rent-a-cop, just to pay my rent. With your pull, even if they charge you with a felony drug death, you'll be out driving your fancy convertible before Christmas. I keep thinking about that opportunity to work for your daddy—the one good chance I ever had...and I blew it. I liked your daddy. He was real people...me and him sort of shared a little secret about that there fancy whorehouse, Madie K's...it was before your time. Your daddy was talking about paying me seventy-five thousand dollars a year...can you imagine that? Why the hell I didn't just take him up on it right there on the spot, I'll go to my grave kicking my ass for that. But then, I guess it's lucky for you I didn't. If I had, I would've been working here for Grail, then you'd have been in the Greensboro jail right this minute, most likely. Maybe I didn't have all the advantages of fancy schools and country club manners, but don't you ever call me a piece of shit, Mr. Graham...*not now, not ever again.*" The Chief looked him coldly in the eye and took a deliberate swallow of his drink.

"Well...uh, now don't get me wrong, Chief...I'm a little stretched at the moment...you can understand." Trip stammered and took another sip of the vodka.

There it was about money and the job again. And the old fox knew about Madie K's? Had the SOB sent Clayton that old photo he'd found?

The bastard had him by the balls, but he'd kept him clear so far. What was the old fart up to?

Trip considered for a minute and asked, "What if the medical examiner just said the cause of death was respiratory arrest...or whatever it was you said? You know...just natural causes? Why does he have to go into the drug tests if they don't really prove the cause of death?"

"Well, it happens that way all the time. In ordinary circumstances, we'd probably just do that...and close the case. We get three or four of these a year...nowadays more, maybe. Unless they're related to another investigation where there's a big drug bust coming down...you know, where we can get the dealers...then we just turn the body over to the next of kin and list it as 'natural causes.' We ain't out to ruin any of the poor common folks' good family name just to make us look good in the public eye. What good is that? But this Claire woman is big news...and worse than that, it happened on a slow news day. I'm sure the medical examiner would rather we handled this case as natural causes, but he won't lay his ass on the line if there's suspicion of a felony. It would all come back on him...."

Trip broke in impatiently, "Bullshit! God knows how many people in Guilford County have a trace of cocaine in their blood right now. And alcohol? Probably twenty percent of the population of the entire world has booze in their blood right this minute...as a matter of fact, two of 'em are sitting in this here automobile..." He laughed a tight little laugh. "Why make a federal case out of this one?"

"Alcohol...OK. But illegal drugs are not that common, and anytime the substance is illegal and there's a death, you're talking felony," the Chief fired right back.

"Even so, it's common enough nowadays...and you just said it yourself, unless you make a connection that leads to a big bust, what's the fucking use? I don't even remember seeing that woman...except two months ago at the Azalea Ball."

"Well, remember it or not, you sure as shit did, and when the press starts to dig into this, those sonsabitches'll make me look like some fucking Barney Fife!" The Chief rolled down the window and spit.

"Well, what if you told the doc to just say respiratory arrest...natural causes? What would he do?" Trip looked him straight in the eye.

"Oh, he'd jump at the chance. The ol' doc doesn't know about the syringe and all the other evidence. The drug issue will just make his life a pain in the ass. When he confirms the rumors that have been building up that there's been a drug death, can you imagine what those reporters are going to do to his life? Worse, my life, too...for the next month?"

"Then why throw me to the wolves? Seventy-five thousand sounds like a bargain for a man of your experience. Maybe this is your lucky day." Trip took a deep breath and put the bribe offer right out on the table. This was his life he was fighting for now.

Almost before the words were out of his mouth, he regretted it. Suppose it was a set up? Suppose Mills was wearing a fucking wire? Well...he hadn't admitted to even knowing the woman...so they really wouldn't have anything. And, after all, Mills brought the subject of money up—a good lawyer would make that obvious. What the hell? Might as well play out his hand.

Mills looked away, out the window. Except to clear his throat, he didn't make a sound.

"What's the matter? Is it too late? Have you let this go too far now? Who else knows about the incident in the motel parking lot? And the off-duty officer at the Steak Barn, what about him?"

"Uhm...well, Mr. Graham...up until now, I've kept a tight lid on this. Except for the off-duty officer, your name hasn't come up. He wouldn't even think about it again if the Medical Examiner says natural causes. Even then, he wouldn't say a word to anyone but me. The matchbook cover and other stuff is right in that there glove box with that syringe. I tried to keep you completely out of this in hope that lab report would point away from a drug death. Now, it's still anybody's call...no, I guess it's my call. I can't deny that. I told the M.E. not to release a statement on the cause of death until I decided if it made any sense to make it a police matter." Mills looked at his watch and turned into a roadside picnic area to turn around. "Every goddamn major news agency is camped up there on our doorstep, right now. They'll be beating down the door in fifteen minutes...howling for blood. I got to call Doc Crawford...he's waiting to hear from me now."

"So, what're you going to tell him? I'll have my secretary give you a letter of employment before you leave town...you can stop by the Tower and pick it up. Seventy-five K. You could take your time, wait a few weeks before you announced that you were resigning to accept the position of Security Director at Grail...maybe even wait 'til after Labor Day. You know, let things kind of cool down and get back to normal. I imagine you've got some vacation time coming to you...a month at Nags Head and some deep-sea fishing might get you rested enough to take on your new position of responsibility. I could come down for a weekend, and we'd fish and talk about organizing the new department. I could have an expense advance...say ten...twenty grand...delivered to you next week. It would cover your vacation rather nicely, I imagine." Trip held his breath. He'd turned his last card.

The Chief slowed the car as they approached the intersection with the Wilmington highway at the bridge. When he stopped for the light, he turned and smiled. He raised his cup in a toast. "It's going to be a real pleasure working for you, Mr. Graham. Uhmm...I wish I could be there to see the look on those reporters' faces...I'd give anything...but, say?...could we make that expense advance twenty-five thousand? I kinda like the sound of it."

"No problem. Consider it done." Trip touched cups with the man, turned up the rest of his vodka and drank it all.

"I'd like that letter of employment to spell out the salary and effective date...say, June 1st? It's OK to make the announcement later, but I don't want to take any chances. My daddy used to say, '...A bird in the hand'...well, you know how it goes. Will you call me Monday about the twenty-five-K...or should I call you? Is there a way we could make that little transaction sorta invisible to the IRS?" The Chief turned the car into the parking lot and pulled up beside Trip's Corvette.

"I'll call, you can depend on it. I'm sure I'll be up to my ass in alligators trying to drain the swamp, so don't worry. I'll arrange for the letter right now before you leave town...and I'll take care of the other money first thing Monday. I have to tell you, though, that our accountants won't fudge on the IRS...but don't worry, I'll make that a personal donation, in cash."

The Chief looked at him in open-mouthed admiration.

"Can I use this?" Trip indicated the car phone. "I'll call my secretary right now."

"Be my guest..."

Trip dialed his number at the Tower and gave Dodie the necessary instructions. "Oh...just say he will serve as special security consultant to Mr. Clayton Massie Graham, III, CEO and Chairman of the Board. Do it now...he's on his way." The matter was settled in less than a couple of minutes.

"That's just awesome...you don't waste any time. Your daddy would be proud. You still headed to the beach, Mr. Graham? Can I reach you there?"

"Yeah, write down the number...and my cell phone, too...just in case. You sure you can handle this now? There won't be any fuck-ups, will there? I mean, are my worries over?"

"Trust me, Mr. Graham. I'm working for you now." He copied intently when Trip gave him the phone numbers and read them back to be certain they were right.

"OK, just drive down to the Tower and take the elevator to the penthouse. See Dodie. The letter will be ready by the time you get there."

"Thank you, Mr. Graham. I'm sure I'll do a good job for Grail." The Chief was a little self-conscious now. He seemed anxious to leave. "Well, I've got to get on this here phone and talk to Doc Crawford. He's waiting to hear from me. I expect he's about to piss in his pants about now, with all those reporters outside the door. Take it easy, Mr. Graham...and again, I can't tell you how sorry I am about your daddy. Oh, yeah...listen to your radio on the way down the road...the Doc will be making a statement in a few minutes...I'll call him now."

Trip nodded and reached for the door handle.

The Chief let go a little chuckle. "My daddy used to say that the sun don't shine on the same dog's ass all the time...I guess I never thought I'd see the day when it was my turn..."

"Looks like we both had a run of luck...." Trip reached over and shook his hand again before he stepped out of the car. Then he stood and watched the Chief back up and turn back out on the highway.

Watching Mills drive away, all at once, Trip felt like the Rock of Gibraltar had been lifted off his back. He'd really put it over. For the first time in his life, he'd saved his own ass. The Chief was right. His daddy would be proud.

Money was the magic word for everything.

And the Chief was also right about a Graham not having to fuck with rules. The rules were made to protect people like the Grahams from people like the Chief.

Suddenly, Trip felt free.

As he drove away, D.C. Mills dialed the car phone and waved out the window at Trip Graham standing in the parking lot.

"Hi, Doc, just thought I'd check in and see if you were ready for your big moment," he said when he heard the answer. "Nothing new is there?...no surprises?"

"Naw," the doctor came back on the phone. "This one is easy. A lot of those bloodthirsty bastards are gonna be disappointed when I tell 'em their story has fizzled...but that's their fault. All that drug stuff was probably press agent bullshit anyway. Hollywood has a movie in the can, and *Playboy* has some magazines to sell. I heard on the news last night that *Playboy* had already doubled their print order." The doctor's voice was almost uninflected, very professional. "Anyway, I'm looking forward to making it short but sweet...answer a few questions from the rumormongers, then head back to Chapel Hill."

"Well...thanks, Doc. Have a good weekend." The Chief hung up the phone.

Heading straight back into town, the Chief's eyes never left the Tower looming ever nearer until it obliterated everything else from his view as he turned into the parking lot. Except for four scattered cars of various descriptions, the lot was virtually deserted. He wondered what it would feel like having an office here. He should've asked that snotty Graham to throw in a membership to that fancy country club.

From the time the Chief left his car until he emerged back outside the building with the envelope in his hand, no more than ten minutes elapsed. He opened the envelope as soon as he got in the car and glanced down at the short letter. He checked off the major points: effective June 1...annual salary of $75,000 plus expenses... expense advance of $25,000...and a company Cadillac! Frigging incredible! He wanted to run into the street, stop traffic and tell the world.

When he was about five miles outside town, the Chief pulled the car into a roadside picnic area and parked under the shade of a tree. Leaving the engine running, he opened the glove box and took out the syringe in the plastic bag. There was a little cosmetic kit and the plastic envelope with the torn matchbook cover, the cocaine and the pills. He gathered them all. He wasted no time in crossing over and dropping it all into a trash can. When he returned and closed the door, he reached behind him and took a manila folder off of the rear seat. The index tab bore the notation EMMA CLAIRE. Opening it with his left hand, he lifted the official medical report and reread the summary statement for perhaps the hundredth time: WHILE THERE WERE TRACES OF ALCOHOL AND OTHER DRUGS IN THE BLOOD SAMPLES, THE LEVELS WERE BELOW SUFFICIENT LEVELS TO CAUSE EXTREME INTOXICATION. THERE IS EVIDENCE THAT THE

DECEASED HAD HAD A RECENT SUBCUTANEOUS INJEC-
TION OF INSULIN. SIGNIFICANT AMOUNTS OF CHLOR-
PHENIRAMINE, DESOXYEPHEDRINE AND ASPIRIN WERE
FOUND UNDIGESTED IN THE CONTENTS OF THE
DECEASED'S STOMACH, WHICH IS CONSISTENT WITH
THE CONCLUSION THAT SHE HAD BEEN TREATING THE
SYMPTOMS OF AN UPPER RESPIRATORY INFECTION. IT
SHOULD BE NOTED THAT THE YOUNG ACTRESS SEEMED
SLIGHTLY DEBILITATED WHICH IS CONSISTENT WITH
SIGNS OF POOR NUTRITION AND SUGGESTS THAT SHE
HAD BEEN DIETING. THE CAUSE OF DEATH IS DETER-
MINED TO BE RESPIRATORY ARREST AND/OR CARDIAC
FAILURE APPARENTLY DUE TO AN OVERWHELMING
INFECTION TO BOTH LUNGS. TISSUE CULTURES SHOW
THAT THE INFECTING ORGANISM WAS KLEBSIELLA PNEU-
MONIAE.

Stuck to the face of the report was a little blue Post-it note with
the scrawled notation: *"Chief: This klebsiella strain is different
from anything we've seen. The CDC lab in Atlanta won't comment. I don't know where this syringe came from but it's been
used to give an insulin injection. Regards, W. T. Crawford, M.D.,
Chief, Infectious Disease, UNC."*

The report and the note were both dated Wednesday, two days
ago.

Funny thing...Monday, when he'd been the first one on the
scene and found that torn matchbook cover under the Claire
woman's body, he'd been certain that it was a drug-related death.

It all added up. Young celebrity, jet-set...the beautiful people.
He had read the report of the ruckus in the parking lot at the
Massie House next door in the night log that morning. It had stood
out because it had been an otherwise slow Sunday night for
Greensboro. When he saw Trip Graham's name on the matchbook
cover, he remembered the yellow car from the beach party Azalea
Festival weekend. It had been a natural to check next door at the
Massie House for Trip. The Massie House was a Grail property,
everyone knew that.

His timing had been off. Trip had just checked out. He'd barely missed him. But he'd found the cosmetic case and the drugs in Trip's room.

It all added up. Wealthy playboy, young actress in Blowing Rock partying, life in the fast lane.

Felony Drug Death written all over it.

When he'd talked to Trip Graham on the phone Tuesday afternoon, he'd been so sure that he had him over a barrel...so sure he had a winning hand.

So goddamn sure, he'd finally found his ticket out.

It certainly had had him fooled, but then, you just never could tell. The whole thing had all been shot to hell with that goddamn lab report. *Felony Drug Death* turned out to be natural causes, and he'd wound up with a busted flush.

Still, had to give himself credit...he'd had the balls to run his bluff, and for the first time in his life, he'd won.

Leaking hints of drug death to that bunch of rumor-hungry bastards from *People*, CNN...all the bigtime media...had been like throwing meat to a ravenous school of blood-crazed sharks. And that story about the off-duty officer had been pure inspiration...maybe he should try his hand at writing detective stories.

The Chief turned and looked fondly back to the Tower shimmering in the distance like a mirage in the midday heat.

Sun sure don't shine on the same dog's ass all the time.

CHAPTER SIXTY-FIVE

WHEN MARILEE HUNG UP THE PHONE, she had a funny feeling things weren't right at home. Something about the way Oleander sounded bothered her. And what was Trip up to anyway? Why had he told Oleander to say that he'd call her back? Drunk?...or well on his way, she feared. No matter...she was powerless to stop him.

After Norris left for the Tower, Marilee went back and excused herself to Mabel, "I'm going next door and check on Trip. He needs to eat something." She gave Mabel's arm a pat and added, "Then I'm going to see about Ivee...this is all very confusing for him. He's trying to be brave and grown up, but it's difficult at his age."

"All right, dear, take your time. Why don't you lie down for awhile? I'll be fine. Nan's here with me." Mabel patted Marilee's hand reassuringly. Marilee could see that Mabel teetered precariously at the edge of exhaustion—in that peculiar near-catatonic state that follows sudden shock.

It would go on for hours, most likely.

Marilee took the shortcut down by the golf course. When Oleander heard her come through the doors from the terrace, she came rushing back through the house to greet her. "Miz Harris just called and said she was going to take the boys to the picture show later and not for you to worry none...Oh, Miz Marilee, you look so tired. Can I get you something?"

"No, I'm OK, Oleander. Really, I am. Did Mr. Graham call?"

"No, ma'am, he di'n't call, but he come back heah right after you called. Then he just left again, mostest 'bout a hour ago. He was kinda in a hurry." The girl looked warily to see Marilee's reaction. She didn't want to cover up for Trip, but she didn't want to start any trouble either.

"Did he say where he was going?" Marilee kept on walking toward the front of the house.

"Well, no ma'am...but he took one of the new keys to yo' Caswell place."

"The beach house? My God, why on earth would he be going to the beach house?"

"I don't know ma'am, but he got a call from a policeman in Greensboro just before he left. I don't think Mr. Graham is acting hisself lately, ma'am."

God, the Greensboro police had called. Marilee wondered if Griff had been contacted. Or Norris maybe...they were probably at the Tower by now. She picked up the phone and dialed Norris' private number. They would most likely be together in Norris' office. She let it ring and finally gave up. She decided not to try him at home. There really wasn't anything Norris could do anyway. She certainly didn't want to take a chance on Agnes answering. Agnes had flown back from her precious daddy's in Virginia for the funeral and had acted very cool today at Mabel's. Reluctantly, she replaced the phone on its cradle and stood there for a minute undecided what to do.

"Did Mr. Graham drink any liquor? You can tell me, Oleander, don't worry."

"Well, ma'am. I think he mighta had a little drink. I just washed a glass that he left on the wet bar, downstairs...and I saw him put a bottle of something wrapped in a sweater in the back of the car." The girl averted her gaze. "He smelled a little like...you know dat smell...he seem to walk all right, though. He just seem a little hard to make up hiz mind...I don't know how to 'splain it."

"That's all right, Oleander," Marilee assured her with a smile. She searched her purse for her keys. The key to the beach house was shiny and new. She had no trouble confirming it was on the ring. "Oleander, I'm going to be out for awhile. If Mrs. Harris calls again, tell her I'll call her early this evening...ask her if she can feed Ivee dinner, will you?"

"Yes'um I'll tell her...where'd you be going, Miz Marilee?" the girl asked.

"Oh, just out for awhile. I have some errands to catch up on."
She hurried down the steps, across to where Dempsey's driver had
left her car yesterday.

Before she headed out, she checked the gas gauge.

Nearly full.

CHAPTER SIXTY-SIX

WATCHING THE CHIEF DRIVE AWAY, Trip felt like running to the Wal-Mart and giving away twenty-dollar bills. Partly from the adrenaline rush from getting the Chief out of his hair and partly due to seeing Norris and Marilee, his thoughts were bouncing around like popcorn in a microwave.

He opened the trunk and fixed himself another drink.

Careful with the booze—no time to fuck up now. Now that he had that cop in his pocket, he finally had it dicked. Chip Merritt would help him stick it up Norris' and Marilee's asses. Once that was taken care of, he'd fix that goddamn blackmailing Dempsey Gearhart.

Sliding under the wheel, he picked up the car phone and dialed Dempsey's number at the air center. He couldn't wait to tell the bastard to get fucked.

Trip listened to the phone ring and ring before he finally gave up.

"Fuck you, anyway, flyboy, are you in for a surprise." Laughing out loud, he headed for the beach.

Trip nursed the single drink he'd poured at the highway market all the way to Route 211 just outside Southport.

The digital clock on his dash showed 2:59. He debated for a moment, then decided he needed to get his act together before he went to see Chip Merritt. If he went straight to Marilee's cottage he could fix a little shooter and think about what he wanted to say to Chip.

If he gave that bitch and Norris enough rope, they'd fucking hang themselves.

All the way down he had kept switching the radio back and

forth, and he never heard another word about that fucking press conference. What could you expect in eastern North Carolina? All you got on the radio was Paul Harvey, holy roller preachers, hard rock, hillbilly music and the fucking farm report. By the time he had crossed the bridge in Wilmington and turned off 17 onto 133 at Leland, he knew the frigging hog and chicken markets by heart.

Finally, as he hung a right to Caswell Beach, the announcer came on with breaking news. "...THE GREENSBORO POLICE ANNOUNCED TODAY THAT ACTRESS EMMA CLAIRE DID NOT DIE OF A DRUG OVERDOSE AS WAS ORIGINALLY BELIEVED. THE MEDICAL EXAMINER'S REPORT FROM THE UNIVERSITY OF NORTH CAROLINA AT CHAPEL HILL CONFIRMED THAT THE YOUNG WOMAN DIED FROM AN OVERWHELMING INFECTION OF THE LUNGS AND BLOODSTREAM BY AN ORGANISM CALLED KLEBSIELLA PNEUMONIAE. MINOR TRACES OF ALCOHOL AND A PRE-SCRIPTION DRUG FOUND IN HER BLOOD WERE WELL BELOW TOXIC LEVELS...THERE WAS NO EVIDENCE THAT ILLEGAL DRUGS WERE INVOLVED..."

Bingo!

The old chief was a man of his word. Who would believe it? That thing about the exotic pneumonia was a real touch of inspiration...the old fart might be handy to have around after all.

In his preoccupation with trying to get a news update on the radio, he'd forgotten all about the flyboy. Trip reached for the phone to call Gearhart again. Now that he was out from under the mess with the Claire woman, he couldn't wait to fire the arrogant bastard.

Ten rings...*Nada!*

Thinking about the Chief, his mind drifted back to Norris and Marilee. Now that he was going to get Chip Merritt to help him set Norris and Marilee up for a big adultery thing, the foxy old Chief might just have some ideas on how to go about it. His main problem was to make sure he kept his own nose clean so Marilee wouldn't have anything to throw back at him in court...if it went to court.

439

Norris was an attorney...probably would want to settle out of court. After all, he was married to the Senator's daughter...had his Boy Scout image to protect. Well, fuck 'em...fuck 'em both. He'd drag the whole thing through the press and smear the bastard. What'd he care anyway? He was the injured party. Everybody feels sorry for the poor husband.

Norris had been on the cover of everything else...how would the bastard like being a new kind of cover boy...on the front page of the fucking *Enquirer*, for chrissakes.

As he turned right onto 133 toward the ocean, he passed a sign that read: Youpon Beach 4. Almost there! He breathed a big sigh just as the car phone rang.

"This is Clayton Graham..." he deepened his voice, trying to sound like his father.

"Ah, yes...Mr. Graham, at last! This is Riley Watson in New York...do you know who I am?" This dude sounded a lot like Mr. William F. Buckley, himself, with that clench-jawed old Buzzy and Binky Yale Club inflection.

"Uh...no...I don't believe I do. How'd you get this number?"

"Getting your number was routine. My business is confidential research relating to matters of corporate security, Mr. Graham. Among other things, I look into people's backgrounds and their comings and goings. I've done a number of investigations for Grail. I'm calling about the New York surveillance of Norris Wrenn that your Mr. Richards requested on Tuesday around midday. The order came from Clayton Massie Graham. Mr. Richards instructed I send the report directly to Mr. Graham at the Grail Tower. But before I even made it back from Sheeps...ah... from my trip...it was in all the papers about your daddy's death. I've tried to get Mr. Richards, but he's been unavailable. Then I got to wondering that since your wife was involved if, under the circumstances, maybe the Clayton Massie Graham who ordered the work was you. I wouldn't want that report to get into the wrong hands."

Surveillance?...Norris?...Marilee?

What the fuck was this guy talking about?

Had Griff ordered Norris followed in New York? And...the

thing about sheep?...did Norris own a farm...?

"Under just what circumstances, Mr. Riley?"

"Well...uh, you know...Mr. Wrenn was with...ah...your wife. Anyway, they were together Tuesday night in New York at Mr. Wrenn's co-op in Manhattan...and all day Wednesday and Wednesday night on that godforsaken island. I knew you'd want this handled with utmost discretion."

Jeezus! Trip felt like he'd been kicked in the stomach—but the shock was quickly replaced by rising excitement.

Marilee and Norris...shacked up on an island? Was this evermore his lucky day?

"Uh...yes, yes indeed. You certainly acted...er...with discretion." Trip tried his best to sound nonchalant. "Send that report to me, Clayton Massie Graham, III and mark it: Personal and Confidential...in red...at the Graham Tower. Don't leave off the 'Third'. Circle that in red, too!"

"Uh...yessir...and Mr. Graham, I was wondering about the fee. Mr. Richards said that since Mr. Wrenn was the CEO and was privy to all corporate expenses, that...uh...I would be paid personally by you. Is that correct, sir?"

"Well, yes...yes, of course." Trip fumed silently. "Just give me the highlights on the phone."

"Well, first I just wanted to make sure you understood the fee, Mr. Graham. That kind of money from a personal bank account isn't an everyday transaction. Since this was negotiated by a third party and by phone, now it's directly in your hands. I don't want any misunderstanding. I like everything to be out in the open. Uhmmm...no, pun intended, of course. But my services are expensive, Mr. Graham. I'm the best, and I got where I am by maintaining my integrity in a business where under-the-table blackmail is common, even at the highest level. *Especially the highest level*," he emphasized, with grave inflection. "I chose my clients carefully...I only work for the very best people."

"Of course, I understand that." This guy had the goods on Norris and Marilee. Why argue over chicken feed. The entire surveillance had only been a matter of two or three days' work.

Money was a minor detail. "Just give me the highlights now, on the phone. I'll pay your fee, Mr. Watson...how much is it, by the way?"

"One hundred thousand plus expenses, which in this case included chartering the chopper to that island...let's see...I'll round it off to one hundred ten thousand," Watson said in his clipped Ivy League voice.

"Jeezus...I, uh..." Trip felt his anger rise—he knew he was being taken.

"Well, if this comes as a surprise, Mr. Graham, I'm sorry, but Mr. Richards is familiar with my fees. When I work, I work mostly alone...particularly in matters involving corporate integrity with people of the stature of Mr. Wrenn. I personally stayed in front of that building across from the Park all night...there are photos. I followed at a discreet distance behind Mr. Wrenn when he jogged for over two miles around the lake just after daylight Wednesday morning—he never left my sight. If you want to consult Mr. Richards, I'm sure he'll vouch for me..."

"No, no...it's OK..." Trip suppressed his resentment. Norris and Marilee...New York...and on an island...two nights together...this would give him complete power over them. And, anyway, there was no need to pay from his personal bank account like Clayt had originally intended. What the fuck! Grail could pick up the tab. What did he care now if Norris knew? *As a matter of fact, he'd make goddamn sure Norris knew!* From now on, Norris Wrenn was in his pocket.

"I'll have a check drawn and have it delivered by courier from our New York offices, late morning Monday...around eleven, OK?"

"That will be fine, Mr. Graham. Just have 'em deliver it to my attorney. He'll FedEx the report Monday as soon as he deposits the check." The flat Yalie voice tried unsuccessfully to affect a friendlier tone. "Take down the address."

"Wait...wait..." Trip slowed and pulled over to a wide place on the shoulder before the Intracoastal Waterway bridge. He opened the glove box, found an old golf score card and a pencil and prepared to write. "OK, shoot," he said. When he finished, he read it back.

"That's it. Call me Tuesday; I'll answer any questions you have after you read the report."

"Wait, aren't you going to tell me any more than that? How do I know that you're telling me the truth? I mean this is serious; that's my wife, the mother of my son...and my best friend...the Chief Operating Officer of one of the biggest companies in the world. If I'm going to have a check cut for that much...I ah..." he sputtered, feeling helpless.

"It's all there, Mr. Graham...and, by the way, Mr. Graham, do you want me to inform Mr. Richards when I've sent the report to you?" Watson interjected.

"Uh...no...goddamnit. Hell no. Keep him out of it. This must remain entirely between us...and there must only be one copy, except for your file. I want to make sure you have a file, just in case...you understand?" He certainly didn't want to tip his hand to Griff. From the conversation he'd heard between Marilee and Norris, it looked like the old fart was in on the plot to hand the company over to them.

"Well, I understand your concern, Mr. Graham. Just let me assure you, you'll get what you're paying for. And Mr. Graham, I have a standard procedure set up with my attorney in cases like this. If something happens to me before the transaction is complete, as soon as your check arrives, the report is released to you anyway. My attorney will keep the file copy. There'll be no slip-ups. I'll be waiting for your call Tuesday, Mr. Graham. Have a good week-end." He hung up before Trip could protest.

Riley Watson picked up the Express Mail Envelope on the desk in front of him, removed the letter dated the previous day and read it again: *Enclosed is a check for $25,500 to cover your professional services and expenses on the Norris Wrenn matter. Please consider your telephone report to me this afternoon as concluding your responsibility in this assignment. Because of the extreme delicacy of this matter, I do not want any written record made of this assignment, not for your records or mine.*

Thank you once again for a job well done.

Sincerely,
Ferebee Griffin Richards, Esq.

Riley discarded the envelope and placed the letter in a folder marked Grail and put it in his file tray. Then he picked up the swimsuit issue of *Sports Illustrated* and a recent copy of *Forbes*...the two magazines were lying side-by-side in front of him. Separate photos of Marilee and Norris smiled back at him from the covers of the respective magazines.

Beautiful!

Each magazine had a mailing label affixed to the cover, bearing the address:

ANGUS ROBERTSON DOUGLAS
LION AND THISTLE
SHEEPSHEAD LIGHT, ME 04639

People in glass houses shouldn't undress in public, he gloated, wryly.

Riley Watson had carefully built his clientele based on his impeccable integrity. Sometimes he wavered...there were extraordinary situations. From time to time there were opportunities to...ah...make his information available to a better advantage, but only rarely did the risk seem worth it. He'd seen greed become the downfall of some of his best competitors. Still, Riley Watson was anything but a fool. He'd known all along that sooner or later the right opportunity would come along...sooner or later there were always those perfect combinations of high stakes and low risk—the prize was always worth the gamble.

Watson picked up the phone and hit a speed dial button. "Jared, I'm on my way. I'm buying today!" He chuckled at the reply and replaced the phone.

There were three copies of the four neatly typed pages of the report. Riley put one into a FedEx Overnight envelope and carefully addressed it as he'd been told, marking it clearly PERSONAL AND CONFIDENTIAL. The other copy he also left flat and inserted it in a brown manila envelope addressed to Jared McBride, his attorney. He affixed an overly generous number of stamps...just in case he got run over by a truck.

Riley made sure the third copy was locked in his desk drawer before he left the room.

"I'll be at my attorney's...in case you need me, we're having lunch at the Algonquin." He walked out with the brown envelope under his arm—he wasn't about to trust this to a courier. Riley Watson gave little notice to the pair of rather preppy-looking men waiting at the elevator.

When he hung up the phone, Trip could barely contain his excitement.

This was just too fucking good to be true. Jackpot again! He was truly on a roll.

He looked up Chip Merritt's number and dialed it before he let the car roll out on the road leading up to the bridge.

"Samuel Merritt Jr.'s law office."

"This is Trip Graham. Put Chip on."

"I'm sorry, Mr. Graham, he's in court. He said to leave your number and he'd call later this afternoon." The snooty bitch's voice had a note of respect, now.

"No...but thanks, anyway. Tell him I'll call him at home later or...maybe in the morning..." His thoughts kept racing ahead.

What was he going to do about Norris and Marilee? That snooty detective said he had pictures. Now that he had them both where he wanted them, his first inclination was to divorce the bitch and send Norris packing. But now that he thought about it, that might be a bad decision. Still...he wasn't about to let them off scot-free.

Their little plot to freeze him out of Grail had just gone up in smoke. With what he had on Norris, he'd have Clayt's will thrown out of court. Norris would be lucky if his sorry ass didn't go to jail.

Still...his daddy was probably right after all. Norris had really done wonders with the Grail corporate profit in the past four years. When he took over, he'd need Norris. He'd be a fool to run him off. And, by god, he had the bastard by the fucking balls. It would be the equivalent to shooting himself in his own fucking foot. He'd take his time. Down the road, he'd find someone else to handle the business end. He certainly didn't want to get bogged down in all that boring shit.

He'd show 'em...look out world, here comes Mr. Clayton Massie Graham, the fucking Third!

Plenty of time to think about the details. At the moment, he needed a drink—quite a lot to celebrate.

After today, no one could say Trip Graham was a fucking alky, anyway. No-fucking-body. He really deserved a pat on the back for how he'd managed his drinking today. After all he'd been through—putting his daddy in the ground, bringing the foxy law-man to his fucking knees...then finding out that his best friend was porking his wife—not even a Baptist preacher could have handled all the shit that had come down on him today without a little nip or two.

He'd be at the cottage in five minutes, and he was going to fix himself a nice tall Stoli and grapefruit...a fucking salty dog! Talk about salty dogs...well he guessed he was one now, all right.

By the time he made it onto Oak Island and turned back north along the ocean, he was not only starting to feel shaky again, he was in grave danger of pissing his pants.

At the cottage, he managed to control his bladder long enough to let himself in and make himself a decent drink. He lifted it shaki-ly and downed it fast before he spilled it all. Then he made another one and carried it with him while he went to the john.

The shakes would pass, but he was feeling a trifle weak—he'd lost all that blood the other day. But this was no time to be think-ing about that.

For the next thirty minutes Trip alternated between trying to reach Dempsey Gearhart on the cell phone, fuming over Norris and Marilee, and refreshing his drink. Pacing nervously back and forth, finally, when the liquor began to take the edge off, he went outside and looked at the ocean from the observation deck. It was a clear day, and, except for the humidity, it was pleasant with the breeze off the ocean—oddly, the beach seemed deserted.

Hmm...his glass was nearly empty.

He blinked at his watch...not yet 4:00. He rubbed the crystal...a little foggy...most likely the humidity. Time to give that fucking flyboy another call. Surprise, surprise. If Gearhart didn't show him some respect, he'd just ask the muthafucker if he'd ever considered becoming a cab driver? Next week, when the asshole came begging on his hands and knees, maybe he'd just let him keep his fucking job. Norris and that goddamn Griff thought Gearhart was such a hot shot. Well...maybe. But first, the flyboy...and everybody else...needed to find out who was boss.

CHAPTER SIXTY-SEVEN

WHEN THE PHONE RANG IN HIS OFFICE around one o'clock, Dempsey Gearhart had gone outside to help Glee with her overnight bag. He rushed back inside just in time to hear Trip hang up. Dempsey shrugged and finished helping Glee. Then, they sat there waiting, getting more and more impatient as the minutes kept ticking by. Finally, it got to be close to three and still no sign of Trip.

"Well, what're you going to do? He won't come now. Something's happened. Take me downtown to that office...the goddamn Tower or whatever they call it. I'm not going back to Jacksonville and wait the rest of my young life for Mr. Griffin Richards to jack me around. Clayton meant for me to have that place at Starfish and, by god, I'm gonna have it before I leave, or...or it'll take 'em all the rest of their lives to clean up the stink I'm going to raise...." Glee kept pacing back and forth, ranting and raving. Finally, she pointed to the clock on his desk again and said, "See? Just see what I told you? He's a freaking no-show. Are you coming with me, or do I call a cab? What's the difference? Norris Wrenn is probably the man to see about this anyway...or the old fart Richards. You know those two stuffed shirts don't want any trouble with the cops or the news people either."

Dempsey had been sitting there listening to her for almost two hours. Not only was she getting on his nerves, but, after awhile, when he thought it over, she made perfect sense.

"OK," he said at last. "Let's go, but just let me do the talking, all right?"

"All right! It's a deal." She grabbed her bag and headed for the door.

Shortly after three, just as they pulled into the parking lot at the Tower, the radio blared the breaking news:

"...AND THE GREENSBORO POLICE ANNOUNCED TODAY THAT ACTRESS EMMA CLAIRE DID NOT DIE OF A DRUG OVERDOSE AS WAS ORIGINALLY BELIEVED. THE MEDICAL EXAMINER'S REPORT FROM THE UNIVERSITY OF NORTH CAROLINA AT CHAPEL HILL CONFIRMED THAT THE YOUNG WOMAN DIED FROM AN OVER-WHELMING INFECTION OF THE LUNGS AND BLOOD-STREAM BY AN ORGANISM CALLED KLEBSIELLA PNEU-MONIAE. AMOUNTS OF ALCOHOL AND A PRESCRIPTION MEDICATION WERE FOUND IN HER BLOOD...AND ALTHOUGH UNCONFIRMED SOURCES SAY THERE WERE TRACES OF COCAINE PRESENT..."

"Shit! What does all that freaking double-talk mean?..." Glee had an uneasy feeling that somehow they'd been defeated.

Without a word, Dempsey let the car roll forward and headed back toward the street. The last time he had felt so lucky was when he'd been shot down in Nam and parachuted from the burning wreckage and had been saved by a rescue chopper.

"It means we don't wind up in jail, thank god!"

"Wait up, goddamn it..." Glee was furious. "Are you just going to let 'em fuck us over?"

Dempsey stopped the car and reached across and opened the door... "Rots-a-'ruck, kid...."

"Demp, goddamn you, you can't just dump me...what's the matter with you?"

"I've never been better. Like my daddy always told me, 'You gotta know when to hold 'em and know when to fold 'em.'" He nodded at the open door. "Now, do you want out here, or do I take you to Raleigh and put you on a plane to Jax? Take my word. In a day or so, Richards will show and give you the deed and a key to your property and bestow upon you a generous list of other bene-fits—the full particulars of which, unless I miss my guess, are going to be your first-class social security for the rest of your life."

Glee was adamant that nothing had really changed about the value of the evidence that Dempsey held involving Trip in the case. "Didn't you hear what they said? The reporters will still be asking where the cocaine came from...I'm damn sure that fucking Griffin Richards and Norris Wrenn don't want the cops to come digging into that...goddamn it, Demp...we may still have 'em by the balls," she fumed. Then she whined, "C'mon, Demp, don't chicken out."

Dempsey remained firm. "It's fucking over, Glee. The Grahams own this state. Forget it happened."

"Then go up there with me while I tell that old fart if he doesn't go through with the condo deal then I'm gonna tell all to Mabel...maybe I'll just sue. C'mon, don't you want to see his face?" she wheedled.

"How many times do you have to hear it from me? If you want my advice, you'll take Griff Richards' word and wait 'til he shows up. If you try to strong-arm Norris Wrenn, then you're gonna wind up with your tit in the ringer. Haven't you fucked up enough already in your young life? Now, come on and I'll take you to Raleigh. There's still time to catch the six o'clock to Jax. Otherwise, I'll help you with your bags and you can call a cab...I'll call you in Jax...if there's enough left of you after they get through with you up there." He looked up through the sunroof to the Tower rising straight above them.

Finally, Glee slumped, suddenly defeated. "OK, you win...take me to Raleigh. But what am I going to do if the old bastard goes back on his word?"

"Then stand up for your rights just like you said you would. You have something coming to you...you earned it. But there'll be plenty of time for that later. Take my word. Griffin Richards...or Norris Wrenn...will be flying into Jacksonville within a week and make you a very happy girl." Dempsey smiled and drove out of the parking lot.

Upstairs, Griffin Richards looked down through the sunroof of Dempsey's car and watched the tableau taking place. He turned to Norris and said, "There's that goddamn Glee Craige down in the parking lot. And Dempsey Gearhart drove her over here. I told her not to come up here to the funeral, and I'm sure that I was unfeeling in trying to restrict her. She must have had some feeling for

Clayton...she made him happy, at least. But I told her this morning that I would get back to her to take care of Clayton's plan about the property and the real estate business. I guess she's on her way up here to make some sort of threat. I'm in no mood for her. What if I just kick her out of here and tell her to sue? What do you think she'd do?"

"Sue us all to hell and back," Norris said. "And I don't blame her." He smiled at his friend. Norris really had a lot of respect for Griffin. "It serves you right if she does read you the riot act. Even mistresses and whores have feelings."

"OK. Perhaps you're right. Anyway, she's changed her mind, it seems. They're leaving now," Griffin said.

"We may be jumping to conclusions here. After all, Gearhart has his office in this building."

"Yeah...OK, OK. Well, back to the issue at hand. Clayton's signature on your contract is duly notarized and his new will leaves the Grail stock in a trust for Ivee—the Board is trustee. Trip, Mabel, Marilee, you—as CEO—and me, we're the Board. Our best bet is to just talk some sense to Trip. You can bet he won't like it. What Clayton feared most has happened. But, now more than ever, Grail...and Ivee...have to be protected from Trip." Griffin looked to Norris in frustration.

"I know. But Trip is going to contest this. Even Mabel might take a stand with him...certainly, if she found out about Clayton's infidelity. A good lawyer would have a field day with the new will, considering Clayton's recent private life. Besides, I'm exhausted. All of a sudden, the prospect of having to put up with Trip's shit leaves me empty. Why should I have to negotiate with the bastard to save his own company? I'm not yet thirty-eight. We're talking about the rest of my life, and lately I've seen a lot of people—who didn't expect it—run out of that precious commodity. There are a lot of places I can go. Almost anywhere I chose, really. I'd just like to sleep on this. It's been a hell of a five days."

"My God, think of yourself...you're just about to get filthy rich, you know? And you're dead wrong about Mabel. She'll support you one hundred per cent. Of course, Marilee will go along...at least the women know how much they need you. Trip won't make trouble...he's too sick."

"Don't bet on it. And what about that, anyway? We should get him back to that fancy drunk farm first thing tomorrow. I'm sure he'd had a drink before the funeral this morning. Unless I miss my guess, he's drunk by now. Clayt's dead, and my old friend Tom Bradley's still in ICU. I've had enough reminders of how precious life is."

"Yeah, it certainly does make a man stop and count his blessings...."

"What about Marilee? Clayt's will doesn't take care of her?"

"I know...not like you'd think...all Clayt thought about was his precious grandson...and Grail. He was afraid to leave Marilee too well-fixed, afraid she'd take Ivee away from Colonial Hall...or become the target of opportunists, I guess. Marilee gets no Grail stock...no property. As long as she remains in Colonial Hall and is of good moral character...no matter what, she gets the use of the house to provide Ivee with a home...and she gets an income of $300,000 a year from a personal trust until Ivee is twenty-five. All Ivee's school and camps...all those expenses...are taken care of separately. Then she gets an annuity of $250,000 for the rest of her life, with cost of living escalations built in...no strings. If Trip is dead or they're divorced by then, she'll get the use of the house for her lifetime; then it goes to Ivee, along with everything else. That's the Graham way...but...it's fair."

"What about the Grail board? What if Trip should die...looks like he's hell bent on it...and Marilee should remarry? Or if Marilee should divorce Trip?" Norris tried to sound offhand.

"Well, in either case, the way I see it, as long as there's no evidence of moral turpitude...at least no public display which would adversely affect Ivee...or Grail...then the deal stands. That will is solid. Still, if Trip should contest it...who knows? He's Clayton Massie Graham the Third. That name is to local law like Moses was to the Ten Commandments. Hell, I don't have to tell you that...you're the attorney who told me how to set up that will."

"Take my word, Griff, Trip Graham's in an ugly mood. He

won't win, but he could stir up a mess. If I stay on as CEO, we won't ever really hear the end of his shit—not as long as he's alive."

Norris walked to the window and looked down on the peaceful town. He did like it here...and he purely hated to lose at anything. Sheepshead Light was a seductive thought, but was he really ready to resign the world and go write books?...just give up the good fight?

"When does Trip go back to the hospital?...do you think he really will?" Norris asked.

"He's supposed to check back in Sunday. He promised...but I have my doubts he'll go without an argument. Still...maybe he's learned his lesson." Griff shrugged.

"Sunday is Mother's Day. Marilee is Mother of the Year, remember?" Norris frowned. "Goddamn!...with all the shit that's going on, I forgot to order my mother's flowers. I must order her flowers. I usually spend the weekend in Sanibel. She'll be disappointed if I don't make it."

"I didn't know your mother was still alive." Griffin had never really thought about it. "In Sanibel, not Raleigh?"

"Yeah, I bought her a house on Sanibel Island four years ago with my first Grail bonus."

"How'd that make you feel?" Griffin asked him. "Buying her the house, I mean?"

"Damn good. I was proud of that. She said my father would be proud of me. Made me feel sort of completed," Norris said, thoughtfully.

"Could you have done it sooner...I mean before you came to Grail? Did all those pictures on the magazine covers bring any real money?" Griffin asked, with seeming casualness. "Was there any real payoff for your plans to save the world?"

"Well...I...uh?" Norris leaned back and thought about it for a moment before he finally answered. "Yeah, sure...I made some money before I came here...but Phoenix was a dream."

"And what stopped you from saving the world, I mean? Phoenix sounded pretty good to me," Griff persisted.

"Well, there wasn't any backing. My team...the so-called 'international moneytrust boys got cold feet. You have to use somebody else's money, especially if you want to save the world...." Norris suddenly grinned. "OK...OK...back off now, you've made your point."

Griff looked back to Norris without a change of expression. "Stick around...stay with the ship. Nan and I will be staying at the big house with Mabel. I'm going to round up Ed Scott, and we'll talk to Mabel. We've got to try our best to get Trip back to Holly Hall on Sunday, right after church. But, whether Trip checks back in or not, I'll stay down here until Monday at least. This is where the work gets done. Remember. The cardinal rule about saving the world is: First save your own ass." Griff got up to leave.

"I can't argue with that." Norris laughed and turned to go back into his office.

CHAPTER SIXTY-EIGHT

TRIP TURNED AND STUMBLED SLIGHTLY as he started across the board-walk, back to the cottage.

Watch it, boy! Slow down.

He headed inside, wondering if there was anything to eat before he fixed another drink. He wasn't really hungry, but didn't want to get seriously knee-walking drunk again.

"Hellooo-o-o, Trip, where are you?..." A ghostly call wafted up to him from somewhere.

Where? Inside? He strained to hear.

Marilee?

No way! Marilee was back in Colonial Hall with Norris.

Fucking ears were playing tricks. He shrugged. He stood still and strained to hear.

The wind, perhaps? It was spooky...made him shiver.

He took another step, stumbled again and grabbed the rail. Goddamn! Maybe he should slow down...still...he felt OK.

"Trip, are you all right?" From the cottage door, Marilee had seen Trip stumble and steady himself on the rail. She could tell that he'd been drinking.

"Whadda fugga you doing here, you goddamn bitch?" His words were slurred. Marilee recalled the scene Monday night at the Club.

"I was worried. I know Clayt's death has been hard on you...and your hemorrhage...you've been ill. It's hard for us all, but Trip...how much have you had to drink? Ed Scott says you should-n't..." Marilee began, totally dismayed.

Trip straightened. To hear this from this cheating bitch was too much. He was sick and tired of being treated like a drunk. Just who the hell did she think she was anyway? And what was she doing following him here?

Running off to New York on the day she'd been named Mother of the Fucking Year...she was "Fucking" Mother of the Year, all right. Shacked up with Norris...that investigator said something about sheeps...and some sort of island? Maybe he should just tell her right here and now that he knew her little secret? Naah...he'd just let her think she had him fooled for awhile longer...it was kind of fun...cat and mouse.

"Quit worrying...I'm OK. One drink won't hurt me. If you listened to Ed Scott, he'd have the whole damn town at an AA meeting. You look like you could use one yourself," he said, finally collecting himself.

"AA? Me?...I don't think so."

"Oh...oh, no, not AA...a drink. How 'bout it?" He walked back to the island counter and picked up the big bottle and sloshed vodka in the glass. He turned and reached another glass from the shelf and looked back to her.

"Well, how 'bout it?"

When Marilee thought about it, the idea of a drink was suddenly appealing. "Well...all right. If you promise you won't have but one. Is that Bloody Mary mix...there, behind you? Please make mine light. It's late, and I've got to get back to Ivee." She turned and looked out at the ocean. What was she going to do? She should call Jaynie. It would be at least 7:00 p.m. by the time she could get back. Why had she come down here, anyway? She wished she had stayed at home. If Trip wanted to drink himself to death what did she care?

As soon as Marilee turned her back, Trip drank the vodka he'd already poured and refilled his glass. This time, he added a little of the Bloody Mary mix to his. When he'd finished fixing the drinks, he walked over to where Marilee was standing and handed her the glass. Goddamn, she smelled good. He casually let his hand drop to her waist, and she jerked slightly and moved just a little so that his hand slid away, brushing across her buttocks as it fell.

The feel of her called up the image of Norris' hand caressing her earlier in the day.

"What'd ja move away for? Have I got leprosy?" He moved a step closer and put his hand back on her waist and let it slide a little so it rested on the upper curve of her hip. "You're still the best-looking woman I know. We need to be closer now...for Ivee's sake." He bent to kiss her as she turned her head away in revulsion.

"Don't..." Marilee gasped. Trip's breath stank of stale booze and rotten fish. She looked closer. Slightly emaciated, hollow around the eyes and sunken in the cheeks, before her stood a grotesque caricature of the man she'd married. She felt nothing for him now...not even pity.

"What the hell's the matter with you, goddamn it? I'm your husband, remember? I guess you don't..." He moved a step closer, but Marilee retreated again.

"Please, Trip...now's hardly the time for this."

"And just why not?" He suddenly remembered the package of clippings he'd found in her room. "Maybe it's because of your hero, my good buddy Norris...is that it?"

"What's Norris got to do with it?" she protested.

"After you went to New York, I found a whole goddamn envelope full of press clippings about Norris in your room. What the hell was that all about?" He watched for her reaction.

"Oh...Ivee wanted to make a book report on Norris' book, *Phoenix Rising*. I sent off for those," she blurted.

"Huh...sounds like overkill to me...." Trip took another step, stumbling forward, slopping his drink all over the front of Marilee's dress, up in her face and in her hair.

"Oh!...Trip...you're drunk. God! Now just see what you've done?" Marilee wailed and brushed at her sodden hair with the back of her hand.

Momentarily embarrassed, Trip moved to the sink and pulled out a lengthy ribbon of paper towels and tore it off. When he turned back, Marilee was bent over, daubing at herself with a cocktail napkin without much success. Finally, she gave up and threw it on the counter in disgust.

"I can't go anywhere like this," she wailed and turned and started toward the stairs. "I have some clothes upstairs. I'm going to jump in the shower and put on some jeans...."

Trip watched her go. The movement of her bottom against the tight fabric as she ascended the stairs was tantalizing. Ignoring the mess on the floor, he went to restore his wasted drink. Upstairs he could hear the shower running. The thought of her naked, soaping herself, hands gliding smoothly over her breasts, rubbing hard between her legs was maddening. Finally, he heard the shower stop. He could stand it no longer.

Stepping into the bedroom, Trip stopped in mid-stride at the sight of Marilee as she emerged from the bathroom toweling herself roughly across the back.

"Goddamn you, get out of here...get out...you hear? I won't have it. I won't have you intruding on me this way..." she tried to cover herself as she screamed with indignation.

"Oh, yes, by God, you will. You'll do any fucking thing I say, lady."

He wrestled her clumsily toward the bed.

Try as she might, Marilee could not fight off his attempt to move her toward the bed. Curiously angry, she was not afraid. She simply despised him. Her only thought was to get away and never see him again.

Renewing her effort, with a mighty twist, she spun him and he fell, taking her down with him.

Trip released his hold on her as he crashed against the corner of the nightstand. Marilee quickly grabbed the towel.

Snatching up the underwear, cotton tee shirt and jeans, she skipped through the door and along the gallery and scampered down the steps. She didn't stop until she reached the door leading out to the deck. Then, she quickly stepped into her panties and put on her bra. By the time she saw Trip appear at the landing at the top of the stairs she had already shrugged into her jeans and was slipping into her tee shirt.

"Goddamn bitch...you'll pay...count on it. You and your precious Norris...you'll wish you'd never been born, both of ya." Trip stood panting at the top of the stairs. He was bleeding from a small gash on his forehead where he'd crashed into the edge of the night-stand.

"Look, Trip...there's no use in talking about any of this now. You're drunk." Marilee's breathing was returning to normal and her words were measured, evenly spaced. "If you want to come with me now, I'll follow you back to Colonial Hall...but I can't wait around...I'm late. Ivee needs me."

"No son needs a common whore for a mother," Trip's voice rasped and faltered. He bent over, staggered and almost pitched forward down the steps. All at once nauseous, with his stomach cramping again, fear gripped him as he fought the violent urge to evacuate his bowels. The memory of the blood gushing out of him flashed vividly across his brain. He straightened himself and ran back down the hall into the bedroom and headed to the bathroom. He had barely dropped his pants and lowered himself to a sitting position atop the commode when the gushing began.

Instinctively aware that he was in extreme distress, Marilee rushed up the steps behind him. She pulled up short as she stood watching in horror what was happening.

"Oh my god," she said and turned to go to the phone. Then she turned back, reluctant to leave him...not knowing what to do first. "Just sit down there. Hold on to the paper holder and the edge of this." She stepped tentatively inside and took his hand and guided it to the countertop of the lavatory cabinet. "Just take it easy...I'll be right back."

"Get your fugga hans offa me, bitch." This time his words came out coldly. "Where'na hell you think you're going?" He made a grab for her wrist and missed.

"You need a doctor. For godsake, Trip, do you want to bleed to death?"

"I don' need a doctor, and I'm not bleeding. Get the hell outa here and close the goddamn door behind you," he commanded, coldly.

Aware that the situation was not as life-threatening as she initially assumed, Marilee backed out of the bathroom and pulled the door closed behind her.

She walked slowly back down the stairs, wondering if she should call Sam Merritt—Chip Merritt's dad. Jellyfish stings, skinned elbows and sunburns, over the years when they were here at the beach, Dr. Samuel Peyton Merritt, Sr. had served them well, both as friend and family physician.

Marilee walked to the sink and vacantly inspected the contents of the half-gallon bottle of vodka. At least one-third empty. The plastic strip which had been the seal of the newly-opened bottle lay curled on the counter top. There was no mistaking that Trip must have consumed it all himself. Incredible. How could he have drunk that much in the space of less than an hour? Her first instinct was to get out of there and go back home. Ed Scott had warned her. Trip was flirting with death. Ed had made it very clear his liver was gone...now she tried to remember all the medical explanations. Ed had said there was danger he could hemorrhage again from the esophagus, and it might be impossible to stop, and he would bleed to death. Marilee tried to recall what else she had heard, but it was all too complicated.

Before she could make sense out of it, she heard the commode flushing upstairs, and Trip came walking along the gallery to the top of the stairs. Standing there, glaring down at her, he looked as white as a sheet. She couldn't just leave him like this. It was her duty to see if she couldn't reason with him.

"I'm going to call Doctor Sam. You need help," she began and moved toward the phone.

"In a pig's asshole. Get oudda here and leave me the fuck alone. All I need is a drink." Trip started down the stairs. "Get away from that phone, bitch." His tone was threatening.

All at once, she became afraid again. Backing away, she moved around the island countertop on the far side of the sink, using it as a barrier. Warily she surveyed her escape routes in case the need arose. She did not believe that he had enough agility to outdistance her in a foot race to either door if she got the first step.

She meant to keep it that way.

Trip eyed Marilee and walked to the kitchen cabinets, took down a glass, opened the ice compartment of the refrigerator and took out a fistful of cubes. Then he returned, unscrewed the cap from the bottle and poured the glass almost to the brim with straight vodka.

"Where's that muthafucking Norris, you whore? I was standing right outside the door when you were playing kissy-feely at the big house this afternoon. What was all that talk about my daddy's will? What kind a plot have you cooked up with that traitor, Griffin Richards?...that two-face muthafucker." The question dripped with venom. "Well, what about it? Why are you here? Is the all-American boy coming to meet you for a little sportfucking?"

"Trip, you know you shouldn't be drinking like that. Ed Scott says it will kill you...you shouldn't drink at all." It was wasted talk, but it was all she could think of to say.

Trip looked her straight in the eye as he tossed off the entire tumbler of straight vodka in two large swallows. She watched with frozen fascination as he refilled the glass and drank from it again.

"Fuck off, whore." He spit out the words like he was ridding himself of insects inside his mouth.

"Trip, are you trying to kill yourself?" Marilee pleaded. "What do you expect to accomplish? Is it your father's death that has you crazy? Please stop this. I'm afraid."

She weighed the possibility of getting to the phone and calling Marcellus. Coming down, she had debated about stopping at his place on the other side of the waterway and bringing him with her on her way in, but at the time it seemed like an overreaction. God, how she wished she had. Still, she really didn't think Trip would attack her physically again.

Marilee lowered her guard and glanced across the room at the phone.

A flash of movement caught the edge of her vision.

Instinctively, she ducked as the glass spewing ice cubes into the air bounced against the wall behind her.

She straightened, and stumbling off balance from the sudden desperate movement, regained her equilibrium and moved to her

461

left as Trip tried to come around the counter and block her from the nearest exit.

Instinctively, she feinted toward him as if to make it by him to the door. The move got him off balance. Taking advantage of the surprise, Marilee broke and ran across the living room.

A mistake. She knew it almost before she started. To make matters worse, her foot slipped on one of the ice cubes scattered about. Halfway across the living room, as she attempted to turn to defend herself, his fist caught her high atop her forehead and sent her sprawling across a low cocktail table. She rolled across the floor and regained her footing just in time to see a blur of light slashing through the air.

Lunging instinctively, she moved aside as he fell across the table, smashing a lamp with a heavy brass candlestick he'd grabbed off the mantle.

My God, he'd swung it at her head! He actually meant to kill her!

"Where's that fuggin' gun? I'm gonna divorce you permanently right now. Blow your goddamn brains out..." Trip struggled to his feet and lurched up the stairs.

Marilee ran headlong through the door, out onto the wide front deck to the top of the stairs leading down to the parking area below. When she glanced back and saw that he had not yet reached the door, she slowed and carefully walked down the steps and started her car, backed it out and headed it toward the street. Then, she put it in park, got out and waited with the motor still running. In a minute Trip came out the door and walked over to the deck rail with a fresh drink in his hands. The candlestick was still clutched tightly in his other fist.

"You go tell Norris he's through. Your ass is grass, too, lady. The free ride is over, whore. Pack your things, you're history with me. The joke may have been on me 'til now...God knows you've got to be the most expensive piece of ass I've ever had...and I've had a lot." With theatrical drunkenness, he measured her cunningly with his eye and let fly with the candlestick. The throw was pathetically short; the candlestick clanged off his steering wheel and landed in the front seat of the Corvette.

"Shit," he exclaimed in disgust. He looked at her, and, turning now with obvious difficulty, he reeled back to the door and disappeared into the house. After two or three minutes, he came back with a fresh glass and staggered to the edge of the railing and balanced the glass there. Reaching behind him, he tugged at something in his hip pocket.

When Trip's hand came up, he had a gun.

Fascinated, Marilee watched, momentarily frozen in horror. Before she could react, he leveled the pistol directly at her and pulled the trigger.

The hammer failed to click.

Trip struggled mightily. No matter how hard he strained, the hammer would not move.

Finally, he raised the gun to eye level and turned it slowly over, trying to figure out how to undo the safety lock. Marilee was turning to the car when she noticed the hollow cavity in the bottom of the pistol's handle.

The magazine was missing. There was no ammunition clip.

Transfixed, she stepped back out on the pavement and watched. Finally, Trip gave up and put the gun back in his hip pocket. He picked up the glass, wiped the sweat from his brow and steadied himself with his left hand on the railing. All at once his expression changed to a look of pain. He bent forward over the rail and violently threw up. Marilee watched in horror as he vomited over and over again, wondering how long one person could maintain such an outpouring of material from his stomach. Then, suddenly, she realized that the vomit had changed color to bright red.

Still very much afraid, she moved around toward the base of the steps. She had crossed half the distance when his heaving slowed and stopped and he stood bent over the railing gasping for breath.

Marilee stopped, hardly daring to breathe. My God, she had thought the hemorrhage would never end. She'd been certain he was going to die right before her eyes.

"Trip, please let me take you into Southport to the hospital. I can call Sam Merritt and have him meet us there. This is serious. Please? Let me come in and call the ambulance. My God, you need some help," she pleaded.

Trip just stood there over the rail, gasping—not saying a word.

"Please, Trip?" she begged.

"Fuck off, woman. How many times do I have to tell you?...fuck off." He took out the gun and waved it. "When I come back out here again, this thing will be working, I promise you. Now fuck off and leave me alone."

Marcellus...she must find Marcellus.

Retracing her steps, Marilee quickly drove away.

Watching as Marilee's car disappeared down the beach road, Trip straightened himself and looked over the rail at the rapidly diminishing pool of vomit as it seeped into the sand.

Bloody Mary mix. *Blood and Sand*...an old Tyrone Power film he'd seen.

Goddamn, he needed a drink again...couldn't get drunk and couldn't get sober. He remembered hearing someone describe the same experience at Holly Hall. But then, he really didn't want to get drunk now, did he? He'd done pretty good...except he'd made a goddamn fool of himself with Marilee. It didn't matter. When he got through with her, she'd be sorry she ever laid eyes on him. If she didn't toe the line, he'd take Ivee and run her ass out of town on a rail. And if Norris even looked the wrong way at him, he'd make a phone call to Agnes' precious daddy, the venerable Senator Dabney Thoughgood Farnsworth himself...and don't forget the media—*People* and the *Enquirer*...and the *Star*...them too. Then the shit would really hit the fan...would it ever. And, that goddamn perennial High Llama at the fucking White House...Chandler or Chambers?...that new airhead, Bible-thumping joker in the Oval Office could hardly afford any more scandal around the Rose Garden. Trouble with everybody around Grail was they'd all come to believe that Trip Graham couldn't live without Norris the Wonderful. Well, now he'd fix the goddamn bastard. He'd show 'em all.

Trip made his way back to the kitchen counter. Swirling the vodka to chill it, he drank it down, refilled the glass and started for the stairs. He'd go lie down...then he'd go up to Long Beach and lay in some food. There'd be a big weekend crowd for Mother's Day...stores would be open late.

When he'd almost reached the top of the steps, he was suddenly taken by an excruciating series of pains that seemed to begin at the base of his throat and bent him double as they radiated downward into his abdomen. Hardly before he could find the banister rail to steady himself, he was struck with overpowering waves of nausea. One after another, they came in a seemingly endless succession. His vision blurred and he felt his knees go weak and his grip loosen on the rail. Lurching against the rail in an effort to maintain his feet, he felt himself losing balance... going...going...over and...over.

He never felt the impact as his limp form crashed headfirst on top of the glass coffee table with a sickening thud. His body came to rest in a pool of bright red blood.

CHAPTER SIXTY-NINE

MARILEE SPED ACROSS THE WATERWAY BRIDGE, straight to Marcellus' place. Chickens, dogs and cats scattered in every direction as she skidded into the sandy drive. When Marcellus came out to greet her, she let out a great sigh of relief. Frantically, she recounted what had happened. Then, noting it was not yet five o'clock, she looked up Dr. Sam's number and dialed her cell phone. Sensing her urgency, the old practitioner's nurse had the doctor on the phone almost instantly.

"He just got home from Holly Hall yesterday on a temporary pass to attend the funeral...he's hemorrhaging badly...come out here and talk to him, Dr. Merritt, please? I'm scared he's going to bleed to death."

"Well, I guess that will always be a possibility for him, but does that mean that you're going to have to keep him under constant surveillance? That's not possible. And, Marilee, from what you describe, it doesn't sound to me like he really had much of a hemorrhage. Sounds like that was Bloody Mary mix you saw...oh, sure there was maybe a little bleeding, probably from the retching. It's not uncommon. At any rate, Marilee, listen to me. Use your head. Think about it. You said he had a gun...said he tried to bash your head in with a drinking glass and a brass candlestick. And you want me to come out there? Do you think this old coot is Superman? You just told me that he forbade you to call me. Call Sheriff Mac Jones and have him locked up. He'll sleep it off. Maybe we can get him back to Holly Hall in the morning," the kindly physician advised with gentle reason.

"But Doctor Sam, I can't call the police...that's Trip Graham. We can't just have him locked up like a common drunk."

"I know who he is, Marilee...what choice do you have?...the

National Guard, maybe? I'm not bulletproof and neither are you, my dear. I think that, most likely, he'll stay put...and from what you said, he may be passed out already. At any rate, he'll just keep on drinking until he passes out. Then he'll sleep it off and feel like hell in the morning. If he's civilized, I'll see him then. I'm sorry, my dear. If you can get him tamed, call me and I'll see him at the hospital anytime night or day. My advice to you is leave him be. If you don't stir him up, he'll probably calm down. Sorry, that's the best I can do...have you tried Ed Scott? Whatever happens, good luck." He hung up.

Marilee put down the phone and put her head between her hands. Marcellus looked at her anxiously and quietly asked. "Want me to go over there, Miz Marilee?"

She raised her head slowly and smiled. "No, Marcellus, leave him alone...Dr. Sam is right. You aren't bulletproof either. I'm going back home and take care of my son and my own life. Nobody can help Trip if he doesn't want help."

At the car she stopped and said, "I'll be home no later than seven, Marcellus. Maybe you could just drive by there after dark and make sure his car is still there. Whatever you do, don't go in. Dr. Merritt is right, let's don't disturb him. Just let him get it out of his system, OK?"

"Yes'm. I'll make sure that he stays put. I'll slip over there and let the air out of his tires after it gets darker...how's that?"

"No, no...I'd rather you didn't in case he needed the car to go for help. Just sort of keep an eye out. If his car is missing, call me. OK? Thanks, Marcellus." Marilee gave him a hug and left.

Unseeing, unfeeling, undecided, Marilee drove numbly down the lane from Marcellus' house. When she hit the main road, she hesitated, then turned back toward the ocean again. She really didn't care about Trip anymore, but she couldn't go off and leave him this way...not knowing.

Before she reached her place, she slowed and pulled into the Wilsons' cottage next door. The Wilsons were summer people. The place was deserted. Marilee walked through the sand around the side of the house and made her way through a wide trough

467

between the series of vine-covered dunes leading to the beach, approaching her cottage from the ocean side. Making sure she could see no sign of movement, she slipped out of the cover of sea oats, high dunes grass and yaupon shrub and crossed the short expanse of sand to the pilings of the high sun deck and went softly up the steps.

Her heart was pounding.

Still barefoot, she crept slowly across the open expanse of deck until she entered the open door leading onto the screened porch. Once inside the porch, she felt less vulnerable. For the few seconds she had taken in negotiating the twenty feet of open deck she had held her breath, wondering if Trip was really crazy enough to shoot her, or if Doctor Sam was right...was he passed out already? But, most of all she wondered why—why she'd come back here again, anyway? She couldn't do anything with him...she didn't even want to...so...why...why...why?

Well, maybe, she told herself, if he gets sick enough, he'll go back to the hospital and I'll get him out of my hair. And maybe...if it comes down to push and shove...the divorce court would not give so much credence to someone who had been treated for drug addiction and alcoholism.

Shielded from the wind now, she stood quietly listening for perhaps two or three minutes.

Nothing...no sound, no movement.

Cautiously, she moved to the door. The top half of the door was paned with glass and she could see back to her left the bottle of Stoli still sitting on the island counter...it was almost half-empty now. Over a quart in just under two hours...my god...how?...

"*Uht...umm...*"

What? She froze.

Imagination?

Her attention was drawn to the half-melted cubes of ice scattered at the bottom of the stairway.

"*Uh...hum-m...*"

A moan...a gurgle...a whisper?...what?...

Praying the door wouldn't squeak, Marilee slowly pushed it

open until it was wide enough to slip through. Making sure she left the door open to accommodate a getaway, she carefully committed her path of escape to memory, took a deep breath and stepped inside. No sooner than she had taken a single step, she stopped dead in her tracks.

Just beyond the bottom of the steps, she could see Trip's foot dangling in the air at a crazy angle. Cautiously, she moved ahead until, mouth agape with horror, she saw all of him. Perhaps six feet out from the side of the open stairs, he lay face upturned, sprawled grotesquely in an enormous pool of fresh blood.

Momentarily she stood transfixed, looking for signs of consciousness. It took her only a glance to tell that he was either unconscious—or dead. Taking great pains to avoid the mess, she circled him. When she had gotten as close as she dared without stepping into the bloody pool, she stopped and watched intently. Was he breathing? Finally, his body give a slight shudder...but still he made no sound. Then, without warning, his body contracted in a violent spasm and a small geyser of blood erupted and fell back onto his upturned face. The expelled air from his nose and mouth made little bubbles in the thick red mucoid mass. Although his eyes were staring half-open, he showed no signs of consciousness.

Suddenly, his body arched upward again, stiffened and fell backward. His foot twitched violently.

Convulsions! She'd seen her daddy suffer them more than once.

Retreating in the same wide circle, she made it back to the door. She stood there for what seemed an eternity. He gurgled once again then went totally limp.

Five minutes passed...no movement now.

At last, she gathered herself and looked at the phone before she quietly left without closing any of the doors.

Funny, she'd never seen anyone die before...yet now she felt absolutely nothing. Utterly numb.

By the time she reached the four-lane expressway north of Wilmington, Marilee was suddenly confronted with the reality that, no matter what, she'd never have Trip to worry about again.

Looking back to see the afternoon in its surrealistic ritual of stark terror, she began to sob. Finally, she started to shake uncontrollably. Overcome, she barely managed to pull off of the roadway. After the tears and the violent trembling passed, she regained her composure and pulled back into the thinning traffic of late afternoon.

What would happen now?

If Trip had remained alive, she couldn't take him to court. But that wouldn't have been the end of the world. Norris had told her the terms of the will. Trip couldn't kick her off of the board.

Poor Ivee. Even his grandfather had realized he must be protected from his own father.

Of course Clayton hadn't realized that Trip was insane—perhaps it was the alcohol, but insane nonetheless. If he had survived, she wondered if she couldn't have had him committed?

Even dead, she hated him. He'd tried to kill her. He called her a whore.

Remembering now, she'd told Sam Merritt about the amount of blood that Trip had lost over the railing. Sam Merritt should have listened. Doctors thought they knew everything. She wasn't to blame. The old coot had told her to leave him. What else could she have done?

Nothing. It was out of her hands.

To lose his father and grandfather in the same week was going to be devastating for Ivee, but in the long run it would certainly be better this way.

To die now, quietly and alone—everyone would be the better for it.

It was his own damn fault...served him right.

She tried Norris again on the cell...she could hardly wait to tell him they were free.

No answer at The Tower.

We're free, Norris, darling...where are you?

Idly, she fiddled with the radio, looking for some music.

"*C'mon baby, make my day.*" The singer's words echoed in the evening air.

470

CHAPTER SEVENTY

WHEN SHE PASSED THROUGH THE GATEHOUSE ON CLUB DRIVE, Marilee looked at her watch and was surprised to see that it was not yet quite seven.

Plenty of time—no need to hurry. She struggled to put her thoughts in order. Ivee was in good hands. Being with his friend Jody was the best thing for him at a time like this.

God! She wanted to see Norris, if only for a minute. But, first, she'd have to go to the big house and see about things with Mabel. Thank goodness, Nan would be staying over for another day at the very least...probably longer.

Trip dead. Incredible!

Poor Mabel!

But why worry about Mabel...it was Ivee who needed her.

Mabel was a tough old bird...of course most of us are a lot tougher than we think, thank god. Still...when Mabel learned Trip was dead, she'd need someone to lean on.

Marilee knew all about alcoholics. Even if, through some miracle, Trip had survived, he was obviously hopeless. He would've wound up the same way as her father...vegetating in the back wards of some loony bin.

Trip was really better off dead than having to rot slowly away. So was everyone concerned.

Still, he *was* Ivee's father. There was no changing that. And to face losing his father so soon after Clayt's death was going to be devastating for Ivee. More than ever now, she needed Norris to step in and take the father role.

She slowed as she passed Norris' house. Agnes' station wagon was parked in front of the garage. The door to Norris' side was open. The space was empty.

Where the hell could he be? She'd tried his unpublished number all the way up the highway with no luck. Maybe he was at the big house with Mabel...waiting for her to show up. Marilee let the car slow and turned into her own drive. She couldn't show up at Mabel's barefoot and looking like this.

There was a light in the downstairs hall and a note from Oleander saying that Jaynie had called to say she was taking the boys for pizza.

Upstairs, she quickly shrugged out of the jeans and slipped into a shower cap for a quick rinse. Donning a loose wraparound cotton skirt, she grabbed a pair of leather thong sandals from the closet and slipped them on one foot at a time as she hopped toward the door.

In less than ten minutes she was moving back out of the drive again.

She drove halfway around the circle at The Club and turned into the drive of Clayt's house.

Clayt's house?...Mabel's house now. That would take some getting used to.

God, what a mess! It was all happening so fast. Nothing would ever be the same again. One thing for sure, Norris wasn't here at the big house either...at least his Riviera wasn't parked in the drive. The only car in the drive up ahead was Griffin Richards' black Cadillac. Nan was forever complaining about how stuffy it looked. She said it suited him!

Norris, where are you? I need you.

As she neared the house, Griff was just stepping out of his car.

Marilee pulled up beside him and rolled down her window. "Are you still here, you poor man? I'm so glad that Mabel...that we all...have you as a friend."

"Well, I just got here. I spent the afternoon with Norris at the Tower. We were trying to chart a plan of action to make sure the corporation won't suffer. I feel that it's in Mabel's...and Trip's...best interest to have Norris assume control immediately."

"Oh, I know you're right. Trip's not competent...no help at all. I don't know what will happen to him now..." Secretly, she felt smug at the lie.

"Well...first we have to get him back in the hospital...." Griff was obviously concerned.

"I'm sure Mabel expects Norris to take charge. Wasn't there to be a contract to that effect, before...before Clayton's accident?"

"Well, yes...actually Clayton left Norris in charge, but everything's in perpetuation...it will go to Ivee. It's all provided for in a trust. It's simple...but complicated. Norris worked it all out. The trustees are Mabel, Trip, you, me and Norris. I hope Trip sees the advantage to Grail...to Ivee. It's all legal, but Norris is worried about Trip making trouble. If he does, Norris says he might not stick around. If Norris leaves, Grail is in for bad trouble...But I'm sure if we reason with Trip...." Griff left the thought unfinished as he reached back in his car for his briefcase.

"Well, I think Norris' worries are unfounded. Trip is in no shape to cause trouble for anyone." She looked him in the eye and shook her head. It was all she could do not to tell Griff that she had just left Trip two hours ago at Caswell, convulsing...choking to death on his own vomit and blood. "He's drinking again. I don't know what to do next. He doesn't want help. Can we have him committed?" She played out the lie...it never hurt to keep one's options open.

"Maybe he'll sober up when the shock of his daddy's death has passed," Griff said without conviction. "Anyway, Ed Scott and I are taking him back to Holly Hall Sunday...I've seen miracles. Maybe he'll be OK after he's been there for awhile."

"I hope so," Marilee said, tiring of the idle chatter. Her mind was racing ahead. Jaynie had suggested that Ivee stay the night...but she really didn't want that now. When word of Trip's death got out, it would be on all the news. Ivee needed to be at home. It had been a rough time for him and now it was going to get worse. His own bed would do wonders.

But right now she needed Norris. It wouldn't hurt to leave Ivee just a little longer, long enough to go to Norris. Griff said he'd left him at the Tower. Maybe she could catch him there.

With a pat on Griff's arm and a smile, Marilee turned toward the house and called over her shoulder, "Forgive me for running ahead, but I have to go tell Mabel that I need to check on Ivee. I hope we can talk more later."

"I understand. Don't worry about Mabel. Nan and I are going to stay here tonight. By the way, do you know where Trip disappeared to? I need to see him," Griff called after her.

"Wherever that is, he's sure to be drowning his sorrow," she shouted back to him and disappeared through the massive front doors.

Inside, she followed the sound of voices straight back through the center hall and into the large keeping room at the rear of the house.

"Oh, there you are, dear." Mabel greeted her warmly enough, but Marilee could see the telltale signs of stress and fatigue written all over her face. Mabel was running on sheer nervous energy now. Nan was a wonder; she always looked fresh as a flower. How did she manage? From the looks of the cups on the table beside their chairs, both women had been drinking either coffee or tea.

My God, Mabel wouldn't sleep a wink.

"We've all been through hell for the past three days. Let me fix you both a drink. God knows, I need one myself," Marilee said as Griff appeared in the door behind her.

"Sounds like a great idea to me. I could use one, too," Griff echoed approval. "What can I get you, Mabel? And you, ladies? I'll go to the kitchen and have Mose fix us a tray."

"Oh, all right," Mabel gave in with a sigh. Clearly, she was too exhausted now to protest. "A martini for me, I think."

"Keep it simple and quick," Nan chimed in. "Just have him bring a pitcher of martinis. That sounds fine to me."

"A large pitcher...double strength...." echoed Marilee.

Griff nodded and left without a word.

"Where's Ivee?" Mabel asked.

"Oh, he went off with the little Harris boy and his mother after the funeral," Marilee said. "I'm sure it was better that way."

"Yes...it's been awful for him, poor thing," Mabel said.

"Are you all right?" Marilee asked.

"I'm tired. I didn't sleep well the last two nights." Mabel looked ten years older.

"You'll sleep tonight, I bet." Marilee hoped that they didn't find Trip until Mabel could get some rest. Tomorrow was soon enough. There was no real hurry now.

"I hate to dash, but I need to get home. I'm exhausted. And I know you are, Mabel. Have you eaten anything all day?" Marilee looked anxiously to Mabel.

"Marilee's right...you have to eat something, Mabel. And then, you should try to rest. Run along, Marilee, we'll take care of her." Nan patted Mabel's arm again.

"Well..." Marilee began, but stopped when Griff came through the door with a tray in his hands. He went to Mabel first. When they had all been served, he put the tray on the coffee table in front of the fireplace.

"*A votre santé*," he said and raised his glass in a token gesture. They all nodded and raised their glasses before drinking.

Gulping her drink in large thirsty gulps, Marilee shuddered at the sudden sting of the raw alcohol on her palate and throat.

I'm here drinking toasts and making small talk, and two hours ago, I left my husband dying. She felt strangely detached.

"I hate to drink and run, but I'll see you in the morning." Marilee was anxious to leave before Mabel gathered her senses and asked her about Trip.

From the look Mabel had given her, it was on her mind.

"I'll call in a little bit, as soon as I can get home and see what's going on," Marilee lied, and patted Mabel's shoulder again. Before anyone could protest, she slipped quickly out of the room. She had to try to catch Norris before he left the Tower. She needed desperately to see him...touch him.

Safely out of earshot, she picked up the phone in the entrance hall at the bottom of the curving staircase. Marilee dialed and waited...afraid. Norris had not answered all afternoon. She'd called the first time around five-thirty...it was nearing seven now. Patting her foot restlessly, she lost count of the rings. She was ready to give up when he finally picked up.

"Norris, thank God, I thought I'd missed you...or worse...that you wouldn't answer the phone," she whispered breathlessly.

"Where are you? I've tried to call..." Norris inquired, obviously concerned.

"I'm at Mabel's. I just got back. Ivee is with Jaynie Harris...pizza and the movies, I think....are you alone...can I come down there?" she spoke in a whisper, a hushed sense of urgency in her voice.

"Yes...uh, yes...but back from where? Where's Trip?" Norris was having a hard time trying to sort things out.

"I just got back from the beach. Trip's at Caswell. Dead. And he knows...I mean, he knew...about Sheepshead...hold on and I'll be right there," Marilee let the words rush out.

"What? He knows? Knew?...? *Dead?*...are you serious?...what do you mean?..." Norris rattled off the questions.

"I can't talk...no one here knows...not yet," she whispered.

"Goddamn it, Marilee, tell me what you mean..."

"I mean he's dead. Just hold tight, I'm on my way. Bye."

As she took the phone away from her ear, she heard Norris' rasp, "Goddamn it, hurry..."

In the fading twilight, the town seemed deserted. Ghostly.

The businesses were closed. The mayor had declared an official day of mourning.

There was practically no traffic on the streets—almost no sign of human life at all, once she got near the business district.

In the peculiar yellowish, virtually shadowless illumination of the sodium vapor streetlights, she was reminded of some old movie about a disaster-devastated world.

It had been a week of high drama...lately her life had been full of it.

The insanity of the afternoon merged with the suppressed memories of her childhood. Recollections of the sad, little, small-town girl cruelly ridiculed by her classmates, tearfully dreaming through the cracked window of the dark room over the shabby pool hall came flooding back. A montage of images flickered in the dark

476

recesses of her psyche like a surreal horror movie.

Until Norris, her life—all of it—had been a bad movie, really.

All the way back from the beach, she had cried and cried, her mind racing endlessly. Somewhere after that first hour, the tears had run out. Since then she had been numb. She had stuffed her feelings down in a dark hole and kept pushing them back with an endless stream of little fantasies about an idyllic life with Norris.

Amazing. Everything was working out the way Clayton had planned.

It was perfect, really. After all...it was all for Ivee.

All that remained now was the matter of timing. Norris would get things settled with Agnes and move her quietly out of the picture.

Too tired to feel any elation—now she was beyond numb.

She pulled the little car into the private lot at the rear of the Tower and parked beside Norris' Riviera.

Crossing the lot, she pressed her thumb on the electronic scanner and positioned her eye in front of the optical ID, which opened the private entrance at the rear. It was a windowless steel door opening into the elegantly appointed foyer which housed the elevator that ran to the executive penthouse.

CHAPTER SEVENTY-ONE

WHEN MARILEE STEPPED OUT OF THE ELEVATOR at the penthouse level, Norris was standing there. Without a word, she stepped into his arms and buried her face into his chest, hugging him hungrily.

Safe at last!

Norris was her fortress. His essence was palpable—the scent of soap, the feel of soft, cotton oxford cloth, a minty vestige of toothpaste, all inimitably Norris Wrenn.

She turned up her face and his mouth found hers. His lips were so achingly sweet...so tenderly loving.

Finally, Norris pulled back and looked warily out toward the reception desk in the outer foyer.

"We don't need any surprises...just let me go activate the elevator alarms." He smiled down at her and kissed the tip of her nose.

"Oh, don't be paranoid...Clayt and Trip are dead." She pulled him back, urged him inside and closed the door to his office.

From this height she could see to the west the scarlet, pencil-thin tracing of the sunset sharply silhouetting the earth's edge. It separated the distant horizon from the intense, eerie electric-blue, which merged like a delicate airbrushing of color into the deeper violets of the night sky. Higher, where the indigoes darkened, the first stars seemed larger than life—like a theatrical set of future time and space. Stretching to the horizon, little ponds, irregularly dotted across the landscape, picked up muted glints of the fading, silvery-blue light. A larger lake, further off in the distance, showed an angry deep red reflection like the glowing cauldron of a volcanic crater at the edge of the earth.

The dawn of creation? Or doomsday, perhaps?

"Do you know we're standing on the surface of a ball with a core of molten fire?" she asked in a hushed whisper.

478

"First time I thought about it today...is that what you came in such a breathless hurry to remind me of?" He laughed and nibbled lightly on her ear lobe. "Now...what the hell is all this about Trip being dead...are you serious?"

"It's true. First he tried to rape me, then he tried to kill me, and, finally, he got sick and started vomiting blood. I went for help, but old Doc Merritt just laughed at me because Trip had been drinking Bloody Marys...said I didn't know the difference between blood and tomato juice. But I assure you, he was vomiting a pure stream of blood...I know the difference...." She stopped short. Should she tell him everything? It would be just like Norris to call the doctor...or the police. She decided to let the matter rest. After all, she didn't have to apologize to anyone...she had already called the doctor, hadn't she?

She pressed herself tight against him, responding to the swell of him thrusting back. Rubbing her lower body slowly side to side, she struggled to get closer.

Finally, Norris pulled back just enough to ask, "Stop that for a minute, damnit, tell me what happened? Why did you go to Caswell? You said he knows about us? I've been worried sick."

"Oh, God, it was awful." She pushed her face against his shoulder underneath his chin, sniffing, snuggling, burrowing in the hollow of his neck. "He knew everything...New York and Sheepshead. But I didn't find that out until after I got there."

"Wait...slow down. How does he know?"

"He had us followed...he knows...he *knew*...everything."

"Oh, shit!"

"Don't worry, he's dead. I'm almost certain."

"You just told me that old Doc Merritt laughed at you...if he'd been worried, he would have rushed out there with full sirens and bells...you can bet on that. He's probably just sick. Trip Graham's probably not dead by a long shot."

"How many times do I have tell you? He's a goner...you'll see..." Marilee pressed her body against him. She was tired of protesting, but she dared not tell him how she knew.

"What in god's name made you go to Caswell? I looked all over for you. No one knew where you were."

"He was drinking at the funeral. Then, afterwards, he left Mabel's and went home alone, to rest, what a joke! Of course, it got worse. After you left, I went home from Mabel's to check on him, and Oleander told me he'd left for the beach. Don't ask me why I went...guilty conscience, maybe. I guess I wanted to help him. It was a big mistake, but I guess I just had to try...It's all such a fine mess," the words came tumbling out of her. "I tried to find you, but you were nowhere to be found."

"Calm down...you're a nervous breakdown about to happen." Norris led her to the furniture in the corner by the window. Then he opened the refrigerator and took out a bottle of Tanqueray martinis and two chilled glasses. He poured the drinks and handed her the glass. "Here, drink this...."

She took a big swallow from the icy glass and gave a little shudder. "Oh, wow! I needed that. This whole day has been a nightmare. Right now is the only good thing that's happened to me." She put her arms back around him and cupped his buttocks and hugged him fiercely.

"This is crazy..." Norris looked over her shoulder at their cars sitting side by side far below in the parking lot. "I really should set the alarm."

Before he could finish, she tugged him away from the window, toward a chair. "Forget the damned alarm and finish your drink...."

Marilee waited until he had drained the glass, then she set both glasses aside. She pushed him into the chair and settled onto his lap facing him with her knees straddling his thighs. Wriggling side to side, she pushed the loose cotton skirt out of the way. All at once, very much the little-girl-lost, she buried her face into that safe place under his chin and gave a little sigh.

"Tell me again, what happened...with Trip, I mean?" Norris tried to sound reassuring, but his tone betrayed his uneasiness.

He waited expectantly, but she said nothing. He wondered if she'd heard his question. Then, just as he was going to ask again, he felt her start to tremble and heard her muffled sobs.

Rocking her gently, he let her cry. "It's OK, baby. I'm here...your lover, your doctor, your daddy...your knight in rusty armor...one size fits all. Go ahead...get it all out. Nobody's going to hurt you now." He crooned the words over and over like a lullaby. Finally, her sobbing stopped.

"Oh, Norris it was a-a-awful," she wavered, but began crying all over again. After awhile, she began to laugh a little at her own predicament. "I'm a mess. How do you stand me?" She sniffled and laughed all at the same time.

"Uhmmm..." He kissed her lightly on the lips. "Yummm..."

Kissing him back, she hungrily began to explore his mouth, probing—trying to taste all the sweetness.

She placed one hand on her breast, guiding his fingertips over her nipple. Little shivers of pleasure coursed through her as his other hand insinuated fingers inside her panty line and found her all warm and wet and open.

The niggling worries about the elevator alarm were replaced with consuming body hunger.

Without a word, Norris loosened the wraparound skirt and let it slip to the floor. Moving a finger back inside the delicate leg band of her panties, he began a gentle, insistent exploration. Lost now and driven, Marilee spread her legs to accept the rhythmic probing. Her back arched and her face lifted in pleasure until her head was tilted upward, stretched taut.

"Ooo-o-o...yes," she whispered in little shudders. "There...harder...god, don't stop."

Possessed by desire now, she helped as he wriggled her underpants side to side and lowered them to fall to her ankles.

Without a word, Norris dropped to his knees and buried his face into the musky sweetness between her legs. She strained against him as she came almost instantly to orgasm.

"OH!" she cried once aloud, then, "oh...god, Norr-i-s-s...yes!" She moved against him harder.

Immersed in the pleasure, piece by piece, they removed the rest of their clothing until, finally, they were naked in front of the expanse of window wall on the deep cushiony carpet.

Cascades of sensation…shimmering waterfalls of pleasure…a shuddering tattoo of little aftershocks. *La petite mort! Jouir!* A celebration of life.…

Panting, sweating, at last they rolled onto their backs, arms spread flat upon the carpet, staring exhausted at the ceiling. Sated. Consumed. Aglow.

After a time, Norris arose and went to the bathroom and ran the shower. Marilee followed him into the enclosure. Wordlessly, she turned her face up, and the tepid water cascaded like crystal summer rain, splashing in their faces. It tickled around the eyes, and they laughed with sheer joy.

He took her face in his hands and kissed her tenderly. "We are like children when we make love. It's remarkable; I saw it in your face in New York. Your whole face changes, and you become a little girl again. Do you know you look like you are about thirteen years old when you are making love? For the first time I know what it is to feel like a boy. I was never a boy before."

Marilee smiled. He'd told her this before. It was true…they *were* like children. She had seen the same changes in his face at Sheepshead.

"Darling, it's true what you said. You're my sweetheart, my doctor…my daddy…my everything rolled into one…Norris Wrenn, my one-man show…the Victor Borge of sexual delight. There was this girl in my hometown, her father was a lawyer—everybody called her Gang-bang Annie. She took on the whole football team one night at a party, after they'd beat up on TeeJay of Richmond for the state championship…you're my one-man gang-bang, quarterback to defensive safety…my whole football team having me in front of fifty thousand screaming fans, under the lights on the fifty-yard line…every girl should have one…I don't know how I ever did without you."

"It's a lot of responsibility to be a whole damn football team." He laughed again.

"I love you so…we're a pair of depraved…incestuous.…"

"You are insane.…"

"God help me.…"

"God help us both...."

Out of the shower, silently and playfully, they went about the room helping each other collect the scattered disarray of clothing. With her inventory of garments complete, Marilee slipped back into the bathroom to restore herself to presentability.

Norris dressed silently in the flickering half-light of the muted TV tuned to CNN.

When he finished, he poured Marilee another drink and took it to her in the bathroom.

"Uhm-m. Thanks." She took the glass and kissed him on the nose before she turned back to the mirror and resumed brushing her hair. Her voice followed him out of the dressing room, "Remember the angel I bought at Sheepshead...when I opened the box last night, the wings were broken off at the back...it was so sad, I cried."

"Don't worry, I can send it back...they'll replace it for you...."

"Oh...I can't do that. I fixed her with some Super-glue."

"That's OK, they'll still take it back...it's no trouble...."

"No...no, you don't understand...I can't send her back...then no one would have her. Our angel would never have a home."

Suddenly overcome by the sheer wonder of this remarkable woman-child, Norris turned and walked to the window and silently brushed away the beginning of a tear.

The phone in the outer reception area began ringing. It persisted for an irritatingly protracted time. At last it stopped.

Not Agnes? She didn't have his unpublished number.

The phone made him jumpy again...he stared down at the two cars side by side in the brightly lighted parking lot...might as well take out a front page ad in the *Observer*.

"Does anyone know you're here?" Norris raised his voice so she could hear.

"No. Of course not." She stuck her head around the edge of the door leading into the dressing room and bath. "What time is it? I have to call Jaynie Harris and see if Ivee is all right."

In a few moments Norris heard her speaking to someone on the phone. Then she came walking back into the room silhouetted against the peach glow of light filtering softly from the bathroom behind her.

"Jaynie's a jewel. She wanted to keep Ivee, but he wants to come on home." Marilee went to the wet bar and put some ice in her drink. "It's going to be awful when he finds out about his father. He knows something terrible is wrong with Trip. God, what will I say to him? How do you tell your son that his father died a hopeless drunk...and hardly before his grandfather's body is cold in the grave?"

"Oh, come on. That may be wishful thinking, I'm afraid," Norris said. He knew she'd had a bad time of it. "Don't you think it might be a good idea to call Marcellus and have him go check on Trip?..."

"Norris, why are you patronizing me like this? Sam Merritt emphatically advised me to let him sleep it off...after all, he had a gun before he started vomiting blood. Do you think I'm a hysterical idiot...?" Her words trailed off. She panicked at the thought of someone bringing Trip back to life.

"A gun?...Trip had a gun?...OK, let's hear it. Tell me everything." It had been a long day, and he was suddenly out of patience —not angry actually, just suddenly very tired.

"Oh, Norris...it was horrible...he knew about Sheepshead... everything...."

"How'd he find out? My God, there'll be hell to pay for that." Norris sobered.

"He had us followed...But it doesn't matter now. He got drunker and drunker...made all kinds of threats...he tried to rape me, and then he tried to kill me. Then he told me that he was going to sue for divorce, and I'd never get custody of Ivee." Marilee sounded like she was on the verge of tears again. "He was crazy...he hit me...and he got a gun. He wanted to kill me..."

"You didn't mention the gun, my god, Marilee...are you serious?"

"Of course...haven't you been listening? But I could see that it wasn't loaded....and you should have seen him...he couldn't find the safety, anyway." She laughed a nervous laugh.

"Listen, damn it, I don't find that very funny at all...I'm glad you got out of there. I agree with you, best let him sleep it off." His thoughts drifted back to the parking lot again.

"He's probably dead by now...or dying. He had drunk a quart or more in less than an hour. Dr. Scott warned him he could bleed to death if he started. Sometimes it's impossible to stop that kind of hemorrhage...even in the hospital. And...I don't care what Sam Merritt said, Trip was spewing blood...a river of it, over the rail. Can you imagine, as soon as he quit vomiting blood, he grabbed the bottle again? That senile idiot Sam Merritt just laughed at me. Trip's dead and it's his own fault. I tried to save him even after he tried to kill me."

"You said he hit you?" Norris was overwhelmed. It had been an all-round unbelievable week. Tonight was no exception. "You mean he slapped you around?"

"He didn't slap me. He hit me with his fist and took a brass candlestick and tried to smash me."

"He attacked you with a brass candlestick? My god, he really could have killed you." Norris reached out to her but she was unseeing...apparently lost in the memory of the afternoon.

"That's right, and he would have. He was raging. Insane. He hit me with his fist and knocked me down and then came after me with that brass candlestick. If he hadn't been too drunk, he would have killed me. I'm sure of it. When he couldn't corner me by chasing me around the living room, he found that target pistol we keep down there. That's when I got out. He really meant to kill me, all right."

Marilee finished her drink and put the glass on the table. Then she told him everything in great detail...the attempted rape...everything...except the part about going back...and seeing him dying.

Norris stood up and took her in his arms. It all sounded so incredible...trying to bludgeon her with a candlestick...and the gun. My god, the SOB *was* crazy.

"Was there any booze left in the house...he won't quit..."

"Of course. There is always enough booze at the cottage to handle a Shriners' convention. It would take the National Guard and a truck to get the booze out of there. My god, Norris...he tried to kill me. Do you think I was going to take a chance on going back in there and try to haul five or six cases of liquor out of there...and in what? And him trying to figure out how to load a gun? No way!" Her voice rose to nearly a shriek.

"Of course not, baby, I didn't mean...it's all right, you're safe now." Norris held her tighter and rocked her gently side to side. Over and over, he crooned reassurance. In a little while, he could feel her relax. Finally, she raised her head and kissed him.

"I love you so much. You're my life now." She hugged him close, then remembered what Griff had told her back at the house. "It doesn't matter anyway. With Trip dead, there's no one to protest your contract with Clayton. You're going to be in charge. Thank God; it's a miracle."

"Yeah...but...more'n likely Trip's just dead drunk. That's all just wishful thinking. We both need rest. It's been a hard day."

She was tired of being patronized. Why wouldn't he listen?

"Well...I'd better get going...." She knew when to shut up.

Norris didn't protest. He wanted her safely out of there. If Trip had had them followed, all hell was going to break loose tomorrow morning.

He edged over to the windows and glanced down at the cars.

"Once you're in charge, everything will be all right." She followed and hugged him from behind. "Oh darling, it will be so wonderful. You can take your time divorcing Agnes. We don't want to make a mess of it, do we?"

"No...we don't want that," he said, absently. No need to remind her of what Trip could do.

"Ivee will love having you all the time. He worships you, you know that. I can hardly wait." She stepped forward and gave him a fierce kiss. "Oh, I love you." Then she quickly disengaged herself, found her purse and started searching for her keys. "Get me out of here. Are you coming now?"

"No...I'm going to stay here tonight. I'm sick of Agnes' whining about my going to Virginia for Mother's Day." He debated telling her that Agnes had said she was taking the girls back to Virginia for good this time. He'd heard that threat before. "Be careful. Lock your car doors."

He kissed her and stepped back as the elevator closed.

Walking back into his office, he stood by the window, watching below while she walked across lot and got into her car. When she cleared the sentinel arm of the electronically activated gate, he followed the red dots of her taillights until they disappeared from view.

He turned, retrieved the green bottle and poured himself a drink.

How many drinks had he had since Marilee arrived?

Go slow...you need to keep your wits...now more than ever.

Well, well...so Trip had had them followed. An icy knot formed in the middle of his gut. Mr. Know-It-All Norris Wrenn had finally fucked up. And Major League at that...it didn't matter that it was his first.

Alpha and omega. In the corporate world, the first was often the last! They gave it names in the inner sanctums above the fortieth floor. Lack of Judgment...Loss of Credibility. They didn't put you in jail...worse. They just swept you under the old Karastan. Conversations stopped in mid-sentence when you entered a room...handshakes lost their firmness...former associates wouldn't look you in the eye...

Was he really through here? Well...maybe. But that wasn't the end of the world. Was it?

He picked up the phone and dialed.

"Washington Hospital Center...ICU..." He identified himself. There was a funny series of clicks as the operator punched him through to an extension.

"Norris..."

"*Tom?...*" Norris couldn't believe his ears. "Tom?...is...is that really *you?...*"

"Yeah...it's really me. Sorry we had to put you through all this. I begged the Attorney General to let me clue you in, but with our military scattered to the four winds, everybody's paranoid. The

Cowboy picked a piss-poor time to close down abortion. Then, on top of everything, the former Chief of Staff Courtland Pike shredded those files amid all the furor over the WTC/Pentagon thing, then blew his brains all over the Mount Vernon Parkway. *Déjà vu.* Congress is talking impeachment and the Oval Office is out to discredit the Special Counsel."

"I...I don't get it...your accident?...you weren't hurt?..."

"No. There was no accident. It was all a game. I had to lay low for a few days. The Special Counsel is in the middle of a shitstorm. Langley's very uptight over Pike's suicide. We needed to debrief those chopper pilots about the President's mysterious fishing trip near Camp Lejeune. The abortion thing in the middle of a war has everybody nuts. To make matters worse, we got wind that Toby Hoskins was hired to make a hit on you. Not to worry now, the little weasel is alligator wrestling in the Everglades."

Was this some kind of bad joke?

"Courtland Pike?...chopper pilots?...Hoskins? Who ordered a hit on me? I don't get it."

"The al-Qaeda hired Hoskins. They declared a jihad on Phoenix. As for the chopper pilots, remember the week you were at the beach for Marilee Graham's party? Remember I told you the President had been flown to Camp Lejeune for some marlin fishing...and you said there was a helicopter at the hotel where the Azalea Queen Emma Claire was staying and how everybody was upset when she left the Azalea Ball early? What I didn't tell you was there was a little surgery arranged for Claire on the Q.T. The Attorney General sent me to Wilmington...hush-hush..."

"Are you telling me the President...Emma Claire?...an illegal abortion?..."

"One and one doesn't always make two," Tom interrupted. "The President is a stand-up guy. The duplicitous Mr. Pike was the one who'd been having an affair with Claire. Apparently the Chief of Staff had been sneaking Claire into the West Wing as far back as her kiddie-porn days. The Company has put a lid on the true nature of those shredded files. But now you know the truth behind Pike's suicide."

So that was it. It had been Courtland Pike he'd seen escorting Emma Claire into the West Wing that late night two years back?

"But why didn't you warn me?...about Hoskins...about any of this?..."

"The Attorney General was afraid you might spook Hoskins. About the rest, the AG's very gun shy. After all, Brookes is the quintessential President's man-at-large...he's served as advisor for every administration since Truman. We weren't sure of his agenda. Now we know the impetus for reviving Phoenix didn't come from the Oval Office. Brookes represents a group who want to restore old-fashioned integrity to government...look, I've got to go now. I'll be in touch...soon."

"But...Tom...wait. What about Phoenix?...and Grail? Are you still with me?...will this?..."

"Don't sweat it...I'll get back to you before the sun goes down Sunday...OK?..."

"OK...but wait...."

"Sorry...later...." The line went dead.

Sitting there trying to sort it all out, Norris' eye was drawn to the TV. CNN BREAKING NEWS was flashing in bold lettering on the screen. As the picture changed to Wolf Blitzer standing on Pennsylvania Avenue outside the White House, Norris reached for the remote and turned up the volume.

"A RELIABLE SOURCE SAYS THE SPECIAL PROSECUTOR'S OFFICE IS FLYING A TEAM OF INVESTIGATORS TO HAW RIVER, NORTH CAROLINA TO THE SCENE OF A ONE-CAR CRASH WHICH TOOK THE LIFE OF DOCTOR W.T. CRAWFORD, CHIEF OF INFECTIOUS DISEASES AT THE UNIVERSITY OF NORTH CAROLINA SCHOOL OF MEDICINE IN CHAPEL HILL. CRAWFORD WAS RETURNING FROM GREENSBORO WHERE THIS AFTERNOON HE'D HELD A NATIONWIDE PRESS CONFERENCE CONCERNING THE DEATH OF MOVIE ACTRESS, EMMA CLAIRE, WHO WAS FOUND DEAD MONDAY IN A GREENSBORO MOTEL. MISTAKENLY THOUGHT TO BE CAUSED BY A DRUG OVERDOSE, CLAIRE'S DEATH WAS ACTUALLY DUE TO AN OVER-

WHELMING INFECTION FROM THE EXOTIC BACTERIO-
LOGICAL AGENT, KLEBSIELLA PNEUMONIAE..."

Jesus! His head was reeling. Too tired to think coherently about anything, Norris sat looking out over the lighted streets below as they faded into inky darkness. Speckled here and there in the distance were twinkling lights of remote farmhouses. Beyond he could trace the faraway glow of traffic on the interstate highway far to the southwest. Off in the near-distance, he could see the blinking lights of a helicopter. To the east, he could see where the bridge crossed the Neuse River and became the Wilmington highway. At the horizon, a soft-peach glow of lightning illuminated a line of soaring thunderheads.

From afar, he heard a faint, almost-imagined, timpani of thunder.

In his numbed state, Norris lost all track of time. He had been sitting there for perhaps ten minutes when his private phone jarred him back to reality.

"This is Wrenn..." he answered, without thinking about the time or who it might be.

"Norris, this is Chatham. I was distressed to hear the news about Clayton Graham. I know you've been through a rough time of it, but I wanted to remind you we are very serious about our intentions up here. With all that's happened, I don't suppose you've thought much about it."

"Well, nothing I'd care to talk about just yet." It was all he could do to keep from asking Brookes if he knew the truth about Tom.

"Can I give you a call Monday, then?" Brookes was used to keeping the ball rolling.

"I'm not sure I'll have any news...you understand."

"Oh, I just thought we might have another chat...it would be appropriate, don't you think?"

"Perhaps. I'll expect your call, but make it late. Things are a mess here at the moment."

"Oh, yes...Norris, there's just one thing. You have to be more careful now. No secret interludes at remote hideaways...no romantic flings with anyone but your wife...as long as you have one. That stuff is for mere mortals...you do understand, don't you? But, never mind, dear boy, nothing we haven't taken care of here." Brookes' voice had a knowing edge. "A word of caution, dear boy...you should not leave the TV on in your office if you're going to engage in such amoral calisthenics. Modern technology is amazing. Look at your laptop; if I'm not mistaken, you're online. I've taken the liberty of downloading a little homespun porno for enjoyment in your old age."

Norris' eyes moved to his laptop. He watched entranced as Marilee undressed him.

"Goddamn you, Chatham...you've gone too far...."

"Stay calm, dear boy...."

"Cut the bullshit, Chatham...." He made no effort to hide his resentment. "By the way, what do you know about that bulletin on CNN just now? That crash that killed Crawford, the infectious disease expert who ruled natural causes in the Emma Claire death? Did Crawford know too much? Is that exotic bacterium one of the Executive Branch's special recipes? And while we're on the subject, what do you know about Toby Hoskins?"

"You're watching too much TV, dear boy. You'll hear from me Monday...."

He hung up before Norris could say another word.

Norris cursed silently. Spies and covert assassins behind every bush; to think he'd believed he had some right to privacy. His *naïveté* had no bounds. So Brookes' spooks knew about Marilee. And still, they hadn't crossed him off the list. When he thought about it, he was glad Chatham had called. In the middle of all this heavy-duty shit, he needed to be reminded he still had options.

Options? What were his options? Looking out at the twinkling lights again, he was filled with a sudden sense of reality. If they could tape him from a chopper, was he really out of the woods? And Trip could still crucify him, if he blew the whistle to Agnes.

Agnes? She was taking the plane back to Washington for Mother's Day tomorrow. Thank God! Trip would surely tell Agnes, even if he no longer had proof.

Unless?...

What about Marilee's escapade at the beach? Could Trip really be dead...or dying?...

Norris picked up the phone and dialed.

"This is Ed Scott."

"Norris Wrenn, Ed...Trip's at it again," Norris quickly told the doctor everything Marilee had told him. "What about it, Ed? Think he's in any real danger?"

"Well, his drinking is serious enough all right. But Marilee shouldn't blame Sam Merritt for not going out there. It's an exercise in futility to try to deal with a drunk in the shape he's in. If Trip had a gun, that's a job for the cops. She should have had 'em lock him up."

"You know the Grahams, Ed. No cops. Mabel would never forgive her for that."

"I know. It rubs off. Under the circumstances, Marilee did the best she could. Most likely he'll sleep it off and we can call down there in the morning...maybe take the chopper and get him back to Holly Hall before he finally drinks himself to death. I'm not looking for a crisis yet, but for someone with esophageal varices, that kind of vomiting really is very dangerous. It could become more than just a superficial bleeding from the gagging...often when they start, nothing, not even surgery can get it stopped. Call me in the morning, OK?"

"OK." He said goodnight and rang off.

Doctors! They talked about life and death the same way old men discuss the weather.

He dialed another number. "Marcellus...this is Norris Wrenn. Sorry to call so late, but Mrs. Graham was worried about her husband. She said you were going to ride by and make sure his car was there...".

"Oh...yessir. I just got back...his car ain't moved all night. You want I should go back and check on him?"

"No...go on to bed. Chances are he'll sleep all night. I'll tell Mrs. Graham first thing in the morning. And thanks again." Norris hung up before Marcellus could protest.

Norris went to his Rolodex and found another number and

punched it in.

"Mack Jones..."

"Mack...this is Norris Wrenn..." Mack was the Brunswick County Sheriff. He lived only a half-mile up the beach from Marilee's cottage. Both Trip and Norris played golf with him on occasion. Norris quickly told him a sugarcoated version of the situation with Trip's drinking. "Mack, I'm concerned for Trip's welfare down there alone at the beach cottage dealing with his daddy's death. Could you personally run by and make sure he's OK? Maybe give me a call back here? Be discreet...I'm sure you understand...."

"I'll get back to you...thirty-minutes max...." After Norris had suffered the sheriff's protestations of regret over Clayton's death, Jones finally assured him he'd discreetly check on Trip's welfare as soon as he got dressed.

9:25...Norris checked the clock on the wall before he walked to the windowed wall and looked out.

The office clock showed 9:52 when the phone rang again.

"Norris...Mack Jones...my god...I don't know how to tell you this...Trip Graham is dead...."

Norris listened benumbed as the old sheriff told him the coroner was on the way.

"Thanks, Mack...I won't keep you...sorry it turned out this way...." Norris rang off.

He dialed Marilee without thinking. "Baby, I should have never doubted you...." He quickly filled her in.

"It's not your fault...I really was afraid to tell you how I knew...you're such a Dudley Doright...." She told him everything about her return to the cottage.

"Norris...you do love me?...don't you?..."

"You know I do...but we've got to be patient...use our heads. This is tricky...the pompous Senator Dabney Thoroughgood Farnsworth won't take kindly to my divorcing his daughter...you have to trust me. There's a lot at stake...."

"Oh...I do trust you...don't worry...I won't cause a mess...."

"OK...best get some rest; poor Ivee's going to need you tomorrow more than he's ever needed anything in his life. This thing is going to turn into a media circus. If you can't get me here, I'll find you. Now, goodnight..." He hung up the phone.

What now?

The enormity of the week's events left him shaking.

Despite his public image, he'd always kept his privacy...now, all at once, his life had become a sequel to *Boogie Nights. So?...what now?...really?* Nobody would control him...he'd make goddamn sure of that.

Did he owe anybody anything?

Agnes?...What did he really owe her? Her dignity...nothing else.

His daughters? That was different.

Marilee?

It was not a matter of owing her.

Did he love her? Well...close enough, he guessed. What did anyone know about love, anyway? Whatever you called it, it was better than anything he'd ever had...or hoped to have.

So?...what's the next move?

Well...when this thing calmed down, he'd waste no time in getting the divorce with Agnes resolved. He had some money. After a decent interval, maybe he'd just take Marilee and Ivee and go to Sheepshead and leave all of 'em to wallow in their own mediocrity.

But what about now? Or tomorrow?

He was still his own man. Right?

Don't answer that, counselor.

Not yet...not now.

Tomorrow. He would figure it all out tomorrow.

The phone rang in Chatham Brookes' office.

"Chatham," the woman said. "We've got him where we want him now."

Special Acknowledgement
My brother, James Harris Robertson, captain of the airways.

Special Appreciation
Charlotte J. Cabaniss

Appreciation
Les Standiford, John Miller, Dan Zeluff, Hal Farrell,
Rick Robotham, Jay Qualeys, Bill W. and Dr. Bob.